D1463641

00189 4830

ORPHANS of TIDE

0 2 NOV 2021

This book is on loan from
Library Services for Schools
www.cumbria.gov.uk/
libraries/schoolslibserv

Cumbria

County Council

Guano Mines

Seagull Roosts

Stilt Town

Market of the
Great Whale

The
Academy

The Shrine of
the God-Bird

Azalea
Markets

Elori Coast

Farms of the
Benevolent God

Kellerman
Mines

Leila's Fury

Astral
Mansions

Shark-fin
Tip

N
W · E
S

TOWARDS THE OCEAN OF
THE GREAT ABOMINATION

The Docks

The
Vile Oak

Ark
Palace

Revelation
Boulevard

The
Shambles

Rioli Coast

Raphaela
Markets

Lorenza Mines

Felicia Markets

Humpback
Crags

Abrami Coast

SHIPWRECK
ISLAND

PUFFIN BOOKS

UK | USA | Canada | Ireland | Australia
India | New Zealand | South Africa

Puffin Books is part of the Penguin Random House group of companies
whose addresses can be found at global.penguinrandomhouse.com.

www.penguin.co.uk
www.puffin.co.uk
www.ladybird.co.uk

Penguin
Random House
UK

First published 2021

001

Text copyright © Struan Murray, 2021
Illustrations copyright © Manuel Šumberac, 2021

The moral right of the author and illustrator has been asserted

Set in 12/17 pt Bembo Book MT Std
Typeset by Jouve (UK), Milton Keynes
Printed and bound in Great Britain by Clays Ltd, Elcograf S.p.A.

The authorized representative in the EEA is Penguin Random House Ireland,
Morrison Chambers, 32 Nassau Street, Dublin D02 YH68

A CIP catalogue record for this book is available from the British Library

ISBN: 978-0-241-38445-9

All correspondence to:
Puffin Books, Penguin Random House Children's
One Embassy Gardens, 8 Viaduct Gardens, London SW11 7BW

MIX
Paper from
responsible sources
FSC® C018179

Penguin Random House is committed to a
sustainable future for our business, our readers
and our planet. This book is made from Forest
Stewardship Council® certified paper.

For Mum and Dad

A Contest of Hopes

The boy spied the pale glimmer of a shark, and his mouth watered. He swam between the rays of moonlight, hoping it wouldn't sense him coming.

Above, he saw a black square on the surface of the sea. Two pale feet dangled at its edge, blurred by the rippling waves. Somehow, the boy knew he mustn't eat them, as surely as he knew he was hungry.

He would eat the shark instead.

He swept his massive tail and the water thundered round him. At the last moment, the shark darted left, right, left, and the boy felt a thrill rush from the tip of his nose to his fins. He snapped his jaws, missed, then snapped again. His teeth grazed the shark's skin and blood filled the water. So close. The shark's tail struck his face and the boy lunged forward and bit down hard, his teeth shredding flesh and bone and –

'SETH!' Ellie yelled, hitting him on the head with the handle of her screwdriver. 'Get off!'

'*Muh?*' said Seth, his eyes wide.

'You're *biting* me!'

'What?' said Seth, scrabbling backwards, causing the whole raft to tilt so that Ellie had to grab the mast. The teeth marks on Ellie's arm glistened with saliva in the moonlight. 'I'm sorry!'

'It's all right,' said Ellie, wiping away his spit with her sleeve. 'You were dreaming.'

Seth rubbed the top of his head. 'I wasn't asleep,' he said. 'There's . . . something underneath the boat. Something big.'

Ellie pulled her feet from the water.

'Did it hurt?' Seth said, eyeing the fading bite marks.

'Yes, a lot,' Ellie lied, picking up the small broken clock she'd been tinkering with. 'You owe me another round.'

Seth groaned, flopping on to his front and burying his face in his arm. 'No. I'm too hungry to think.'

'But we need to *distract* ourselves from food. Especially now you're turning into a cannibal.'

'It wasn't you I thought I was eating, it was that shark.'

'What shark?'

'I saw a shark. But I wasn't me. I was . . . something else.'

'You were in the sea again?' Ellie said, and Seth nodded. Ellie felt strangely jealous whenever Seth cast his mind out into the sea. She worried that he was doing it to avoid her. They were often arguing these days, over the silliest things, only to make up again a few minutes later. It was hard being in one person's company all the time, Ellie had discovered – even someone she liked as much as Seth – and by her count they'd been at sea for at least three months.

'You go first,' she said.

'Do we have to?' Seth rolled on to his back. He was so tall he had to fold in his legs to fit on the raft.

'Yes, because you bit me,' said Ellie.

The mast gave a mournful creak, the sail fluttering in the warm breeze.

'Fine, okay,' Seth said. He sat up, his brows furrowing irritably. 'I wish –'

'Hope,' Ellie corrected softly. The word 'wish' was not a pleasant one for her any more.

'Hope,' said Seth, looking out to the horizon. In the moonlight, he resembled a pen-and-ink drawing, all sharp angles and messy black hair. 'I hope . . . that on this new island we find a pair of proper beds, with pillows, where we can sleep until noon, without wolves trying to eat us.'

'That's not very imaginative,' said Ellie. 'I'm sure you've used that one before.'

'I still see those wolves in my dreams, you know. Their glowing red eyes.'

'Their eyes did not glow red,' said Ellie, though they hadn't been friendly, either. They'd woken Seth and Ellie with their howling, on a tiny islet a month ago.

'Okay, it's my turn,' said Ellie, rubbing her hands together. 'I hope that on this new island we find lots of people who need me to invent things for them, so I can create amazing machines to turn the island into a paradise where everyone is happy all the time and nobody suffers.'

Seth stared at her. He had large, wintry blue eyes and sometimes it was like being stared at by a cat.

'I think mine wins, don't you?' said Ellie brightly, fetching a penknife from one of the countless pockets of her old, stitched-together coat. She crawled on her elbows to one corner of the raft, where many vertical lines had been scored into the wood, some beneath a crudely inscribed letter E, others beneath the letter S. Taking the knife, Ellie scored a new groove under E.

'Why not hope the island is already a paradise?' said Seth.

'What?' said Ellie, cheerfully blowing the hair away from her face.

'Why hope to find somewhere you can turn into a paradise? Why not hope for an island that already *is* a paradise?'

Ellie wrinkled her nose. 'But then . . . what use would I be?'

Seth studied her. 'Let's just focus on getting to the island,' he said, glancing suspiciously over his shoulder. 'And fast.'

'Seth, for the last time, no one is following us.'

4

'I saw a sail, Ellie. A black sail. It must be the Inquisition.'

'Why would the Inquisition be following us? They think I'm dead.'

'Maybe they figured out that you faked your death. There was definitely a ship – I could sense it in the water.'

'Just because there was a ship doesn't mean it was following us. Now come on, let's play another –'

Seth jerked to one side, his eyes fixed on the sea.

'What is it *now*?' said Ellie. 'Inquisitors chasing us on the backs of dolphins?'

'No, it's that shoal of fish.'

'What shoal of fish?'

'The one I told you about earlier,' Seth said excitedly. 'They've come back. I think they're drawn towards me.'

Ellie rolled her eyes. 'Yes, because you're so interesting. Why not try catching one?'

'With what, my hands?'

'Your *powers*, Seth. You should really be practising every day so you don't forget how to use them.'

Seth looked at the sea like it was filled with writhing worms. 'I don't *like* using them,' he said, pouting petulantly.

'Fine. Stay hungry.'

He glared at her, then hunched forward over the water, closing his eyes and gripping the edge of the raft. His fingers tightened, nails digging into wood.

Then, dark swirls appeared on the surface of his arms. He grimaced, like he was in pain.

5

'Seth?' Ellie said, inching towards him.

Seth's eyes flashed open and he held out one hand above the waves. There was a *splosh* and something small and glossy wriggled free of the ocean and straight into his outstretched fingers.

'That was amazing!' said Ellie, clapping, then wincing as Seth whacked the fish hard against the mast. It stopped wriggling after that. He grabbed the penknife and quickly sliced off the fish's skin, then presented its flesh to Ellie. It glowed in the moonlight.

'I think I'll wait until we can build a fire,' said Ellie, though her stomach whined. Seth tore into the fish, slurping it down.

'You're disgusting,' Ellie said.

Seth shrugged, and Ellie kept watching, then shuffled over to him. 'How did you do it, then? Did you make the water spit up the fish, or did you convince the fish to jump out?'

'Not sure,' said Seth, his mouth full. 'You really don't want any?' He pulled a bone from his teeth, then dangled the mutilated fish in front of her.

Ellie inspected it suspiciously. 'Uncooked fish can make you sick.'

'Not eating can make you dead.'

Ellie took the fish. Its head was hanging at an angle, held on by a sliver of spine. She sniffed, then took a bite. It tasted salty and sweet at the same time, the flesh melting on her tongue.

Seth smiled, and his eyelids drooped. He got tired whenever he used his powers over the sea. A few times during their journey, he'd needed to calm the wild sea, or propel the raft along when there'd been no breeze. He'd collapsed afterwards every time, his skin cold as morning frost.

'Shall we play one more round?' Ellie said brightly. She knew it was selfish, but she didn't want Seth to fall asleep and leave her alone. When she slept, she dreamed she was being chased along twisting alleyways. When she was alone, she thought she could hear a voice on the wind. 'Please?'

Seth looked at her through half-shut eyes.

'Okay,' he sighed. 'I hope . . . that on this new island, you can find someone else to play this pointless game with.'

'*Seth!*' Ellie batted his arm. 'Be serious.'

Seth tried and failed to suppress a sleepy smile. 'Sorry. I hope that on this island, I can learn how to fish properly, without using my . . .' He looked at the fading blue swirls on his skin. 'You know.'

Ellie waited, expecting more. 'That's it?' she said eventually. 'Why *wouldn't* you want to use your powers?'

'Because they make me tired.'

'Don't you want to make new friends on the island? *They* could teach you how to fish without using your powers.'

Seth hugged his legs. 'I don't trust people.'

'They won't be like the people in the City,' said Ellie. 'They might be nice. And you trust me, don't you? And I bet you trusted your brothers and sisters.'

7

'My brothers and sisters weren't people, they were gods. And they're all dead. Except for the Enemy.'

Ellie winced, her chest tightening.

'Sorry,' said Seth.

'But . . . we don't know for sure that they're all dead. I mean, everyone in the City thought only the Enemy was left, but then you turned up. Maybe if we found other gods, they could help you get your memories back? Help you remember who you really are.'

'I know who I am. I'm Seth. I'm happy that way. Your turn,' he added curtly.

Ellie glowered at him. 'Fine. I hope that on this new island –' she paused to think – 'there are people who . . . are like me. Like my mum. People who want to invent things – who want to make the world better. I hope there are people there who'll see that I'm special.'

As she spoke, she felt the hairs on her neck stand on end, and her chest twisted with painful longing. Seth looked down at his hand. He seemed to have become very interested in a small cut on his finger.

'What?' Ellie said flatly.

'I don't think this game is good for you. You're getting your hopes up too much. We've no idea what we're going to find on this island, if it even exists.'

Ellie felt a stab of irritation. 'But we *saw* it – on the map in the Inquisitorial stronghold.'

'Yes, and the Inquisition has *always* been trustworthy,' Seth said, rolling his eyes.

Ellie took a deep breath. They'd had this conversation many times. But she understood why Seth was so wary, given that the Inquisition had tried to burn him to death.

'And if it *does* exist,' Seth grumbled, 'it might be dangerous. Why else would the Inquisitors keep it a secret?'

Ellie frowned. 'Maybe because it's a wonderful, amazing place, and they don't want everyone in the City to try and escape to it?'

'That doesn't sound very likely.'

Ellie scowled and turned away, finding she didn't want to see his face any more. 'I think I won that round,' she announced, picking up the knife and scoring another vertical line next to the thirty already beneath the letter E. She looked at the six lines below the letter S. 'You're doing terribly,' she added.

'I really don't care, Ellie.'

Ellie felt a surge of fury bubble in her gut. She grabbed the mangled remains of the fish and hurled them at Seth's head. He ducked and they fell into the sea with a *splosh*.

The water rose up in a black, glistening mass that split across the middle to reveal sharp teeth and a fat pink tongue. The mouth snapped shut and the fish was gone, but the creature kept rising, spraying water from its sleek surface. Its white stomach fell against the raft, rocking it so hard that Ellie slipped and rolled backwards, the raft vanishing from under her. She choked on salt water as it rushed up her nose and into her mouth and all the spaces between her skin and her clothes.

She opened her eyes, and through the murk she saw it: a killer whale, white patches on its side, a tall fin on its back. It looked at her for an instant, then twisted and swam away in a flurry of foam. Relief rushed through Ellie as it vanished into the dark. She kicked up towards the surface, risking a glance down into the depths, frightened that a shark might have been drawn by the commotion. But there was just an endless emptiness that sucked away the light.

Ellie frowned, blinking against the salt water. Because there *was* something – she could have sworn it. Deep down in the dark, somehow even blacker than the gloom.

A figure. Something in the shape of a human.

For long seconds she stared, trying to decide if what she saw was real. It kept fading in and out of her sight. When it was there, it was motionless. Not swimming, but fixed in place. She could feel it watching her.

She blinked, and the figure was gone, and then something rushed up against her from beneath, and she was rising, rising. The waters parted and warm night air swept against her skin and filled her lungs. The moon shone above her, and Seth's bright eyes did too.

He pulled her off the back of the killer whale and on to the raft, wrapping her long sealskin coat round her. There was a splash as a dark tail rose above them, then vanished with a watery *glug* and a pop of froth.

'Are you okay?' Seth asked, patting her on the back. Ellie coughed, seawater gushing from her nose. She shook her head.

'It's fine,' said Seth. 'The whale was never going to hurt you. I think it came here because of me. Let's light the oil lamp.'

'It's not the whale, Seth,' said Ellie, shivering and huddling close to him for warmth. 'I think I saw it.'

'Saw what?'

Ellie took in a trembling breath, and Seth swallowed. 'Oh.' He was quiet for a moment. 'Did it look like your brother?'

'No. I don't think it can take Finn's shape again, after what I did to it. I could only see a shadow, really. But it was definitely . . . *it*. It was looking right at me.'

'But it can't hurt you any more, Ellie. You won. So long as you don't ask it to grant any more wishes, it can't regain its power.'

'Yeah,' said Ellie, managing a weak smile. 'Yeah, you're right.'

'And you've not made any more wishes, and you're not going to. So it can't ever hurt you again.'

Ellie nodded. 'Thank you, Seth,' she said, pulling her coat more tightly round herself. She risked a glance down into the deep, but saw nothing but her own reflection.

When she looked up, Seth was still watching her. There was a mischievous twist to his smile.

'I hope,' he began, 'that on this new island, there are nice people who will let us live there with them, who'll feed us and welcome us. That it's an island where you can make friends, and invent amazing new machines, and where no Inquisitors can find us. Where no one has ever heard of the Enemy.'

Ellie smiled too, wiping a strand of wet hair from her eyes. 'I think you win that round, to be honest.'

'But you didn't hope for anything?'

Ellie picked up her penknife, and scored a line beneath the letter S. 'Nothing could beat that,' she said, looking back up at him.

But as their eyes met, Seth was distracted by something over Ellie's shoulder, gazing in sudden wonder. Ellie turned to look too.

It lay upon the horizon. A dark, jagged shape, picked out by the moonlight.

A new island.

Praise Her

For hours, the island sat on the horizon. It didn't seem to be getting any closer, just bigger, and Ellie wondered if they'd ever reach it at all. She pulled a telescope from her coat pocket, rubbing the lens with her thumb. She squinted into the eyepiece.

'The island's got something growing out of it.'

'A mountain?' said Seth.

Ellie frowned. 'No. The shape's too regular. Like it was made by people.' She passed him the telescope. 'It sort of looks like –'

'A ship,' said Seth.

'Yeah,' said Ellie. 'A *huge* ship.'

'What's a ship doing on top of an island?'

'I don't know. Maybe it got stuck there? But how . . .' Ellie's palms prickled. 'Wait! Seth, maybe it's an

Ark. One of the four giant ships people used to escape the Drowning!'

The sun rose as the raft approached, painting the eastern sky pale orange, washing the darkness from the massive structure that rested atop the island. It was almost crescent-shaped, as if the moon had crashed down from the skies above. Ellie and Seth looked at each other – there was no doubt it was an Ark.

The island itself was shrouded in mist, except at one side, where a volcano jutted out at an angle. Even this was dwarfed by the Ark, which rose and rose until it was a swollen shadow above them. The raft drifted through the humid mist, leaving hot beads of condensation on their faces.

Then, houses appeared.

At first, Ellie thought that they were floating impossibly above the water. But, as the mists cleared, she realized they were raised on stilts – a village of wooden homes with straw roofs, connected by rickety bridges and narrow walkways. The mist parted, and sunlight struck the village, revealing a world of bright paintwork: cherry reds and cornflower blues and egg-yolk yellows, and lurid carvings of whales and fish and sharks that poked from the rooftop corners, grinning down at the sea.

A woman opened her door with a musical clatter of wind chimes, stepping out on to a walkway.

'Morning, Alistair,' she called, to an old man in a rocking chair on his front porch. 'Looks like a lovely day.'

'Aye, no doubt. Praise Her.'

'Praise Her,' beamed the woman. Her eyes glanced down at Ellie and Seth as their raft passed beneath. 'Look at the state of you two,' she said with a smile.

'Did you come all the way from Ingarth Island on *that*?' said the man.

'Oh,' said Ellie. 'I mean, um . . .'

'Yes,' Seth said stiffly. 'We came from . . . Ingurf Island.'

'Hope you've got a place to stay,' said the woman. 'You look like you could both use a good bath.'

'We do, don't we?' said Ellie, faking a laugh. 'It must be all that mud we have on Ingarth Island.'

'And a meal for you, skinny one,' the woman said to Ellie. 'Though it seems you've brought breakfast with you!'

Ellie followed where she was pointing, and saw a carpet of glittering fish trailing their raft, like a thousand shards of blue crystal.

'Been a long time since I seen a shoal that big this close to the island. Perhaps our fortunes are changing, praise God,' the man declared. 'Praise Her.'

'Praise Her,' echoed the woman.

'Praise Her,' said Ellie, since it seemed like the right thing to do.

The raft floated lazily on between algae-covered stilts, beneath walkways and rope bridges. Seth was crouched on all fours, eyes darting from one house to the next.

'We should have kept that spear,' he said.

'It's fine,' said Ellie. 'We just have to act like we belong here.'

An old woman drew a trap up from beneath her house as the shoal passed by, laughing at all the fish wriggling inside. She spotted Ellie and Seth and narrowed her eyes. Seth threw his arm out protectively in front of Ellie, and Ellie batted it away.

'Smile,' she whispered, forcing one herself. 'Look friendly.'

Seth gripped the edge of the raft so tightly that the wood splintered beneath his fingers. '*Ow.*'

'Seth, relax.' Ellie pulled some tweezers from her coat. 'Don't worry.'

'Why not? The last time I arrived in a new place, all the people there tried to kill me.'

'Except one,' said Ellie, plucking a splinter from Seth's palm. She smiled at him, but he just rubbed at a scar on his arm – a legacy of his interrogation by a particularly brutal Inquisitor called Hargrath.

'It'll be okay, Seth,' Ellie told him. 'We're together, we can do this.'

The raft drifted further through the village. Cats stalked overhead, licking their lips as they watched the shoal of fish. One man paddled behind the raft in a canoe, fishing net at the ready, ignoring the looks Seth was giving him.

Finally, a strip of beach appeared through the gaps in the stilts, the colour of burnt sugar. Golden sandstone buildings hugged the island above it, climbing in rows towards the massive bulk of the Ark. Some huddled close like dear friends, others stood alone, surrounded by colourful potted plants. And trees – actual *trees* – erupted from the ground, not wizened and emaciated like those few sad specimens that grew in the City, but lush palm trees so tall they sagged over at the top, weighed down by clutches of fat, hairy coconuts. They sprouted between the buildings, and in some places *through* the buildings, bursting from the thatched rooftops.

'It's *beautiful*,' said Ellie.

'That doesn't mean it's not dangerous.'

The raft washed against the beach. Before them was a large lime-green wooden house. A little girl sat on the doorstep, chewing a blade of grass.

'*See* – nobody here wants to kill us,' said Ellie.

Seth grumbled, glaring at the girl like she might be concealing a harpoon gun. Ellie used the mast to hoist herself to her feet. 'What should we do with the raft?'

'I suppose we could just leave it.'

'What if someone steals it?'

They looked at the raft, barely more than a bundle of sticks tied together with dead vines, then laughed. It was hard to believe they'd spent three months on such a dismal thing. They'd abandoned Ellie's underwater boat after only two weeks at sea, its mechanisms corroded by salt water. She sighed at the memory – it had been arguably her greatest invention, even if it had only worked in the first place because the Enemy had fixed it. They'd left it on a rocky islet, along with the small collection of tools and prized books she'd brought from the City. Now all she owned were the clothes she was wearing, the contents of her coat pockets, and the coat itself: a drab grey thing stitched together from scraps of cloth and sealskin. She pulled it on, despite the clammy heat, comforted by its familiar weight.

'You're going to be too hot,' said Seth.

Ellie gave him a warning look, and Seth nodded in understanding. Wearing her coat made Ellie feel more like an inventor – more like her mother – and, most importantly, it put another layer between the world and the terrible secret she carried everywhere.

'Here you go,' said Seth, picking up a long, polished rod of wood, which they'd salvaged from the rudder of the underwater boat. Ellie glared at it resentfully.

'Thanks,' she grumbled, using the cane to lower herself from the raft. She had hurt her right leg while fleeing the City three months before. It wasn't healing, and Ellie worried this was something to do with the Enemy. Soon after her injury, the god had almost taken a physical form inside her – a process that would have killed her had she not found a way to stop it, with the help of Seth and her best friend, Anna.

Ellie crossed the beach to join Seth, the sand fluffy beneath her bare feet. Seth was inspecting a tall wooden statue of a woman that sat outside the house. She had purple hair down to her waist, large yellow eyes and a kind smile. Bunches of lilacs grew by her feet, and she wore a chain of wilted daisies on her head.

'Who do you think this is?' said Seth.

'Maybe it's the woman everyone keeps praising,' said Ellie, leaning in close to admire the carving.

'That's not how you do it!'

The little girl shoved between Ellie and Seth, kneeling before the statue.

'Thank you, Divine Queen, for bringing the fish and the flowers and keeping our island safe. Please could you bring me a new puppy and fix Grandma's hip.'

The girl looked at them scathingly, a blade of grass still sticking out of her mouth.

'Who is –' Ellie started to say, but Seth clapped a hand over her face and pulled her aside.

'We shouldn't ask obvious questions,' he whispered. 'If people realize we're not from here, they might think we're dangerous.'

Ellie scrunched up her nose. 'She's only little. Anyway, that man asked us if we were from Ingarth Island. And he hardly seemed worried by the idea, did he?'

'It's rude to whisper, you know,' said the girl. 'Especially in front of the Queen.'

'Sorry,' said Ellie. 'Um, praise Her,' she added.

The girl's face lit up. 'Praise Her,' she said, then bent to pull a wad of grass from the sand.

Ellie and Seth walked away along the beach, glancing back at the girl, who was kneeling before the statue once more.

'She's a queen?' said Seth.

Ellie nodded. 'But that girl's *praying* to her. In the City, people prayed to the saints, but . . . did you hear what that old man said?'

' "Praise Her",' said Seth, shrugging.

'Before that. He said, "Praise God".'

Seth grimaced.

Ellie checked around to make sure there was no one listening. 'What if the Queen is a god, like you?' she asked, excitement tickling the back of her neck.

'How do we know that's a good thing?' Seth said, eyeing the statue with a dark expression. The little girl was now gathering daisies, making a new chain that she placed on the statue's head to replace the old one.

Ellie had known two gods. One had saved her life, and she trusted him completely. The other had spent three years trying to destroy her.

'What kind are you?' she whispered.

Leila's Diary

4,753 days aboard the *Revival*

I want to cry but I can't because I've got to write this down first. Feels important.

Blue Eyes wasn't himself this morning. A seal swam right by his mouth and he didn't even take a nibble, so I thought I'd see if that old medicine woman could do something about it. I dug my heels in and swore at Blue Eyes until he swam us back to the Ark, on to the sea-soaked platform sticking from its side. I tore my feet from the stirrups and leapt from the saddle.

'Get the Crone!' I roared, splashing ankle-deep through the water. Timothy looked at me in terror. 'NOW!'

He scarpered up the rickety staircase towards the Sky Deck. I knelt at Blue Eyes' side to check him over. His black skin was scarred and bumpy as usual, but the big white patch on his side was yellow as old paper.

The staircase creaked and I looked up and saw the ancient woman, a wild cloud of wispy grey hair and a face lined ten thousand times. She had a big hump for a back, and her eyes were a tight bunch of wrinkles, like shrivelled walnuts.

'How'd you get here so fast?' I said.

'She was already coming down the stairs!' said Timothy behind her.

'My whale is sick,' I told the Crone.

She hobbled towards me on a crutch made from a tree branch. 'Your whale isn't sick, child.'

'It is so. And don't call me child – I'm thirteen years and eight days – don't call me child.'

'Your whale isn't sick, old child.'

'Then why won't he hunt?'

'Because *he's* old. Much too old for a whale of his kind.'

'Fine – you're a healer. Heal him.'

The Crone closed her eyes intently, like she kept secret knowledge behind her eyelids. 'Old things must die. This one especially.'

'No!' I snarled. 'We are bonded – we will hunt together until I am as wretched and wrinkled as you are. He will not die!'

'My child. He is already dead.'

'He's not, he's breathing, look!' I pointed at his side, which was clearly rising and falling.

'That is not him,' said the Crone. 'A new life comes. We must help it.'

She moved too fast for something so old. I saw a flash of metal, then a thick red slash across Blue Eyes' side. I raised my fist to strike the Crone, then screamed when I saw what was reaching out from the cut she'd made.

A hand.

Shipwreck Island

'Come *on*, Ellie,' said Seth. 'I can smell food, and I'm starving.'

Ellie lingered, studying the statue of the Queen.

'Mm? Oh, oh yeah, I'm coming.'

She was about to turn when she noticed something else far along the beach, where the mist still clung to the shore.

A dark shape, blurred like a mirage at its edges.

'Seth, is that a ship?' she asked. It was always worth checking whether he could see the same things she could.

Seth frowned. 'Yes.' His eyes widened. 'With a black sail.'

'It's not the one you saw following us, is it?' Ellie asked.

'I . . . don't know.'

They watched as the ship slid up the beach. It was small, built for two or three people at most. As Ellie watched, a tall figure leapt down from the deck and looked around.

'Can you see that as well?' Ellie whispered. It reminded her all too much of the dark shape she'd seen beneath the waves.

Seth nodded, squinting through the misty haze. 'Come on. Whoever it is, I doubt they want to help us.'

They hurried along the beach to the bottom of a wide, splintery wooden staircase that rose out of the sand, built into the side of a low cliff face. Ellie could smell sizzling tomatoes, sweet vanilla and rose perfume, and hear the bustle of a crowd above. She glanced over her shoulder, and saw the dark figure had stopped further up the beach.

'Are they . . . watching us?'

She took Seth's hand, leading him up the staircase to the top of the cliff. Into a land of music and colour.

Children darted past, giggling and throwing oranges at each other, then tumbling to the ground in a heap and wrestling across a yellow sandstone street like excitable puppies. Beyond was a market square teeming with shoppers in tunics and dresses the colours of autumn leaves. Every person was smiling or chatting or happily haggling, crowding round an assortment of lace-covered market stalls that spilled over with creased leather shoes, glittering threads of pearls and carelessly piled hats.

In the centre of the market was a whale.

It lay on its belly with its tail curving up and its head rising to meet it, glittering with jewels that studded its hide like barnacles, a beard of green and blue paper streamers trailing from its jaw. Its eyes were made of black coal, its body from grey wood. Its mouth gaped open like a cave, and inside was a small orchestra of flutes, lutes and violins. Two women in floor-length embroidered dresses were singing, their hair tied up in yellow ribbons. Their voices vibrated deep in the belly of the wooden whale, as if *it* was singing. A crowd of children sat rapt in its shadow.

Ellie blinked, trying to take it all in. How could such cheerfulness exist? Seth took a few careful steps forward, and Ellie watched as his scrunched-up, tightly wound frame relaxed, his shoulders settling, the white of his knuckles returning to brown as his fists unclenched.

'Looks like this island might be everything we hoped for,' said Ellie.

'What if we've been followed?' said Seth. 'That ship . . .'

'Well, what better place to hide than an island full of people? I hid *you* in an island full of people, didn't I? From three hundred Inquisitors.'

Seth stared round the market. 'It is nice,' he admitted.

Ellie breathed in a wave of smoke from chicken legs searing over a fire pit. The smell made her stomach squirm with hunger.

'We need money,' she said.

'Huh?' said Seth, watching a woman teeter by on stilts, tossing flowers to children below.

'*Money*. For food.'

Seth shrugged. 'I can just catch fish.'

'We need more than fish, Seth. We don't even have any shoes! And where are we going to sleep? We should get jobs. Then we can get money *and* blend in. In case someone really has followed us.'

Seth squinted into the distance, then pointed. 'Look at all those fishing boats! That must be the port. Come on!'

The crowd parted to let Seth through, smiling at him approvingly and whispering to each other through half-hidden grins. They didn't part for Ellie, or even look at her, except to frown. She found this irritating. She caught up with Seth, panting for breath and scrutinizing his appearance. With his unblemished skin, large eyes and symmetrical features, she was forced to admit that other people probably thought him attractive. She found this irritating too.

'Look,' said Seth.

They'd reached the top of a hill overlooking a bright ocean dotted with boats. Each one was sleek and as riotously coloured as the rest of the island, sails dyed and hulls splashed with garish murals, so the docks appeared like some water-drenched flower garden.

'We can get a job on one of those,' said Seth.

'Oh,' said Ellie, pulling at the tattered hems of her coat sleeves. She pictured them on a boat, Seth hauling in huge mountains of fish, Ellie tangled up in a fishing net, helplessly stuck while sailors pelted her with questions about who she was. 'Um, they'd never let a woman fish. Even Castion didn't allow women on his ship.'

Seth pointed to the wooden jetties stitched between the boats. 'Ellie, half the sailors are women.'

'Well . . .' Ellie raised her cane. 'What about my bad leg!'

'That woman there only has *one* leg. Come on,' said Seth, dragging her down a rickety wooden staircase. The sea was green like molten emeralds, and Ellie spotted tiny glittering fish and blushing coral beneath the gentle waves. There were no spires or rooftops poking above the surface, like in the City – all the buildings here must have been built after the Drowning. Maybe the Ark had crashed into the island, and its occupants had decided it was as good a place as any to build a new home.

Ellie and Seth wandered the docks, watching sailors carry cratefuls of gleaming fish along the walkways, to be hauled up the hillside on a system of primitive winches that Ellie eyed critically, dreaming up plans for improvement. They came to the end of one jetty, where a huge man sat in a chair. He had a square, weather-beaten head and thick dark limbs, scarred and knotted like bark. He sank down behind a large sheet of paper, as if hoping to make himself invisible.

'I'm looking for work,' said Seth.

The man grumbled, then scratched at his eyepatch, studying Seth carefully.

'Fine,' he said. 'Grab a mop. The deck will need cleaning when Viola gets back.'

'I don't want to mop,' said Seth. 'I want to fish.'

The man rolled his eye and retrieved a pipe from the pocket of his jerkin, which he began stuffing with tobacco. Ellie peered round Seth's shoulder, annoyed that the man hadn't even looked at her. 'You're from the outer islands?' he said.

'Ingarth Island,' Seth said with confidence.

The man snorted. 'Islanders always come here thinking jobs will fall on their heads. Just arrived, have you?' He looked at Ellie for the first time. 'Seem a little young for newlyweds.'

Seth let out a low laugh that Ellie found insulting.

'We're not newlyweds,' she said, punching Seth's arm. 'My name's Ellie L—' She winced, thinking of the dark figure on the beach. 'Ellie Stonewall. And this is Seth. We're . . . brother and sister.'

'Really?' The man looked from Ellie to Seth in surprise. It was true that it would be hard to find two people who looked less alike — Seth was tall and strong, while Ellie was small and sickly-looking, her hair lank and thin, her body almost vanishing inside her oversized coat. The only sensible explanation would be that Seth was adopted, Ellie decided.

'She was adopted,' said Seth, and Ellie scowled at him. 'Someone left her on our doorstep. My parents were horrified.'

The man chuckled. 'I can see why,' he said, and Ellie scowled at him too. 'It's mopping or nothing. Ah, here's your chance.'

A small boat with two sails drifted in alongside the jetty, pulled on a rope by a sailor. Carved on its prow was a disgruntled pig. A crate was lowered from the deck by two more sailors, and the old man peered inside. His eye widened in horror.

'It's barely half full!' he cried.

'That's because there are *barely* any fish, Dad,' said the last sailor to climb down from the boat. She was about the same age as Ellie, with thick black hair and dark brown skin, and her long arms looked capable of beating even Anna in an arm-wrestle. A tiny grey kitten was perched on her shoulder. Ellie thought it was a stuffed toy pinned to her tunic, until it gave a plaintive miaow. 'Not today, not yesterday, not for the last month. And it's more than just the fish – Jessica said her mum's farm's struggling, and the price of barley's so high Molworth thinks he's gonna have no ale left by autumn.'

'It'll all be fine after the Festival of Life,' said the man, wringing his hands. 'The Queen will provide. Praise Her.'

'She'll provide for Herself,' the girl snorted. 'She's probably stealing all the food for Her and Her rich friends.'

The kitten miaowed loudly, as if in agreement.

'Stop that blasphemous nonsense *right* now,' the man snapped. 'You'll get yourself arrested again.'

The girl rolled her eyes. 'Who's this?' she asked, nodding at Seth. She didn't seem to notice Ellie at all.

31

'No idea,' said the man. 'I'm trying to convince him to scrub the deck. He's from the outer islands so I doubt he expects much pay. Also –' he leaned towards his daughter and whispered – 'I don't think he's too bright.'

'Let me go out in this boat,' Seth said firmly. 'I'll find where all the fish are. I . . . I have a special technique,' he added, when the girl continued to look unimpressed. 'I'm the best fisherman on my island. I'll . . . bet you tonight's dinner?'

Ellie grabbed him by the wrist.

'*Seth*,' she hissed in his ear. 'If they see you use your powers, they might get suspicious.'

'I won't use them,' Seth whispered. 'The fish will come to me. They followed me before – and that whale did too. I didn't even have to use my powers.'

The old man had already lost interest, and was muttering to himself over the half-empty crate. The girl was eyeing Seth curiously.

'What sort of dinner?' she said.

'Viola, stop talking to that sea-sponge,' said her father. 'Take the boat out again and fill the rest of this crate!'

The girl yawned, stretching out her arm so her kitten could crawl along it. 'All right. But I'm taking the sea-sponge with me.'

'What?'

'Either he's telling the truth, in which case we get a better catch, or he's crazy and I'll get a free dinner out of it. My name's Viola, by the way,' she added to Seth, with a slow, easy smile. 'This is my dad, Janssen.'

Seth shook Viola's hand. 'Seth,' he said.

'My name's Ellie,' said Ellie, though nobody seemed to hear her.

Viola swaggered off towards the boat, beckoning for Seth to follow. Seth looked back at Ellie. 'You coming?'

'Oh,' said Ellie. 'I . . .' She looked at Viola and the other sailors, and again pictured being tangled in a net, unable to stop them from questioning her. Finding out who she really was. 'I think I should stay here.'

Seth frowned. 'Why?'

'I . . . It's very hot. I'll get burned in seconds. Here, I have something you could use.'

She rummaged around in her pockets and, after pulling out a handful of pencils and a vial of sheep's blood, she found two hole-spotted gloves.

'Thanks,' said Seth. 'But they don't go with my outfit.'

'They're to cover the blue marks on your skin, *seasponge*,' she whispered. 'Just in case you get in trouble and *do* have to use your powers. Actually . . .' She looked at Seth's bare arms. 'Maybe you should take this too.'

Nervously, she clutched the lapels of her coat.

'Ellie, really, you don't have to do that,' Seth said, looking slightly alarmed.

'Better than you getting put on a bonfire again,' she said, and with a deep breath she removed her coat and

33

handed it to Seth. She wrapped her arms round herself, immediately conscious of the breeze on her neck, and of eyes, *eyes* everywhere.

Seth pulled it on. Despite being much too large on Ellie, the coat was nearly too small for him, though it covered his arms well enough.

'Come on, mate, tide's turning,' Viola called. Seth strode off towards the boat, and Ellie felt a sudden emptiness, like she herself was somehow lacking, without all the parts necessary for a human being.

Maybe it was because she'd given him her coat.

The Abomination

Ellie watched Viola's boat sail away, absently tapping her cane against the edge of the jetty.

'Are you in pain, girl?' came Janssen's gruff voice. 'What happened to your leg?'

The boat had fast become a speck on the horizon.

'I tripped,' said Ellie. She turned to look at the Ark perched proudly upon the tip of the island, an eagle in its roost. Green tufts burst from its curved grey belly, like stuffing from a child's toy. At first, Ellie thought it was moss, then realized they were gardens, growing on massive balconies. 'Is that where the Queen lives?'

'Of course,' said Janssen. 'Are you simple, girl?'

'I'm an *outer islander*, remember? Have you ever seen Her?'

Janssen snorted. 'I've *seen* Her, but not up close – why would they let me anywhere *near* Her? I'm not worthy to breathe the same air. Assuming She even needs air.'

He snatched up his paper, clearly considering the conversation at an end. Ellie scanned the headline:

LOREN SAVES SAILOR FROM DROWNING – MAN DELIGHTED TO MEET HIS HERO

Ellie gazed back at the Ark thoughtfully. What special inventions did they use to make the gardens grow? What other miraculous devices were hidden inside? She pictured the Queen: a tall, luminous being, gifting food and medicine to her people. She saw herself by the Queen's side, not half starved and hobbling on a cane, but wearing a gleaming new coat lined with hundreds of pockets . . .

A snore from Janssen snapped Ellie out of her daydream. She glanced down at her watery reflection, remembering the dark shadow she'd seen beneath the waves, and that figure on the beach. Feeling suddenly exposed, she hurried back along the jetty towards dry land, passing houses with chipped orange shutters swaying lazily in the breeze. Elderly men and women sat on benches, gossiping and sipping tea. Further on, she found three children playing in a doorway. One girl – the tallest of the group – pointed to the boy.

'You've been found guilty of treason by me, the Queen. Your punishment is that you get your head cut off. Gemma, pass me the head.'

A shorter girl handed over a misshapen cloth sack with a face stitched on it. Grinning, the accused boy pulled his shirt up to cover his face, and the taller girl balanced the sack on his head. She raised a large, heavy stick, then smacked the head back off again. The boy giggled.

'But this *isn't* right,' said the short girl. 'The Queen is *kind*.'

'Not always,' said the tall girl. 'She once had someone's head cut off for stealing a goat.'

The short girl shook her head. 'Not the Queen. Never.'

Ellie cleared her throat. 'Um, sorry, can I ask something?'

The children turned as one, saw Ellie, and took a step backwards.

'Are you a ghost?' said the tall girl.

'Are you very unwell?' said the short one.

'No.' Ellie bristled. 'I just wondered . . . what does the Queen look like?'

'She's the most beautiful Queen or King that ever lived,' said the short girl, 'and the gentlest. *She'd* never cut anyone's head off.'

'She would too!' the tall girl cried. 'Thieves and murderers, and anyone who comes from the Island of the –' She frowned, her lips struggling to frame the next word. 'The Abom– Abom–'

'The Abobdiman?' the short girl tried. 'The Abdomen?'

'The Abomination,' said the boy, his voice still muffled by his shirt.

'Exactly,' said the tall girl. 'The Abom– the Abom– Well, you know.' She leaned in close to Ellie, and whispered. 'The *Enemy*.'

Ellie staggered, clutching a hand to her stomach.

'Are you okay?' said the short girl, putting an arm round Ellie's waist.

'I'm fine,' Ellie lied. A shard of ice had pierced her chest. For a few moments she couldn't breathe.

'Don't be afraid, miss,' the tall girl told her. 'People *do* keep trying to come here from the Enemy's City. Because they have such a bad life there and because their god is evil. But the Queen executes them all. And the Abdominal One itself can never come here.' She straightened proudly. 'The Queen keeps us safe.'

'Wait,' said Ellie. 'What do you mean?'

'*Ohh*, you must be an outer islander.' The girl gave her a condescending smile. 'The Enemy is afraid of the Queen, miss. You see, the god inside Her is the God of life and creation. It doesn't even have a proper name, because it's so important. The Enemy is the god of death and destruction – of *course* it fears Her.'

The girl's words settled in Ellie's mind, her fear swept away by an urgent excitement. *The god inside her . . .*

The Queen wasn't a god. She was a *Vessel*.

Ellie gripped her cane and pushed off against the paving stones, racing back towards the docks.

'Sir!' she cried, skidding to a halt at the end of the jetty. 'Um, Janssen!'

The huge man woke with a yelp. 'Mother!' he cried. He noticed Ellie. 'Who are you?'

'How do you know that the Queen is a Vessel?'

Janssen looked at Ellie like she was a loaf of mouldy bread. 'You outer islanders are such heathens. I *know* because it's true. I know because there are fish in the sea and wheat in the fields. I know because, when I was a boy, I saw the miracle of Her power at the Festival of Life.'

'The Festival of Life?'

'Queen's mercy, are you thick, child? Once in a generation, the Queen appears to the people, to heal the sick and make the fields and gardens bloom. My own mother, bless her soul, she had a wasting sickness, and the Queen took her hand in Hers –' Janssen halted, tears leaking out from under his eyepatch. 'Mum lived ten more years. Ten! Thanks to the Queen, she lived to see me become a man. *Praise Her!* And do you know, whenever She uses Her power like that, it drains a little part of Her forever? She gave a bit of Herself, just for my old mum. And She's going to do it again for all of us, six weeks from now at the Festival of Life. Then there'll be fish in the sea again, and crops in the fields.'

He collapsed into his chair. 'Praise Her,' he whispered, then squawked in fright as a crate slammed on to the jetty. Ellie jumped too. She hadn't even noticed the boat return.

Viola and Seth hopped from the deck, beaming like two burglars who'd pulled off a spectacular crime. Viola's kitten mewled triumphantly.

'Dad, have you been crying?' said Viola. 'Was it about those puppies again?'

Janssen leaned over the open crate. 'QUEEN'S MERCY!'

Ellie stood on tiptoe to see inside. It was full to the brim with glistening white-bellied fish.

'Miraculous!' Janssen cried.

'Dad,' said Viola, gripping his shoulder. 'Look at the boat.'

Janssen turned. He grunted, then let out a shrill, hysterical laugh. Ellie caught Seth's eye, and he hid a grin behind his hand.

The entire deck was overflowing with fish.

Leila's Diary

4,754 days aboard the *Revival*

The Crone has a garden deep inside the Ark. Nobody can tell me how anything grows in there without sunlight, but I guess there's more important stuff to worry about. They say the Ark-Captain's losing control, and there'll be fighting soon. Worse, there are whispers that the Enemy is on the Ark with us.

'Where's the boy? I will strangle him,' I told the Crone.

The room was hot and humid, and smelled like sweat and soil. The Crone was leaning over to inspect some plant, rubbing a person-sized leaf between her fingers.

'He didn't kill your whale,' she said. 'In fact, you might say he *is* your whale.'

'Where is he?'

The Crone sighed, lifting her oil lamp and leading me between rows of bean shoots and berry bushes. 'Please refrain from violence – we will need him if we're going to survive this voyage.'

The boy lay sprawled on the floor. He had a sharply drawn face, brown skin and messy black hair. He looked like he'd be useful in a fight, if only he'd wake up.

'What you keeping him for?' I asked.

'You won't believe me, but this boy is a god.'

'Impossible. The gods are gone.'

'I said you wouldn't believe me.'

'He's not my whale, either. Blue Eyes was useful. He brought us fish and seals.'

'Girl, this boy will bring us all the fish and seals we could ever need. He *is* the sea.'

'He's the sea, he's my whale, he's a god. Decide, Crone.'

'You are a mean-spirited child.'

'My whale is *dead*,' I scowled. 'We were bonded. We brought food to the Ark. What am I without him?'

'Perhaps you could help me with my garden instead.'

'I'm a hunter. I won't water plants. Why is this boy my whale?'

The Crone smiled and bent over him. 'Look.'

With a soil-encrusted thumb, she lifted one of his eyelids, revealing an eye the colour of a dark sea. I took a step back.

'*Blue Eyes*,' I whispered. 'What is the meaning of this?'

'Your whale was a Vessel, child. A mortal soul twinned with an immortal spirit.'

'Nonsense. Foolishness. What do you mean?'

'I know the signs, child. I know them better than any.'

'How?'

The Crone touched the boy's cheek tenderly.

'Because I'm a Vessel too.'

The Vile Oak

Seth's grin faltered.

His eyes went out of focus. Ellie rushed to stop him falling and he crumpled against her like a sack of potatoes.

'Seth? Are you okay?' Ellie struggled to keep him upright.

'Has he drunk enough water?' said Janssen, fussing over Seth like he was a prize-fighting walrus. 'HANDYL!' he roared along the jetty. 'WATER!'

'I'm fine.' Seth strained to open his eyes. 'Just tired.'

Janssen nodded vigorously, slapping a jangling purse into Viola's hand. 'Get him a room at the Oak.'

Viola waved for Seth and Ellie to follow. 'It's okay,' Seth said, as Ellie helped him along the jetty. 'I can manage.'

'What happened?' she asked, then lowered her voice. 'Did you have to use your *powers*?'

'No . . . but I saw something.' He grimaced. 'I think I was a whale again. And there was a girl . . .'

'Did you fall asleep for a minute?'

'No, I did not fall asleep,' Seth snapped.

'Oi!' Viola shouted from up the street. 'You coming, or you gonna faint again?'

'I did *not* faint!' Seth said.

'You outer islanders are all soft,' said Viola. 'And there I was thinking I could recruit you for the Revolution.'

Seth and Ellie shared a glance. 'Um, what's that?' said Ellie.

'When the people rise up and take back control of the island from Her Royal Uselessness,' said Viola, pointing an accusing finger at the Ark.

'Who have you recruited so far?' said Seth, as they clattered up some wooden steps.

'Just me and Archibald,' she said, stroking her kitten's ear. 'People get pretty angry when I bring it up. But if you ask me we shouldn't have a god in government. Gods don't care about us little people.'

'You don't know that,' said Seth defensively.

Viola tutted. 'Another Queen-lover.' She gave a long sigh. 'And I had such high hopes for you.'

She punched him in the arm and ran off ahead, smiling mischievously. Seth rubbed his arm, but was smiling too. Ellie felt a hot twinge in her chest.

'Seth, listen,' she said, partly to get his attention back. 'I found something out about the Queen, actually. She's not a god. She's a *Vessel*.'

Seth gave her a long stare.

'Apparently there have been other Queens and Kings before her,' Ellie continued. 'But they must have contained the same god, passing from one person to the next. Another Vessel, Seth! Like me!'

Seth frowned, but stayed silent.

'What?' said Ellie. She searched his face, but his eyes were far away, like he was doing complex sums in his head. 'Why aren't you excited?'

'She's not like you. She's a Queen.'

'But she has a *god* inside her – one of your siblings.'

'Ellie, the only one of my siblings we've met keeps trying to kill you. Maybe Viola's right not to trust the Queen.'

'But that's the other thing,' she said. 'The Enemy's *afraid* of her. She's the most powerful person on this island! In the whole world, maybe! What if she can help us?'

Seth looked at her with a mixture of pity and affection. 'Ellie, you don't know anything about her. What do you expect her to do if you turn up and say, "Hi, I'm a Vessel too, and, by the way, my friend here is a god"?'

'Well, obviously I'm not going to say *that*,' said Ellie.

'Powerful people are dangerous, Ellie,' said Seth. 'Have you forgotten the Inquisition?'

Ellie crossed her arms. 'Just because she's a Vessel doesn't mean she's dangerous. Besides, you're powerful. And you're not dangerous.'

Seth gave her another long stare. 'We shouldn't draw attention to ourselves. We need to be careful, in case the person on that ship really did follow us here.'

Ellie shrugged. 'If they did, they should watch themselves – apparently, people from the City have been executed here before.'

Seth's eyes bulged. 'Then we definitely need to be careful.'

'We're here!' Viola announced.

They'd come out of the street, and were standing directly in the shadow of the Ark's belly. The island was almost vertical on this side, a sheer hill rising towards the bottom of the Ark, cluttered with colourful, cosily packed houses.

'This part of the island is called the Shambles,' Viola said fondly. Ellie thought this a very appropriate name. It was a wall of tiered streets, homes piled on top of each other like ill-fitting jigsaw pieces, stacked so steeply that anyone racing out of their front door would likely tumble to their death.

They climbed tight little staircases, chickens strutting across the drystone walls, pecking up tiny, jewel-coloured insects. There were no palm trees here but thick, fierce oaks, which looked considerably older than anything else on the island, except maybe the Ark itself. One unfortunate building had a tree growing all the way through it, though it might have been more accurate to say the tree had bits of building growing round it. It was a particularly burly and menacing oak, clutching fragments of the building in its branches, like a child that has broken its favourite toy. The largest part of the building was at street level, wedged into the trunk, from which many staircases wound out of and up the tree's sides, following the branches to where other ramshackle huts sat like birds' nests.

A metal sign dangled from one branch. THE — OAK, it read, the middle word obscured by rust.

'The Vile Oak!' said Viola proudly.

'That's not a good name for an inn,' said Seth.

'Its real name is the Royal Oak, but no one calls it that except Molworth the innkeeper. He gets *really* angry when you don't use its proper name.'

Bells tinkled as they opened the front door, into a wide room that smelled of stale beer and oranges. In places, the walls had been ripped open by the tree, branches pressing in to fill the gaps. Behind a polished bar stood a small boy, his pale round face only just peeping above the counter.

'It's . . . nice,' said Ellie. 'Where's the innkeeper?'

Viola frowned. 'There.'

'Where?'

'*Here*,' said the boy. He raised himself up on to the bar, glaring at them with eyes like deep puddles. He had wispy black hair, a single curl plastered to his pale forehead. He

wore a black jacket with silver buttons, which looked expensive, and a pair of ragged trousers, which did not.

'This is Molworth,' said Viola. 'He owns the inn.'

'How old are you?' asked Ellie.

'Twelve,' said Molworth. His voice was surprisingly deep. 'How old are you?'

'Thirteen. What's a twelve-year-old doing owning an inn?'

'What's a thirteen-year-old doing asking stupid questions? And why aren't either of you wearing shoes? Viola, why've you brought me an idiot and a mute with no shoes? Also, didn't I bar you?'

'I'm not mute,' Seth muttered.

'I *won* the inn,' said Molworth, crossing his arms. 'In a game of cards.'

Viola rolled her eyes. 'You did not. Your dad left it to you in his will.'

'Only because I beat him in a game of cards. Now, if you can't afford shoes, I doubt you can afford rooms, either. And I don't sell beer to children.' He paused. 'Not any more.'

'My dad's just given the healthy one a job,' said Viola, jangling Janssen's purse. 'They can afford one of the top rooms.'

'Healthy one?' said Ellie.

Molworth let out a long groan. 'Fine.' He bowed. 'Let me fetch the key, and I'll lead you to your room, loyal subjects.'

He flopped gracelessly from view. Behind the bar, Ellie noticed, was another tall statue of the Queen – the most intricate and well crafted she'd seen. Other queenly statuettes sat in cubbyholes round the walls, between dusty bottles, and pinned to the shelves were dozens of drawings of a beautiful face with yellow eyes and purple hair. Scribbled in the corner of one were the words *Molworth, aged nine and a half*.

'You *really* like the Queen,' said Seth.

Molworth's head reappeared, his eyes narrowing suspiciously. 'Who doesn't?'

'Me,' said Viola.

'And that's why I barred you!' Molworth snapped. 'Only a fool like Viola wouldn't love the Queen – She is our beloved provider and protector.' He climbed on the counter and threw his hands above his head, reminding Ellie of the preachers back in the City. 'She is the Vessel!' he proclaimed. 'The physical container of our kind and benevolent God, who brings the harvest and the fish! She is the watcher of the horizon and the source of life itself, and we are not worthy of Her grace! She is divine and beautiful and in six weeks She will return the island to greatness at the Festival of Life!'

'Please shut up, Molworth,' said Viola.

Molworth glared at her balefully. 'I will *not*,' he said. 'And another thing: stop leaving those leaflets of yours on my tables. Nobody cares about your stupid Revolution.

You're an ungrateful heathen and one day I'm going to take that cat and –'

Viola rushed over and tickled him under the arms.

'No, don't!' Molworth protested, laughing hysterically.

'There are *other* things in life besides the Queen, you know,' Viola said, grabbing the key from Molworth's fist and leading Seth and Ellie away from the bar, leaving Molworth crumpled against the counter.

'Nothing worth my time,' he said, in a faraway voice.

Ellie and Seth followed Viola up a narrow winding staircase high into the oak, its leaves shimmering around them, to a branch that was as thick as a whale, sanded flat to accommodate a long wooden hut. Inside was a humid corridor.

'You're down the far end,' said Viola, handing Seth the key. 'I better get back to Dad. See you tomorrow, Seth. Be at the docks by dawn – we sail with the tide! Oh and I'll bring some of my leaflets for you to read. Bye, Jennifer,' she added to Ellie.

The room looked like a ship's cabin, smelling of pine and tobacco, the ceiling so low that Seth had to hunch. Ellie hung her coat on the single hook in the wall, which promptly fell off, clattering to the floor and taking her coat with it. A black liquid seeped from the pockets.

'Ellie, try to keep *this* room clean, will you?' Seth said.

'That wasn't my fault!' she said, then noticed Seth was smiling.

'And no experiments, either,' he added archly.

Ellie huffed and inspected a crude painting of a horse on the shelf, the name *Molworth* scrawled in one corner. She picked up her coat and searched the pockets, removing a flat parcel of dried seal intestine, inside which was a water-damaged drawing of a boat in coloured pencils. On the boat was a girl with ginger hair, a girl with blonde hair, and a boy with green eyes. Ellie placed it on the shelf and nodded approvingly, until thoughts of Anna made her sad and she looked about for a distraction.

'We have a door!' she announced, grinning and pointing at the flimsy piece of wood, badly set into the wall.

'And a window,' Seth said, opening it and eliciting a disgruntled squawk from the seagull nesting outside. He leaned back on one of the two beds, his face bathed in warm honey-coloured daylight. 'It's weird that I get to live here and it doesn't have to be a secret.'

Ellie smiled, delighted to see him happy.

She hobbled over to the other bed. It was child-sized, with a single pillow spilling feathers, and a metal frame crusted orange with rust. It was beautiful.

'A bed,' she said. 'An actual bed. Isn't it great, Seth? Seth?'

Seth's eyes were closed and his mouth hung open. Ellie tucked the sheet round him, then yawned. Her bed drew her towards it like a current, her head hitting the pillow.

CRASH.

Ellie and Seth both jumped to their feet in terror.

Janssen stood in the doorway, a huge smile on his face, a frightening sparkle in his eye, and Molworth tucked under one arm. He pointed at Seth.

'There he is! My saviour. Come, boy, we're celebrating!'

'Please let me go,' said Molworth, his voice muffled by Janssen's armpit.

'They need sleep, Dad,' said Viola, appearing from behind Janssen. 'Look – they're exhausted.'

But Janssen hoisted Seth up and jogged from the room, ferrying Seth and Molworth under each arm. The door slammed shut, and Ellie was alone.

The silence pressed in on her, shocking and sudden, like she'd only dreamed the others had just been there. She looked at Seth's empty bed, frowned, then pulled on her coat and crept after them.

The bar felt half the size it had done before, crowded by singing and shouting and the smell of fish. Fifty men and women in jerkins and torn trousers were taking it in turns to introduce themselves to Seth. He kept running a hand through his hair and smiling bashfully, and sometimes he would say something and everyone would laugh. Ellie had never noticed how good Seth was with people before, although admittedly back in the City everyone had wanted to kill him. Even Anna.

Ellie's heart ached at the thought of Anna threatening to slip poison in Seth's breakfast. She stood alone in a corner, afraid someone would glance over and take note of her aloneness. She felt very aware of her hands, and didn't know what to do with them; they seemed huge and conspicuous. She spotted Viola leaning against the bar, holding up a saucer of milk for Archibald to drink from.

'Hello, I'm Ellie,' she said, hurrying over.

Viola's eyes narrowed in confusion. 'I know. We . . . we've met.'

'Oh, yes. I just . . . you know, in case you'd forgotten.'

Viola looked at Ellie, and Ellie swallowed, finding her head empty of thoughts. Anna had once told her that a good way to make friends was by telling jokes, or by finding something you had in common. But Ellie had never been good at jokes – she always overthought them. She scratched her head, opened her mouth, then closed it again. The lump in her throat swelled to the size of a cannonball.

'So . . . do you like . . . fish?'

Viola frowned. 'Here, have one of these,' she said, offering Ellie a plate of round sugar-coated buns. 'My mum used to make 'em. Dad's never got the recipe right.'

Ellie took one gratefully. 'So . . . why doesn't your mum make them any more?'

'She's dead.'

'Oh great!'

Viola's eyes widened.

'I mean.' Ellie winced. 'My mum's dead too. So's my brother,' she added, as if this might somehow mean they had *more* in common.

Viola gave Ellie a long stare. 'Wait, I thought Seth was your brother?'

'Oh, oh right, yeah. He *is* my brother. My other brother. I have two brothers. I mean . . . I *had* two brothers. No, wait –'

Viola continued to stare.

'Um, I should go and check Seth's doing okay,' Ellie said hurriedly.

But Seth *was* doing okay – much more than okay, even. The sailors clamoured round him, telling stories that involved a lot of dramatic hand gestures and booming laughter. Seth just listened quietly as they vied to impress him – somehow, they'd already accepted him as one of their own. Molworth, meanwhile, was darting around at waist height with a cloth and a look of panic, mopping spills and snatching up empty glasses before a careless hand could knock them flying.

'Come on then, lad – what's your secret?' one man asked Seth.

'Oh,' said Seth, rubbing the back of his head, smiling that same bashful smile. 'Well, you know. I just ask the fish really nicely.'

The roar of laughter was so loud Ellie had to cover her ears, while Molworth dropped a glass, miraculously catching it on the tip of his shoe. Ellie frowned – it wasn't even a good joke! She wondered if being handsome meant people always laughed at your jokes, even if they weren't funny.

Viola joined the circle. 'Did you tell 'em about the great white shark we saw?'

'Oh yeah,' said Seth. 'It was massive. Its teeth were like carving knives and it came right up next to the boat.'

Ellie felt another hot stab in her chest. Why had Seth not mentioned to her that they'd seen a great white shark?

'Seth threw a fish straight in its mouth,' said Viola, miming the action. 'Thought it was going to take his arm off – you could see right down its big throat.'

The crowd listened intently, and the way Seth and Viola spoke it was like they were the only two people in the bar.

'How long do you think it was?' said Seth. 'The length of this room?'

'And it had these dead lifeless eyes,' said Viola. 'Almost jumped in the water just to see what it would do. Always fancied myself a shark wrestler. What I'd do is, I'd punch it right in the head, then –'

'I saw a great white shark once,' said Ellie.

Viola blinked at the interruption. 'Yeah?'

'Yeah,' said Ellie. All the sailors turned to stare at her. She cleared her throat. 'It was dead.'

'Oh,' said Viola, her smile faltering. Seth scratched his head. The other sailors muttered to one another.

'Yeah,' said Ellie. Her throat seemed to be closing up. 'It smelled bad too.'

There was a moment's silence, and if there'd been a great white shark in the bar, Ellie would have leapt straight into its mouth.

'Excuse me,' she said, and hobbled for the front door. 'I, uh . . . need to check on a . . . tree.' She fumbled with the door handle. 'It's outside.'

'Your sister's an odd one, isn't she?' Janssen said. The door closed behind her, drowning out the sound of their laughter. Ellie stepped into the baking daylight, looking down at the sea and the huge new island around her.

And somewhere, deep inside her mind, crawling from one slimy, secret corner, she heard something else laughing.

The Spy

Ellie didn't know where she was going, she just knew she didn't want to be at the inn. She took the first alley she could find, away from the Shambles and towards the rest of the island.

'You'll be much too hot in that coat, girl,' said a man on a pile of straw, a cat nestled in his lap.

Ellie scowled and pulled her coat tightly round herself stubbornly. She realized suddenly but with complete clarity that she *hated* this island, with its stifling heat that made sweat get in her eyes, and its people who crowded round Seth adoringly while ignoring her altogether.

It was a few streets before she realized her feet were taking her upward, towards the island's peak. Towards the Ark. She stopped, and was annoyed to find a tear on her cheek. She looked up at the Ark, its prow stabbing the sky.

Surely, if anyone on this island was going to understand her, it would be a Queen. A Queen who was wise, and wanted to protect her people. A Queen who was a Vessel.

Ellie hurried onwards, not caring that her leg hurt. Performers capered atop tall stilts, covered in shimmering purple feathers, tottering around to the delight of small children. She passed what looked like guards, or soldiers maybe – men and women in polished silver armour and ornate conical helmets, with plumes of feathers issuing from the top, a deep onion red. Always she watched the alleyways, searching for the tall figure from the beach.

She was pretty sure she'd come to the richer part of the island. The buildings up here were less ramshackle, though just as colourful, and the people would have shamed even the whale lords with their extravagance. They were clothed in dresses shaped like church bells, the colours of saffron and wheat, turtle green and parrot turquoise. They wore huge, gem-studded hats, which looked likely to cause neck problems in later life.

Strangely, Ellie couldn't always see the Ark this far up the island, what with the streets being packed so high. She caught glimpses of it between rooftops as she passed by, but only after climbing for what felt an hour, as she turned on to a long, broad street, was it revealed entirely.

It pointed majestically at the sky, as if preparing to ascend heavenwards on one final voyage. It was the size of a hundred whaling ships joined together. Though it must once have been made entirely from wood, parts of it had been built over in stone, as if it had petrified with time, transfiguring it from a ship into a palace.

What had once been its topmost deck was now its front wall, painted with a vast mural: hundreds of people in a garden of fat, fruit-bearing trees, so luscious that Ellie expected the plants to grow even as she watched. At the very top of the mural, right beneath the prow of the ship, a glowing, angelic figure had been painted to gaze lovingly upon the garden. Neither male nor female, it had immense, swanlike wings that spilled down the sides of the mural, sheltering the humans within their embrace, feathers changing to leaves, then vines, then roots that curled into the soil.

Ellie walked towards two huge doors set within a great archway at the bottom of the mural, from which a staircase issued like a tongue. An iron gate rose before the stairs, and one of the armoured men stood next to it, tapping a rhythm on his gauntlet and humming softly to himself.

'Um, can I go in?' Ellie asked.

The gatekeeper didn't look at her. 'Do you have official business?'

'Uh, I'd like to speak to the Queen, if that counts?'

'It does not.'

Ellie grumbled. She grabbed the gates in both hands and squeezed her head partway through the gap, staring at the massive closed doors at the base of the mural.

'Please don't,' said the gatekeeper. 'You wouldn't believe how many children I've had to pull from these gates.'

'Does she ever come out?' said Ellie.

'Yes.'

'If I stay here, will I see her?'

The gatekeeper shrugged. 'Maybe. She's unlikely to see you, though.'

Ellie sighed, trying to will the doors to open. Instead, a much smaller door opened at one side, and a line of eight girls emerged, each a replica of the other. They wore silver face paint, and long purple dresses with black flowers on each shoulder.

'Who are they?' Ellie asked the gatekeeper.

'If I tell you, will you stop asking questions?'

Ellie nodded.

'They're the Queen's handmaidens. They serve Her Divine Majesty in all Her tasks.'

'What tasks?'

'That sounds like another question to me.'

The handmaidens mounted the stairs towards the main entrance in perfect synchrony, and the doors were pulled open by two more guards in silver armour.

Ellie gasped as she caught a glimpse inside. White marble walls. Gleaming black tiles. Glittering crystal chandeliers. She could hardly imagine what exquisite lives the handmaidens must lead as servants of the Queen; a woman who could rule an island larger than even the City, despite being a Vessel. Ellie pictured herself walking through the palace with her head held high, assisting the Queen and impressing her with all her knowledge. The hairs on her neck stood on end.

Then the doors slammed shut.

Ellie's eyes narrowed. 'I'll be back,' she told the gatekeeper.

'I look forward to it,' he replied. 'Though maybe wear some shoes next time.'

Ellie slouched away, feeling even more alone than before. She drifted down the street, dropping into a heap in front of a jeweller's shop. Her heartbeat echoed through her whole body, like a clock ticking inside an empty cathedral.

She thought of Seth, a smile on his face for everyone but her. She groaned, sliding down the wall until she was almost horizontal. A girl with a mess of curly ginger hair walked by, and Ellie wished dearly that Anna could be here with her right now, to lift her up and lead her off on some poorly thought-out and dangerous scheme.

But Anna was a thousand miles away. In a city that thought Ellie was dead – that had *wanted* her dead. She tried to remind herself that, in a way, Anna *was* still with her. That friendships lasted beyond time, beyond circumstance. Beyond death. Anna had taught her that, and it had saved Ellie's life. She tried to imagine Anna there with her now. Tried to picture her face.

But it was so hard.

She let out a long sigh, which took some of the pain with it, then eased herself up with her cane. She glanced down, then squinted.

Something glistened on the paving stones. Many somethings, in fact.

There were bloody footprints on the ground, dotted with white pinpricks of sunlight.

A child's.

Ellie placed her bare foot next to one. It was about the same size as hers. The footprints trailed along the alley, and Ellie was afraid that a child nearby was hurt. She followed the footprints round a corner, down the street and into a dead-end alley, where they vanished beside a pile of crates.

Ellie frowned, wondering where the child could have gone. Then she glanced up, and saw that, kneeling upon the highest crate, was a girl.

She had tanned skin and long, messy dark hair. She wore a weathered blue cloak, black shoes and socks, and was watching something through a window.

'Excuse me,' said Ellie. 'Have you seen an injured child?'

The girl's head turned sharply in Ellie's direction. She didn't seem surprised by her sudden appearance, just annoyed.

Shut up, she mouthed, then returned to staring through the window.

'Can't you see all these footprints?'

The girl swiped her hand angrily through the air. She was pretty, about Ellie's age or slightly older. Her cloak fell open as she gesticulated, revealing a glimpse of pale lilac beneath. Ellie gasped.

'You're one of the Queen's handmaidens!' she whispered, noticing a smudge of silver make-up beneath the girl's right earlobe. 'Are you here on royal business?'

'*Shh!*' said the girl.

Ellie crept on to the crate. Up close, the girl smelled of honey and lavender. Ellie peered through the window, into a cosy kitchen. There were children's paintings on the wall, racks of spices and herbs, and a wooden counter covered in coconut husks, tomato seeds and fish skeletons.

A mother, a father, and three daughters sat round the kitchen table. The father presented the youngest daughter with a toy dolphin made from felt, which the girl clutched tightly to her chest. She wore a hat of flowers, and Ellie supposed it was her birthday. The man leaned back in his chair, watching his daughter with satisfaction. He had a warm face and kind eyes, which just then glanced up to the window, spotting Ellie and the other girl.

'YOU!' His roar made the glass tremble. He leapt from his seat and darted from view. Fabric brushed Ellie's face as the handmaiden sprang down from the crate and raced along the alley back towards the street.

A great shadow appeared, blocking the girl's path.

'I told you I'd hand you over to the Wardens if I caught you spying again!' said the father.

The girl stood frozen, hands trembling. Ellie looked from her to the huge man and back, then reached into her coat pocket. She retrieved a small metal sphere, praying it would still work after so many months at sea, then hurled it at the ground by the man's feet.

It exploded immediately, spouting a massive cloud of smoke that filled the alley. Ellie rushed forward, reaching out and finding a slim arm, and a hand, which gripped Ellie's with surprising strength. A massive dark shape flailed above them as they snuck by, and then they were through the smoke and sunlight burst all around them.

They hurried across the street and down another alley, hearing the man's shouts behind them. Ellie clenched her teeth as she struggled to keep up with the girl, her right leg aching fiercely. As she turned a corner, her foot caught a box of empty flowerpots, and she tripped, nails and screwdrivers spilling from her pockets, her cane clattering away across the paving stones.

Ellie heard a deep shout echo from close by: the man was chasing them. She looked up, and saw the handmaiden racing down the alley. Ellie groaned – her one chance to meet the Queen was slipping away.

Then the girl glanced back over her shoulder.

She saw Ellie on the floor, hesitated, then rolled her eyes and hurried back, snatching up Ellie's cane. She pulled Ellie out of the alley and down another, through a bewildering riot of dangling laundry and drying fish hanging from wooden frames. Finally, they stopped in the cool shadow of a statue of the Queen. The girl sat down, eyeing Ellie suspiciously. Her cheeks were tinged pink, but she was otherwise composed. Ellie, meanwhile, was leaning on her cane and coughing.

'Th-thank you,' Ellie spluttered. 'For coming back for me.'

'How did you make that dark cloud?'

'Oh,' said Ellie, still struggling to breathe. 'It was . . . was one of these.' She pulled another metal sphere from her pocket. 'I call them smoke bombs. They contain . . . sugar, saltpetre and saleratus.' She paused, waiting for the girl to be impressed, but she just stared at her. The girl's eyes were large and brown with golden specks. 'I make them myself,' Ellie added.

Still the girl said nothing, just stared.

'I'm an inventor, you see.' Ellie's mouth had gone very dry.

The girl did not appear to ever blink.

'My name's Ellie.'

The girl's ears twitched slightly. The rest of her was as still as the statue above them.

'Um, what's yours?' Ellie said.

'Kate,' she said. 'Can I see that?'

Ellie passed her the smoke bomb. The girl turned it over in her fingers, studying it.

'Um . . . Kate?' said Ellie. 'You work for the Queen, don't you?'

Kate looked up, a hint of danger in her eyes. A suggestion of imminent violence.

'I just mean, um,' Ellie stammered. 'The thing is, I'd like to work for her too.'

Finally, Kate blinked, slow and controlled. 'What can you do for the Queen?'

'Well, like I said – I'm an inventor. I make things. I made a boat that can go underwater. Do you think you could maybe ask her if I . . . you know . . .'

'What would She want with *you*?'

'Well, I think I could be useful,' she said. 'And I want to be part of something good. You work for the Queen, you must know what I mean?'

Kate watched Ellie with that same dangerous stare.

'You don't want to work for the Queen, Ellie,' she said, rising to her feet. 'The Queen cannot be trusted.'

She threw the smoke bomb at the floor.

Smoke rushed up Ellie's nose. She coughed and reached out into the grey blanket around her. But her fingers touched bare wall, and when the smoke cleared, Ellie found herself standing in an empty alleyway.

Alone.

Leila's Diary

4,756 days aboard the *Revival*

I bring the Crone water for her plants and for the boy. I buy fish from the fishing clans. Now that Blue Eyes is dead, I belong to no clan. I've no money either but the Crone gives me beetroots and onions to trade with, so plump and juicy that I reckon they'd spout water if you stabbed a hole in them. Not like the ragged vegetables the farming clans grow on the Sky Deck.

'What's your secret?' I asked, watching her prune a cherry tree in the dim candlelight.

'I have a god living inside me. Here, take this.' She handed me some of the offcuts to collect in a bucket.

'What's it called?'

'It doesn't call itself anything.'

'I thought gods had names. The Enemy has a name.'

'That is the name *we* have given it, much to its delight, I'm sure. What's *your* name, girl?'

'Leila,' I said. 'Leila the whale rider.'

'You'll need a new name now.'

'I don't want a new name.'

'It doesn't describe you.'

'So? You call yourself a Vessel, but I've yet to see any evidence.'

'Hold this,' said the Crone, putting a pot of soil in my hands.

'I don't even know why I waste my time here,' I said, feeling my temper rise. 'You've brought me nothing but misery, and a boy who stole my whale's eyes and who sleeps all the –'

Something touched my wrist and I dropped the pot. I expected a crash of clay, but . . . nothing. The pot was suspended a foot above the wooden floor, a branch curling from the soil, wrapping round my arm. I watched as sharp leaves uncurled from its tightly packed buds.

The old woman looked at me.

'You stay here because you think you have nothing else, child. No parents, no siblings and now no whale. The god in me, though . . . it lost this whole world. But with this one –' she looked down at the sheepskin rug where the boy lay utterly still – 'we might be able to make it new again.'

The Crone passed her hand over the branch round my wrist, and a brilliant purple flower burst forth.

A Lesson in Guano

Seth left the Vile Oak early each morning to work on Janssen's boat. Sometimes Ellie would be woken only by the sound of him closing the door on the way out, and would crawl from the sheets, grouchy and alone, the bedroom massive and empty.

She stumbled down to the bar one day to find Molworth mopping the floor. The room stank of stale beer and wine and there were puddles of both everywhere, and a shattered violin for some reason. A man was asleep on a table by the window, his perfectly round stomach eclipsing the sun as it rose and fell.

'Um, can I help?' Ellie asked. Molworth prodded the man with the handle of his mop, eliciting nothing but a burp.

'You'd only get in the way,' said Molworth, pulling a fork from his pocket and inspecting the points in the sunlight. 'What *do* you do, anyway?'

'Well . . . nothing at the moment,' Ellie said, sticking her hands deep in her pockets. 'I've never had nothing to do before.'

'Pray to the Queen, and She will show you a path,' said Molworth, holding the fork over the man's bare stomach. 'And maybe try brushing your hair occasionally.'

Ellie grumbled and stepped out of the pub. There was a high-pitched yelp from behind her, scattering chickens and seagulls.

With nothing to do while Seth was fishing, Ellie wandered the island. She found a blacksmith's by the Humpback Crags, where skinny, blue-furred goats leapt from rock to rock. The forge was hot and smoky and Ellie breathed deeply, imagining she was back in her workshop. She half expected Anna to appear, to hug her or punch her arm.

'What do you want,' said a huge woman, rising from behind the bellows. Her skin was a map of old burn scars.

'I'm looking for work.'

'Can you cook?'

'A little? Though I don't —'

'I need someone to make my soup.'

'No, you don't understand, I'm an inventor.'

73

'Then invent me some soup.'

'I could . . . make you a machine that sharpens your tools, or . . . clears all this smoke? I could improve that forge of yours. It looks very old.'

'You telling me how to do my job?'

'Exactly!' said Ellie. 'I can tell you all sorts of ways you could do your job better.'

'I don't want sick-looking pains-in-the-neck, I want someone to make my soup.'

'But please, I need a job!'

The blacksmith rolled her eyes. 'Pray to the Queen, and She will show you a path. Now get out.'

So Ellie wandered south to the Abrami Coast, where old men and women sheltered in the shade of palm trees, and children frolicked and squealed in the shallows. She entered an apothecary's, a cramped shop stuffed with shelves of colourful powders, the ceiling hung with a hundred bunches of dried plants. It smelled of rot and rancid fruit.

The gaunt man behind the counter peered over the paper he was reading. On it were printed block capitals:

LOREN DONATES GRAIN TO THE POOR. POOR OVERJOYED TO MEET THEIR HERO

'Queen's mercy, what's wrong with you?' the man said, eyes widening in horror. 'Why haven't you come to see me sooner? You need Sprig of Marbel to put the colour back in your cheeks.'

He held up a purple flower. Ellie made a face.

'That's nightshade. It's extremely dangerous.'

'Child, I know a bit more about plants than you do. Take this.' He held out something small, round and red. 'It will fix that leg of yours in minutes.'

'That's a radish. You're selling these things to people as *treatments*? I'm surprised you haven't killed someone!'

'You watch your tongue, girl. Doreen Willis was getting on in years. And she had those warts on her face *before* she came to me.'

'Look, can I have a job? I know a lot about plants.'

The man looked her up and down. A big smile spread across his face.

'No.'

After that, Ellie tried a candlemaker, a cake-maker and a seamstress, none of whom had need of her help. She tried a chef, who thought she'd come to babysit her son. She tried an elderly clockmaker, who threatened to have her arrested. She tried a timid shoe-shiner.

'I could invent a machine that shines the shoes *for* you,' she told him excitedly. He had a brush in hand and a queue of extravagantly dressed noblemen waiting impatiently.

'Oh dear, I think you should go,' he mumbled. 'You don't look well – you might need a Sprig of Marbel from the apothecary.'

'Ooh, it could have *eight* arms, and each one could have a hand that spins very quickly and shines the shoes, so you can just sit back and relax!'

'But I like shining shoes.'

'Please,' said Ellie. 'I really need a job.'

The man looked deeply into Ellie's eyes.

'Pray to the Queen, and She will –'

'Oh, I'll tell you what she can do with her path!' Ellie yelled, then scarpered as the noblemen rushed at her, like a flock of seagulls to a fish.

~

The bedroom door swung open a few inches, then got stuck. Seth's tired face appeared through the gap.

'Why won't the door open?' he said wearily.

Ellie hurried over and shifted a large metal pot, taking care not to disturb the liquid inside.

'What's that doing there?' said Seth.

'I borrowed it from the kitchen.'

Seth frowned, then looked round their room. 'Ellie, what have you done?'

The floor was packed wall to wall with pots, tin cans, clay bowls, mugs, glass jars, and the empty turtle shell that Janssen liked to drink his beer from. Every container was filled to the brim with a murky grey-green liquid, and the room had a musty smell even though the window was open. Only Seth's bed remained undisturbed, with a foot of clear space left around it as a sign of respect.

'It's guano,' Ellie said proudly.

'What's guano?'

'They have these guano mines on the north side that are just *full* of the stuff.'

'But what is it?'

'Oh, well . . . it's bird droppings.'

'Bird droppings!' Seth exclaimed, then put a hand to his mouth. '*Bird droppings?*' he hissed. 'Did you tell Molworth that that's what you needed his pots for when you asked to borrow them?'

Ellie laughed. 'Oh, don't worry about that.'

'Good.'

'I never asked.'

'*Ellie!*'

'Well, he wouldn't have lent them to me if I *had*.'

Seth gingerly navigated his way across the room. 'I'm going to take a bath.'

'Um . . . I wouldn't recommend using the bathtub right now. It's . . . occupied.'

Seth's shoulders stiffened. 'Didn't we agree: no experiments in the bedroom?'

Ellie shot Seth her most winning smile. 'It's all part of my new plan.'

Seth grumbled, hopped over the last few pots, and collapsed on his bed. Ellie took a long wooden spoon and stirred the liquid in one bowl.

'Aren't you going to ask me what it's for?' she said, holding up the spoon and inspecting it.

Seth buried his face in his pillow.

'If I leave the guano in water overnight,' Ellie explained, 'it will form these special crystals, you see.'

She waited a few seconds. Seth sighed deeply. 'What are the crystals for?'

Ellie savoured the moment. 'Gunpowder.'

'GUNPOWDER?' Seth cried, wedging himself into the corner of the room, eyeing the pots in horror.

'I haven't *made* it yet,' said Ellie. 'The crystals need to be mixed with charcoal and sulphur before they'll explode.'

'Ellie.' Seth shut his eyes tightly. 'We're supposed to be keeping a low profile. Remember the person from that black ship? Don't you think they might notice if you blow up half the island by mistake?'

'Oh, I think we're being paranoid – we haven't seen any sign of them for days. It was probably just a sailor. Nobody could have followed us all the way from the City. Besides, I'm not going to blow anything up – I'll only make a *little* bomb, to check the powder works. And I promise to set it off somewhere there's no one about.'

'*Ellie.*'

'The rest is for *fireworks*. They don't have them here – maybe they've forgotten how to make them?'

Seth rubbed his hands over his face in exasperation. 'Good, yes, start setting off fireworks all over the place. Nobody's going to notice that.'

'Well, maybe I *want* her to notice,' Ellie snapped.

'Her?' Seth said. 'Who's "her"?'

Ellie looked intently at the bowl of guano she was stirring. She could feel Seth watching her.

'Please don't tell me you mean the Queen,' he said.

Ellie's cheeks flushed.

'How do you think the Queen can help you?'

'Maybe she knows how to defeat the Enemy,' said Ellie. 'Why else would it be afraid of her?'

'Ellie, that's just an old story the people here believe. Some of Janssen's crew also think it's good luck to wash your face in squid ink on a Monday.'

'But if there's even the slightest chance the story might be true, I need to investigate. Besides, she's a Vessel *too*, like me. And she's clearly doing okay – she's the Queen. So maybe she can help me to be okay too.'

Seth took a careful step towards her. 'But you are okay, Ellie.'

'I'm *not*,' Ellie said, stirring one pot so violently that guano-water slopped over the edge. 'I saw it. Underwater, the day we arrived here. What if it comes back?'

'Ellie, it's not coming back,' said Seth gently. 'You don't need a Queen to help you – you already defeated the Enemy by yourself. And you're not going to make any wishes, and that's the only way it can get any power.'

'But what if this Queen knows something we don't?' Ellie felt a surge of annoyance. 'I don't understand why you're not more excited. She's a *Vessel*, Seth. She's got a *god* living inside her mind. One of your brothers or sisters.'

Seth winced. 'I told you – I don't want anything to do with other gods. I just want to fish. I don't want to have to feel the *sea* all the time. And I don't want these dreams, either.'

'What dreams? You mean like that vision you had the other day?'

Seth nodded. 'They keep happening.'

'What do you see?'

'I'm . . . this other person, and I'm inside the Ark. Only the Ark is out at sea, not stuck on an island. And at first I was in this killer whale, or I *was* the killer whale, but then I'm just a boy. And there's this girl called Leila, and this old woman called the Crone.'

'But, Seth, these must be *memories*. It's one of your past . . . *lives* or whatever they're called. That killer whale was your Vessel, and the boy was one of your past manifestations.'

'I know they're memories,' said Seth, looking at his feet. 'I still don't want them.'

Ellie put down her spoon and stood up eagerly, nearly slipping in a puddle of guano. 'But maybe if you write down more of the next –'

'I don't want to remember, Ellie,' said Seth, an edge of irritation in his voice. 'And I don't want to hear those voices, either. I don't care who I was.'

'But what about your brothers and sisters?' Ellie said. She couldn't understand why he wouldn't want to remember them – Ellie had fought so hard to remember her own brother, and it had saved her life.

'My brothers and sisters are down there, Ellie.' Seth pointed through the window towards the docks.

Ellie squinted. 'You mean . . . the sailors?'

'Yes. They don't hunt me and they don't try to force me to be something else. They just let me *be*.'

Ellie took a step back. 'I don't try to force you to be something else. But . . . don't you want to know who you really are?'

'I know who I am.'

Ellie turned away, finding she couldn't look at him. She almost wished they were back at sea, just the two of them.

'I . . . *I* don't know who I am here,' she said quietly. 'Not without anything to do.'

'Then come and work on the boat with me,' said Seth. 'Think how much fun it will be – we'll get to spend all our time together.'

Ellie remembered the first night in the bar, the way the sailors had laughed at her. Her body twisted with embarrassment. 'I need to be *useful*.'

'You can be useful on a fishing boat,' said Seth.

'No, *you* can be useful on a fishing boat,' Ellie snapped. 'I'd just get in the way. Besides, the crew all love you.' A sudden, hot feeling bubbled into her stomach. Tears itched her eyes. 'I wish Anna was here.'

As soon as the words were out, she wished she could pull them back in. They filled the room, foul as the smell of guano. Seth stared at the floor, brow crumpled. Guilt prickled at the back of Ellie's neck, but she clenched her fists.

'Don't you want to spend time with me?' Seth said, in a small voice. 'You could . . . help repair things?'

'Look.' Ellie sat back down. 'I'm an inventor. I can't be fixing boats all day.'

Seth's eyes went wide. 'You think you're better than they are,' he said. 'You don't want the Queen to help you, you just want someone to tell you how *special* you are.'

The pain in Ellie's stomach curdled into a swift storm of rage. 'Don't lecture me! You can't imagine what I've been through.'

Seth opened his mouth to object.

'No!' Ellie spun to face him. 'The years of hiding – hiding the darkest secret there is! It wasn't easy, Seth, but I did it! I saved your life. I defeated a *god* –'

She took an angry step towards him, and her foot plunged straight into a large pot, liquid soaking through her sock and between her toes.

Slowly, Ellie extracted her foot, dripping globs of guano on the floor. Her cheeks burned.

'I'll fetch some clean water,' said Seth, nimbly stepping over the pots towards the door. 'And some soap.' He bowed deeply. 'Your *Majesty*.'

The Man in the Marketplace

Ellie pretended to be asleep the next morning when Seth got up for work, keeping her back turned and her eyes fiercely shut until he'd closed the bedroom door.

Molworth watched her suspiciously as she ate breakfast in the bar.

'Seth looked unhappy when he left,' he said, leaning on his mop.

Ellie crunched down hard on a radish.

'I heard arguing last night.'

'I don't want to talk about it.'

'That's what Seth said too. I wish I had a best friend.'

'We're brother and sister,' Ellie corrected.

'No you're not. Don't lie to me – I spend my whole life in here watching people, I know best friends when I see them.'

'You're creepily grown up for a twelve-year-old,' said Ellie.

Molworth leaned in so his face was an inch from Ellie's. 'Friendship is prized above all else. So the Great One says – She who is wisest of all.'

Ellie leaned away from him. 'But he's friends with all the sailors now, and they're always together. I've tried talking to them but . . . I'm not very good at talking to people.'

'I know,' said Molworth. 'I've seen you.'

Ellie scowled. 'Maybe you'd have a best friend if you were nicer.'

'I'm just being honest. Honesty is prized second only to friendship, so the Great –'

'All right, all right,' said Ellie. 'What should I do?'

'Why not get him a present, to say sorry?'

'That's a good idea.'

'I know. Now get out – I need to practise my violin and I can't do it when there's people listening.'

So Ellie wandered to the Raphaela Markets south of the Shambles, where a hundred colourfully dressed people danced to a band of drummers, like a field of rippling wild flowers. Every eighth beat they cried out, 'Praise Her!' in unison. Ellie hummed along to the music as she explored the stalls, admiring piles of honey cakes with purple icing, animal statuettes, and leaf-shaped brooches. Ellie picked up a small humpback whale, carved from crystal – the same sort of whale she'd pulled Seth from months before. It was perfect.

'Aren't you too hot in that coat?' said the stallholder. Ellie bit her tongue and searched her pockets for money, grabbing the whale and rushing down towards the Shambles. Seth wouldn't be back from work for hours, but Ellie was brimming with excitement as she approached the Vile Oak, picturing Seth's face when she gave it to him.

As she walked along a high path, she looked down and saw, in a little garden of lilies and hibiscus, a circle of girls and boys her age, all of them laughing and joking.

And there, sitting among them, was Seth.

He was wearing a green cardigan she'd never seen him in before, laughing so hard that he started to cough. Ellie frowned. He'd left work early but hadn't thought to come and find her? She waved timidly and his eyes flickered towards her – she was sure of it – but then he just carried on listening to the next joke.

Ellie stood rooted to the spot. She'd never seen Seth laugh that way before, and *she'd* certainly never made him laugh like that. In fact, now that she thought about it, she wasn't sure she had *ever* made him laugh. Lately, he just disapproved of everything she said and did. He didn't want her doing experiments, he didn't want her to meet the Queen. He didn't want to spend time with her.

Spinning on her heel, Ellie marched back to the markets, her cane smacking a man's leg so that he yelped and dropped his sandwich. Ellie was too angry to apologize. She wished she'd never come to this awful place. She wished they'd found a quiet little island, with no sailors to take Seth from her, and no Vessel-Queens to ignore her, either.

Ellie rounded the corner of a bread stall, and stopped dead.

'No,' she whispered.

She searched the shifting crowd, trying to convince herself she hadn't just glimpsed a man in a long black coat, on the other side of the market square. A woman on stilts strode by in a purple gown, trailed by giggling children. Ellie squinted – the gown *did* look a bit like an Inquisitor's coat. She sighed in relief.

Then the stilt-walker passed by, and Ellie cried out.

The man was hugely tall, with broad shoulders, skin the colour of a corpse, and eyes like angry inkblots. Eyes filled with pain and fury.

Eyes that stared right at her.

Hargrath.

9

Letters of Love and Friendship

'*LANCASTER!*'

The roar broke across the tranquil marketplace. Ellie dropped to the ground, hiding beneath the shoulders of the crowd.

'No,' she moaned. Of all the Inquisitors who could have followed her here, why did it have to be Hargrath?

'*LANCASTER!*'

The cry was oddly shrill for a creature of such size. Ellie spotted him parting the crowd like a ship cleaving through water. She darted from the marketplace, to a point where the street divided into three. She flung a smoke bomb at her feet, so Hargrath wouldn't know which path she'd taken, then ran left and kept going until her bad leg seized up and she collapsed into a tight alleyway.

She listened for footsteps, but heard nothing.

She took a moment to catch her breath, then pulled herself upright. She closed her eyes, but saw only Hargrath's demonic glare, and Seth's laughing face. Her body felt crunchy and sore, like it was full of gravel. She looked down, and saw bloody, child-sized footprints on the paving stones.

Ellie checked over her shoulder, then followed after them, eager to put more distance between her and Hargrath. They led her past a pig snuffling at a pile of cabbages, then two women arguing loudly, oblivious to the bloody splotches right by their feet. Between tall sandstone buildings she came to a strange, empty passage, with a curving roof made from tightly wound tree branches. Thousands of scraps of paper had been nailed to the walls, most of them aged to yellowness.

For my beloved, one said.

Our love is forever, said another.

Thank you, H, you helped me through the hardest of times.

A gentle wind blew through the passage, rustling the letters so they glimmered like the scales of a giant paper fish. Ellie wondered why they'd been put there in the first place, rather than sent to the people they were meant for. Perhaps those people weren't around any more.

Ellie gently removed the nail holding one letter to the wall.

Dear Ellie,
 I'm glad we're not friends any more.
Seth

A skewer of hot pain pierced Ellie's heart. She blinked, and read again.

Dear Edith,
 I'm glad you were there with me.
Sarah

Ellie frowned, glancing up and down the passage. She went to return the paper to the wall, but noticed that on the bare patch behind it was a red splodge. She put her finger to it. It was sticky and thick like blood, but cold. When she blinked, it was gone.

Ellie felt a single droplet of ice water land on the back of her neck, trickling down her spine.

'Go away,' she whispered. 'Leave me alone.'

A wind fluttered through the tunnel again. The papers rustled.

Alone, they said.

Ellie shivered inside her coat. 'I've got enough problems without *you*.'

A small bulge appeared in the wall next to her, like an air bubble beneath the papers. Ellie pushed it back in, but more cold blood leaked out through the gaps between the letters, soaking her fingers. She rubbed her hands against her coat, but the blood left no marks.

A new bulge grew from the wall.

Alone, the papers whispered again.

'Go *away*!' Ellie roared, pushing back the blister.

Ellie, the papers whispered. *Alone. Ellie, alone. Ellie, alone.* They breathed in the word *Ellie* and breathed out *alone*. A bundle of letters came away in her hands, but the paper didn't *feel* like paper. It was rougher, like fabric or bandages.

Ellie, alone. Ellie, alone.

More letters bubbled all over the wall. Ellie yelled and shoved them back, but her hands were wrenched inside the paper, vanishing up to her wrists. The mound of letters was inches from her face, and Ellie thought she saw the outline of eyelids beneath the paper, and a nose. She screamed and the wall released her, and she toppled on to her back.

A tiny, brittle figure pulled away from the wall, picking bits of paper from itself. It looked like a child, covered head to toe in bandages. Just its neck, its shoulders, its chin and mouth were bare, its skin the colour of snow. Hair stuck out of the back of its bandaged head in thick, blood-matted locks.

'No,' Ellie whispered. 'You can't be back.'

She scrabbled to her feet and slammed the figure against the wall. Only instead of hitting the wall, the child went *through* it, sucked in by the paper.

Ellie turned round, her gasping filling the empty passage.

The child emerged from the wall opposite, smiling, and tilted its head towards her. Ellie could feel it looking at her, though its eyes were hidden behind a single flat stretch of bloodied fabric.

'I *defeated* you,' she said.

'But not destroyed, Ellie,' said the bandaged creature. Its voice was like two voices speaking together – one a child's, the other deep and ancient. 'Never destroyed. I'll always be here for you, when you need me.'

'I *don't* need you.'

'You need a friend, don't you? Seth is so happy with *his* new friends. Though . . . ah –' the child breathed deeply in satisfaction – 'you'd prefer he didn't have any friends apart from you, wouldn't you? Oh, Ellie, and I thought *I* was the monster.'

'Be *quiet*,' Ellie hissed.

A wet gurgle bubbled up from the child's throat. It sounded nothing like human laughter. 'I've missed you, Ellie, how I've missed you!'

The act of laughing seemed too much for it, and it fell against the wall, fingernails scraping paper as it struggled to stand.

'What are you doing here?' said Ellie. She wanted to cry, but refused to show any weakness in front of it.

'You can't hide your sadness from me,' it said, pointing to her head. 'I'm right in here with you. Who else knows you as well as I do? Anna knew you a little, I suppose, but you left her behind on that evil, rotten island. Brought *me* with you, though . . .'

'If I could have it the other way round, believe me I would,' said Ellie.

'*This* island, though, it's almost paradise, isn't it? And this Queen, why, I hear she's a Vessel, just like you.'

Ellie clenched her fists inside her pockets. 'The islanders say you're afraid of her.'

'Rumours,' said the child. 'You think maybe she can rid you of me? Destroy me, even? But who will you talk to then? Seth? He's moved on to better things. Ahh . . . but this Queen. You think *she'll* be your friend? You think she'll be wise, creative, thoughtful. Like you, I suppose? Is that what you think, Ellie? That she'll value you, respect you. *Praise* you. That's what you want, isn't it? Praise for little Ellie. *Praise Her!*'

'Shut up.'

It smiled. Its teeth were tiny and pointed like a piranha's. 'Poor, clever, brilliant Ellie. No mother or brother or Anna to tell her how *good* she is, and now no Seth, either. And if you're not doing good . . . then you're doing badly. And who knows what could happen if you're doing badly? The last time you were doing badly, why, you almost died.'

'Because *you* almost killed me!' Ellie spat.

'Go ahead, waste your time. The Queen can't help you. You cannot destroy suffering. You cannot destroy me.'

'Leave me alone.'

The child hugged itself. 'Oh, I've missed hearing you say that! Takes me back to our old adventures. Remember when I threw Hargrath in the sea, and you thought I'd killed him? But he just keeps returning to chase you, doesn't he? I guess something really drove him insane. Say, why not ask me to kill him for good this time?'

'No more wishes,' said Ellie. 'I beat you. We're done.'

'We are *not* done. You need my help, or someone is going to die.'

Ellie growled. 'You can't kill anyone. I haven't made any wishes. You don't have any power.'

'True, I can't kill anyone right now. But people have a habit of dying anyway.' The child bared its pointed teeth in a hideous grin. 'This person very soon.'

Ellie's heartbeat picked up. 'Who?'

'No, not dear Seth,' said the child. 'A miner, trapped underground, and soon to be consumed by a fire.'

Ellie shook her head. 'You're lying.'

'Oh . . . so you're just going to let him die, then? That's so like you.'

'*Nobody* is dying,' said Ellie.

'Why would I lie? Ask me to save him – if he's not really in danger, I won't be *able* to save him, and I won't gain any power. You win either way.'

'I've never gained anything by asking for your help.'

'Oh, I'm sorry – was it *you* who rescued Seth from on top of that bonfire?'

'Leave me alone!' Ellie cried.

'Nobody else here can help you.'

'That's not true,' said Ellie, struck with an idea. She looked the child in the place its eyes should have been. 'There is someone else, and he's always with me.'

The child's smile dropped.

'Not him, don't do that.' It pawed at Ellie's arm. 'Please, you *need* me. That man is going to –'

'Finn,' Ellie said.

Hope flared in her chest as the memory of her brother filled her mind: his bright green eyes, freckled face and kind smile. A golden warmth blossomed out to her fingertips as she remembered sunny afternoons in a rowing boat, and evenings playing board games in the orphanage. As she remembered the moment her brother had saved her life, and broken the Enemy's power.

The child hissed and fell on its front, unleashing a high-pitched squeal and a roar like an avalanche both at once. Its body curled up tight, then tighter still, folding in on itself. Vanishing to nothing.

Ellie leaned on her cane, feeling both elated and exhausted, like she'd been laughing too hard. She allowed the embers of happy memories to glow a little longer in her mind, idly reading the papers on the wall. One stood out.

Dear Luis,

   You are the most annoying brother, and the most loved.
Dora

Ellie smiled.

There was an angry chime as a bottle spun towards her across the paving stones, kicked accidentally by a man thundering along the paper-covered passageway. He was pale and frightened and there was grey dust in his hair and on his clothes. He shot past Ellie without looking at her.

Ellie watched him vanish round the corner, then walked cautiously along the passage in the direction the man had been running from, listening for sounds from the streets beyond.

'Help! Help! Warden! I need a Warden!'

Ellie's chest tightened at the distant call. She picked up her pace.

With a clatter of metal, one of the silver-armoured soldiers appeared, marching in the same direction as Ellie. A woman ran towards him, her eyes red rings in a face powdered white by dust.

'Help me, Warden!' she cried, grabbing the man's armoured wrist. 'Please, you've got to help. My brother, he's trapped in the mine. He's trapped and there's a fire!'

Brother, Ellie thought. *Her brother needs saving.*

Stalactites

Ellie hurried after the Warden and the dust-coated miner. At the end of a quiet street, the sandy paving stones gave way to bare, jagged rock and wagons piled with broken stone. A tall, cavernous mouth was carved from the island's side, discharging grey fumes like a man belching tobacco smoke. As Ellie got near, a panicked cry echoed from the darkness.

She raced inside. The tunnel was so narrow the Warden's armour scraped the sides, but soon opened on to a wider, torchlit cavern, where cruelly spiked stalactites speared down from above. A host of frightened miners huddled round a massive rock wedged into the cavern wall, smoke seeping round its edges.

'I've brought a Warden!' the woman shouted.

'This rock fell when we were running from the fire,' another miner explained to the Warden, stifling a cough. The cavern stank like burning compost, and Ellie tried not to breathe in too much.

'My brother's trapped on the other side!' said the woman.

The Warden inspected the fallen boulder, then looked at the miners.

'Don't you have pickaxes?' he said uncertainly. The miners gawped at him.

'You think we haven't thought of that?' one said. 'Do something!'

'What can I do? You're the miners – mine!'

Ellie hurried to the rock, knowing she had to act before the others wondered what she was doing. She pulled a fist-sized bundle from her pocket: a clay sphere with a short piece of rope sticking out of it. Seth's disapproving voice rang in her mind, but she trampled it quiet, dragging a match across the stone, then lighting the tip of the rope. It fizzed like a sparkler.

'What are you doing here, child?' cried the Warden, noticing her at last. 'It's not safe!'

Ellie tucked the clay sphere into a wide crack at the base of the rock. She heard a feeble cough from the other side. The Warden grabbed Ellie's sleeve, but she slipped free, kneeling down by the thin space between the rock and the cavern wall.

'Can you hear me?' Ellie called.

More coughing, then, 'Y-yes?'

'Stand well back.'

She faced the other miners, whose gazes drifted from her to the little clay sphere.

'What is that?' said the Warden.

'A bomb,' said Ellie. 'You should probably take cover.'

The miners lurched backwards.

'Girl,' the Warden growled, 'you don't know what trouble you'll be in. The use of fire powder is blasphemy! The Queen Herself will find out.'

Ellie glanced at the fizzing rope. There was still time to extinguish it.

The Queen Herself will find out.

'Everyone,' said Ellie, 'STAND BACK!'

She rushed away from the bomb, grabbing the Warden's wrist. They joined the miners on the far side of the cavern, huddling behind an empty cart.

'Won't he get hurt?' said the trapped man's sister, her voice trembling.

'I don't think so – it won't be a very big bang. I only used –'

Noise stabbed Ellie's eardrums and bright light filled her eyes and something great and powerful knocked her on to her back.

She disentangled herself from the tumble of miners, coughing as ash slipped into her lungs, her ears filled by an insistent ringing. She hobbled towards the boulder.

Only it wasn't in the place it had been before, but rather in several places around the cavern. The now-open tunnel spewed smoke. And, limping from inside it, came a man.

His sister raced to catch him as he stumbled and fell into her arms. As they hugged and laughed together, a tingling sensation raced out to Ellie's fingertips.

There was a creaking from above like old bones. Dust trickled on to Ellie's shoulder.

'Watch out!' the woman cried.

Ellie flung herself aside as a chunk of stalactite landed heavily beside her. She lay on her back, panting.

'We need to leave, now!' roared the Warden.

There was another creak, and Ellie watched as a second stalactite detached itself from the cavern ceiling. Watched as it hurtled down towards her. Watched as it landed on her left arm.

At first she felt nothing. But only for a heartbeat. She looked at the rock, her arm underneath it, and she screamed and she screamed until everything went black.

Leila's Diary

4,758 days aboard the *Revival*

The Crone spends so much time tending the boy that her plants have started wilting. I water them regularly and scold her for her laziness.

'I think you're a liar, Crone. If you can make a garden grow in darkness, why can't you wake him up?'

'His mind resists me, idiot girl. It is a swirling chaos.'

'What does *that* mean?'

The Crone stroked the boy's cheek. 'At the height of his powers, this child held dominion over the sea. But since the Drowning, the sea is full of the memories of the dead, and the terrible suffering of their final moments. The boy is the sea, and so the boy *is* that suffering.'

'Have you tried hitting him?'

'I have a task for you. The captain keeps some rare elixirs in his quarters – relics from before the Drowning that even I am incapable of brewing. One may have the power to soothe his troubled mind: the Spirit of Osha. Offer him this bag of willow bark in trade. Now go! The boy is a god, but his shell is mortal. He will die of thirst if we don't wake him soon.'

I hurried through the Ark with the massive sack in my arms, along the big corridor-street that runs right through the Market Deck, straight towards the Ark-Captain's quarters. I cursed the Crone but secretly hoped the boy would be okay. He was all I had left of my whale.

I told the guards what I had come for and they let me right in. The Ark-Captain sat in his wooden throne, before the massive wheel that controlled the ship. His men stood round me, stroking their swords like they were very proud of them.

'The whale rider is here,' he said, smiling kindly. He was all muscle and scar tissue.

'No whale rider any more,' said the First Mate, an ugly and even more muscular man with few teeth and a wooden leg. 'Whale's dead.'

I fixed the Ark-Captain with a scowl. 'The Crone wants your Spirit of Osha.' I dumped the bag at his feet. 'She'll trade you this.'

The First Mate spat on the floor. 'Why trade? We should just take what we want from those old bones and her mouldy plants.'

I stepped towards him. 'If you come to her garden looking for a fight, I'll rip off your wooden leg and beat you to death with it.'

The men all looked at me in disbelief, and then at each other, and they kept doing that until the Ark-Captain stood up.

And started to laugh.

Loren

Ellie's mind was in her arm. The rest of her body could have been removed entirely, she wouldn't have known. She was a thin slice of meat, searing in a pan on a hot stove.

But she was floating, somehow. When she opened her eyes, she saw stalactites passing overhead; or stalagmites – she couldn't tell which way up she was. A faint light appeared ahead, blindingly bright, and she felt herself being lowered carefully to the ground. She smelled a strange but pleasant aroma, like woodsmoke and raspberry jam.

'This will help with the pain,' said a clear, musical voice. Gentle fingers daubed something cold against the ragged landscape of Ellie's arm, and she sobbed in relief. The pain faded, and the rest of her body came back to her – shoulders and hands and the old ache in her leg.

'Am I dead?' she croaked.

'No, dear child,' the voice said. 'I've rubbed essence of willow bark into your arm. It will keep the pain at bay for a little while.'

'He saved her!' cried a woman. 'Loren saved her!'

Ellie opened her eyes to see a forest of boots, ankles and colourful trousers, then gazed up into a canopy of smiling faces. Some were looking at her, but most stared at the man kneeling at Ellie's side. He had long, curling hair like sun-drenched gold, his face tanned and unblemished, and he was watching Ellie with twinkly blue eyes. He was so impossibly beautiful that she feared it was the Enemy in a new form.

A portly man sat wheezing to one side, a heavy book filled with thousands of ink-stained pages resting on his lap, which appeared to be the cause of his breathlessness. His hair was patchy, like he'd pulled out chunks of it in distress. Ellie wondered if the book was the cause of that too.

'Excuse me?' Ellie asked him, her voice slurring. 'Can you see this pretty man?'

The scribe blinked several times, then rapidly scribbled something in his book. Ellie read upside down:

Brave Loren saved the girl from certain death. She was a sickly waif of a child, and not sound of mind.

'Hey!' Ellie protested.

Standing behind the scribe was a tiny third man with a purple-feathered hat and a lute. He began to sing:

> *'Bravest Loren rescued the girl from certain demise.*
> *She was a sickly child. A waif of a child.*
> *And clearly not sound of mind.'*

The crowd cheered and joined in the singing, badly out of key. The handsome man got to his feet.

'Please, friends, though I am flattered, it is this girl we should be praising.' His voice seemed always on the cusp of breaking into laughter. 'Her quick thinking saved one of my own miners from a fiery demise.'

The crowd fell quiet and nodded solemnly. Ellie watched the scribe as his quill danced across the page.

> *When the crowd tried to give*
> *credit to Loren, he humbly requested*
> *they acknowledge the girl's own*
> *heroism.*

The bard sprang into action:

> *'When the crowd tried to give all –'*

'That's enough singing for now, friends,' said Loren. 'We must get this child the necessary medical attention. I will pay the surgeon's bill, of course!'

There was a frenzy of applause, then a clatter of metal as the Warden staggered from the mine, armour smeared with soot, his helmet missing. He clutched his head, checking for blood, then glared at Ellie. He grabbed her broken arm, puncturing the cloud of relief the willow bark had offered. Ellie screamed.

'What do you think you're doing!' yelled a man. 'This girl is a hero!'

'She almost killed us all!' the Warden snapped. 'She used blasphemous *sorcery* to blow that rock up.'

'Sorcery?' Loren smiled, dimples forming on both cheeks. It was impossible to guess his age – he could have been twenty or fifty. 'My dear friend, there's no such thing.'

'It was gunpowder,' Ellie offered. 'I made it from sulphur, charcoal and guano.'

'Fascinating,' said Loren, and the way he said the word made Ellie's heart leap. 'You did that yourself? Where did you learn the method?'

'From a book,' said Ellie. She could remember reading it, though it had been years ago, in her mother's old workshop.

'*Fascinating*,' he said again, and Ellie's heart leapt further. 'A scholar, no less. And so young. Your parents must be very proud.'

'I don't have parents,' said Ellie.

'Well, someone is proud, I'm sure. And *I* am terribly impressed.'

Ellie smiled, feeling dizzy. She'd almost forgotten about the pain in her arm.

'Impressed?' shrieked the Warden. 'She could have brought the whole mine down on us. She belongs in prison.'

The crowd booed, and the Warden loosened his grip on Ellie's arm.

'Now, friends.' Loren's bright blue eyes searched the crowd. 'This man is only doing his duty. I believe I have a solution. The Queen will shortly be meeting with Her Royal Court, of which I am a member.' He turned to Ellie. 'What's your name, young scholar?'

'Um . . . it's Ellie. Ellie Stonewall.'

'I will take Ellie before the court and plead her case.' His voice grew sombre for the first time. 'Do not fret, fellow servants of Our Most Glorious Vessel, I shall make sure fairness prevails. Praise Her!'

'Praise Her!' the crowd roared.

'Is that agreeable with you, loyal subject?' Loren said to the Warden. The man's face was purple, his hand straying to the hilt of his sword. He looked at the crowd, scowled, then nodded.

'We must keep your arm steady, brave Ellie,' said Loren. 'Probably best I carry you, if you don't mind?'

Ellie nodded dumbly, and Loren lifted her, filling Ellie's nose again with the smell of jam and woodsmoke. The bard broke into song, but was drowned out by the cheers of the crowd as they swept through the streets, parading round Loren, Ellie and the disgruntled Warden. The scribe followed too, walking and writing at the same time. Ellie read over Loren's shoulder:

> Brave Loren carried the sickly hero through the streets. The crowds flocked round them, golden-voiced children singing Loren's name. Men and women danced and embraced, and it was as if the gods themselves had returned from death to celebrate.

There were no golden-voiced children that Ellie could hear, just an endless off-key chanting of 'LOREN, LOREN, LOREN!' and people were not embracing or dancing but jostling each other to get closer to him, kept back by four burly men in leather armour.

'Sariah!' Loren called, reaching out to the crowd. 'How is your grandfather's elbow? Did that Essence of Ambrose do the trick? My word, Malma, is that your son? Look how tall he's grown!'

The crowd swelled as they processed through the streets, passing beneath painted paper constructions of whales, peacocks and octopuses strung from one building to the next. People threw flower petals from their balconies, so the air shimmered white and purple.

'Thank you, thank you, dear friends!' Loren said, laughing as petals fell on his face. The buildings around them turned grander, straw-roofed huts giving way to sandstone houses, vivid murals embellishing their walls.

'We're going to the Ark,' said Ellie. 'We're going to see the Queen?'

Loren smiled. 'Indeed we are.' Nerves prickled Ellie's neck, like hailstones on glass. 'Tell me, Ellie, I don't suppose you're looking for employment? Assuming I can convince Her not to throw you in a cell, I think the Queen may have a use for your talents.'

Ellie looked up at Loren, dumbfounded. She nodded. 'Yes,' she said. 'Yes, please.'

'Excellent!' Loren declared. The street opened up on to Revelation Boulevard, and there was the Ark ahead of them, heat shimmering across its sprawling grey-white surface. Ellie looked nervously at the crowd, offering a hesitant wave that was met with fresh cheers. Her face flushed with joy.

'*LANCASTER!*'

It was like the roar of a wounded bull. Heads turned, and Ellie wriggled in Loren's grip, her stomach twisting.

Hargrath marched through the crowd, black coat fluttering behind him. His eyes were bright red, his skin clammy. He looked as if he had never slept.

'OUT OF MY WAY!' he snarled.

'What is this?' said Loren, frowning at the commotion.

'Let me through!' Hargrath demanded, as the crowd jostled him. 'How *dare* you touch me! I am an –' Hargrath swallowed. 'An –'

But even Hargrath seemed to have realized that, on this island, announcing he was an Inquisitor from the Enemy's City was a bad idea. 'You don't know what you're doing,' he growled. 'She's dangerous!'

'She's a hero!' cried a woman. 'Get out of here, monster!'

Hargrath shrieked and drew his sword. Screams pierced the air. Loren laughed. 'Another crazed fan. Gregory, Aidan, could you deal with him?' he asked two of the burly men in leather armour.

'*I'll* handle it,' said the Warden, reaching for his sword, but Loren put a hand on his shoulder.

'Sir, you've had a trying ordeal,' he said politely. 'Let my men take care of this.'

'I don't take orders from a preening fool like you!' yelled the Warden, flecking Loren's face with spit. Up close, Ellie saw the shadow of a frown mar Loren's perfect features. He laughed softly, dabbing his face with the sleeve of his gown as his two bodyguards leapt upon Hargrath and wrestled him to the paving stones.

Loren leaned in close to the Warden, whispering in his ear. The Warden stuttered. 'You know my name?'

Again Loren whispered.

The Warden's face paled. 'I, uh, well —'

The crowd laughed and whooped as Loren's guards pulled off Hargrath's coat, revealing the stump where his left arm would have been. Hargrath lashed out wildly, ripping his coat back from them then fleeing down an alley, Loren's men in pursuit. He looked over his shoulder, and his black eyes met Ellie's one last time before he vanished round a corner.

'Well, I'm glad that's sorted,' Loren said. 'There are some peculiar people in this world, aren't there, Ellie?'

Ellie glanced about. The Warden seemed to have vanished too.

'*LOREN, LOREN, LOREN!*' The chanting swelled as Loren carried Ellie towards the gates of the palace. The mural on the front of the Ark reared overhead, the winged, angelic figure staring down at them.

The gatekeeper smiled at Ellie. 'You're back. And look at that, you're wearing shoes this time.'

Loren raised a hand to the crowd. 'Friends! Sadly this is where we must part, but rest assured this child shall receive the accolades she deserves!'

The crowd cheered as Loren carried Ellie through the gates. The double doors swung open, and Ellie shielded her eyes against a new flood of light.

At last, she was inside the palace.

The Room of a Hundred Animals

The air was cool and clean; all Ellie could smell was the woodsmoke and jam of Loren's strange perfume, and her own sweat. This was not how she'd imagined this moment – she'd been walking tall, her hair brushed at least, not being carried, coated in dust, with an arm that resembled a shredded steak.

Portraits of men and women hung from the walls, every one of them beautiful, surrounded by flowers and with a dog or a cat or a colourful bird in their lap. Their hair was sleek and dark, and they had halos of gold leaf round their heads.

'The Queen's ancestors,' said Loren. 'Now prepare yourself, you're about to see the Grand Atrium.'

He carried her through another door, and for a moment Ellie thought they were outside again. She looked up into a world of white light.

It felt like every other building on the island could have fitted inside this chamber. A thousand circular windows shone like shards of precious stone glinting on a white-sand beach. The walls were painted white, with white marble staircases that stretched endlessly over their heads. The cleanness of the place made Ellie feel even dirtier: a smudge on a fresh sheet of paper.

The chamber echoed with the patter of footsteps, and somewhere cellos played a gentle melody. Boys and girls dressed in white shirts and black trousers hurried up and down the staircases, in and out of a hundred doors, and Ellie felt she was in the glittering, pumping heart of some giant, pristine sea creature.

Servants opened another set of double doors, and a new corridor stretched away into darkness. Loren set Ellie down, and she tugged at her collar.

'What is the Royal Court?' she said.

'Ah, it's nothing to worry about,' said Loren. 'Merely the council that advises the Queen, made up of the most respected and wealthy people on the island.'

'That sounds like something to worry about,' said Ellie.

Loren laughed. 'It'll be fine – they're terribly fond of me.'

They entered the corridor, the doors closed, and darkness enveloped them.

A dim orange light lay ahead. Ellie heard voices, and tried to make out what they were saying, but the pain in her arm turned her thoughts thick like syrup.

'Do you have any more of that essence of willow bark?' Ellie whispered, and Loren shook his head in apology.

'Whatever you do,' he said softly, 'don't look Her in the eye.'

They emerged into flickering candlelight, and a new chamber appeared to Ellie in parts: a great darkness, high above, where there should have been a ceiling. An elephant. A black marble floor, with some stubby white candles to light the entire chamber. A horse. Shifting figures in chairs. A bear.

A bear was glaring at her with fierce black eyes.

Ellie jumped a step back. The bear did nothing. She breathed deeply, then realized the bear was dead, and stuffed, and that there were a hundred other dead animals in the room, along with a smaller number of people, who were still alive.

'Beetroots,' croaked a dry, whispery voice from the darkness. 'Yield down three per cent, all sources.'

There was the sound of a page being turned.

'Aubergines. Yield down twenty-two per cent, all sources.'

Old men and women were seated round the chamber, squeezed between the animals. It was clear the animals had come to the room first: they'd taken all the prime spots. Ellie wondered whether they'd been stuffed before the Drowning. There were lots she'd only ever seen in illustrations – the elephant for one, and a mountainous rhinoceros. Suspended from the ceiling was what looked like a squirrel, only it had a furry lining between its arms

and legs, like an outstretched cape, like it had once been able to fly, or at least glide.

'Onions. Yield down thirty-one per cent, all sources.'

An ancient man sat behind a large, shrivelled tortoise, his body arched over like a wilting plant, a thick, tattered book open in his lap. Each time he spoke, his tongue swept across his bottom lip, unsticking itself with a wet *pop*.

Ellie looked around, searching for the Queen, but finding only the handmaidens, gathered at the centre of the room in their purple dresses.

'Now, the fishing,' the man with the book droned on. 'Mackerel, all sources –'

The handmaidens held their breath hopefully.

'– down forty-five per cent.'

They let out a small, collective groan.

'Anchovies,' the man said, with the same wet *pop*. The handmaidens breathed in again. 'Down forty-eight per cent.'

Again they groaned.

'Tuna.'

The handmaidens breathed in.

'Down eighty-seven per cent.'

The handmaidens gasped.

'*Stop. That.*'

The voice cut through the chamber, straightening spines as it passed, making the hairs on Ellie's neck stand on end. She had never heard a voice so melodious and yet so deep and commanding.

Loren stepped forward. 'Your Divinity, I bring an urgent matter before you.'

Something shifted in the darkness, and Ellie noticed a shadowy figure behind the handmaidens, much taller than they were.

Ellie swallowed.

'Andre Catlos, how do we fix this?' said the voice, ignoring Loren entirely. The shadow raised a long, trailing sleeve, and Ellie saw a finger glinting with jewellery, pointing to a prim, upright man with a long neck, sitting next to an ostrich.

Catlos scratched his neck. 'The Academy is looking into it, Your Divinity, and I think we have some promising leads.'

'And what are they?'

'Oh.' Catlos clutched his knees. 'I'd . . . have to consult my colleagues, you see.'

'Yes, I see,' said the voice. 'Your leads are so promising that you can't remember what they are.'

Ellie rubbed her throbbing arm, the air suddenly stifling. This was not a person who would look kindly on her setting off a bomb.

'Your Divinity?' said Loren.

'*Silence.*'

The jewel-covered hand fell on a huge snow leopard, frozen forever in time with its teeth bared.

'Benevolent Protector?' said a thickset, grouchy-looking man near the rhinoceros. It occurred to Ellie that everyone in the room was sitting next to an animal that in some way resembled them. Ellie wondered if the Queen had arranged this on purpose.

'Speak, Cassor,' said the voice.

'Well.' Cassor shifted uncomfortably. 'I'm not sure why we are concerning ourselves with these shortages. It has been many years now since the last Festival of Life – of course the harvests are poor. But the next Festival is just weeks away. You will make the island fertile again.'

The shadow turned sharply. Ellie gasped and lowered her gaze.

For a moment, she'd seen them. Piercing golden eyes.

'Of course I will,' said the voice. 'But in the meantime I will not let my island starve.'

'Your Divinity, I have some help I'd like to offer?' said Loren, smiling bashfully, but keeping his eyes on the ground.

'Speak again without my say-so, Loren Alexander,' said the voice, 'and I will have your tongue removed.'

'Beloved Provider, forgive me, but has my help not been instrumental so far? It was *my* artisans who made all the false plants now filling the island's public gardens.'

Ellie looked at Loren in shock. She'd spent a lot of time moping in the gardens, and would never have guessed the plants weren't real.

'You forget your place,' said the voice. 'Your wealth and popularity may have won you a position in this court, but

I don't need your help. And I certainly don't need a sickly girl with a fondness for blowing things up.'

Ellie shivered as she felt the golden eyes on her. Loren frowned. 'The news has already reached you?'

'That fire in *your* mines spread to a hidden cache of grain – a secret royal supply that could have kept the whole island fed for a month. Matters are now –' the voice paused – 'much worse.'

'Your Divinity,' said Loren, 'I have a large store of grain on my estate in the outer islands. I can have it brought to Shipwreck Island in days. Then –'

'The girl must be punished,' said the voice. 'The recipe for fire powder is a divine secret. Its creation is blasphemy.'

'But I can help!'

Ellie froze as her own words echoed in her ears, sounding feeble and small. She felt like even the dead animals were staring at her.

'Please, Your Divinity. I . . . I'm an inventor. I know I'm young, but I've invented all sorts of things, um, back on Ingarth Island. I made a device for trapping wild animals in a net. I made a boat that can swim underwater. I know lots about plants too – I can help with the harvest problem!'

Ellie could hear her heartbeat, feel the pain pulsing up and down her arm. She risked a glance up, and found those golden eyes staring back, filling her mind.

'So be it, inventor,' said the Queen. 'You shall remain our prisoner. Prove that you can create such wonders as you describe, or I will have you publicly executed.'

The New Workshop

Ellie had never been in prison before, but she was certain they didn't normally come with chandeliers, balconies or four-poster beds. She doubted they had mahogany wardrobes or gilded bathtubs, either, or a fruit bowl larger than her head.

Ellie's prison had all these things. She hobbled around, admiring the lace pillows, then a tall suit of armour made from segmented plates of black metal. It had a spear, a purple cape, and a reflective mask that was smooth and featureless, like the face of a mannequin. She touched a finger to the mask, and an armoured fist grabbed her hand. Ellie yelped and leapt backwards, as the suit of armour clasped its spear again, and was motionless.

The door swung open, and the tiny, tortoise-like man shuffled in, carrying a wooden trunk.

'That suit of armour just moved!' Ellie told him.

'That's because there is a person inside that suit of armour; you are honoured to stand in the presence of one of the Seven Sentinels. Perfect warriors devoted to the protection of the Queen.'

Ellie studied the armour, feeling strangely reassured to have a perfect warrior watching over her, in case Hargrath should find his way up here. 'Doesn't it speak?'

'They have taken a vow of silence, so as to never divulge the Queen's secrets.'

'How does it see through that mask?'

'Young lady, I am here to mend your arm, not answer silly questions.' The man pointed to a cushioned chair.

Ellie sat down. 'It's fractured, and the muscle has contracted round the bone,' she told him. 'You need to pull my arm to fit the ends back together, then tie a splint to it.'

'Where did you learn that?' said the man, opening his trunk.

Ellie shrugged. 'I've dissected a lot of rats. Is the Queen going to come and see me?'

'Absolutely not. The Queen isn't interested in the activities of –' he looked at Ellie over his glasses; her torn clothes, dusty hair, the dried blood on her arm – 'whatever you are. Now come on, let's get this over with. And please try not to scream too loudly. I have sensitive ears.'

~

An hour later, Ellie was led from her prison, clutching protectively at her arm in its silk sling. A Warden guided her down a dank spiral staircase, deep into the Ark's belly, and she felt a swell of disappointment as they emerged into a grimy, moss-smelling corridor, empty but for a mop and bucket, and a faded painting of a man that someone had drawn a moustache on.

The Warden pulled Ellie through a doorway, and she stood in a spacious, candlelit room filled with four squat workbenches, several desks and a large kiln in one corner.

'A workshop,' Ellie whispered, awestruck, then realized she was speaking to nobody – the door slammed shut behind her.

A shiver of excitement ran up her neck as she investigated, flinging open every drawer, inspecting the materials she'd been given – screws and nails and wire, sheets of brass and copper, saws and wrenches and vices, and even an axe for some reason. She wasn't sure who'd prepared the room or what they thought she'd be doing in it – on one desk lay an arrangement of parrot feathers, a chunk of red gemstone, and three turquoise birds' eggs sitting in cotton wool. Ellie picked one up, wondering if the room had once belonged to a scholar of some sort. She hoped they had retired by choice.

There was a small cough from behind her and Ellie dropped the egg, fumbled to catch it, then fell over in the attempt, crushing it beneath her thigh.

A tall, tanned girl with sleek hair stood over her, wearing the purple dress of a handmaiden.

'Kate!' Ellie said. 'What are you doing here?'

'I'm your assistant,' said Kate, helping Ellie off the floor. 'The Queen thought you might need an extra couple of arms, since you only have one of your own.'

Kate was immaculately clean, without the messy hair and smeared silver make-up from that day in the alley, though she had a terrible slouch that surely wasn't befitting a handmaiden. Ellie felt a stab of annoyance, remembering how Kate had abandoned her in a cloud of smoke.

'I don't *need* an assistant,' Ellie said, raising her chin with a petulant sniff. She wanted to fold both arms in front of her, but could only fold one, making the gesture less impressive. 'I can manage fine, thank you.'

Kate's smile broadened. She glanced around, picking up a jar of nails with a screw-on lid. 'I'll leave you to open this, then, shall I?'

Ellie scowled and took the jar with her good hand, wedging it into the nearest vice. She gave Kate a forced smile, then tried to unscrew the lid. She grimaced and strained. It didn't come off.

Kate removed the jar from the vice, unscrewing the lid with a single twist. Ellie glowered at her.

'I did warn you the Queen couldn't be trusted,' Kate said. 'Now you're going to be executed.'

'Don't sound *too* happy about it.'

Kate raised herself on to a workbench, sitting on her heels like someone in prayer. 'Impressive that a little girl managed to get the attention of Loren Alexander, the Royal Court, *and* the Queen, all in one day. You're already in one of Loren's stupid newspapers.'

Kate picked up the axe, turning it over in her hands.

'I'm not a "*little girl*",' Ellie said, snatching the axe from her. 'I'm probably the same age as you. And the Queen's not *going* to execute me, because I'm about to build an incredible machine that will really impress her.'

'What machine?'

'I haven't figured that out yet,' said Ellie, and Kate laughed. 'Oh, I'm glad my execution is funny to you! You're certainly much more cheerful than you were the other day,' she added snidely, watching with satisfaction as Kate's smile dropped. 'Who was that family you were spying on, anyway?'

'That's royal business,' said Kate. 'And none of yours.'

Ellie could see she'd touched a nerve, and felt a reckless desire to keep digging. 'Royal business? Why would the Queen send *you* to spy on people? She must have proper grown-up spies.'

Kate glared at her.

'You weren't supposed to be there at all, were you?' said Ellie, pointing a wrench at her accusingly. 'That's why the Queen's made you my assistant. As a punishment.'

Kate smirked. 'Quite an imagination you have, Ellie Stonewall of Ingarth Island. Why don't you put it to work *inventing something.*' She studied Ellie a moment. 'You don't seem very afraid of being executed.'

Ellie spread out a piece of paper on a desk, dipping a quill in ink. 'I've been threatened with death before.'

Kate nodded as if this made perfect sense, then hopped down from the workbench. 'The Queen's already *got* drawings, you know. Loads. By proper artists.'

'This is a *schematic*,' Ellie said, savouring Kate's look of confusion. 'A plan of what I'm going to build. You have to plan complex, ingenious, brilliant inventions extremely carefully.'

Kate blinked once, then peered expectantly at the blank paper. She looked at Ellie, then back at the paper. 'Go on, then.'

'I can't concentrate with you watching!'

Kate grinned. 'This isn't a punishment, by the way. It's a nice break from all the boring ceremonies I have to go to, with the Queen. Listening to people drone *on* and *on* . . .' She looked Ellie up and down. 'That coat is horrid . . . it's like you're wearing a dead animal.'

Ellie fiddled with the flap of one pocket. 'It *is* a dead animal. Several – it's made from sealskin.'

'I meant a *recently* dead animal.'

Ellie wrinkled her nose. 'Well, you look like . . . like a . . . like . . .' She gave a frustrated growl.

Kate's eyes widened in delight. 'Maybe stick to inventing machines, not insults.' She glanced down at the blank paper. 'How *do* you know about machines, anyway?'

Ellie pulled the paper away from Kate. She wished the Queen had sent someone more helpful to be her helper.

'My mum was an inventor,' she said, and clutched her coat. 'This was hers before she died.'

Kate took an abrupt step back, kicking a screwdriver with her heel and sending it clattering across the workshop. 'Oh . . .' she said. 'Oh . . .'

'What's wrong?' said Ellie.

Kate's cheeks were tinged pink. She stared at the floor. 'I was only joking. I'd never have said anything if I'd known it was your mum's.'

Ellie felt a sudden need to comfort her. 'It's all right. I know it's a ragged old thing, but it reminds me of her. And it's very practical.'

'It does have a lot of pockets,' Kate said, with a tiny smile. She swallowed. 'My mum's dead too. I loved her dearly.'

Ellie picked up the screwdriver from the floor. 'I loved mine too,' she said.

They watched each other in silence, until Kate shuffled her feet. 'Ellie, I'm sorry I made fun of your coat. I spend all my time in the palace, I forget sometimes how to talk to people.'

'It's okay,' said Ellie. 'Really.'

But Kate didn't meet Ellie's eye, tugging at her fingers instead, as if to check each one was still there. It was an odd habit, but it gave Ellie an idea.

'I know what we're going to make,' she said.

Ellie began sketching, though it was slow work, since she wasn't used to drawing right-handed. She was aware of Kate at her shoulder the whole time. She smelled of soap and lavender.

'Um,' said Ellie, as Kate's breath whistled in her ear. 'Why don't you gather some materials?'

Kate nodded. 'What do you need?'

So Ellie called out one thing after another as she drew, and Kate dashed about the workshop, eyes darting from tabletop to shelf to drawer.

'Copper sheets!' Ellie called, and Kate vaulted a bench like a ballerina, rolled across the floor, and rose with a bundle of shiny squares in her arms.

'Copper sheets,' she said, blowing a strand of hair from her face.

'Um, thanks,' said Ellie. 'You don't have to be so . . . acrobatic.'

Kate shrugged. 'I know. But it's fun,' she said, though Ellie suspected she was just trying very hard to make it up to her.

Ellie looked at the finished schematic. The hand was supposed to work like a real one, with tendons made from wire, and skin made from the sheets of copper, cut and folded into segments.

Ellie spread the sheets out in front of her on one of the workbenches. Then, using a brush and black paint, she drew the shapes for the hand's outer shell. She tried to cut the copper right-handed, but fumbled the scissors and dropped them, nearly impaling her foot.

'Here, let me do that,' said Kate. She took to the task with zeal, cutting out the shapes with the care of a master seamstress, leaving no jagged edges and never once going over the lines. Ellie put the skeleton of the hand together, joining the brass bones with tiny screws. When she looked up, she saw tears on Kate's cheeks.

'Did you cut yourself?' Ellie asked.

'What? Oh no, I'm fine.' Kate hastily rubbed an arm across her face. 'Almost finished.'

But Ellie wasn't convinced. There was a distant look in Kate's eyes, as if she was grappling with an inner darkness. Ellie considered herself something of an expert on the subject.

She picked up a small steel bolt, and flung it at Kate.

Kate looked up in surprise as it bounced off her forehead, her mouth opening in outrage.

'Hey!' she said, and Ellie threw another. This time, Kate caught it. She smiled wickedly, and threw it back, hitting Ellie's shoulder. They began circling each other, hurling tiny metal bolts back and forth across the workshop. Kate was an incredible catch, plucking them out of mid-air. Ellie was less good at catching them, and indeed never caught one.

'It's not fair!' she complained. 'I only have one usable arm.'

Kate found Ellie's inability to catch extremely funny, launching the little bolts in slow arcs, and watching in delight as Ellie flailed. Soon, Kate was slumped over a workbench, wheezing, her cheeks bright red.

'*What* is so funny?' Ellie scowled.

'It's . . .' Kate paused to catch her breath. 'The look on your face.' She did an impression of some furious gargoyle. 'It's so determined. Then when I throw, you change to a startled rabbit, and just sort of . . . flap your hand about.'

Kate was overcome by a fresh attack of laughter, keeling over. Ellie frowned, but also felt a confusing joy in her chest.

'Hey!' said Kate, as she caught the empty matchbox Ellie threw at her head.

Ellie glanced at the clock, then the unfinished hand. 'We should finish up. I don't know when they'll come to take me back to my prison.'

'Yes, right.' Kate looked at Ellie, and Ellie thought she saw something like pity in her eyes.

'It is a very nice prison,' Ellie added.

Kate gave her a sad smile. 'Still a prison. Come on, let's finish it together.'

So Ellie held the wires in place while Kate threaded them through the little hoops attached to the brass bones, with exacting care. They wound the wires round the tiny dials on the side of the wrist, which would control the movement of the fingers.

'It's *perfect*,' Kate said, gasping as the fingers twitched.

The door opened, and a Warden strode in, grabbing Ellie by her bad arm. She yelped.

'Be careful of her!' Kate snapped, and the man's grip softened.

'*Thanks*,' Ellie whispered. The Warden pulled her from the room, and Ellie stole a final glimpse at Kate before the door shut. She was carefully studying the metal hand, with an enchanted, faraway look.

The Warden stuffed Ellie back inside her prison, locking the door. A bowl of soup and bread had been left on the round mahogany dining table, and a bath had been filled. The air smelled richly of rose petals, and Ellie was pleased to see that the living suit of armour was gone. She realized she was still covered in the filth of the mine, and felt a hot embarrassment that Kate had seen her that way. She dipped a cloth in the bath, rubbing the worst of the dirt from her coat, then hung it over the balcony to dry, risking a glance below.

Her legs wobbled. The island spread out beneath her in the light of the setting sun, a shifting, breathing map. It was blurred at the edges where the froth of the sea met white beaches, grew darker with black soil and grey boulders, then turned colourful with rooftops of chalk blue, red and orange, like clusters of coral reef. Palm trees and shrubs burst from the wide spaces in between, and in the market squares the crowds appeared like constellations of swirling tea leaves. Ellie could almost see straight down the volcano on the southern coast.

Below her, the curving grey belly of the Ark was covered with strange, squat statues, studding its surface like barnacles on a whale. They had round, blank faces, the features worn away by centuries of wind and rain.

Ellie took a step back, afraid some mad impulse would take her over the edge. She wished she had wings, to swoop above the beautiful world beneath. Instead, she hungrily slurped down her dinner, and took an awkward bath, trying not to get her sling wet. Then she pulled on a nightdress she found in the wardrobe and climbed on to the huge bed, listening to the rhythmic chorus of seagulls, rising and falling in time with the waves . . .

Ellie woke to the sound of crumbling stone. A hinge creaked, and a shadow stood by the open balcony window. Ellie yelped and grabbed for the candlestick on her bedside table, afraid that Hargrath had found her. The shadow took three steps towards her, then crumpled to the floor.

Ellie peered over the edge of the bed, holding the candlestick above her in readiness. Moonlight fell on the figure. Ellie gasped.

It was Seth.

Leila's Diary

4,761 days aboard the *Revival*

The Crone was sleeping, but I couldn't, so I was watching the boy instead. I've decided his name is Varu – I got it from a song I heard some kids singing, about a boy who could turn into a dolphin. I put the bottle of elixir under his nose every few minutes, trying very hard not to punch him in the arm. I felt angry at him for making the Crone so tired, with his stupid mind that she couldn't fix.

I was holding the elixir by his nose again when suddenly Varu wasn't there and I was on my back somehow and the bottle was skidding across the floorboards and I could feel footsteps shuddering away from me. I flipped on to my front, grabbed the elixir and sprang after him. He was fleeing the garden, wearing only the grubby trousers the Crone had dressed him in.

I chased him through the corridors, hurling all the best curses I knew, and people came out of their cabin-houses to see what the fuss was. I raced up the rickety stairs on to the Sky Deck and the night air filled my lungs and the crashing waves filled my mind. The sea was so loud tonight.

Varu fell on his knees, howling, clutching his head like the noise of the waves was inside him too.

'Shut *up*,' I hissed, glancing around. There weren't many people on deck, just a few groups of friends drinking wine, but they looked at us strangely. There were still rumours that the Enemy was onboard and I didn't want anyone getting suspicious. 'Be *quiet*, silly boy. Listen – my name's Leila. Your name is Varu.'

'That noise,' he said. 'That *noise*!'

'It's the sea,' I said.

'It's everywhere!'

'That's because the world drowned, stupid. Now shut up or I'll beat you into silence.'

The boy ran to the rail and stared in horror at the seething mountains of water three hundred feet below. I went to grab him but his hand shot out and clutched my wrist, twisting my arm behind my back. I can beat most boys at arm-wrestles but not this one.

'Let me go!'

'What are those screams?' he cried. 'There are people down there. They need help!'

'They're already dead, idiot. They drowned.'

'*No*,' Varu whispered, and I seized my moment and shoved the bottle of elixir under his nose. He snorted and let me go, stumbling about cross-eyed.

'That'll teach you to twist my arm.'

'Wait . . .' Varu squinted at me. 'Your voice. I remember it. We used to ride the waves together. We used to hunt.'

I took a step back. 'No,' I said. 'That was Blue Eyes.'

'Yes, that was my name,' he said. 'We used to hunt beneath the sea for seals and sharks. You could hold your breath for so long, for a human. We were good friends, weren't we?'

I found tears on my cheek and dashed them away.

Varu glanced around. 'Where are they?'

'I told you, they drowned.'

'No, not them. Where are the others – where are my brothers and sisters?'

And he collapsed on his back and was asleep again.

14

The Boy Who Climbed the Ark

Ellie rolled Seth over with all the strength she could muster in her good arm.

'Seth, are you okay? How did you get here?'

Seth opened one eye. 'Climbed,' he whispered.

'Climbed!' said Ellie, and looked at the balcony. 'But we must be thirty storeys up! And the surface doesn't look safe.'

'One of the statues broke and fell when I was climbing,' he said, in a distant voice. 'It's probably in a billion pieces.'

Ellie lifted one of his hands. '*Seth*,' she groaned: his palms were crisscrossed with cuts, like he'd been wrestling a tiger.

'It took a thousand years to get here,' he said dreamily. 'I must be very old now.'

'Old and foolish,' she scolded. 'These cuts will get infected. Hold on, I think I have some alcohol in my coat pockets.'

'Thanks, but I don't drink,' Seth mumbled.

'For your *cuts*!'

Ellie rushed to the balcony and rifled in her pockets, her legs wobbling again as she peered over the edge, down the moonlit curve of the Ark. She could see the ruined stump of the statue he'd broken, now just a pair of stubby legs. If Seth had fallen with it, he would certainly have died. What was he thinking?

Her eyes widened – he'd come to rescue her! He must have seen her coat on the balcony and climbed up here, thinking she was in trouble. A flood of warmth spread from her chest to her fingers and toes. She smiled, then noticed Seth's eyes were both closed. 'Seth?'

He leapt to his feet. 'Leila!' he cried, looking round the room. 'She was right here.' Seth rubbed his head. 'Talking to me.'

'You were having another vision.' Ellie held the bottle of alcohol in her teeth and soaked a napkin from the dining table. 'What happened?'

'It felt so real. I could hear them,' said Seth, flinching as Ellie dabbed at the cuts on his hands.

'Who?'

He closed his eyes tightly. When he opened them again, they glistened. 'The voices in the sea. The people. They were drowning.'

'Seth, that all happened in the past. The Drowning was more than seven centuries ago.'

'It felt like they were suffering now.' He stared intently round the room, then noticed Ellie's sling. 'What happened?' he said, patting the rest of her to check for injury, leaving a bloody smear of alcohol on her wrist. 'Did they do that to your arm? I'll kill them! Wait, why is it so . . . nice in here?'

'Keep your voice down,' Ellie said, nervously eyeing the door. 'I'm okay.'

Seth grabbed Ellie's good wrist and pulled her towards the balcony. 'We have to get out of here. They're going to execute you, Ellie! It's all anyone in the Vile Oak is talking about. Now come on, jump on my back. I'll climb you down.'

'Well . . . I'm not *definitely* getting executed,' said Ellie, and Seth frowned. 'They'll only execute me if I can't invent something impressive, and I think I've already done that.'

Seth gave her a fierce look. 'Ellie, they tortured you.'

'They didn't *torture* me.'

'Look what they did to your arm! And your nose!'

Ellie put one hand on her hip. 'I've told you before, my nose has always done that! And nobody broke my arm – I set off a bomb and a stalactite fell on it.'

Seth's eyes widened. 'That explosion in the mine. *You* caused it?'

'I saved a man's life.'

'You could have been killed. And now you *are* going to be killed. Come on.' He took her hand. 'I'll help you climb down.'

'Seth, there's no way you can climb back down.' She prodded him gently and he nearly fell over. 'See? You can sleep under the bed – nobody will find you. We can figure out how to sneak you out in the morning.'

Seth frowned. 'Sneak *us* out.'

'Seth . . .' Ellie let out a sigh. 'I can't go – I need to impress Kate,' she said, then shook her head. She didn't know why she'd said that. 'I need to impress the *Queen*.'

'Who's Kate?' Seth said suspiciously.

'Besides, I think maybe I'm safer in the Ark. Seth . . . Hargrath followed us here.'

'*HARGRATH?*' Seth cried.

'Shh!' Ellie scolded. 'Yes. He's here on the island. And not doing a good job of hiding who he is, either.'

Seth paced back and forth, rubbing at the scar on his arm that Hargrath had given him.

'This is bad,' he said.

'I know.' Ellie swallowed. 'I hoped the City would never follow us here, but . . .' The image of a child wrapped in bandages filled her mind. Her bad leg began to ache. 'Seth, I'm worried the Enemy is getting stronger. I felt very lonely earlier and . . . and it spoke to me.'

Seth's face was grave. 'It's okay,' he said, after a long pause. 'Whatever it said – so long as you don't make a wish, it can't gain any power. But now we need to leave. If Hargrath gets caught, he might tell the Queen who you are. We can't trust her.'

'She needs my help, Seth. The island is running out of food.'

'Ellie –'

'*Please*, Seth, I'm really close to –'

'No, I hear footsteps. Come *on*.'

Seth dragged Ellie towards the window, but she pulled away from him.

'Get under the bed,' she said through gritted teeth. The bolt on the door slammed aside. The handle turned, and Seth dropped to the floor. Ellie leapt on to the bed.

The door opened. 'What's going on?' said a reedy voice.

Ellie pretended to wake. 'Huh? What?'

'I heard voices.'

'Sorry, sometimes I talk in my sleep,' said Ellie.

'I heard a *boy's* voice.'

Ellie blinked. 'Sometimes I do impressions.'

The voice sighed. Through the darkness, Ellie could see it belonged to the tortoise-like, bespectacled man who had fixed her arm.

'Well, kindly *don't*. Some of us are trying to sleep.'

The door closed and Ellie waited until the footsteps had retreated along the corridor, then gathered up a pillow and the extra blanket from the end of her bed, sneaking them underneath. 'Here you go.'

The pillow was snatched from her hand. Ellie heard a snort. She lay back in bed.

'Seth?'

There was a rustle of fabric, then silence.

'I'm really glad you came to rescue me.'

There was another snort. Then, Seth's hand reached up from below, holding a crushed parcel tied with string.

'What's this?' Ellie asked.

'Chocolate. In case you're hungry. You always forget to eat when you're inventing.'

'Thank you,' said Ellie. She took the parcel and held it tight. And though she didn't eat the chocolate, it filled her with warmth all the same.

The Flying Machine

The tiny, bespectacled man delivered a huge platter of cheese and bread for breakfast – more than enough to feed both Ellie and Seth.

'I'm still hungry,' said Seth, swallowing the last hunk of bread and dabbing his finger into the crumbs.

'Well, you did climb all the way up the Ark. Now, we need a plan for how to get you out again.'

'I'm not going anywhere,' Seth said sternly. 'What if the Queen tries to execute you?'

'But you'll miss work?'

Seth shrugged. 'Janssen's not going to sack me – thanks to me, his boat is bringing in more fish than any on the island.'

There was a knock at the door. Ellie looked meaningfully at Seth.

'How I've missed hiding in tiny, spider-infested spaces,' he growled, then crawled under the bed.

'Just stay there. I'll be back as soon as I can.'

Seth's mood aside, Ellie was in high spirits as she was marched back to the workshop. Kate was there already, slouching as usual and wearing a look of concern.

The metal hand lay on the workbench, a piece of paper folded between its fingers. Ellie snapped the paper from its grip.

I am disappointed. How is this any more useful than a hook for a hand? Also, if you need to use a hand to operate it, you still only have one usable hand! Try harder next time.

'Try harder,' said Ellie, her voice hollow. 'Try *harder*?'

She picked up the hand, glaring at it. She didn't understand – what was there not to like? It was beautiful and complex and the way the fingers moved was almost lifelike. She gripped her cane tightly.

'I'm sorry, Ellie,' said Kate, then she shrugged. 'Though the Queen does have a point.'

Ellie's head turned slowly in Kate's direction. 'What.'

'Well, it's not exactly useful to Her, is it? She has two hands already.'

Ellie blinked. 'You could have said something yesterday – I thought you liked it!'

'It *is* very beautiful,' Kate said, patting Ellie on the shoulder. Ellie was about to thank her, then realized Kate was patting her with the mechanical hand. Kate laughed.

'This isn't *funny*.' Ellie scowled. 'Have you forgotten she'll execute me if I don't give her something she likes?'

Kate affected a dainty cough. 'Sorry. So what are we going to do?'

'I don't *know*. You spend time with the Queen – what would impress her?'

'Well, Her island is slowly dying, so something to stop that, probably.'

'Oh, I've got lots of ideas already for that, but they'll take time. I need something quick. And *really* spectacular.'

Ellie paced back and forth, massaging her temples to help her think. She tried to imagine herself as the Queen, with the whole island stretching out beneath her. What was the thing Ellie would want most if she was stuck up in the Ark all the time?

'Kate,' Ellie said carefully. 'The Queen . . . um . . . she doesn't have wings, does she?'

Kate blinked. 'No, She doesn't have *wings*.'

'The mural on the front of the Ark shows a figure with wings.'

'That's not the Queen, that's the god who lives inside Her.'

'So *it* has wings?'

'Of course!' said Kate, in disbelief. 'Are outer islanders so ignorant? When a Queen or a King gets too old, or uses

145

their power too much, they undergo something called *manifestation*. They die, and the god takes a physical form and flies round the island for a few hours, making all the plant life bloom. Sometimes it looks like a winged person, other times it's the God-Bird – a giant purple bird bigger than a horse.'

'Oh,' said Ellie. This sounded a lot like what happened when the Enemy weakened its Vessel so much it could take a form of its own. 'Then what happens?'

Kate's eyes narrowed suspiciously. 'The god takes a new Vessel. Usually it's the previous Vessel's child, but sometimes another person is picked, if the Queen or King doesn't have a child of their own. The next Vessel is marked in the great Ritual of Succession – they really never taught you all this? The schools on your island must be appalling.'

'Oh, they mostly just taught us about fish. That's why I came here. So, um, the Queen can't fly. But what . . .' Ellie licked her lips. 'What if she could?'

Kate opened her mouth, blinking rapidly. 'But She can't.'

'But what if she *could*?'

'Ellie, I think you've broken.'

'We'll make her *wings*. So she can fly! She must have everything she's ever wanted, being a Queen. But I bet she'd love to fly – *everyone* dreams of flying.'

'People can't fly,' said Kate.

'But birds can, so it must be possible.'

'Birds are much smaller than people.'

'You just said the god can be a bird bigger than a horse, and it can fly!'

'That's because it's a *god*.'

'There are laws governing all things, even gods, I bet. What goes up, must come down, right?' Ellie pointed at the crushed shards of the bird's egg she'd dropped the day before. 'Unless . . .' She picked up one of the intact eggs. 'Something pushes it up with enough force to counterbalance its own weight.'

Kate cocked her head to one side. 'The people on your island only learn about fish, do they?'

'I need some lightweight fabrics,' Ellie announced. 'And some very big, hollow tubes. Bird bones are hollow, you know. And if the wings are *big* enough, and can push with enough force, then the person can *fly*!'

Ellie threw her hand into the air, forgetting she was still holding the egg. It flew up and smashed against the ceiling.

Kate looked at the trail of yolk dripping to the floor, then at Ellie. A smile spread across her face.

'You're insane, Ellie Stonewall. Let's do it.'

~

Ellie set to work bending bits of copper into tubes, and Kate hurried up into the palace, returning half an hour later with a pile of sumptuous silk dresses.

'Where did you get these?' Ellie asked.

'They're old cast-offs,' Kate said carelessly, placing the pile on the largest workbench. They were the colour of bright jewels, as gauzy as spider's web, trimmed with lace and with buttons made from seashells. Ellie peered at them, noticing how long they were – obviously meant for someone very tall. Her eyes grew wide.

'These belonged to the Queen?'

Kate hesitated, then nodded.

Ellie scrunched one of the dresses in her hands. It was pale purple, soft as butter, and it seemed a crime to tear it into pieces.

'Um, Ellie,' said Kate, as the sound of ripping fabric filled the workshop. 'If people could fly simply by wearing a big pair of wings, wouldn't they have done it already?'

'Well, actually, I thought we'd just give her wings that will let her glide, instead of fly – like wearing a big kite. Although, now you mention it, if we strapped a mechanism to her back, and some kind of engine that burned oil, then perhaps . . .'

An hour later, Ellie and Kate were frantically trying to put out a small fire in the centre of the workshop.

'I'm sorry!' Ellie cried, as she rushed from the sink with another bucketful of water. 'I didn't think it would explode like that!'

Kate ripped another dress at the seams, flinging it over the burning heap of metal and wood, stamping on the pile.

'Excellent idea!' said Ellie.

Kate yelped, swiping an ember from her wrist.

'Oh no, are you okay?' Ellie cried, rushing to Kate's aid. 'Let's run cold water on that.'

Kate pulled away. 'It's fine,' she said. 'Just a tiny burn.'

Ellie reached for Kate's hand, where an angry welt had blossomed. 'No, I really think we should –'

'Don't touch me!'

Kate straightened up to her full height and slapped Ellie's hand away, fixing her with a ferocious glare. Ellie stared in shock.

'I'm – I'm sorry.'

'No, no,' Kate stammered, slouching again and staring at her feet. 'I'm sorry. It just hurt, that's all.'

But Ellie couldn't forget what she'd seen in her eyes. She looked down at Kate's hands, noticing for the first time how clean and smooth they were. On every finger was a band of pale skin, like tan lines left by heavy rings. Ellie examined her own hands. They were scratched and blistered, the nails bitten to nubs. Kate's nails were immaculate. Her arms were strong, her eyes sharp. Every part of her had been well nourished and well cared for.

'Straighten up,' said Ellie, without really thinking. Slowly, Kate obliged. Now that she wasn't slouching, Ellie realized how tall Kate was. Ellie lifted one of the unburnt dresses and held it out in front of her. It would have fitted perfectly.

Ellie dropped the dress to the ground.

Kate looked at Ellie, her gaze unwavering. Her lips were small, her ears a little large, so the tops of them poked out through her hair. And her eyes. Her eyes bored into Ellie, almost golden in colour. Looking at them was like staring into the sun.

'You're . . . you're the . . .' Ellie stammered.

'Yes,' said the Queen. 'I am.'

Leila's Diary

4,762 days aboard the *Revival*

I tied Varu to a chair so he wouldn't run off again, but he didn't wake up until the next day.

I pushed a mug of water to his lips. 'Drink.'

'Where am I?' Varu said, looking round the torchlit garden. The Ark creaked and groaned.

'You're on the *Revival*,' I told him. 'It's a really big ship.'

He tried to raise his hands to his head.

'I'll cut those ropes,' I said, kneeling with my knife. 'But if you try anything, I'll throw you overboard.'

I sliced the cords binding Varu's wrists, and he clutched his head. 'The sea . . . it's . . . it's *everywhere*.'

'It's all that's left,' I said. 'Nothing but sea, and more sea, and this Ark. There were three others, but nobody knows if they survived. They all got separated during the Drowning.'

'The Drowning?'

'When the seas got raised,' I said. 'Years ago, before I was born, there was a big war. Like the biggest you can imagine. One of the gods started it, but it was people who fought. And it got so bad that the only way to stop it was to flood the whole world.'

Varu looked at me, blinking. 'What's a god?'

I frowned. 'You really don't remember anything, do you? A god is like a . . .' I stopped, realizing I wasn't even sure how to describe one. 'They're like, the most powerful things in the world. Spirits that float about until they find someone, like a person or an animal, that they can *live* inside, until eventually they can take a form of their own. That's the way it's always been.'

'So where are they?'

I rubbed the back of my head. 'Er, the Crone has one god inside her, and, um . . .' I looked at Varu, feeling guilty for being the one to tell him. 'She says you're another.'

The boy was quiet for ages. 'So what about the rest?' he said eventually. He sounded calm, but his hands were gripping his chair really tight. 'Where are my brothers and sisters?'

'Look, it's okay,' I said, trying to speak softly. 'Me and the Crone will look after you. I don't care that you killed my whale.'

The Ark creaked louder than I'd ever heard it; the seas must have been very angry.

'Where are they?' Varu said, his eyes big and fierce.

I swallowed. 'Well, the gods thought they could survive the Drowning, but something went wrong. I'm really sorry.' I put my hand on his. 'They're all gone.'

16

The Queen

Ellie's body was rigid. It was like she'd glanced away from Kate a moment, then looked back to find a snarling wolf in her place. She was afraid to even move.

'I . . . I don't understand,' she managed. 'Why didn't you tell me?'

Kate smiled sadly. 'Because look how you're acting now. You're terrified.'

'You said you'd have me executed,' said Ellie.

'And I imprisoned you so we could spend time together, and said your mechanical hand was worthless so you'd have to stay longer. I told you I couldn't be trusted.'

Ellie took three deep breaths. 'So . . . are you going to execute me now?'

'What?' Kate's eyes widened in shock. 'I was *never* going to execute you, Ellie. I just wanted you to take this seriously.'

Ellie's fists clenched so tightly her nails dug into her palms. 'That's the cruellest thing I've ever heard.'

'I have to appear strong in front of my court. Especially Loren, he's a snake. Speaking of which . . .' She glanced at the clock. 'I'm supposed to be meeting them now.'

She clapped her hands twice, and the doors swung open. Eight handmaidens in purple dresses entered the workshop.

'Were they outside this whole time?' said Ellie.

Kate nodded. 'You're surprisingly unobservant for an inventor,' she said, raising her arms.

The handmaidens crowded round Kate, pulling her dress off over her head so she was just in her underclothes. Ellie glanced away, though Kate didn't seem the slightest bit embarrassed. The handmaidens attended to her like fastidious doll-makers. One applied a file to her left hand, another to her right. One rubbed a white paste into her cheek; another drew a line of gold across her collarbone. One spread an amber-coloured ointment across the burn on her wrist, another to a cut on her knee. Two more stood upon chairs and drew combs made from bone through her hair, smoothing it to gleaming sheets of darkness. It was only with so many handmaidens around her that Ellie realized *just* how tall Kate was.

'Oh, and on the subject of cruelty,' said Kate, 'were you planning on leaving that boy trapped under your bed *all* day?'

'Seth!' Ellie took a step forward. 'What have you done to him?'

The handmaidens threw her filthy looks. 'You will address the Queen as "Your Divinity",' one snapped.

'I didn't *do* anything,' said Kate coolly. 'I'm not a monster. He's probably still there. A servant saw him asleep under the bed while they were sweeping. How did he get in, anyway?'

'He climbed the Ark,' said Ellie.

Kate jerked forward, causing a handmaiden to drop her nail file. '*Climbed?* That's extremely dangerous – the stonework is brittle and old. Those statues are always breaking off.'

'Oh really?' Ellie said, tugging her collar.

The handmaidens began to draw earthy red, swirling patterns like plant roots along Kate's bare arms, while others weaved thin ribbons of gold through her hair, parting it into five long tendrils that spilled down her back. Kate kept her eyes on Ellie the whole time, though Ellie found it hard to look back.

'Ellie, stop pouting and tell me what you're thinking.'

'I don't like being toyed with.'

Kate rolled her eyes. 'I'm sorry, okay? I wasn't sure I could trust you – I thought maybe you were one of Loren's spies. But now I know you and you'd make a terrible spy.'

'I would *not*,' said Ellie. 'I can be very sneaky.'

'With a limp and a broken arm?'

'Besides, why would Loren spy on you? He seemed nice to me. If a bit full of himself.'

'A *bit*?'

'I've been thinking, though – everyone keeps talking about the Festival of Life, and how you're going to use your powers to make the fields bloom, and fill the seas with fish again. If things are so bad right now, why not just have the Festival early?'

Kate turned suddenly, causing one handmaiden to gasp as she smeared red ointment down Kate's cheek, like warpaint. She now looked like some demonic warrior, eyeing Ellie dangerously.

'Get out,' Kate whispered to her handmaidens.

'Your Divinity!' one complained. 'We're not finished –'

'OUT!'

The handmaidens yelped and fled the room. The door slammed shut and Ellie and Kate were alone again.

'I'm sorry,' Ellie said hurriedly. 'I didn't mean to make you angry. I'm going to help, okay? I'm going to invent things that will fix everything. I'm sorry I mentioned the Festival of Life.'

Kate clenched her fists. She took a step towards Ellie, and Ellie took a wary step back. Just for a second, she saw a flash of Seth in Kate's frustrated expression, and in that moment was struck by a new thought. 'You . . . you *do* know how to use your powers, don't you?'

Kate took one more step towards Ellie, breathing in deeply. Then, all the anger drained from her face and she fell to her knees, burying her face in her hands.

'Oh, oh dear,' said Ellie, dropping down at Kate's side. Kate's hands were smeared with red face paint, her tears turning red as they dripped to the floor. 'Don't cry,' said Ellie. 'It's okay if you find it hard – maybe I can help?'

'I'm the Queen, Ellie!' Kate snarled. 'Of *course* I can use my powers.' She got to her feet and stormed from the workshop, slamming the door behind her.

Ellie chased after, but paused at the door, pressing her ear against it, listening to the sobs that echoed down the corridor.

17

The Crystal Whale

That Saturday morning, Ellie sat at a table in the
empty bar of the Vile Oak, working her way through
a pile of books she'd borrowed from the palace. She took
extra care not to let the books touch the sticky patches of
orange juice on the table – things with Kate had been left
on such a tense note she was surprised she and Seth had
been let out of the palace at all. She didn't want to give
Kate any more reason to be cross with her.

Molworth was mopping the floorboards, glaring at the
clock, flinching at every whoop or whistle from outside.

'What's wrong?' said Ellie.

Molworth shivered. 'The weekend crowd arrives at
noon. They can be . . . a handful.' His knuckles paled as he
clenched the mop.

'Have you ever thought of selling this place?' Ellie asked. 'Doing something you enjoy more?'

Molworth's eyes widened, like she'd announced she was about to murder him. 'What could I possibly enjoy more?'

The door slammed open and Molworth shrieked, holding up his mop in defence. But it was just Seth and Viola, laughing and shoving each other as they came in. Viola slapped a piece of paper down on Ellie's table, which Archibald immediately sprawled himself across. Viola rolled him aside.

LOREN HEROICALLY RESCUES INNOCENT GIRL FROM CAPTIVITY

'You're famous,' said Viola.

Ellie scanned the newspaper. 'But . . . it doesn't say my name anywhere? Get *off* me,' she added, shooing Molworth away as he tried to dab a drip of orange juice off her chin. Ever since she'd returned from the Ark, he'd been treating her with the same devotion he gave to his statues of the Queen.

'Tell me again what She looked like?' Molworth said.

'Stop asking that,' said Ellie.

Molworth bowed deeply. 'I live to serve. Can I fetch you more oranges?'

'This is great,' said Viola, rubbing her hands together. 'Now that you're working for the Queen, you can help me with the Revolution. Steal back all the food She's been keeping in the palace.'

'Right, that's strike ten billion,' said Molworth, putting his face right up to Viola's. 'You are barred from the inn forever.'

Viola stared at him, unblinking.

'For two weeks,' said Molworth.

Viola cracked her knuckles.

'Two days,' said Molworth. 'Would you like an orange?'

The door slammed open, and Molworth shrieked again as a crowd of thirty sailors thundered into the pub, led by Janssen. He scooped Molworth up in one arm, depositing him behind the bar. 'Beer for all!' he declared.

Viola raced over to greet the newcomers, while Seth picked up a tall sunflower that was lying across the table.

'From Molworth again?' he said, then frowned. 'Wait . . . is this made of paper?'

Ellie nodded. 'It's quite realistic, isn't it? About half the flowers in the public gardens aren't real, but you wouldn't notice without getting close. Loren did it to help the Queen.'

Seth sniffed the flower experimentally. 'Why?'

'To stop people from panicking, I guess. The island isn't nearly as fertile as it looks. The harvests have been declining ever since the current Queen became Vessel.' Ellie lowered her voice. 'I think she might not know how to control her powers properly.'

Seth laid the sunflower back on the table. 'Oh, by the way. The Crone in my visions. She's a Vessel. To the same god as the Queen, I think.'

'What?' Ellie shot up. 'Why didn't you tell me sooner!'

Seth wrinkled his nose. 'I only found out this morning. It's not like I can control the visions.'

'Has the Crone mentioned anything about how she uses her powers?'

'No. It's mostly Leila who talks to me. Last time, she was talking about the Drowning.'

He looked distantly at the window, then frowned and shook his head. 'You've been spending a lot of time at the palace this week. I've barely seen you.'

'I've been learning all sorts of things in the library,' Ellie said excitedly. 'Did you know there was once an animal called a flying squirrel, that could glide for over three hundred feet?'

Seth grunted, watching Viola and the other sailors. 'How's that supposed to help the harvest?'

Ellie's brow crumpled. 'Anyway . . . it's safer for me to be in the palace. Hargrath could walk in here at any moment, and tell everyone who I am.'

Seth's eyes flicked to the door. 'They'd probably think he was a maniac.'

'But he could still attack me.'

'You're well protected, though,' Seth said, lifting his chin.

'That's true. The Queen will protect me.'

'I was talking about me!'

'Oh right.' Ellie winced. 'Yes, of course.'

'You do actually *like* her, though? The Queen, I mean.'

Ellie shifted uncomfortably, and Seth's eyes narrowed. 'What happened?'

'Nothing, I, um . . . I haven't really seen her, since she got angry with me.'

'I don't know why you're bothering to help her, if she's not even going to treat you nicely.'

'She's just . . . in a difficult position. Imagine ruling a whole island. It can't be easy.'

Seth raised his eyebrows. 'You need to stand up for yourself.'

'Oh, by the way,' said Ellie, leaping on the chance to change the subject, 'I've been meaning to give you something.'

She reached for a small box wrapped in blue tissue paper – the crystal whale she'd bought for him. Her stomach jittered as she picked it up. Would he like it?

'Seth!' Viola cried, rushing over and clamping both hands on his shoulders. 'Tell Handyl about the giant flying jellyfish you saw that time.'

'I didn't see a flying jellyfish,' said Seth.

'Yeah, but I've been telling Handyl you did. Just make something up, will you? You're a hero to him.'

Seth followed Viola to the centre of the pub, where he began to recount a ridiculous saga about the jellyfish he and Viola had ridden beyond the outer islands. He didn't look back at Ellie once.

Ellie hugged the present close. It was a while before she noticed the girl sitting at the table with her. She wore a weathered blue cloak, a hood pulled down over her eyes. She placed both hands on the table, and Ellie recognized the bands of tan lines on the fingers, the fingernails still flecked with purple nail polish.

Ellie pushed her chair back with a scrape. 'What are you doing here?'

'A pleasure to see you too,' said Kate, pulling back her hood. 'Can I get a beer here?'

Ellie swallowed. 'Molworth stopped serving beer to children, after the Apple Pie Riots. How can you be here?'

'Nobody recognizes me if I'm not dressed up. And I wanted to see what weekends are like.'

Molworth stumbled over, rubbing his runny nose on his sleeve. 'Ellie, I'm going to the loo. If anyone tries to steal anything, there's a cutlass behind the bar.'

'Okay. Um, Molworth, this is, uh, this is . . .'

'Kate,' said Kate brightly, extending her hand. Molworth grunted.

'You have a ladybird in your hair,' he said, then walked away.

Kate pulled her hood back. 'He's right!' she said cheerfully, holding out her finger so the ladybird could fly away. She looked at Ellie, then at her lap. 'Look, the real reason I came here was to say sorry. For how I acted the other day.'

'Oh.' Ellie shuffled in her seat. She put Seth's gift back on the table, trying to think of something to say.

'Is that for me?' said Kate, peering at the box.

'What? This?' Ellie glanced at Kate and saw the hopeful glint in her eye, then looked at Seth, surrounded by his audience of smiling sailors. 'Yes, yes, it's for you.'

Kate unwrapped the present, gasping as she lifted up the whale in both hands. Ellie could see Kate's golden eyes reflected in its crystal surface.

'That's . . .' Kate opened her mouth, closed it. 'Thank you. That's so kind of you.'

'Seth's present!' Molworth announced, reappearing by the table. 'You finally gave it to him, then? Did he like it?'

Ellie felt an overwhelming desire to hit Molworth with her cane.

Kate blinked at Molworth, then back at the crystal whale. Her smile fell. On the far side of the bar, Viola had placed Archibald on the mantlepiece and pulled two wooden swords from the wall, challenging the other sailors to duel with her.

'What are you talking about, Molworth?' said Ellie, forcing a smile. 'I got it for Kate.'

Molworth frowned. 'No you didn't.'

'I *did*!'

Kate fixed her with a knowing look. 'Ellie.'

Ellie sighed. 'I'm sorry. You just . . . you seemed so happy when you thought I'd got it for you, and . . .'

There was a cheer as Viola casually flicked the sword from the hand of her opponent – a seven-foot giant with shark-tooth scars scabbing his chest.

Kate smiled. 'I think that's maybe even kinder. But I really can't accept this now.'

'What's going on?' said Seth, wandering over and frowning at Kate. 'Who's this?'

'Ellie was giving her your present!' Molworth said brightly.

'*Molworth!*' Ellie cried.

Seth looked at the humpback whale in Kate's hand.

'No, it was a misunderstanding,' Kate explained. 'I thought it was for me. Ellie was only being kind.' She presented the whale to him. 'Here you go,' she said, flashing a brilliant smile.

Seth stared at the whale. 'You got this for me,' he said flatly.

Ellie fiddled with her sling. 'Yes.'

'But you were going to give it to her?' he said, his brow crumpling.

'Quite insensitive, if you ask me,' said Molworth.

'Well, nobody *is* asking you, Molworth!' Ellie yelled, whacking him with her cane.

Seth stared at Kate. 'Who are you?'

'I'm Kate,' she said, putting the whale down and offering Seth her hand.

Seth's eyes flitted between her and Ellie. 'Why would Ellie . . .' he began, then took a step back. 'Wait.' He looked at Ellie. 'Is she –' He looked at Kate. 'Are you –'

'From the palace?' Ellie said quickly, giving Seth a meaningful glare. 'Yes, she works there.'

Molworth squealed. 'You're from the palace? You should have said! Is it true the Queen can turn flour into cake just by clicking Her fingers?'

Kate winked at him. 'Only chocolate cake.'

Molworth's face turned red. 'I know you're teasing me. But I don't care. Come, I have a much nicer table for you – you don't want to sit with these idiots. Here, I got you a gift.' He picked up the crystal whale and presented it to her.

Seth snatched it from Molworth's hand, glaring at Kate. 'You were going to execute Ellie,' Seth whispered, as Molworth shuffled miserably back to the bar.

Kate's smile flickered. 'That was just for show. I would *never* hurt Ellie.'

'Why should I believe you? You barely even know her. And you can't go taking things from her that aren't yours. Though I guess that comes naturally to –'

'*Seth*,' Ellie hissed.

'Which of you scoundrels is next?' said Viola, swaggering over with a wooden sword in each hand, Archibald balancing on her head. 'Oi, Seth.' She prodded him with a sword tip. 'Fight me.'

'Not right now,' said Seth.

'What's put you in a mood this time?' said Viola. 'Ellie, you'll fight me, won't you?'

'Um, I don't think I'd make a very good opponent,' said Ellie, pointing to her sling.

Two red-faced sailors behind Viola began chanting, 'El-*lie*, El-*lie*, El-*lie*!'

'No, really, I –'

The chant spread, echoing deafeningly from the low ceiling. 'EL-LIE! EL-LIE! EL-LIE!'

Ellie's face went hot. Her stomach squirmed.

'I'll fight you,' Kate said quietly.

The whole pub cheered.

'OTHER GIRL! OTHER GIRL! OTHER GIRL!'

Viola grinned and tossed one sword to Kate, who caught it neatly in mid-air. The sailors fell into a frenzy of bet-taking.

'Wait,' said Seth, grabbing the other sword from Viola's hand. He narrowed his eyes at Kate. 'I want to fight.'

'But you *just* said you didn't,' said Viola, making a face.

'Um, maybe this isn't a good idea?' said Ellie, wary of the glare Seth was giving Kate.

'I've protected you from worse than her,' Seth muttered, out of the corner of his mouth.

'I'll put ten silver pieces on the beautiful one,' Molworth was telling a sailor.

'His name is Seth,' said the man.

'What's got into him?' Viola asked Ellie, and Ellie looked guiltily at the crystal whale.

The sailors cleared a space, and Seth and Kate faced one another. Kate stood perfectly still, her sword held calmly in both hands. Seth swung his in theatrical arcs, his lips set in a line. Janssen clapped his hands once and Seth rushed at Kate, sword raised over his head.

'Stop!' Ellie cried, but her voice was swallowed by cheering. She closed her eyes, hearing a scuffle and a thud. When she opened them again, Seth was on the ground, with Kate's sword tip resting on his nose.

The room fell deathly silent.

'Good God,' said Molworth.

There was an explosion of applause. Kate turned a little pink and bowed as three fishermen lifted Seth from the ground, brushing the dust off him. Seth batted them away furiously and whirled round, marching for the door.

'My turn!' Viola declared, picking up Seth's sword to face Kate. Ellie lurched after Seth, but tripped over a root that curled from the floorboards. As she staggered to her feet, a musical voice swept through the pub.

'Why, look at all these smiling faces!'

Loren was dressed in a sky-blue robe lined with spotted animal fur, his bard and scribe close behind him. The sailors drew in their breath as one.

'It's Loren Alexander,' Molworth whispered, then fell on his back.

A crowd clamoured towards Loren, and he shook their hands one by one, gifting a man with a bead necklace and a woman with a golden brooch. Both were immediately set upon by the others.

'Now please, loyal subjects, I've come to see my dear friend Ellie Stonewall, if you don't mind. Ah, there she is.'

The sailors parted to let him through, then crowded round to listen attentively.

'Ellie,' Loren said. 'How are you?'

'I'm okay. Um, how are you?'

'Thriving, just thriving!' Loren announced. 'And so pleased that the Queen has accepted you into Her employ. On which subject, I do have a small request to make of you.'

'Uh, of course?'

Loren glanced round at the eavesdropping sailors. 'Oliver, how about a song?'

The bard strummed a chord on his lute, and the sailors launched into a rousing rendition of 'Loren the Great'.

Loren leaned in close to Ellie. 'By virtue of your new position,' he said, 'you will be privy to much that goes on in the palace. It would be helpful if, now and then, I could pick your brains about Our Beloved Queen's activities.'

Ellie stiffened uncomfortably and glanced at Kate, who'd abandoned her swordfight and was eyeing Loren warily.

'Oh, um . . .' Ellie cleared her throat. 'I don't think so. That sounds like spying.'

'Ellie, the Queen needs help from Her advisors. But we can't help Her if She won't tell us what She's up to. She is . . . unstable, Ellie. She did threaten to execute you, after all.'

'That wasn't a real threat. I'm sorry, I don't think I can spy on her.'

Loren frowned. 'Ellie, it's really the least you could do. Without my help, you'd probably be in a prison cell still. You owe me.'

The words were chillingly familiar to Ellie. She sat up straight. 'I'm sorry, but I'm not going to do it.'

Loren studied her a long moment, then smiled. 'Very well. Personally, I'm just glad the Queen has someone as talented, imaginative and –' he patted her on the shoulder – '*principled* as you in Her confidence. She will need the help of intelligent people in the weeks to come.'

From his robes, he produced a newspaper, which still smelled of fresh ink.

QUEEN USES FAKE FLOWERS TO HIDE TRUTH OF POOR HARVEST

The sailors spotted the newspaper and gasped, muttering to one another in disbelief. Kate marched over and snatched it from Loren's grip. Her fingers trembled as she read.

'Pardon me, I don't think we've been introduced,' said Loren, holding out his hand. 'Loren Alexander.'

'I know who you are,' said Kate, not meeting his eye. Loren studied her a moment, then smiled.

'And what is your name?'

'Kate.'

Loren's smile broadened, his eyes crinkling. 'Charming, most charming.'

Ellie felt a tightness in her chest, but couldn't say why. Molworth appeared at Loren's elbow with a quill, an inkpot and a stack of his own crudely drawn portraits of Loren. Loren began signing them, one after the other, without even looking at them.

Kate gripped the newspaper furiously. 'Why would you tell everyone this?' she said, her voice low and serious.

'Me?' Loren blinked. 'Dear friend, I don't print these newspapers.'

'Then why are they always going on about how great you are?'

'They simply report the truth,' said Loren, as Molworth passed him another picture to sign. Kate snarled and knocked the inkpot aside. Molworth yelped and ran to grab his mop, as Loren calmly dabbed black specks from his face.

'You can't tell everyone that the Queen's been lying to them,' Kate yelled, 'when it was *your* idea to put those fake plants everywhere in the first place.'

The pub had fallen silent. Loren winced at his bard, who promptly began to play again, then leaned in towards Kate, his hand falling on the open box still sitting on the table.

'A present?' he asked, picking up the whale. 'How lovely.'

'Put that down,' said Kate.

Loren continued to study Kate. He lowered his voice. 'The Queen should know better than to threaten me in front of Her Royal Court. If She's not going to show *me* respect, well . . . then I can be very disrespectful of Her. Take from Her the things that matter most.'

He turned the crystal whale over in his hand, then slipped it into his pocket.

'Don't you –' Kate raised her fist.

'You'd be amazed,' interrupted Loren, adjusting the sleeves of his robe, '*just* how many secrets some people keep. Why, I bet even little Ellie here has secrets.'

He smiled at them both, and an icy hand gripped Ellie's heart. 'Now, if you'll forgive me, I must be going. The Royal Court has tasked me with hiring musicians for the Festival of Life. Can you believe it's only forty-one days away? Forty-one days, and the Queen will put all this nasty business with the harvest to rest. Won't she, Kate?'

Kate's lips paled as Loren watched her, his eyes dancing with laughter. He removed a purple rose from his pocket, and placed it in Kate's hand.

'Praise Her,' he said.

18

A Question for the Dead

The farms of Shipwreck Island covered its entire western side: a patchwork of fields that stretched from the Guano Mines in the north to the volcano in the south, punctured by rocky spires from which seagulls scanned the water's edge for their next meal. Despite the warm sun, the land was a grey bed of dead earth, with only the occasional clump of wheat or barley.

Grim-faced men and women worked the soil, sweat glinting on their bare shoulders. Ellie, meanwhile, was watching a small mechanical device crawl across an empty plot. She bit back the desire to swear as it fell on its side for the fifth time.

Ellie righted the tilling machine, so it could continue on its path. She had built the prototype over the last few days, with Kate's help. It lacked the grace of her mother's crablike oyster-catchers, which had seemed almost alive. Its cogs were exposed, its many limbs twitching as it walked, like a jittery spider. It tumbled over again, and there was a collective groan from nearby.

'Bad luck, miss.'

Three small children were watching at a safe distance, torn between their fascination of the machine and their fear of Ellie.

'If you want, you can come closer. I'm not a ghost.'

'You do look like one, though, miss,' one called.

'You don't have to call me "miss", either. I'm thirteen.'

'What does it do, miss?'

'It's for improving the soil. To help the plants grow,' she added. The machine fell over again.

'Miss, is it true we've only got two weeks to live?' said one little girl.

'No! Where did you hear that?'

'My mum says that's when the food's going to run out.'

'Well, even if that was true, we wouldn't die straight away. It takes a long time to die of starvation.'

One small boy burst into tears.

'Making friends again, I see.'

Ellie turned to find Seth, then spun away from him, lifting her chin. They hadn't spoken since he'd been so grumpy in the pub at the weekend.

'Wait, I've got news!' he said. 'I spent all day sailing round the island. That ship we saw, with the black sail – Hargrath's boat? It's gone.'

'Gone? Why would he go?'

Seth shrugged. 'You said that crowd attacked him. He must have got spooked and fled.'

'Or else he's gone back to get more Inquisitors,' Ellie said, stroking her chin.

'They probably won't believe him. He's insane. It's good news, though, isn't it?'

Ellie narrowed her eyes suspiciously. 'I'm still angry with you,' she said. 'This doesn't make up for your behaviour on Saturday. Wait, what are you –'

She yelped as Seth pulled her to the ground.

'Shh!' Seth hissed. 'There's something at the edge of the field, watching us.'

Ellie squirmed out of his grip. 'It's one of the Seven Sentinels,' she said, standing up and brushing herself off. 'Kate's bodyguards. That one's protecting me from Inquisitors and strange boys.'

'It's not doing a good job – I just tackled you to the ground.'

'Probably doesn't think you're very threatening,' Ellie said, and Seth scowled. The three children had crept closer to gaze up at Seth.

'I *am* very threatening,' said Seth, and he growled at the children like a wolf. They fell about laughing. Seth glanced over to where the Sentinel stood in a tree's shadow, a dark suit of armour with a cape and a featureless, reflective face. 'How does it see through that mask?'

Ellie studied the bodyguard thoughtfully. 'Back in the City, Altimus Ashenholme invented a kind of glass that could only be seen through in one direction – all it takes is a thin layer of silver on regular glass. The Inquisitors used it in rooms where they were interrogating people, so the suspect couldn't see who was talking to them.'

'Altimus Ashenholme is a stupid name,' said Seth.

'He was my mum's mentor,' said Ellie. 'Though she was much smarter than him,' she added hastily. 'I've been thinking about him a lot lately, because *he* invented a way to take nitrogen out of the air.'

She waited patiently for Seth to ask what nitrogen was, but he wasn't listening. 'Nitrogen can be used to make plant fertilizer. If I could figure out how Ashenholme did it . . . You know, I think I had some journals of his, only I left them in the underwater boat –'

'What's that?' said Seth, pointing to a tall cylinder wedged into the soil, with three dials on its side, a piston-driven pump, and six nozzles sprouting from the top.

'It's for spraying fertilizer on the fields. When I figure out how to make fertilizer from the air, *that's* what I'm going to put it in.'

'So what's inside it now?'

'Bird droppings.'

Seth sighed. 'Of course. So these machines are going to improve the harvest? Janssen thinks people will be eating each other by the end of next month.'

Ellie knelt down to wind up the tilling machine. 'I hope they'll improve it, if I can just get them working.'

The machine walked round in a tiny circle, then fell over. Ellie groaned. 'But, more importantly, I need to talk to Kate about what the problem is with her powers. Hey! Could you keep it down?'

The children had gathered to inspect the dropping-sprayer and were giggling and shoving each other to get a closer look.

'When I use my powers, it makes me feel sick.' Seth put a hand to his stomach. 'And leaves me tired. Maybe it's the same for her.'

'Wait,' said Ellie. 'That's it! Maybe *you* could help!'

'Me?'

'You've been learning how to control your powers all this time – you can teach her.'

Seth stared at her, aghast. 'But we can't let her know who I really am. And anyway, my powers are completely different to hers – who knows if they work the same way?'

Ellie massaged her head, trying to think. The children continued to giggle.

'Okay, well . . . what about the Crone? You said she contained the same god that lives in Kate. Maybe she can tell us something.'

'Ellie, the Crone lived seven hundred years ago. She's dead.'

'Yeah, but the way you talk about your visions, it's not like they're memories, it's like you're really there. Maybe you can ask her questions and get answers.'

Seth blinked. 'That might be the craziest idea you've ever had. Worse than when you tried to inflate that puffer fish to help the raft float.'

'Sometimes I can change my dreams if I think hard enough.'

'But these things actually happened. They're not dreams!'

'We might as well *try* it.'

'You mean, *I* might as well try. I don't like the visions.'

'Don't you like seeing Leila?'

'Yeah, but I don't like hearing the sound of a whole world drowning. Wait, what are they doing?'

The three children were fiddling with the dropping-sprayer, one of them cranking the largest dial on the side.

'Stop!' Ellie cried, as the machine began to rumble, the piston pumping angrily and the nozzles trembling. 'Get away from that!'

The children shrieked and scattered, but nothing happened. The machine just rumbled away, with nothing coming out of the nozzles.

'Eurgh, *that's* not working, either,' said Ellie, stepping towards it and pulling a screwdriver from her coat pocket.

'Ellie, wait!' Seth cried, grabbing her by the shoulder. The machine had begun to rumble louder, rattling wildly like someone was trapped inside. 'It's going to –'

There was a bang, and a wet squelching sound, like custard flung against a wall. Ellie braced herself, expecting to feel bird droppings leaking down her shirt. But the feeling never came.

The tall dark Sentinel stood in front of them, facing the wreckage of the machine, sword raised high. Ellie stepped round the motionless figure, between scraps of twisted metal. The Sentinel's entire front was caked with bird droppings.

'Are . . . are you okay?' Ellie asked. The Sentinel looked round, but their mask was covered in droppings too, like globs of egg white flecked with black speckles. They tried to scrape some away with an armoured fist.

'Here,' said Ellie, taking a cloth from her pocket.

'Why can't it talk?' asked Seth.

'They've taken a vow of silence to keep the Queen's secrets,' said Ellie, then leaned in close. 'They're a bit scary, to be honest. Like they're not even human underneath.'

The masked head turned sharply in Ellie's direction, looking as insulted as it was possible for a blank face to look. One armoured glove clamped on to the other and pulled, revealing a pale, muscular hand underneath.

'Well, I guess they have human hands at least,' muttered Ellie, and she thought she heard a quiet 'huff' beneath the mask as the Sentinel turned and marched away. The ruined dropping-sprayer burped a final glob of guano. Ellie winced.

'Seth, what if my machines never work? We *have* to help Kate use her powers. Please, just try to ask the Crone?'

Seth grimaced. 'All right. But only because it will help everyone, not just Kate. I still don't trust her.'

'Thank you, Seth,' said Ellie. 'Can I do anything to –'

'No, I need peace and quiet.'

He sat down in the dirt, and took several deep breaths. He closed his eyes.

Leila's Diary

4,783 days aboard the *Revival*

Varu was acting even stranger than usual today.

It was long past breakfast but he was still sleeping in his bedroll by the orchid patch. He is very lazy. I was watering the potato plants, navigating thick curtains of spider's webs. I'd asked the Crone three times to let me get rid of the spiders but she refused.

There was a sharp cry, and I turned to find Varu looking at me like I was a ghost.

'L-Leila?'

I threw a potato at his head. 'Who else would I be?'

'What's the matter?' croaked the Crone. I hadn't even noticed her sitting in her chair among the tall sunflowers.

'I . . . I could see something,' said Varu. 'A huge ship.'

'You're *in* a huge ship, fool,' I said.

He shook his head. 'No, this ship grew out of an island. I was there.'

'It's called a dream,' I said. 'Someone who sleeps as much as you should be used to them.'

'*No*,' Varu said, drumming his knuckles against his head. 'This was real. There was a girl talking to me, only she didn't call me Varu. She wanted me to ask you something.'

'Me?' I said.

'No, not you.' Varu scowled, and threw the potato back at me. He looked at the Crone. 'She wanted to know what it is you do to use your powers. To make plants grow. To heal the sick.'

The Crone studied Varu. 'Can she be trusted?'

Varu nodded immediately, then seemed surprised, like he hadn't meant to. 'She's . . . trying to help someone. She's trying to help *everyone*.'

'Wait.' I glared at the Crone. 'You're not taking this seriously, are you? It's just some stupid dream.'

The Crone got to her feet with a clicking of bones. 'It's not so different to how you control the sea.'

'But . . . I haven't controlled the sea,' said Varu.

'Not in this manifestation, no, but you have, and you will.' She put a hand on his shoulder. 'To control the sea, you must *become* the sea in your mind. You must forget your own self: your thoughts must turn to currents, your emotions to tides. Of course, you must be able to find your way back again: if you forget yourself entirely, your mind will turn to nothing, and your mortal body will die. And the more power you use, the harder you will find it to return.'

Varu blinked. 'So that's what I tell her? She has to imagine she's a plant?'

I snorted.

'She must surrender her identity for a time, yes,' said the Crone, ignoring me. 'All Vessels share one thing – each time they call on the power of the god that lives inside them, they give that god a piece of themselves. For some Vessels, this is a wondrous thing – they gradually become one with the god, and live on within them for evermore, a part of the Divine Cycle. For others, it is the worst kind of death you can imagine. The god feeds on the Vessel's soul until it is rent apart.'

'The Enemy,' I whispered. Varu and the Crone both looked at me. 'That's how the Enemy claims its Vessels,' I said. 'My mum told me.'

'The Enemy.' Varu frowned. 'I've heard of it before.'

'Everyone's heard of the Enemy,' I said. 'It's the god that drowned the world.'

'The Enemy did not drown the world,' said the Crone. 'Though it played its part.'

Varu was lost in thought. 'No. *They* know the Enemy. The pale girl. She's terrified of it.'

The Crone nodded. 'She should be.'

Varu looked at the Crone, deadly serious. 'It lives in *her*. It causes her –' Varu winced – 'so much pain. Can anyone help her?'

The Crone hobbled back to her seat. 'Not anyone. But someone. The Enemy was determined to destroy all the other gods, after it learned that one among them had the power to destroy *it*. The Enemy did not know which god that was, but I do.' She looked at Varu a long time, then tapped her chest. 'It is the god that lives in me.'

19

Experiments with Seeds

Ellie's mouth hung open. Light glittered in her vision.

'The Queen can destroy the Enemy,' she said.

Seth nodded. 'That makes sense. The same god that lived in the Crone lives in Kate.'

A bubble rose inside Ellie, turning to sudden laughter as it left her lips. '*Kate* can destroy the Enemy.' She leapt at Seth and hugged him tight. 'Thank you, Seth!'

'I didn't do anything,' he said, patting her uncertainly on the back.

'Yes you did! You went back into your vision-memory things, and talked to your past self!' Ellie bent to pick up her cane.

'You're going now?' said Seth.

'Of course! There's no time to lose. If I can help Kate learn how to use her powers, she'll be able to fix the island *and* destroy the Enemy!'

After a moment, Seth nodded. 'Okay. I'll come with you. I'll help too.'

'No, trust me – this isn't something she'll want to talk about in front of someone she doesn't know. And, well, you didn't make the best first impression on her.'

'All right, but be –'

'Careful, yes, I promise!' said Ellie, beaming excitedly, then racing into the streets. She stopped briefly at a market along the way, then hurried up to the palace.

'I need to see the Queen!' she told the first Warden she passed. 'It's, um . . . a royal emergency!'

The Warden eyed her sceptically, then motioned for her to follow him upstairs. Ellie's leg sang in pain by the top of the first staircase, screamed by the time she'd climbed the tenth. But she didn't care. She was led to the highest level of the Grand Atrium, where the upper deck and the hull of the ship merged together in a sharp point. At the top of the final staircase was a tall pair of golden doors flanked by two Sentinels.

They swung back the doors, and Ellie had to shield her eyes. It was like opening a box of polished jewellery in the blazing sun. For half a moment, Ellie thought the chamber was filled by a crowd of people, then realized only one of these people was real.

Statues had taken over the chamber. A boy and girl peeked slyly between ebony pillars; an austere man stood atop a varnished gold-edged bookcase. A watchful old woman leaned heavily on a silver bathtub. They were all staring at the girl who stood alone at the centre of the room, so fixedly it seemed that if she took a step their marble eyes would follow.

'Oh, hello, Ellie,' said Kate.

Ellie glanced around, noticing a statue of a particularly tall woman, who closely resembled Kate, staring sadly at her clasped hands. Ellie was sure it must be Kate's mother. 'These are the previous Vessels.'

Kate nodded. She was dressed in a purple silk robe and was tugging at her fingers with the same nervous intensity that Ellie had noticed before. Her eyes were puffy from lack of sleep, and there were smears of make-up on her face.

'Are you okay?' said Ellie.

'Oh yes,' said Kate, sniffing, then rubbing her nose. 'Yes, I'm fine. Fine.' She got to her feet. 'Yes, I'm fine.'

'Okay . . .' said Ellie slowly.

Kate stared at the floor, leaving a great empty silence that filled the chamber. Ellie rubbed the back of her neck, searching for something to say. She glanced up, and nearly screamed in fright.

A gigantic bird hovered over the chamber, bearing down on Ellie like it might be about to pick her up in its beak. It was bigger than a horse, with wings as long as a fishing boat, curling up and around so the tips of its feathers met to form a circle. Beyond the circle was a round stained-glass window, and beneath this was a platform, flanked by two golden staircases, on which sat a four-poster bed.

Like the statues, the bird appeared alive at first, its feathers glittering in the sunlight. But as Ellie stared, she saw its entire surface was studded with purple amethysts, with orbs of menacing coal-black onyx for eyes.

'That's what the god inside you looks like, between its different Vessels? That's its physical form?'

Kate looked up, and wrinkled her nose. 'The God-Bird,' she said. Ellie thought it must be strange for Kate to be constantly reminded of what she'd turn into when she died.

'Here,' said Ellie, unslinging the sack from her shoulder. 'I brought you some things.'

She removed three plant pots, a bag of soil and a pouch of seeds. Kate inspected them curiously. 'Ellie, it's fine – you don't need to make up for that crystal whale with this . . . bag of dirt.'

'No – they're for you to practise with!' Ellie explained, trying to sound cheerful.

Kate's lips pressed tightly together. 'Practise what?'

Ellie nibbled her fingernail. 'Your powers,' she said quietly.

Kate stiffened.

'Look,' Ellie said hurriedly, 'I know this isn't something you like to talk about, but –'

'What could you possibly know?' Kate spat, fists clenched.

'I think you've been struggling to use your powers. That's why you're frightened about the Festival of Life.'

Kate took one long, loud breath. Ellie took a step back towards the door.

'Get out,' said Kate.

Ellie swallowed. 'Look, why don't you just have a go? It couldn't hurt, could it?'

'Yes, it *could*, Ellie. If I can't do it then it will be *extremely* hurtful.'

Ellie knelt by the plant pots, filling them each with soil and pressing a seed inside with one finger.

'I'm *not* doing this, Ellie,' Kate insisted, folding her arms.

'Oh, I almost forgot,' Ellie added, rummaging in the sack and pulling out a small wire cage. A startled mouse scrambled madly inside.

Kate's eyes widened in adoration and she leapt on the cage. 'Oh, it's so cute!'

'I thought you could try healing it,' Ellie explained, as the little mouse sniffed Kate's finger.

Kate looked at Ellie quizzically. 'But there's nothing wrong with it?'

'No.' Ellie shrugged, fishing out a pair of pliers from her coat pocket. 'Not yet.'

Kate hugged the cage close. 'Ellie, I will not let you harm an innocent mouse for some bizarre experiment!'

'It's *not* an experiment – it's *training*.' She looked at the mouse, and at Kate, then moved the pliers towards the cage. 'Practise on the seeds, or else this little fellow's ankle might have an unfortunate accident.'

Kate snatched the pliers from Ellie's hand. 'No! Anyway, I don't *need* to use my powers any more. Your machines are going to fix the harvest.'

Ellie grimaced. 'We don't know that for sure. It's good to have a backup plan. Besides, wouldn't it be good for you to learn how to use your powers?'

Kate closed her eyes tightly, and Ellie felt a twinge of guilt, which turned to horror as tears rolled down Kate's cheeks. Kate put a hand to her face, and scowled resentfully at her own tears. She paced over to a golden cabinet, opening it to reveal many shelves of shimmering crystal vials.

She selected one, unstoppered it, then ran it up her cheek, collecting the tears. She caught the look of astonishment in Ellie's eyes.

'The Cabinet of Tears,' Kate said, gesturing to the cabinet. 'These are the tears of all the previous Queens and Kings. They're supposed to have magical properties.' She picked up another vial and swished it around suspiciously. 'But I'm pretty sure most are just seawater.'

'I bet your ancestors had things to cry about,' said Ellie. 'I bet some of them struggled to use their powers too.'

Kate looked round at the statues, then sighed. 'None of them. Not even my great-great-great-uncle,' she added, pointing to the small boy sitting cross-legged on the cabinet. 'And he choked to death on a chicken bone.'

'Well, if he could do it, you definitely can.' Ellie picked up one of the plant pots. 'Now, the Vessel needs to empty their mind and *become* the plant they're trying to grow.'

'How do you know that?'

'It's –' Ellie fiddled with the fabric of her sling. 'It's an old legend from Ingarth Island.'

Kate touched the hand of the statue that resembled her. 'My mum said something like that once. But it sounds so ridiculous. How can I pretend to be a plant?'

'But you're *great* at pretending! You pretend to be the Queen.'

Kate's head turned sharply. 'I *am* the Queen!' she snapped.

'I know,' said Ellie, wincing. 'What I mean is, you still have to *act* like the Queen in front of people – the way you stand, your tone of voice. It's terrifying.'

Kate stood a little taller, her cheeks slightly pink. 'Thank you.'

'Look, just give it a try, okay? I really think you can do this.'

Kate stared at Ellie for a long moment, then sighed. 'Fine, I'll play along. If only to keep you from harming small animals.'

Ellie bounced excitedly, placing one of the plant pots at Kate's feet. 'Just have a go. If nothing happens today, there's plenty of time.' Ellie forced a smile.

Kate took several deep breaths, then fixed her gaze on the pot.

Ellie watched the soil intently. Kate frowned. Her nose started twitching. Her breathing grew heavy. Her eyes closed.

Ellie felt a hot excitement in her chest. This was exactly how Seth looked when he was controlling the sea!

Kate's hands trembled. A vein pulsed in her forehead. Her eyes opened wide.

'This is ridiculous!' she roared. 'How am I supposed to imagine myself as a seed?'

She kicked the plant pot. It flew across the room, colliding with the face of a tall moustached statue, spraying soil everywhere.

'Sorry, Grandfather,' Kate muttered, then spun round. 'I can't *do* this, Ellie.'

'Imagine you're curled in a tight little ball, with all these . . . possibilities inside you. A small thing that will turn into something great. What *were* you imagining?'

Kate's lips twitched. 'Me, standing in front of all my subjects, trying to make one silly seed grow.'

'Well, that's not good,' said Ellie, casting around for ideas. She noticed a map sitting on an easel nearby, and frowned. The outline looked familiar, but it took her a moment to realize why. It was a map of a place Ellie knew very well.

'It's the Enemy's City,' Kate explained, following her gaze.

A chill travelled up Ellie's spine, lingering at the base of her neck. The map was drawn badly, as if from a vague memory, but she could still pick out features she recognized – the Salvation Waterfront, where she'd gone fishing with Finn in their little boat; the Flats, where the orphans waded through the mud, hunting for expensive relics. The northern tip where she'd faked her own death, by the Chapel of St Bartholomew.

Words were scribbled on the map. By the Minor Docks was written: *Vulnerable?*

Ellie shivered. 'You're not . . . thinking of attacking it, are you?'

'I'm not *foolish*,' said Kate. 'The Enemy's City is defended by a fleet of massive ships. They use them to hunt and kill whales, even though whales are sacred. "Whale kings" they call themselves, or something stupid like that. They're masters of seafaring. It would be lunacy to attack them.'

'How do you know all this?' said Ellie.

Kate picked up the cage, smiling at the mouse inside. 'We've sent spies there in the past, though not for a long time. The last two . . . Well, one was captured and executed and the other barely escaped.'

Ellie rattled the pouch of seeds in her hand, trying to keep her voice steady.

'So . . . do you think the Enemy's City knows about this island?' She thought of Hargrath. 'Would they ever attack us?'

'I doubt it. They have ships, but from what we know, little in the way of an army. Whereas *I* have a thousand trained Wardens,' she said proudly, 'and the Seven. A war between us would be too costly for both sides.'

It was strange to see Kate discussing military strategy while cooing over a mouse. 'Would you like to see more of my maps?' she added, a little too eagerly.

Ellie cleared her throat. 'No, no we should really keep practising,' she said, picking up another plant pot. 'Try not to destroy this one.'

In Kate's defence, it was at least fifteen minutes before the second plant pot sailed into the face of her great-grandmother. For the third and final pot, Ellie tried different ways to motivate Kate. First, she rewarded her with sweets for every full minute she stayed focused. Next, she tried hitting her lightly on the leg with her cane every time her concentration lapsed.

'*Ow!*' Kate complained. 'You know I normally execute people who touch me!'

'You couldn't even hurt a mouse – I doubt you've ever had anyone executed.'

Kate bared her teeth. 'There's a first time for everything.'

'Shh,' said Ellie. '*Focus.*'

Finally, Ellie tried blindfolding her, figuring it would be easier to imagine *being* nothing if she couldn't see anything, either. But even blindfolded, Kate was able to kick the plant pot straight across the room, towards the face of the servant boy who'd brought her lunch. He ducked just in time, miraculously spilling not a drop of soup.

'This isn't working, Ellie!' Kate cried, ripping off her blindfold as the servant beat a hasty retreat.

Ellie stroked her chin. 'We could try dressing you up like a plant?'

'Dressing –' Kate clutched her head, eyes bulging with indignation. 'That's the stupidest thing I've ever heard! I can't concentrate in here. Let's go outside.'

'But how do we *get* outside on our own? Won't the Seven Sentinels try and follow you?'

Kate snorted. 'I've got a secret route. Besides, the Seven have to do everything I say,' she said, pulling off her gown and shoving her arms into a shirt. 'My father trained them that way.'

'Your father?'

Kate flung on her blue cloak. 'The Seven Sentinels were his idea. Although they loved my mother much more. Everyone loved my mother.'

'I'm sure the Seven love you too. And I *know* everyone else does.'

Kate frowned, tugging again at her fingers. 'Come on, let's go.'

They hurried down a damp spiral staircase, then along a dark tunnel that led out of the Ark through an abandoned butcher's shop. The streets and alleys were golden in the sunlight, the air humid, thick with the smell of sun-baked stone.

'Let's find a quiet garden for you to practise in,' Ellie said, eyeing the alleyways, in case Seth was wrong and Hargrath was still lurking on the island.

'In a minute,' said Kate. 'I want to go to the Azalea Markets since we're here. Sometimes they have the most amazing sky dancers – you *have* to see them.'

Ellie grumbled, convinced that Kate was pretending to be more excited about the dancers than she really was. She hobbled after her into a busy square, rife with cheerful haggling. Sandstone buildings rose to the sky, their balconies draped with colourful sheets and gossiping neighbours.

'There they are!' Kate cried excitedly.

Between the buildings hung thick ropes, and swinging from these were muscular dancers dressed in costumes of blue ribbon, spinning round one another in mid-air, seeming to defy the physical laws that demanded they fall to earth.

Kate took Ellie's hand, leading her through the shoppers. 'Let's find somewhere to sit.'

'I know what you're doing,' said Ellie.

Kate smiled innocently, perching on the edge of a fountain in the centre of the square. 'Look at them, though, aren't they amazing? I wish I could do that.'

'We came out to practise.'

The shadows of the dancers crossed Kate's face. 'Your head is too full of cogs and numbers to appreciate art.'

'That's not true!' Ellie said. 'I used to do lots of drawings back home.'

'Of cogs?'

Ellie grumbled and joined Kate on the fountain, staring up at the dancers. She was forced to admit that they *were* impressive, but tried very hard not to let this show.

'I see that wonder in your eyes,' said Kate, smirking.

Ellie huffed. 'Right, come on, we're –'

'NEWS! NEWS!'

The cry pierced the square from somewhere unseen. Ellie looked around as the noise of the crowd quietened to a low mutter. There was a rustle as a sheaf of papers was hurled into the air, dipping and weaving overhead. Kate leapt up and caught one, holding it out for them both to read.

FAMINE IS COMING! LOREN SAYS: 'BUY EVERYTHING YOU CAN!'

'What is he doing?' Kate snarled. 'It's not like the food has *already* run out. This will only cause panic!'

Even as she spoke, a scream tore apart the quiet. Shoppers fell on the stalls like seagulls on the carcass of a whale, streaking the ground with flour and smashed fruit, sticky shards of honey jars and cracked eggs that bubbled on the hot paving stones. Ellie felt a stab of terror as a distracted sky dancer missed the rope he'd been jumping to, crashing into a stall below and ripping through its cloth roof. She sighed in relief as the dancer pulled himself up, then gasped as a tiny girl was knocked to the ground. The girl wailed, a crush of boots trampling round her.

Kate darted forward, sweeping the girl up in her arms. Ellie steered them out of the churning crowd.

'Meredith!'

A pale-faced man pulled the girl into a tight hug, without a word of thanks. Kate gazed unblinking at the chaos behind. When Ellie took her hand, she could feel it trembling.

'Kate, if you can figure out how to use your powers, we can stop all of this.'

Kate nodded, a fierce look in her eye. 'Come on.'

They ran along the street, Ellie struggling to keep up. Kate stopped outside a dressmaker's, and Ellie sighed in gratitude as she caught up with her, then yelped as Kate grabbed her by the arm and threw her into an alleyway.

'What is it?' Ellie whispered. Kate leaned against the corner, peering into the street. Ellie stood on tiptoe to see over her shoulder.

They had come to a familiar building – the house Ellie had found Kate spying on the day they'd first met. On the doorstep sat the three daughters and their mother, who was reading to them in the afternoon sun.

Ellie noticed Kate's shoulders relaxing as she watched them. The mother was putting on funny voices for the different characters, causing the youngest daughter to shriek in hysterics and roll about giggling. Each time she laughed, the corners of Kate's mouth rose.

Ellie felt she was intruding on something private, and wondered again why Kate had been watching the family that day. 'Who are they?' she whispered softly.

The mother closed the book and lifted the youngest girl on to her lap, stroking the tears of laughter from her cheeks. Kate raised a hand hesitantly to her own cheek, and touched it.

'I've no idea who they are, Ellie,' she said. 'They just seem to be having such a nice time.'

Footsteps drew their attention along the street: the father, returning from the market. His daughters rushed to greet him, hugging his waist. He forced a smile, failing to hide the sorrow in his eyes. He placed an empty bag in front of his wife, and they exchanged a frightened glance. Then he gathered up his smallest daughter in his arms, and the whole family went inside.

Kate breathed heavily. 'I must do something.'

'You *are*,' said Ellie. 'You're going to figure out your powers, and I'm going to get my machines working.'

Kate turned, and Ellie saw hope shining in her eyes, and knew she must do whatever she could to make sure that light did not go out.

'Then everything will be okay. Won't it, Ellie?' Kate's voice quivered slightly. 'Everything will be okay?'

Ellie nodded. 'Yes, of course it will.'

Kate smiled, then walked towards the house. From the pocket of her cloak, she removed four gold rings studded with gemstones. Ellie frowned, then realized what Kate was doing. She rummaged in her own pockets, and found a drawstring pouch. Kate put the rings inside, placed the pouch on the doorstep, then knocked on the door three times.

'Come on,' she said. 'Let's make things right.'

And they raced away from the house, hand in hand.

20

Signs of the Enemy

That night Ellie went without sleep, tinkering away in the dimly lit workshop until her eyes hurt. At dawn, she returned to the fields to test her work, the streets already full of Wardens as they patrolled the markets, trying to restore order. Ellie placed a new spiderlike tilling machine on the dusty soil, clapping as it walked in a straight line, then whooping with delight when the improved dropping-spreader didn't explode, dancing in the shower of guano.

The next day, Kate enlisted an army of blacksmiths to come to the palace, so that Ellie could teach them how to build her machines. By the end of the day, they'd built three soil-tillers and seven dropping-sprayers. The day after that, they had four times as many.

Soon, the farms of Shipwreck Island were crawling with the twitchy but dependable mechanical spiders, while the dropping-spreaders sprayed clouds of guano over the fields. Unfortunately, the island's supply of guano was now being used faster than the seagull population could replenish it, so Ellie turned her mind to solving the puzzle of how Altimus Ashenholme had turned nitrogen from the air into fertilizer. She spent days pacing her workshop, poring over books and occasionally setting things on fire.

'I've got it!' she finally declared, flinging her hand out in triumph.

'Ow!'

Ellie turned to find Kate standing behind her, rubbing one eye.

'Oh, sorry!' Ellie cried. 'I didn't know you were there!'

Kate glared at her with her other eye. 'I've been standing here a full minute saying "Ellie", over and over again.'

'I was thinking.'

'You were drooling.'

'I've made a breakthrough. I think I know how Ash – I mean, I think I know how to get nitrogen from the air,' she said. She didn't think it was a good idea to mention Altimus Ashenholme in front of Kate, since he'd come from the City. 'That's what this big machine is for.'

The workshop had been transformed since Ellie's arrival. It was now a messy, dangerous place, littered with shards of metal and broken inventions with jagged edges, reeking of gunpowder, burnt wood and a pungent scent of chemicals. It felt like home.

On the central bench sat a misshapen, ramshackle machine, stretching up to the ceiling; a chaotic assembly of beaten copper canisters and curling pipes, some of which sprouted straight through the wall, sucking in air from outside the palace.

'I've been trying to come up with a good name for it,' Ellie explained. 'So far the best I've managed is "fertilizer-making machine".'

She hoped this might raise a smile, but Kate only nodded.

'It's almost exploded twice,' Ellie added. Still Kate just nodded. Ellie wondered what was distracting her – she often visited the workshop to watch Ellie work, but sometimes she was so quiet it was as if she wasn't there at all.

'So . . .' Ellie ventured. 'Shall we practise?'

Kate screwed up her eyes. While Ellie's work had been progressing at a rapid pace, Kate's practice had not, unless progress was measured in smashed plant pots and frightened servants.

'Maybe later.'

Ellie bit her lip. 'I know you don't enjoy it, but it's important you keep trying.'

Kate looked at her feet, her brow a furrowed frown. Ellie felt a stab of guilt – she wasn't sure if she was pressuring Kate to practise for the good of the island or the good of Ellie Lancaster. Ever since she'd learned Kate had the power to destroy the Enemy, Ellie had lain awake every night, imagining a life without the Enemy. Without the constant fear it would return and tear her life apart again. 'There's a chance my machines won't work, you know.'

'You said everything would be okay.'

'I mean, I'm sure they *will* work,' said Ellie, anxiously eyeing the fertilizer-making machine. 'But there's still the Festival of Life to worry about. People are going to expect to see you using your powers.'

Still, Kate stared at the floorboards.

'But I do have some thoughts about that too, actually,' Ellie said. 'Just in case you can't get them working in time.' She pointed to a wooden rack of glass vials containing colourful powders, from pale pink to luminous green. 'I've been sending Seth and Viola to the outer islands to collect the strangest plants they could find. Some plants have remarkable properties, you know.'

Kate offered a weary smile, then looked at the piles of boxes at the back of the table, a sheet thrown over them. Kate wrinkled her nose at the smell. 'What's that noise? Are those . . . oh, Ellie. Not *more* mice,' she said, as Ellie flung the sheet aside to reveal twenty tiny, scurrying pouches of fur, in twenty wire cages.

'I got them from Molworth,' Ellie explained. 'He's named them all, can you believe that?'

Kate grimaced. 'I'm afraid to ask, but what exactly –'

'I've been feeding them the plants,' Ellie said proudly.

'*Ellie!*' said Kate.

'I grind them up in this mortar and pestle, then mix them with cheese to trick the mice into eating them. I've found one plant in particular that's *really* special. See that mouse there?' She pointed to the leftmost cage. 'It used to have a broken paw.'

Kate looked horrified. 'You didn't.'

'*No* – it was broken when Molworth gave it to me! But look at it now.' Ellie poked the mouse with her pencil, and it squeaked and scurried nimbly away. She selected a vial of blood-red powder from the rack. 'It was this plant,' she added, unstoppering the vial. 'I think it might make my arm heal faster, maybe even help my leg. And if it works on humans, we can give it to people at the Festival of Life and say it was *your* power that did it.' Ellie grabbed another lump of cheese, dipped it in the powder, then popped it in her mouth.

Kate glanced at Ellie, back at the cages, then turned in alarm, realizing what Ellie had done. She leapt forward and grabbed Ellie's jaw.

'*Don't swallow!*'

Ellie looked up at Kate guiltily. 'Too late,' she managed to say. 'It's all right, it didn't do anything bad to the mouse.'

'Humans aren't *mice*, Ellie,' Kate admonished her. 'And some plants are *extremely* poisonous.'

'It's okay – I tried a little bit before. Nothing happened, and I swear my arm was less sore afterwards. Kate? What's wrong?'

Kate's lips had paled, her eyes wide. 'Ellie,' she said, in a hollow voice. 'Ellie, spit it out.'

'I can't spit it out, I've swallowed it.'

'Then you need to vomit it up.'

'Why?'

Kate pulled her over towards the mirror on the wall. Ellie gasped.

Her skin had gone snow-white – even whiter than it had been months before, when the Enemy was at its strongest. And her eyes . . .

Her eyes had turned red. Blood red.

'Have you got any salt?' Kate said, frantically searching the workshop. 'If you drink lots of saltwater it can make you be sick. Wait! The vials of tears in my chamber – they've got saltwater in them! Silvia!' she roared at the door. 'Silvia! Fetch the Royal Physician!'

The door swung open and Viola and Seth came in, giggling, each carrying a crate of exotic plants in their arms. They saw Ellie and gasped, Archibald hissing from atop Viola's shoulder.

Seth threw his crate aside and raced over, pulling Ellie away from Kate.

'What happened?' he said, holding Ellie's face and glaring at Kate. 'What did you do to her?'

'Nothing!' Kate snarled. 'It was the plants *you* brought back that did this.' She grabbed Ellie and tried to tug her away from Seth.

'Please,' Ellie managed, as her head jerked back and forth. 'Really, I'm fine.'

The door swung open again, and Molworth bounced inside, carrying a crate of plants and grinning from ear to ear. He saw Ellie and screamed.

'The Enemy!' he cried, dropping his crate and throwing out an accusatory finger. 'The Enemy has come!' He turned to flee, but tripped over a broken mechanical spider.

Ellie winced, sharing an uncomfortable glance with Seth.

'She's not the Enemy,' said Kate.

'Everyone knows the signs of the Enemy's Vessel!' Molworth shrieked. 'It has red eyes and pale skin, and worms and rats spring from the ground wherever it walks. And look!' He pointed to the cages by the wall.

Viola squinted. 'Those are mice.'

'*Your* mice,' said Seth.

'I just ate a weird plant, that's all,' said Ellie, taking a step towards Molworth, who cringed and shrank into a corner. 'And stop acting like that! The Queen could walk in at any moment,' she said pointedly. 'What would She think if She saw you cowering on the floor?'

Molworth scrabbled to his feet. 'Really, She might come here? But I'm not wearing my good trousers!' he yelped, rubbing furiously at a stain on his shirt.

'You don't *own* any good trousers,' said Viola, scooping up Archibald, who'd been trying to find a way inside the mouse cages. 'Now come on, Molworth, I need you to help me look for secret passages. Somewhere around here there'll be huge chests of gold we can give back to the people.' She eyed Kate warily. 'I mean, let's take a look around and . . . admire the artwork.'

Kate pressed a finger to Ellie's cheek. 'Hmm, I *think* there's a little more colour in your face now – though it's hard to tell. I've never met anyone so pale. Promise me you'll stop eating strange plants.'

Ellie rubbed the back of her head. The door swung open.

'It's the Queen!' Molworth screeched.

In fact, it was Quentin, the ancient, shrivelled man who so resembled a tortoise. He readjusted his glasses, scanning the workshop. He saw Ellie and screamed.

'The Enemy!' he cried, dropping his heavy book and clutching the doorframe. 'The Enemy is here!'

'Control yourself, Quentin,' Kate snapped.

'But it is; the pale skin, the red eyes – these are signs of the Enemy!'

'What do you want?'

The old man looked round at the assemblage of strange children. 'I . . . I was told the Queen was here.'

'I am her handmaiden,' said Kate. 'Give me your message and I will convey it to Her.'

He hugged his book protectively. 'It's the farms,' he said, smiling nervously. 'The farmers say they've noticed an improvement. The crops are growing faster.'

Kate turned to Ellie, her eyes growing wide.

'It's still early days,' Ellie said quickly. 'We'll need to wait a bit before –'

'YOU DID IT!' Kate cried, flinging her arms round Ellie and hugging her fiercely. Ellie hugged her back, feeling the tension drain from Kate's body.

'Thank you,' Kate whispered, nestling her chin into Ellie's shoulder. 'Thank you.'

Leila's Diary

4,798 days aboard the *Revival*

Tonight I wandered through the Ark, clutching a blue orchid from the garden. On the Market Deck, I saw Aaron Sacco being thrown out of his bakery. A huge brute hobbled behind him on one wooden leg. The First Mate.

'Word is, you're the Enemy's Vessel,' he said.

'What?' said Sacco, lip trembling in horror. 'No, that's not true.'

The First Mate laughed. 'Not what I heard. Heard you've been talking to it.'

'No, please.' Sacco got on his knees.

'Tell you what, give me all your grain, and your shop, and maybe I won't tell anyone.'

I rolled up my sleeves, ready to march forward, but then the Ark-Captain strode out from nowhere, big and angry. He helped Sacco back into his shop, then pinned the First Mate against the wall.

'What are you doing?' the Ark-Captain spat.

'We need food,' said the First Mate.

'You can't go around accusing people of being the Enemy's Vessel! Things are bad enough as it is.'

'Whale girl,' whispered the First Mate.

The Ark-Captain turned and saw me. 'On your way, Leila,' he said. There was a big vein on his forehead and I could tell he wasn't messing around, so I ran off up towards the Sky Deck.

The sea was all silver in the moonlight, wind whistling in my ears. Gripping the rail, I edged down the stairs on the outside of the Ark, to the wooden platform where Blue Eyes had died. The Ark battered its way through the ocean.

I laid the orchid on the water's surface, but the sea whisked it away before I had time to say the words I'd prepared. I bowed my head and said them anyway.

'I miss you, Blue Eyes. I don't know what to do without you. I look after the garden, and the boy, only I don't know what I can do to help him. And I'm worried about what's happening on the Ark. Everyone's turning against each other. When you were here, things were simpler. I don't belong to anything any more.'

I looked out at the horizon, waiting. I wasn't sure what I was waiting for, because I knew Blue Eyes was gone. And what else was there except the ocean and this horrible ship?

A jet of water sprayed high in the air.

A dark fin cleaved through distant waves, and my heart leapt. Then another fin, and another. I counted ten, then twenty.

'I heard them calling for him yesterday.'

I almost fell into the sea. Varu was standing at my side, smiling. I listened harder, over the crash of the sea. There was a faint song, made of clicks and chirrups. A song I recognized.

'Blue Eyes,' I said.

Varu nodded. 'They're his family, I think.'

'But Blue Eyes never had a family? He was alone when I found him.'

'They must have been separated by the Drowning.' Varu closed his eyes. Faint blue shapes swirled across his skin. 'They've been searching for him a long time.'

Jets of water split the night air again. The song was sweet, and sorrowful.

'They must be so sad, to have come all this way for nothing.'

'They're not sad. They've found the part of him that lives on still.'

I frowned. 'You?'

Varu shook his head. 'Not me.'

The sleek black shapes rose and fell. Their song grew louder, until I could feel it rattling my bones, warming my heart.

'What are they doing?' I said. 'What's this for?'

Varu smiled. 'They're honouring you.'

21

The God of Life

'Hail the Great Inventor!'

'Not again,' Seth moaned.

The market sellers had stopped setting up their stalls to cheer Ellie as she passed through the Azalea Markets. Ellie pushed her hair behind her ears, her whole face breaking into a smile. Seth rolled his eyes. 'This is why you wanted to come this way, isn't it? Even though it takes twice as long.'

'I don't know what you're talking about.'

'You're going to struggle getting through doors with a head that big.'

'Oh, just because they're not staring at you for once.'

Seth grumbled, but couldn't quite hide his smile when a little girl rushed up to present Ellie with a crumpled flower from her tiny fist.

'Thank you,' said Ellie, and the girl smiled bashfully, then ran away.

A riot of squawking drew Ellie's attention to the Ark high above, pale in the morning light, where seagulls nested among the army of statues dotting its surface. The gatekeeper bowed to Ellie as she hurried up the steps, Seth following behind with a boxful of tools in his arms.

Seth always looked out of place inside the palace, like a lion at a ballroom dance. He stared intently at the servants as they rushed by, ferrying an army's supply of crockery: each bowl filled with a single massive barnacle, floating in a blue-coloured soup.

'Who are they feeding?' he said. 'A whale?'

'Kate is entertaining the Guild of Lawmakers for breakfast,' said Ellie. 'And you wouldn't find barnacle soup in a whale's stomach.' She gave Seth a wry smile. 'Just strange boys.'

Seth waved her away as a timid servant sidled over, eyeing Ellie nervously. 'Um, Miss Stonewall? The Queen asked to see you the moment you arrived.'

'Oh, thanks,' said Ellie, ushering Seth up the mighty staircase to the top of the Ark. A Warden peered suspiciously at Seth as they hurried past.

'You did get permission for me to be here, didn't you?' asked Seth.

'Of course! I mean, I think so,' Ellie said. 'But it doesn't matter, because *I'm* with you,' she said, placing a hand to her chest and feeling very humble.

'Stop looking so pleased with yourself.'

They stepped inside Kate's chambers and were confronted by the massive God-Bird perched above, which stopped Seth dead with its glare.

'It's not real,' said Ellie.

'I *know* that.'

From the state of the chamber, it seemed Kate's handmaidens had not dressed her that morning without a struggle: there were streaks of gold face paint on the statues, a smashed clay pot leaking gritty ointment on the marble floor, and Kate, lying on her back with a happy smile and purple make-up smeared erratically across her cheeks. She wore a long black gown, and a headdress of purple feathers. Her eyes flicked to Ellie. 'You're here!' she cried cheerfully, then noticed Seth and sat up. 'I mean,' she added, in a much deeper voice, 'you may enter.'

'It's only Seth,' said Ellie. 'You don't have to be a queen in front of him.'

'Only Seth,' said Seth. 'How nice.'

Ellie pointed to the mess. 'Um, did your handmaidens attack you?'

Kate scowled. 'They were being annoying. Felicity kept going on about how *handsome* Loren Alexander is. And then Yasmin asked me if I was excited about the Festival of Life. As if that even matters any more – thanks to your machines, the farms are green and gold as far as the eye can see.'

'Well, actually, we *do* still need to figure out how you're going to perform convincing miracles at the Festival of Life, if you, um, can't get your powers working in time,' said Ellie. 'I'm building a device that will let you shoot flowers from your sleeves. And I've found a species of plant that looks dead if you don't water it, then springs back to life in seconds when you do.'

'Wonderful, wonderful,' said Kate, then she let out a long yawn. Ellie noticed bags under her eyes. 'Sorry, I didn't sleep well, I was too excited. I've been worried for so long, it's weird now to feel such relief instead. Oh, and speaking of your hard work . . .'

Kate leapt to her feet and raced up one of the golden staircases to her bed.

'There's seawater in there,' said Seth. He was frowning at the Cabinet of Tears.

Ellie blinked in surprise. 'They're supposed to contain Kate's ancestors' tears, but she does suspect they're mostly seawater. Wait, you can feel that?'

Seth rubbed his arm. 'I can always feel the sea.'

Kate hurtled back down the stairs, clutching a bundle of lilac cloth. 'Here!' She unfurled it, revealing a long coat. It was the exact same shade as the handmaidens' dresses.

'It's . . . it's lovely,' Ellie said, her throat dry.

'I don't mean for it to replace your mother's coat,' Kate said hastily. 'But, well . . .' She scanned Ellie's old coat, pockmarked with huge holes that were growing every day. 'I think one more explosion might finish it off for good. This coat has just as many pockets, look.'

She held it out and Ellie rubbed it between her fingers. The fabric was so soft it was hard to be sure she was even touching it. 'You . . . you made this?'

Kate nodded. 'Now come on, try it.'

'Oh,' said Ellie, shifting uncomfortably.

Kate glared at Seth. 'It's not polite to look when a lady is changing.'

Seth frowned. 'It's only a coat.'

'It's fine,' said Ellie, unbuttoning her coat one-handed, then trying to shrug it off without hurting her broken arm. Seth and Kate both went to help her, but Kate got there first.

'Your poor arm,' she said, easing off the coat. 'The bone is taking a long time to mend, isn't it?'

Ellie felt the humid air pressing on her skin. Her body felt like a brittle, flimsy shell wrapped round an ancient, terrible secret. She looked nervously at Seth, waiting for Kate to say something. Instead, Kate draped the new coat round her shoulders, delicately avoiding Ellie's broken arm and helping the other through the sleeve. It was light as sea foam, and when Ellie moved, the folds fanned her with cool air.

'I made it with silk from the silkworms of Bianca Island,' Kate said proudly, scanning Ellie up and down. 'Perfect,' she said, smiling so broadly that dimples formed on her cheeks. 'Just perfect.'

'I prefer the old one,' Seth muttered, and Kate either didn't hear him or pretended not to.

'I thought you could wear it . . .' she began, then her smile faltered. 'At the Festival of Life.'

Her eyes grew wide, and she was silent a long moment. Seth and Ellie shared a glance.

'Kate,' said Ellie delicately. 'If you don't feel ready for the Festival of Life yet, then why don't you postpone it? That way you have more time to figure out your powers, and I have longer to figure out how to fake a miracle. You know, just in case?'

Kate stared at Ellie. 'Postpone the Festival of Life? It's not a dinner party, Ellie. I can't simply *postpone* it. Loren will leap on that – say I'm weak. Eugh, he's going to be at this awful breakfast. Though at least I don't need his help any more. If your machines hadn't worked, I would have had no choice but to ask him to bring grain from his family estates. I'd rather eat my own fingers.'

'Please don't eat your own fingers,' said Ellie. 'And it's still fourteen days until the Festival of Life. That's plenty of time for you to learn to control your powers. Actually, I've had some thoughts about that.' She knelt by the box Seth had brought. 'Now I know you were sceptical about dressing up as a plant, but –'

Kate tilted her ear to the window.

'Focus, Kate,' Ellie said. 'You're not wriggling out of this again.'

'*Quiet!*' Kate snapped.

Ellie strained to hear. 'What is that?'

'It sounds like seagulls,' said Seth. 'Or is it – someone crying?'

Kate's lips went white. 'It's not one person crying.' She ran to the window and stuck her head outside. Ellie could hear it more clearly now – the noise of people wailing, like at a funeral.

'It's coming from the farms,' said Kate, snatching up her blue cloak from a chair to hide her gown, pulling the hood over her headdress and darting from the room. Seth and Ellie exchanged a worried glance then hurried after her, down the staircase and out through the palace gates.

The sound of wailing was louder in the streets, burbling between the buildings like a flock of injured birds. Kate raced ahead, Ellie falling behind as she hobbled on her cane. The alleys teemed with people drawn by the cries.

'Keep close to me,' said Seth, the crowd parting before him. Ellie peered over shoulders, straining to catch a glimpse of whatever was causing the terrible sound. Finally, the western coast of the island stretched out beneath them.

What before had been a gleaming, luscious land was now a putrid swamp. Once-golden fields of wheat had turned the colour of rust, while green crops of maize and sugar cane had faded to pus-like yellow. Puddles of milky water pooled round the stems of wilted plants, and the air was filled with a sour, vinegary stench. Ellie covered her mouth, feeling like she was going to be sick – from the smell or the shock, she wasn't sure.

They found Kate hunched in the soil, her cloak heavy with mud. The crowd was swelling now, spreading along the edge of the fields.

'Save us!' a man cried.

Next to Ellie, a woman kept muttering 'She protects' under her breath. Farmers knelt desolately in the grey, grainy soil, friends picking their way through the marsh to console them.

'Ellie, Seth!'

Viola squeezed through the crowd, Molworth scurrying behind. 'Queen's mercy!' he squeaked, when he saw the fields.

'What on . . . ?' Viola started, clutching Archibald protectively to her chest. 'How did this happen?'

Ellie helped Kate shakily to her feet. Her hands were trembling.

One of the fertilizer-sprayers nearby hissed out a cloud of greenish vapour, and the smell of vinegar grew stronger. Ellie sniffed. 'That's not my fertilizer,' she said. 'Someone's switched it for something else. Who would do that?'

Kate's eyes were glassy. '*Him.*'

'MY FRIENDS!'

The voice rang out as clear as a trumpet call. Loren was standing above the crowd, on a rickety platform that seemed to have been hastily built for this exact purpose. He was dressed in a black gown.

'Oh, friends,' he said, the crowd falling silent. 'Grieve with me! What a terrible tragedy to have befallen our island. Our crops, shrivelled and dead. Grieve with me, friends!'

He met the miserable faces tilting up to him, one by one, and their sobs pierced the air. Ellie squinted. There was water on Loren's cheeks, but his eyes were not ringed red like someone who'd been crying.

'I'm afraid, friends, that I know why this happened. I am fortunate enough to be a close friend of the Queen. I told Her that it was foolish to trust an untested "inventor" with the future of the island. A *child*.'

'It was your idea!' Kate hissed. 'You brought her to me!'

'Now, whether by accident or design, this girl has poisoned our crops and we will *all* suffer.'

Ellie froze, rooted to the spot. She yelped as Kate pulled her roughly towards her, tugging off her new coat.

'What are you doing?'

'No one must recognize you,' Kate said, throwing the coat to Molworth. 'Hide this. We need to go *now*.'

Viola began pushing back through the crowd. 'Out of my way! Coming through! Jenkins, shift that humongous son of yours,' she growled. Ellie tried not to meet anyone's eye as she followed.

'But, friends,' Loren continued, 'do not judge Our Divine Queen too harshly for this terrible lapse in judgement. She did only what She thought was right for Her people. Praise Her!'

'PRAISE HER!' the crowd roared back, spit flecking the air.

'Now, friends,' said Loren. 'I ask you, as a humble servant of Her Divine Majesty – do you trust me?'

'YES!'

'Then know that I will fix this famine. I will ask the Queen to abandon these reckless *experiments*. But first I shall bring grain to our island with all haste, so no one shall go hungry!'

There was an eruption of applause, and the crowd took up the chant of 'LOREN, LOREN, LOREN!' He waited for everyone to settle down, beaming round at them.

'One last thing. This is hard for me to say, dear friends, but I do what I must for the safety of the Queen. We cannot trust this inventor, Ellie Stonewall.'

Kate and Ellie shared a panicked glance as they neared the edge of the crowd.

'Hurry,' Kate said. Without thinking, Ellie glanced up at the woman next to her. The woman's eyes narrowed.

'Wait . . .' she said.

'Come on!' Kate urged, tugging Ellie out of reach.

'That's her!' the woman cried. 'That's the girl!'

'*Go*,' Viola growled, shoving Kate and Ellie in front of her and blocking the woman's way. 'What are you talking about, Griselda? I think you've been drinking old cactus juice again.'

Kate, Ellie, Seth and Molworth hurried up the street, but others were following now: a group of twenty or more peeling off from the back of the crowd.

'*Go*,' Molworth hissed, pointing them into an alley.

'That's not the quickest way to the palace,' said Ellie.

'Shut up, hamster-face, and trust me!' he cried, flinging Ellie's coat back at her.

They hurried down the alley, and Ellie looked over her shoulder to see Molworth grinning happily as the pursuers caught up with him. 'Would you like to see a dance I just invented?' he said, starting to caper round in circles.

'Out of our way, fool,' said a burly man.

'Are you after the pasty girl with the funny nose?' asked Molworth. 'She went towards the Royal Oak,' he said, pointing up the street away from Ellie and Kate. 'I hear it serves delicious orange-peel pie. And the prices are very reasonable too.'

Kate stormed up the street towards the gates of the Ark, flinging off her hood and cloak. Tears streaked the swirls of purple make-up on her face.

'It's fine,' she muttered. 'Everything's fine. We don't need his grain.'

'Really?' said Ellie hopefully.

Kate nodded. 'There are three more royal grain caches hidden around the island, besides the one that the fire in the Lorenza Mines destroyed. We'll use those to feed the people while we get the farms back to health.'

The palace doors swung open as they hobbled up the steps. The Seven Sentinels came clattering out, and though Ellie couldn't see their faces, she could tell from their jerky movements how agitated they were. One scrutinized Kate for injury. Another drew their sword and pointed it at Seth.

'Put that away,' Kate snarled, pushing past and into the Grand Atrium. Quentin hobbled to her side, clutching a bundle of letters and nervously readjusting his glasses.

'My Queen, I have –'

'*Quiet!*' Kate snapped. 'The royal grain stores. We must open them *now.*'

The colour drained from Quentin's face. 'But that's what I was going to say. The stores . . . they're ruined. Destroyed.'

Kate fell utterly still.

'I sent Wardens to check,' said Quentin. He swallowed. 'Some potent poison.'

Kate's fingers trembled. 'The locations of those stores were a secret,' she said, in her queenly, emotionless voice. 'Even from my Royal Court. Loren could not have known about them.'

'Loren, Your Divinity?'

'Kate,' said Ellie. 'Loren must have started the fire in his own mines deliberately. That's why he was right there to rescue me! It wasn't an accident – it was sabotage.'

'Who told him?' Kate shouted. 'Who has been spilling my secrets?'

The handmaidens burst from a door nearby and threw themselves at Kate's feet, weeping in relief. The Seven formed a tight circle round them all, and Kate let out a savage roar.

'GET AWAY!' she cried. 'You're all useless – *useless*. Seven of you can't speak, and the rest of you I wish *couldn't* speak.'

'Kate,' said Ellie. 'They didn't do anything.'

'You must address the Queen as *Your Divinity*,' hissed a handmaiden, throwing Ellie a filthy look.

'Oh, who *cares* about that!' Kate yelled. 'Loren has destroyed me! He has poisoned the farms and the grain and ruined *everything*!'

She stormed up the steps, scattering the servants who'd been watching the spectacle from above. The Seven and the handmaidens hurried after. 'Leave me!' she bellowed. 'All of you, just leave!'

The handmaidens fled and the Seven shrank away as if scolded by a parent. Kate took five more steps, then sank to her knees, tugging at her fingers one after another, her body shaking like a sapling in a storm. The servants, the handmaidens and the Seven all stood paralysed, too afraid to go near. Kate's quiet sobs filled the chamber.

Ellie rushed up the steps, helping her off the ground and up the staircase. Kate was stiff and heavy, clinging so tightly that her nails dug into Ellie's arm. Her eyes were closed, and occasionally she let out a stifled groan, like someone fighting back against a nightmare.

They hobbled into Kate's bedchamber. Ellie guided Kate to the bottom of one of the spiral staircases, where she sank into a beautifully dressed heap. Carefully, Ellie removed Kate's headdress, wincing to see a drop of blood inside the headband, where it had dug into her scalp.

Kate grabbed Ellie's wrist, looking at her pleadingly, her breath coming in fevered starts.

'Slowly,' Ellie said. She took in a deep breath, and released it gently. Kate breathed with her. Finally, she rose, stepped over to the balcony and opened the glass doors, letting in the morning air.

'LOREN! LOREN! LOREN!'

A thousand voices chanted the word so forcefully it made Ellie's throat hurt just to hear it. Kate watched the streets with a glassy, disbelieving stare. She closed the balcony doors.

'Kate?' Ellie said gently. Kate stood in the shadow of the amethyst God-Bird, her nose and lips twitching. There was a second of total silence, and then a wretched, blood-freezing scream tore its way out of her. Her face contorted like a hissing cat's, her cheeks bright red, her every muscle tense. She sank to her knees and fell quiet.

Ellie put a hand on her shoulder.

'It's –'

'It's *not* okay, Ellie,' said Kate. 'Nothing is okay. It's over.' She hugged her knees. 'They see how weak I am. I've got no choice now but to accept Loren's help, and everyone is going to love him for it. He wants to rule the island, I know it. He's going to turn them all against me.'

'Not if we can *prove* Loren's behind all this. Prove what a monster he is. And we will. And we're going to keep practising with your powers too. Nobody's going to think you're weak when the Festival of Life comes. You're going to show them just what you're capable of.'

'Oh, Ellie. My practice is going terribly, and you know it.'

Ellie knelt beside her. 'You're so determined, I really believe you can do this.'

Kate looked at Ellie a long moment, then rested her hand on Ellie's. 'You have such faith in me,' she said, with a sad smile. 'I wish you'd come to me sooner. The last six years might not have been so painful.'

She closed her eyes, squeezing fresh tears down her cheeks. 'You know, you even managed to make *me* believe. To hope. That maybe I'd been wrong all along. That just maybe I *could* do all the things they think I can.'

Ellie frowned. 'But you *can* do those things,' she said. 'You're the Vessel. You're the Vessel to the God of Life.'

Kate flinched and looked away.

'No, Ellie. I'm not.'

The Expedition North

Kate gave half a sob, strained to contain it, then burst into tears.

'What . . . what do you mean? Of course you're the Vessel.'

'I've *never* been a Vessel, Ellie.'

Ellie took her hand from Kate's shoulder. 'But . . .'

'I've been terrified someone would realize. For six years,' Kate whimpered. 'I'm a *lie*. And now they're all going to find out.'

Ellie stepped away from Kate, her head spinning. Kate *was* a Vessel – she had to be. All this time they'd spent together, their connection. Kate *did* have powers; she had to. She was going to destroy the Enemy.

'I need air,' Kate mumbled, getting to her feet but staggering aimlessly. Ellie guided her towards the balcony, but felt she was watching some other girl guide her, some other girl undo the latch on the window, and help Kate outside.

'Kate,' Ellie said, 'how . . . how do you know for sure?'

Kate grasped the handrail, purple make-up running in two curving arcs down her cheeks.

'Because the God has never spoken to me, like it spoke to my mother.' She managed a smile. 'The island adored her, Ellie. The harvests were always plentiful.'

'I don't understand,' Ellie whispered. 'If your mother was the Vessel, then surely you are too?'

Kate gritted her teeth bitterly. 'No.'

'But then . . . what happened?'

Kate's knuckles blanched. 'My father happened. Nobody knew exactly where he'd come from, but he was clever, and the nobles loved him. He became my mother's advisor, and then her husband. Would you believe, he was an inventor too? But he wasn't interested in helping people, like you are. He was always locked in his study, day after day, and would not be distracted. When I was five, he poisoned my dog after she barked through the night.'

'That's horrible,' said Ellie, her voice hoarse.

Kate nodded. 'Then, one day, my mother told me that she and my father were going away for several months. A crucial expedition, Father called it. I was so upset – everyone was. No Vessel had ever left Shipwreck Island before. She must have really loved him to leave her people's side for so long. They were going to take a ship, with the Seven and a handful of servants, and sail north towards the Enemy's City.'

Ellie felt a chill rise up her spine.

'I didn't want to be left alone, so I tricked my nursemaid, escaped the palace, and stowed away on the ship, below deck where Father kept his strange machines. He found me a day later, asleep inside a giant suit of brass armour. I'd never seen him so angry. But he refused to turn back – the voyage was too important. So we travelled on for weeks. And every day I asked Mother where we were going, and why, and she said it was for the good of our island.

'Finally, we dropped anchor in the middle of the ocean. Mother and Father put on the brass suits of armour. They were going underwater, attached to the ship by two tubes that they could breathe through. I screamed and yelled at Father not to risk Mother's life, but the Sentinels restrained me, and I was forced to watch my parents vanish beneath the waves. I cried for seven hours, and then they came back.'

'Mother was barely alive. She was pale and wheezing, and her skin was hot as burning coal. Father, though . . . he was . . . *happy*. He kept saying, "It worked. It worked." Like he didn't care that Mother was sick. I told him we had to return to Shipwreck Island immediately. Father just laughed. He said his work wasn't done yet. Mother collapsed, but Father didn't care. It was . . . like he'd been

using her. Like she'd just been another experiment . . .'
Kate swallowed. 'He ordered the Seven Sentinels to throw
me and Mother overboard, and all the servants. But they
did nothing. They loved Mother like I did. When Father
went to grab me, the Sentinels hurled him into the
ocean instead.'

Kate took a trembling breath, and closed her eyes.

'We returned to the island, and within the year, my
mother was dead. But when she died, the God-Bird did
not appear. And though I prayed and pleaded and cried,
her power never passed to me. Whatever happened to
Mother, down in those depths, the god was taken from
her. Her power was extinguished. The next year the
harvest began to dwindle. Each year it's been worse and
worse. Until now . . .'

Kate's head drooped forward and Ellie felt a swell of
pity rising in her chest. Kate had been keeping this secret
hidden for so long, even as it ate at her from inside. She
gripped Kate's shoulder tightly.

Kate blinked, like she was coming out of a dream. She
shivered, and squeezed Ellie's hand.

'Come on, your pale skin shouldn't be out in this sun,'
she said, helping Ellie to her feet and back indoors.

Kate wove between the statues of her ancestors, then sat
down by the one of her mother. Ellie tapped her cane
absent-mindedly, thinking. 'Kate . . . why do you suppose
your father wanted to take your mother's power?'

'I don't know. He didn't need to: she would have done anything for him. I've sometimes wondered if he was a spy of the Enemy's.'

Ellie's eyes widened, her fingertips tingling. She could feel ideas connecting in her brain, sparking like electricity as they collided. 'You said the Seven Sentinels were your father's idea. Did he also design the masks they wear?'

'Yes. Why?'

'Oh, nothing. Um, Kate, what was your father's name?'

Kate's nose twitched, her lips framing the words like a poison.

'Altimus Ashenholme.'

Ellie tripped, catching herself on a statue's arm. She looked into its cold marble eyes, her mind racing. Kate's father had come from the City. He'd been Ellie's mother's own mentor. And, somehow, he had taken the god that had lived in Kate's mother.

Kate curled up in a ball. 'What can we do, Ellie?' she sobbed. 'They're going to find out. I know it.'

'We'll figure something out.' Ellie clenched her fists. 'I promise.'

'Oh, Ellie,' said Kate, watching her fondly. 'Always trying to fix things. But what if some things cannot be fixed?'

Ellie knelt at Kate's side. 'Then they were never broken.'

'You know, you almost made me feel like . . . like I *could* still wield that power, even though a part of me knew I couldn't.'

'You do have power, Kate. Maybe not the same as your mother's. But you do.'

Kate fell silent, her face aglow with sunlight. 'I wish that was true. I would give everything to my people, Ellie. If I had anything to give.'

Kate lay down on Ellie's lap, and Ellie stroked her hair, trying to think of something to say – anything to make Kate feel better again. But nothing came. Long minutes passed, and Kate's eyes closed, and soon her soft, rhythmic breathing matched the rise and fall of her chest. The tears on her cheeks dried, and Ellie watched, and still could think of nothing to say.

With great care, Ellie removed Kate's hand from hers, and rolled up her new coat into a ball. She eased Kate from her lap, resting her head on the makeshift pillow. She felt more alone than she had in months. She glanced at the statues of Kate's ancestors casting long shadows in the sunlight: the tall, muscular woman with the gentle smile, the round-cheeked man frozen mid-laugh. The frail, pearly white child staring straight at her.

Ellie narrowed her eyes, cold fear dripping down her neck. But the statue remained unmoving. Ellie sighed in relief.

'They're going to destroy her.'

The voice hissed from all around. Ellie's shoulders tensed.

'Today was just the beginning.'

Ellie rose warily to her feet, her heart pulsing in her palms. 'Did you do this?'

The chamber laughed at her, two voices together: one deep and grating, the other high-pitched and childish.

'*Me?* Ellie, you're not using your head. I can't do anything without your say-so. I barely have the strength for these little chats of ours.'

Ellie turned round, searching the shadows and sunbeams. When she turned back, the statue of the frail child had vanished.

'What –' Ellie's mouth was almost too dry to speak. 'What do you want?'

'Funny, isn't it? An orphan, who couldn't live up to her brilliant mother's reputation, hiding this horrible, destructive secret for years. I guess you two have more in common than you realized?'

Ellie saw movement out of the corner of her eye. When she turned, the statue of the child was standing ten feet away, in shadow. She couldn't see its eyes – it didn't seem to have any – but she could see its smile.

Ellie licked her lips. 'Did you take her mother's power? Was Altimus Ashenholme your Vessel?'

'It does sound like my work, doesn't it?' hissed the voice. 'But no. I do remember dear Hestermeyer mentioning an Ashenholme, though. He was not especially fond of him, and with good reason it appears! What a thing to do to your wife and child.'

'What's going to happen to Kate?'

Laughter split the air, cutting into Ellie's mind. 'They will tear her down, piece by piece, until nothing remains.'

'They won't.' Ellie gritted her teeth. 'The people love her.'

'*Loved* her. After this morning, I'm not so sure. And when the Festival of Life comes, and they find out how weak she really is? Why, if *only* there was someone who could help her. Someone who really *was* a Vessel. Someone who could perform miracles, just by speaking a few words.'

Ellie felt breath on her ear, and turned to find the statue of the frail child standing right by her side, its wide grin and the flat surface where its eyes should have been. But even as she watched, the marble melted away like dripping paint, and the creature underneath was revealed. Snow-white skin, a bandaged, frail body. Fabric pulled taut against its eyes and nose.

'With my help, you can save her. Stop anyone from ever hurting her.'

Ellie looked down at Kate, her brow furrowing in restless sleep. Her hand still gripped tightly on to nothing, where it had been holding Ellie's hand before.

'You want to help her, don't you?' said the child. 'You can perform the miracles, and she can think it was her. The whole island can think it was her.'

Ellie's lips trembled. 'If I ask you to grant a wish, then you'll have a wish of your own. And you'll use that power to put Kate at risk. That's what you always do – attack the ones I care about.' She took a deep breath and stepped between Kate and the child. 'I don't need you. I'll fix this. I'll stop Loren. Even if Kate's not a Vessel, my inventions can make it *look* like she is.'

The child's hand hovered by Ellie's cheek. 'Ever determined. But I know what's coming, and, believe me, you are not equal to it. When it comes, well . . . You will fail.'

The Enemy leaned forward, baring a hundred pointed teeth. 'And by the end, my dear, dear Ellie, you will beg for my help.'

23

The Hoarder of Secrets

The Vile Oak was so quiet that night that Ellie could hear it creaking under the weight of its dour, silent patrons. The sailors were huddled in the corner furthest from Ellie and Seth, shooting Ellie disgruntled looks over teacups of ale. Molworth had locked away the tankards and instituted rationing – no one was allowed more than a single cup an evening.

Seth and Ellie were sitting at their table by the window. Seth, who usually had at least three dinners, was hugging his stomach while trying to savour the single radish on his plate. He raised a thin slice to his mouth, then broke into a huge yawn.

'Oh lovely,' said Ellie. 'I think I just saw your lunch.'

'How?' Seth grumbled. 'I could barely see it when I was eating it.' He watched the miserable sailors. 'What if the food does run out? Is everyone really going to starve?'

'I . . . I don't know,' said Ellie. She felt too guilty to look in the sailors' direction. Janssen had explained to them that the poisoning of the farms wasn't Ellie's fault, but it was clear they were searching for someone to blame. Loren's grain had arrived on the island, but whoever it had been given to, the sailors had seen none of it. Meanwhile, the price of even a loaf of bread had skyrocketed.

Seth stifled another yawn.

'Did you not sleep?'

'More visions. I'm worried something bad is going to happen to Leila and . . . me.'

'Well, whatever it is, it's already happened.'

Seth glowered at her.

'Sorry,' said Ellie. 'That's not very helpful.'

'The voices in the sea are getting louder too.' Seth massaged his temples. 'I don't know why – I barely even use my powers any more.'

'Maybe the visions and the voices are linked. You're remembering things from your past lives.'

'I don't want to,' Seth said, staring resentfully at what remained of his radish. 'I wish the past would just leave me alone.'

Ellie winced.

'What?' said Seth.

'I saw the Enemy yesterday,' she confessed. Seth's eyes widened. 'That's the second time since we got to the island.'

Seth pushed back his chair, as if the Enemy might be hiding under the table. 'What did it look like?'

'Ill. And weak. The first time I saw it was the day after we –' she swallowed – 'had our big argument.'

'Are you okay?'

Ellie shrugged. 'I'm okay now, but yesterday I felt so lonely.'

'Maybe when you're upset,' Seth said, his brow furrowing, 'the Enemy is able to appear?'

'Maybe.' Ellie took a deep breath. 'I think I can manage it, though. It helps when I picture my friends,' she said. She thought of Kate, about how she had trusted Ellie with her darkest secret. She might not be a Vessel, but she was still a friend.

'You are doing really well,' Seth said, smiling encouragingly.

Ellie shifted in her chair. 'Thank you.'

A shadow fell across the table. Ellie turned, and gasped.

'Charmed to see you too,' said Kate, taking a seat. Her hair was messy, and there were new, dark shadows under her eyes.

'Sorry,' said Ellie. 'It's just . . . always a bit of a shock seeing you here. Like finding a swan in a swamp.'

Kate frowned. 'I *think* that's a compliment?'

'It's more than I ever get,' Seth huffed.

'If you want revenge, you should try throwing things at her,' said Kate. 'She's a terrible catch.'

Seth laughed and did an impression of a startled seal clapping its flippers. Kate snorted.

'While I'm glad you're both getting on so well,' Ellie snapped, 'we have planning to do.'

'Planning for what?' said Seth.

'You haven't told him yet?' said Kate.

'No, I wanted to wait until he'd eaten something,' said Ellie. 'He's less grouchy then.'

'Tell. Me. What?'

'All right, losers?' said a voice, and they looked up to find Viola standing above them. 'My dad said you wanted some kelp. I know a seaweed merchant over on the west side, though it's probably going to be really expensive now that –'

'I said we want your *help*,' said Ellie.

Viola rolled her eyes. 'I keep telling Dad his hearing's going.'

'Wait, she's coming with us?' said Kate. 'It could be dangerous.'

Viola laughed. 'I'm not afraid of anything.'

'Viola knows the island better than the rest of us,' Ellie explained.

'Excuse me,' said Kate. 'Nobody knows the island better than me.'

'Well, I thought Viola might actually know where Loren lives.'

'*I* know where he lives,' said Kate. 'I've been there.'

'Oh,' said Ellie. 'Sorry. I just thought . . . you *are* inside the palace most of the time.'

'Everyone's always underestimating me, Ellie. Please don't you start too.'

'WHAT ARE WE DOING?'

The whole pub turned to stare at Seth, who was glaring at Ellie, a vein pulsing in his forehead.

'Breaking into Loren's mansion,' Kate said simply.

Seth butted his head against the table. 'That is an extremely bad idea,' he said, as Archibald hopped down from Viola's shoulder, and began to lick Seth's ear.

'We don't have a choice,' said Kate. 'We *have* to find evidence to prove he poisoned the fields. We're going to uncover his darkest secret, and we're going to *destroy* him.' She punched her palm for emphasis.

'I don't want to die hungry,' said Seth.

Ellie beamed. 'So you'll come with us?'

'Hold on,' said Viola. 'Why are we sticking our necks out for the *Queen*? She could fix this famine with a snap of Her fingers, but She doesn't. For all we know, She was in on this whole plan with Loren.'

'Viola,' said Seth, 'Kate is the Queen.'

'*Seth!*' Ellie hissed.

'She deserves to know who she's risking her life for!'

Viola rose slowly from her chair, watching Kate with wide eyes. 'Y-you?'

Kate leaned forward. 'And I would never hurt my people,' she said, in a low, dangerous whisper. 'I would do *anything* for them.'

'But . . . you're so . . . normal,' said Viola, struggling to find the words. 'I thought you'd be . . . You seem *nice*.'

'She *is* nice,' said Ellie. 'It's Loren who's making the island worse.'

'But. . .' Viola slumped into her chair. 'The Revolution . . .'

'Can still happen,' said Ellie. 'It's just Loren we're overthrowing, not the Queen. *He's* the greedy one. He poisoned the fields to make her seem weak, because he wants all her power for himself. Help us break into his mansion, and we can figure out what he's planning next, and find a way to stop him. Or maybe even find some incriminating evidence against him! And *no one* will be risking their life.'

'Well, they might, actually,' said Kate, gritting her teeth. 'People have been killed trying to rob Loren's mansion before. He's at a banquet for the Guild of Merchants tonight. If I know nobles, he'll be there until morning, greasing palms and spreading lies. There are two guards standing watch outside his front door. The windows are all barred, so the only way in is to get past them.'

'But what about once we're inside?' said Ellie. 'What if he has more guards or, I don't know, trained *tigers* or something?'

'Trained tigers?' Kate said, and her lips twitched.

'Well, you never know.'

Kate grinned. 'I promise, if there are trained tigers, or bears, or an army of sword-wielding squirrels, then I will name my first child Ellie. Even if it's a boy.'

Ellie smiled. 'Could we use the Seven to get past the guards?'

Kate shook her head. 'Then Loren will know I'm up to something. They're not exactly inconspicuous.'

They sat in silence, trying to think up ideas. Seth watched two of the sailors, who had leaned in close to pat each other on the back. He let out a pained sigh.

'Can't think of anything?' said Ellie.

Seth shook his head. 'No, I have an excellent idea. I'm just afraid that if I tell you, you're going to go ahead with this stupid plan.'

~

Loren's home was on the southern side of the island, where the mansions of the nobility grew round the base of the volcano like architectural fungus. Every house was trying very hard to look different from the others. There was one shaped like a peacock, another that resembled the Ark in miniature, while a third was tiered like a wedding cake.

Loren's mansion looked almost normal by comparison. Built like a castle, it gleamed silver in the moonlight, its battlements adorned with statues of robed men and women, frozen in a complex dance. Two guards flanked the front door, carrying tall spears.

Kate, Ellie, Seth and Viola crouched behind a thick palm tree on the edge of the property. They wore black cloaks over their clothes, and Ellie was sweating under her coat, her leg already aching. She had left her cane at home to look less conspicuous.

Kate rubbed her hands together. 'You know, I've never broken in anywhere before.'

'Oh yeah,' said Ellie, sharing a guilty glance with Seth. 'Me neither.'

'Amateurs,' said Viola, then frowned at the others when they turned to stare.

'Viola, is that a *sword*?' said Seth.

'Yeah.' She pointed indignantly at Kate. 'She said Loren's killed people who broke into his house!'

'I brought one too,' said Kate.

Seth rubbed his forehead.

'Let's try to avoid sword fights if we can,' said Ellie. 'Oh look – here they come!'

Twenty hooded figures were hurrying along the beach, towards the mansion. Their leader was hugely tall, with massive broad shoulders. Running at his side, and struggling to keep up, was someone exceptionally tiny.

'Why did your dad bring Molworth?' said Seth.

Viola grimaced. 'I made the mistake of saying this was a top-secret mission for the Queen.'

As the hooded sailors approached, the guards stared in confusion, then held up their shields as the sailors pelted them with pebbles.

'Give us the grain you promised us!' a sailor roared. 'Give it to the poor!'

'Yeah!' came a squeak. 'Especially innkeepers!'

'Won't this noise attract the Wardens?' Ellie whispered.

Kate shook her head. 'I ordered them to avoid this side of the island tonight.'

The two guards marched down the steps of the mansion, spears lowered. The sailors retreated, flinging more stones. Ellie bit her lip as the guards kept advancing, leaving the doors unattended.

'You're impressed, aren't you?' said Seth.

'No,' Ellie snapped.

'You wish you'd come up with the idea.'

'I am *slightly* impressed – are you happy?'

'Come on, now's our chance!' said Kate.

The four of them dashed up the stairs. On the beach, Ellie saw Molworth trip and roll, until Janssen scooped him up and placed him on his shoulders.

'What if one of them gets hurt?' said Ellie.

'They'll be fine – it's us I'm worried about,' said Kate.

Ellie knelt by the keyhole, her fingers trembling as she held up two lock-picks. Seth leaned in. 'You can do it,' he said.

'This was always more Anna's thing,' Ellie whispered, burying a pang of longing to see her again.

'Come on, Ellie,' called Viola. 'They can't have many pebbles left.'

'I'm trying!' said Ellie, biting her lip as she rattled the picks in the lock.

'The guards are catching up with them!' said Kate.

Ellie breathed deeply. 'I just need a bit more time.'

'Smash the door down!' Viola said. 'Come on, all of us, on three.'

'That won't work!' said Kate. 'Ellie, the guards are going to turn round any moment and see us!'

CLICK.

'Hurry!' Seth cried, as the doors swung inwards. The four of them collapsed inside, listening to the whoops of the sailors drift into the distance.

They were standing in a giant chamber, dark orange in the light of nearly spent torches: a wide, three-storey room with tall marble columns and a glass roof framing the starlit sky. Swathes of red velvet hung from the balconies, while in the centre was an empty bath big enough for dolphins to play in, carpeted with a layer of dried flower petals. At the head of the bath stood a golden figure, lean and muscular, as tall as the room itself, with a familiar smiling, dimpled face.

'Disgusting,' said Kate.

'Says the girl with statues of herself all over the island,' said Viola.

'Those don't even look like me!' said Kate.

'*Shh*,' said Seth, glancing nervously back at the door. They circled the chamber, hugging the walls. Portraits hung above them, but it was hard to be sure if they were of Loren's ancestors, or of Loren himself in a variety of elaborate wigs and outfits.

Ellie peered closely – framed between the portraits was a series of quotations written in an elegant, sloping hand.

'Triumph is fleeting, but obscurity is forever.'
Loren Alexander

'He's quoting . . . himself?' said Ellie, sticking out her tongue. She passed a shelf of books, scanning the spines. Every one of them was written by Loren. She pulled one out, and found that most of its pages were blank.

'None of this is incriminating,' Kate said, picking up a crystal bust of Loren's head. 'You can't execute someone for being self-obsessed. Hold on . . .'

She pointed to a desk by the feet of the golden statue. On it was a chess set, only all the pieces were little statues of Loren.

'How would you even *play* that?' said Ellie.

'Not that, *this*,' said Kate. Beside the chess set was a quill, an inkpot, and a very large book. 'It's much more worn than any other book here. And look how worn the leather on this chair is – he clearly spends a lot of time here.'

She opened the book, Ellie peering round her shoulders to see. The pages were filled with rows and rows of names, written carefully in black ink.

Mirko Brooke – has an illegitimate child with Maria Easton.

Desiree Smith – poisoned Alessio Carter with deadly nightshade in his wine.

Selena Orsel – stole a prize-winning goat from Zachary Tristan.

Some people had an X next to their names. Ellie dreaded to think what this might mean.

'It's a book full of people's secrets,' said Kate, in disbelief. Ellie tugged at her collar, suddenly afraid that her own name might appear.

Viola thrust her head between Kate and Ellie, poring over the pages.

'I know him!' she said. 'Elias Marcellino – he's on Denzel's boat. "*Defacing the statue of the Queen in Kaiden Square.*"' She flipped through more pages. 'And *she* works in the Lorenza Mines – great story about her cabbage tattoo, remind me to tell you later. Why do some of them have an I by their name – what does that mean?'

'I'm not sure,' said Ellie.

'*Informant*,' said Kate sourly. 'They're his spies. I think Loren is blackmailing people – they have to do his dirty work or else he'll reveal their secrets!'

Viola turned more pages. 'We should steal this book.'

'Yes!' said Kate, eyes wide and hungry. 'We can use it to *crush* him.'

'For the people!' added Viola.

'But if we take the book he'll *know* we were here,' said Ellie. She pulled some scraps of ink-smudged paper from her pockets, and a chewed pencil. 'Viola, read out the names of the informants you recognize.'

Viola began flicking through pages, reading names aloud as fast as she could.

'Hey,' said Kate, pointing. 'That's one of my servants! Loren's got eyes *everywhere*.'

'Wait.'

Seth's voice broke above them as they pored feverishly over the book. 'Viola,' he said, eyeing the pages like they were about to burst into flame. 'Are any of the informants sailors? Sailors we involved in tonight's plan?'

Viola looked round at Seth, then at the book. She flicked rapidly backwards. She gulped. 'Yeah.'

There was a *slam* from deep below, then a rush of footsteps.

'Quick,' said Ellie, pointing to the gallery above. 'We need to climb up there – we can unlock those windows from the inside!'

The footsteps were coming nearer.

'There's no time!' said Kate, shoving Ellie behind a bookcase, while Seth and Viola ducked down by a hideous centaur: the bottom half a taxidermy horse, the top half a statue of Loren.

Ellie could feel her own pulse against Kate's palm. She shot Seth a fearful glance, and he jerked his head at the front door. He and Viola began to creep towards it on hands and knees, vanishing from sight behind a cabinet. Kate and Ellie crawled through the maze of mahogany tables, round the tall sides of the massive bathtub. Ellie listened to the footsteps, expecting a shadow to cross her path at any moment.

The footsteps fell silent. Kate crossed a gap between one bookcase and the next, then gestured for Ellie to follow.

Ellie risked a peek through the gap, and saw Seth all by himself, crouching beside the statue of an angel. He glanced furtively at something Ellie couldn't see, then beckoned for her to come towards him. Ellie tugged on Kate's trouser leg, mouthing for her to follow. Kate shook her head vehemently, and tried to grab Ellie as she crawled towards Seth.

'HEY!'

The cry split the silence, and Ellie looked up to see a man with a sword glaring right at her.

'Oh no,' Ellie whispered.

Kate seized Ellie's elbow and they raced for the door.

'No, wait – *Seth*,' Ellie said, turning her head to search for him.

'I'm right here,' said Seth, appearing at her side with Viola.

'What were you doing?' said Ellie. 'You led me right into his path!'

'HELP!' roared the guard. 'There are thieves in here!'

The front doors slammed open, and the other two guards stood against the starry sky, gaping in bewilderment.

'Stop them! The master gave orders to kill any intruders! They must not escape!'

Before the guards could react, Ellie flung a smoke bomb down at their feet. She grabbed Kate's hand as Seth grabbed Viola's, and the four of them tore through the hissing, billowing cloud of smoke.

The night air was warm, the seas leaping and seething like an endless shoal of fish. They hurtled down towards the beach, but already Ellie could hear the heavy tread of the three guards behind.

'I can stop this!' sang a voice from above. 'Ask me!'

The bandaged child was swinging from a palm tree. 'Someone's going to get hurt, Ellie,' it said seriously.

Far along the coast, windows glimmered in the moonlight – the street that would take them up to the rest of the island. To safety. But it was so far, and Ellie's leg was screaming in pain.

'Ellie, get on my back!' Seth said. Ellie leapt on to his shoulders, arms round his neck. Seth took off at an astonishing pace, with Kate and Viola running alongside.

But Loren's guards were still closing on them. Ellie grabbed a fistful of smoke bombs and hurled them at the guards, but they landed on the soft sand and didn't explode. The sea rumbled deeply, flecking her face with saltwater.

'Seth, I'm slowing you down!' Ellie cried. 'Leave me!'

'No!' said Kate, unsheathing her sword. 'You three go – I'll hold them off.'

'No way,' said Viola. 'No one left behind.'

'Shut up, all of you,' Seth snarled. The sea rumbled again, as if echoing his words. 'I'm trying to concentrate!'

One guard was getting nearer. 'Stop, thieves!' he yelled.

'Ellie,' said Seth, panting heavily. 'Tell me when they're close – like a spear's length away.'

'Okay,' said Ellie uncertainly. Tiny blue patches swirled on Seth's arms, sweat dripping from his hairline.

They hurtled along the beach, their feet kicking up saltwater as they dashed through the shallows. Ellie glanced behind; the guard's spear looked sharp enough to cut skin from flesh with the merest touch. He got closer, closer, closer. He pulled his arm back.

'Now, Seth,' Ellie cried. 'NOW!'

The man's arm shot forward and the spear did too, but at the same moment there was an eruption like a mountain bursting from the sea. Ellie's vision was filled by a dark shape that glistened in the moonlight, a white patch down one side and a monstrous, tooth-filled mouth.

A killer whale.

The spear flew wide and the guard screamed as the whale slammed into the sand in front of him, blocking his path. Ellie laughed in shock and amazement, and hugged Seth a little tighter. Only Seth staggered, and fell to his knees.

'Come on,' she cried, leaping from his back. 'We're so nearly there!'

'Where did that *whale* come from?' Kate cried.

Together, Ellie and Viola pulled Seth to his feet, and they hobbled and stumbled through the sand. There were wet, sloshing footsteps behind, and Ellie saw the other two guards appear from behind the killer whale as it thrashed in the shallows. One picked up the fallen spear, and was about to launch it through the air when Seth let out a wordless shout and a second killer whale burst from the sea, then a third, right over their heads. Ellie looked up to see its white belly, so close she could make out the scars on its skin, before it too crashed into the sand between them and the guards.

Seth collapsed on his back, shivering furiously. His skin was pale, and the blue marks were spreading – obvious now even in the darkness. Ellie pulled off her cloak and flung it over him, trying to hide the marks from Kate and Viola.

But Viola noticed, dropping down at his side.

'What . . . what's happening to him?' she said, voice trembling. She put a hand to his forehead and pulled away in fright. 'He's like ice! He needs a surgeon!'

'He's all right,' Ellie lied, eyeing Kate. 'Don't tell anyone about this, okay?'

Kate launched herself at one of the guards as he came

tumbling over a flailing tailfin. She swung her sword with a furious cry, cutting the man's spear in two.

'Leila? Where are you?' Seth muttered. The whites of his eyes had turned blue, and his pupils had vanished, both of them like dark whirlpools.

'Leila's not here, Seth,' said Ellie. 'It's me, it's Ellie.'

'They're hurting,' he said, then let out a moan. 'I can hear them.'

'That was a long time ago, Seth,' said Ellie. 'Everything's going to be okay.'

The other guards had joined the first, bearing down on Kate with swords and spears. Viola growled and raced to Kate's side, as the whales thrashed and rolled back into the sea.

Ellie pulled Seth on to her knees. 'Come on, Seth,' she said. 'We need your help.'

Seth's mouth opened and he let out a cry of pain.

'Seth!' Ellie cried, shaking him. 'Please, wherever you are, come back!'

'They wouldn't stop hurting each other,' Seth said, his voice distant and weak. 'I had to do something.'

One guard swung at Kate with his sword, and she struck it from his hands with a ring of metal. Another threw their spear at Viola. She leapt back, but not before it scraped her arm.

'Seth!' Ellie cried. 'We need you now!'

'They're gone,' Seth whispered. 'They've left.'

'They're *not* all gone, Seth,' said Ellie. '*I'm* here.'

Kate fell backwards as another spear swept towards her. Ellie felt Seth wriggle on her lap.

A rush of water struck the beach like a comet, hitting the three guards and dragging them away in a swirl of foam and darkness, far into the distance.

Seth was standing now, his hands out by his sides. Ellie could see the veins in his arms and on his neck. His skin was milk-white, swirling with blue mist.

Kate and Viola staggered to their feet, searching for the guards in shock.

'What happened?' said Kate, panting for breath. 'Where did they go?'

Ellie looked at Seth, and managed a weak smile. The blue mist had drained from his skin.

'Are you okay?' she said.

Seth collapsed to the sand.

Leila's Diary

4,805 days aboard the *Revival*

Trying to get Varu to listen can be hard work.

'Oi, I'm talking to you!' I yelled. 'Pass. Me. The. Watering. Can.'

Varu blinked at me. 'Leila?' he said, like I was a dead person come back to life.

I rolled my eyes. 'How can someone with no memories spend so much time in his own head?'

'I saw them again,' he said. 'That boy. Me. And that girl. They . . . know about us, too.'

'Look, we've got gardening to do. It's not fair to make the Crone do all the work. You heard what she said – the more she uses her powers, the closer she gets to dying. Maybe that's why she's so hideously ugly. For all we know she's the same age as me.'

'And just as hideously ugly,' croaked a voice behind me.

I jumped. 'I thought you were asleep!'

Varu stepped towards the Crone. 'How can I see that other me? How can he see us?'

The Crone peered into Varu's eyes like she was trying to see through to his brain. 'Your mind is fragmented. Broken into shards. It might be that the shards have been scattered across time. Perhaps the fragments of your mind are calling to each other.'

Varu frowned. 'My mind is . . . broken?'

'That would explain a lot,' I said, and Varu put out a leg and tripped me to the floor, pinning me under his foot. 'Let me go!'

'Who would break my mind?' Varu asked.

'I'm not sure,' said the Crone. 'But it has done great damage to you. It's why you have so few memories. I suspect it has also made you much weaker.'

'Yeah, weakling!' I said, batting against Varu's foot.

'You will struggle to control your powers,' said the Crone, 'until the pieces of your mind are restored.'

Varu looked at the Crone seriously. 'How?'

'I don't know,' she said. I stopped bucking and squirming.

'So if I get my mind back together,' said Varu, 'I'll be able to remember my brothers and sisters? Will I be able to quieten the people out there, the voices in the sea?'

The Crone took a deep breath. 'My boy, if you can restore your mind, then your powers will be so great you could reverse the Drowning itself.'

The First Queen of
Shipwreck Island

Ellie peered down the dark alleyway, seeing only a starved-looking rat, twitching its nose inside an empty honeypot.

Viola and Kate were carrying Seth between them, hoisted on their shoulders. 'I didn't even see them hit Seth,' Kate whispered, nudging Seth's head away from hers. 'They've knocked him out cold. Any sign of them?'

'Nothing,' said Ellie. 'Why did they want to kill us so badly?'

'That book,' said Kate. 'It contained *everything*. All the spies working for Loren, and the secrets he has on them.'

Ellie fished out the ink-smudged paper from her pocket. 'But what should we do, now we have the names?'

'Figure out what they're up to, of course!' said Kate. 'Whatever Loren's planning to do next, it will involve the informants in that book. They're the army he used to destroy the fields, and the grain. We need to catch them in the act!' She grimaced. 'How is this boy so heavy?'

She and Viola lugged Seth up the final staircase through the Shambles. Ellie noticed that Viola kept glancing at Seth with a wary, worried look. Above them, the branches of the Vile Oak rattled in the night breeze.

Molworth's tiny head appeared from his bedroom window, a white nightcap flopping over his eyes. 'Thieves!' he shrieked. 'Stay away from the beer cellar or I'll empty my chamberpot all over you!'

'It's *us*, Molworth,' Viola said, dragging Seth through the door. Archibald came skidding across the floorboards, tumbling over in his excitement then leaping up on to Viola's shoulder.

'What *I* don't understand is where those whales came from,' said Kate.

'Oh, yes, that was . . . very strange,' said Ellie, meeting Viola's gaze.

Molworth appeared behind the bar. 'You *did* get into the beer cellar,' he said, eyeing Seth suspiciously.

'He's not drunk, Molworth,' said Viola.

'He needs leeches,' said Kate. 'That's what the Royal Physician always recommends. Molworth, do you have any?'

'Of course,' said Molworth. 'Hundreds! Follow me, loyal servant.'

Kate leapt over the counter and vanished, while Ellie and Viola heaved Seth up to the bedroom and dropped him on to his bed. Ellie knelt down, panting. Viola hadn't even broken a sweat. She watched Seth carefully, touching a finger to his skin.

'Those blue marks,' she said.

'Please, Viola, you can't mention them to anyone. Even Kate.'

'He called those whales. Didn't he?'

Ellie looked at Viola sharply, then swallowed.

'I'm not stupid, Ellie. I spend every day with him on the boat. The sea and him . . . they're like twins – twins that don't always get on. When he's moody, the sea gets choppy. When he's happy, the boat glides along smoothly, and the fish swarm round us. He's like Varu.'

'Who's Varu?'

Viola sat down, and Archibald hopped on to Seth's pillow. 'He's from a story my mum would tell me when I was little. He moved the seas, and could turn into a whale. He was a friend of Leila's, the first Queen of Shipwreck Island.'

Ellie's eyes widened. 'Leila becomes the Vessel?' she said, but Viola didn't seem to be listening, just staring at Seth with a faraway look. Archibald curled up against his neck and began to purr.

'He's a god,' said Viola. 'He's an actual god.'

She snatched Archibald up in her arms, causing him to mewl in protest.

'Seth's not dangerous,' said Ellie.

Viola looked at the tiny kitten in her arms, then at Seth, and seemed to realize what she'd done. 'But . . . he controlled the sea. He swept those men away, like toys.'

'To save our lives. He's still just a boy, really. He's still your friend.'

They watched Seth in silence, the sound of his breath like a chill wind. Ellie was struck by an idea – Leila had known Seth, or at least one of Seth's previous manifestations, so maybe she knew how they might make Seth better. 'I don't suppose that Leila, uh, wrote any books about her life, did she?'

Viola shrugged. 'I dunno. Maybe your so-called *friend* has some in her library.'

'Kate *is* my friend.'

'She's a Queen, Ellie. They don't get to have friends. Queens aren't people.' She looked at Seth. 'Gods aren't people.'

'Look, I trust Kate,' said Ellie. 'She wants to do what's best for the island, but Loren doesn't. That's why we have to stop him.'

Viola chewed her tongue, rubbing Archibald's head. Kate's footsteps clattered up the branch towards them.

'Please don't tell Kate about Seth,' Ellie whispered. 'I don't know why, but I get the feeling she wouldn't understand.'

In fact, Ellie had a strong suspicion Kate would be jealous of Seth's powers.

'If you trust her,' said Viola, 'then why can't you tell her?'

The door smashed open.

'Okay, I got the leeches,' Kate said, holding up a jar. 'Hold on! These are pickles!'

'Kate,' Ellie said, trying to sound casual, 'do you know of anyone called Leila, who lived on the Ark when it was still at sea?'

Kate jerked upright, taken aback by the question. 'Course I do,' she said. 'She's my ancestor. Why are you asking?'

'Um, you know, just, um, Molworth mentioned her the other day. Makes sense – you know how obsessed he is with the Royal Family.'

Kate cocked her head to one side. 'It never ceases to amaze me how little you outer islanders know about your own history. Leila's diary is one of the most prized volumes in my library.'

'Oh,' said Ellie. 'Can I read it?'

'Ellie, I think there are more important things to worry about at this moment. Now help me put this pickle under Seth's nose.'

'LEILA!' Seth jerked up in bed, gasping for breath.

'Seth! Are you okay?' said Ellie, hugging him in relief. He felt a little warmer now.

'Did he just say "Leila"?' Kate asked.

'He must have heard us talking about her,' Viola said, catching Ellie's gaze.

Seth looked around through tiny, tired eyes. 'Where . . . what happened?'

'One of those guards must have bumped you on the head,' Ellie said quickly, before Kate could start asking difficult questions. 'Are you okay?'

Seth nodded.

'Good!' Kate said, punching her fist in the air. 'There's no time to lose – we need to follow Loren's spies, and find out what they're up to. Any ideas, oh Great Inventor?'

Ellie blushed slightly. She watched Seth as he rubbed his eyes, then rolled them around as if to get them working again.

'What?' said Seth, catching her staring at him.

'I have a plan,' Ellie said slowly. 'But, Viola, I'll need your help. For the good of the people.'

Viola gave Ellie a sour look, then glanced at Kate, who smiled back uncertainly.

'I guess the Revolution can wait. What's the plan?'

'Well,' said Ellie, 'I'm afraid you're going to have to lose some sword fights.'

Viola shrugged. 'First time for everything.'

25

A Seam of Seawater

The mood in the Vile Oak that afternoon was tense. Viola circled her opponent, a bead of sweat on her brow, a flood of sweat on his. She let out a cry and leapt forward, wooden sword swinging in a wide arc. But she'd left herself open; the man's sword tapped her waist, and the crowd yelped in shock.

'She's really off her game today,' Janssen grumbled, readjusting his eyepatch.

Seth grunted.

'You look terrible, son,' Janssen said, clutching Seth's face in both hands.

'Maybe he's possessed by the Enemy,' said Molworth. 'Like Ellie was the other day.'

'I was *not* possessed by the Enemy,' said Ellie, shifting in discomfort.

'She was too,' Molworth said, raising his chin authoritatively. 'She had red eyes and white skin, and worms and rats burst out of the floor.'

Janssen's eyes bulged. 'Just like the old rhymes!' he said, inching his chair away from Ellie. The sailors next to them picked up their table, moved it several feet away, then sat down again, eyeing her suspiciously.

Ellie's mouth was dry. 'That's not what happened. And there weren't any worms or rats.'

Molworth grumbled. 'You're no fun.'

Viola clapped her opponent on the shoulder and presented him with his prize – a golden bracelet inlaid with a single sparkling crystal. He shoved it on, grinning smugly and rotating his wrist for all his friends to see.

Viola swaggered back to the table, swishing her sword. Seth pulled out a chair for her, and she glanced at it, then sat down in the chair next to her dad. Seth's face fell.

'You can cross Aaron Pulis off the list, Ellie,' Viola said proudly.

They'd spent the day travelling to all the pubs on the island, from the Laughing Octopus by Shark-fin Tip to the King and Whale Inn on the Rioli Coast. Viola had lost fights at every one of them. Ellie scanned the sheet of ink-smudged paper, striking a line through Aaron's name. Then she turned, yelped, and fell off her seat.

'Am I *really* that frightening?' said Kate.

'How do you always sneak up on me like that?' said Ellie, clutching her chest as Kate and Seth helped her back up.

'I have good news!' Kate announced. 'I just held a royal ceremony, where I rewarded Loren for "Official Services to the Island".'

'That doesn't sound like good news,' said Ellie. 'He poisoned the farms and the grain, and he's certainly planning worse. Why would you reward him?'

'Well,' said Kate, reaching into the box on the table and pulling out a golden bracelet, waggling it meaningfully, 'what do you think I rewarded him with? He shoved it straight on his wrist in front of me. How do these work, anyway?'

'Oh,' said Ellie, swallowing. 'You know. Complicated inventor stuff.'

In truth, threaded through every bracelet was a seam filled with seawater. Just enough, Ellie hoped, for Seth to be able to sense it with his powers, like he'd done with the vials of seawater in Kate's chambers. After Viola's amazing run of 'bad luck', each bracelet was now on the wrist of one of the informants from Loren's book.

That night, Ellie and Seth wandered the island, hooded and cloaked.

'Feel anything yet?' Ellie asked, as they walked beneath the Revival Archway.

Seth kept swiping his hand through the air, like he was trying to swat a fly. The voices in the sea tormented him constantly these days.

'No,' he said, then kicked a clamshell, scattering a flock of seagulls.

'Um . . . are you okay?' said Ellie.

'I think Viola knows about me.'

'Oh,' said Ellie, rubbing the back of her head. 'Yeah, she does. She saw the marks on your skin, and figured out it was you who made those killer whales rescue us. She . . . she knows you're a god. But it's not like she's stopped being friends with you or anything – you spent the whole day with her!'

'And she didn't say a word to me.' His face fell. 'She's acting strange, not making jokes like she usually does. Like she's . . . scared of me or something.'

'I think it was just a bit of a shock. Give her some time.'

Seth crossed his arms fiercely and marched off. Ellie hurried after.

'Maybe . . . if you talked to her about it, you could help her understand?'

Seth stopped dead in the middle of the street.

'What?' said Ellie. 'I think that's a good idea.'

'No,' said Seth, pointing. 'Two of the bracelets are down there.' He darted along an alleyway.

'*Seth!*' Ellie whispered. 'Wait for me!'

Two men were dragging a burlap sack out of the door of a faded blue wooden house, a tiny dog yapping at their heels. A woman hurried after them in her nightdress.

'Please, I've been saving that! It's all the grain we have left!'

'Consider it a service,' said one man. 'You're going hungry so your betters can be fed.' He pointed at his accomplice's wrist. 'Hey – where'd you get that?'

The man grinned. 'Won it in a sword fight. Against a woman ten feet tall, arms thicker than my head.'

'Ha! Me too.' The other raised his wrist to reveal another golden bracelet, crystal glittering in the darkness. 'Pretty, isn't it?'

'I'll . . . I'll call for the Wardens!' said the woman.

'You do that,' said one man, raising his boot over the tiny dog, 'and we won't be so genial.'

The woman sank to her knees, hugging her dog close.

'Give it back,' said Seth. His voice was deep and strangely emotionless.

One man smiled, like Seth was an infant who'd said something profound. 'Run along, boy. You don't know who you're dealing with.'

'You're Loren's men. You think you have his protection. But he can't protect you from me.'

The two men shared a look, then dumped the sack of grain and drew knives from their belts.

'*Seth!*' said Ellie, hobbling forward and grabbing a smoke bomb from her pocket.

Seth cocked his head to one side.

Both men were yanked sharply away from each other, by an invisible force that seemed to have gripped their wrists. Seth cocked his head again, and the men were pulled back together, their heads colliding with a heavy *thunk*. They collapsed in a pile, mouths open and eyes half closed. Ellie crouched to inspect them.

'They're fine,' said Seth. 'I can feel their pulses through the seawater.'

He picked up the sack of grain and handed it back to the woman. 'Here you go,' he said gently.

The dog growled at him, and the woman snatched the grain from Seth's hands.

'Get away from me, monster!' she snapped, dragging the sack into her home.

Seth turned back to Ellie. Blue mists swirled across his skin.

'She's just frightened, Seth.'

'I know,' Seth said, his voice slightly broken. He let out a long sigh, then looked at the men. 'Let's find some Wardens to deal with these two. *Wait.*'

He closed his eyes, brow furrowing and unfurrowing.

'What is it?' said Ellie.

Seth's head snapped up, blue mist still swirling on his arms.

'I can feel them,' he said, then clamped his hands to his ears. 'Quiet!'

'I didn't say anything!' Ellie protested.

'Not you, the voices in the sea,' said Seth. 'I can feel more of Loren's men. *All* of them.'

'Where?' said Ellie, looking around and holding up her cane like a sword. Seth touched her elbow.

'No, Ellie,' he said, and pointed down.

'What do you mean?' said Ellie. 'How can they be underneath us?'

'I don't know. But they're all heading in the same direction.' He opened his eyes wide. 'And I know where they're going.'

~

Ellie slapped the huge crumpled piece of paper down on the table.

'Seth and I have been following Loren's men these last few nights,' she announced, pointing to the lines she'd scrawled over the map. 'They're using tunnels to move around under the island.'

'What tunnels?' said Kate, eyeing the map suspiciously. 'There are no tunnels there.'

'Well, they're not moving through solid stone,' said Ellie. 'Now listen, this is where it gets really interesting.'

'Evening, loyal subjects. What's this, a map?' said Molworth, peering over Seth's shoulder.

'Molworth –' Seth wrinkled his nose – 'are you wearing perfume?'

'Absolutely not, why would I do such a thing?' He bowed to Kate. 'Evening, Oh Handmaiden of the Queen. Would you care for some orange-peel pie? I don't have many oranges left, but I'll gladly spare them for you.'

'Yes, Molworth,' said Ellie, shooing him away. 'Please go and make a pie. And take a *long* time about it.'

She jabbed her finger down on the map, on the edge of the island.

'The volcano?' said Kate. 'What about it?'

Ellie grinned. 'Loren's men gathered there last night.'

'Inside the volcano?'

'It's not an *active* volcano,' said Ellie. 'But that's where all the tunnels lead. I reckon that's where Loren's meeting his informants, to give them their instructions. Like . . . his very own council. He's destroyed the fields and the grain, and now his men are robbing homes and spreading fear. Next, I think he'll probably try to attack *you*, Kate. Maybe not to kill you, but to show everyone how weak you are. To make the people think you're not fit to protect them.'

'So that he can step in,' said Kate. 'That's genius, Ellie. How did you figure that out?'

Ellie scratched the back of her head. She had past experience of trying to second-guess a monster. 'Oh, you know . . . reading stories. Now, we need to get into that volcano. If we can listen in on what he's planning next, we can figure out how to stop it.'

'How are we going to get in the volcano?' said Kate, raising an eyebrow. 'Fly?'

Ellie scratched her chin thoughtfully.

'That wasn't a serious suggestion! Remember the last time you tried to build a flying machine?'

'Well, maybe we could glide? Like that stuffed squirrel in the palace, with the flaps of skin between its arms and legs.'

'Why don't we just use the tunnels,' said Seth, slumping over the table. Kate and Ellie shared a look. Seth had been in a particularly bad mood all evening.

'I suppose we could,' said Ellie grudgingly. 'Now here's where it gets really, *really* interesting.'

'Would you like cinnamon on your pie?'

'Go *away*, Molworth!' Ellie cried and Molworth scurried off. She jabbed her pencil at the map. 'See this X near the Kellerman Mines? Well, according to my, erm, special inventor bracelets, someone keeps going to this point, deep underground, again and again. But only one person.'

Kate narrowed her eyes. 'Do you think it's Loren?'

Ellie nodded eagerly. 'It could be, if he's still wearing the bracelet you rewarded him with. But why? What could he be keeping there?'

Kate stood up, gripping the map and staring fixedly at the cross. 'If he's not letting anyone else see it, then I bet it's something *really* incriminating. Let's go find out.'

'We can't go now,' said Ellie. 'We should wait until it's very late. You'll come, won't you, Seth?'

Seth nodded, still resting his head on folded arms.

'And . . . you could ask Viola to come too?'

Seth sat up. 'I'm going to bed,' he said. 'Wake me up when it's time to leave.'

He slouched off without another word.

'What's wrong with him?' said Kate.

'I think he and Viola had some kind of falling out.'

The front door swung open, and two men came in, looking miserable.

'If you ask me, it's all the Queen's fault,' one grumbled to the other. 'Thieves aren't scared of Her, so they're just doing whatever they please. Wouldn't happen if a man was in charge.'

There was a loud rip, and Kate looked down at the map in her hands, which was now in two pieces.

'Come on, let's get some sleep,' said Ellie, touching Kate's arm. 'We'll need it.'

'That reminds me,' Kate said, picking up a cloth bag from by her feet. 'Some bedtime reading for you. I'll meet you at the entrance to the Kellerman Mines at three o'clock.'

They hugged goodnight, then Ellie climbed the branch to her bedroom. Seth was snoring lightly as she lay down in bed. Ellie turned on to her side to watch him, hoping his sleep was dreamless, then lit a candle and opened the bag Kate had given her.

Inside was a pile of yellowed paper, bound by string and tucked in a leather folder. Ellie read the first page.

Leila's Diary: A horrible time on a horrible ship.

Leila's Diary

4,807 days aboard the *Revival*

At night the Crone goes on long walks around the Ark, so the moment Varu's steady breathing filled the garden I snuck out after her. I found her alone on the Sky Deck, a tiny shrivelled shape beneath the massive white moon.

'You're lying to him,' I said. 'You *do* know who broke his mind. And you know how he can fix it too.'

The Crone glanced over her shoulder at me. 'You're far cleverer than you look, child.'

'You must tell him.'

'He's not ready,' said the Crone. 'He needs to be nourished, loved, or else he will break beneath the truth.'

'What are you talking about?'

The Crone gazed across the endless, tranquil sea. 'The boy has died a thousand times, and will die a thousand more. He is a god. But even gods have souls, and even their souls can be broken. His soul must be mended, before his mind can be.'

All her words were making my head hurt. 'But *how* can he fix his mind?'

'By remembering the truth.'

'But you just said the truth would break him!'

'I did.'

I growled in frustration. 'You're so annoying. Can't you talk like a normal person for once? *Who* broke his mind?'

The Crone studied me. 'If you care for him at all, you must promise not to tell him.'

I gritted my teeth. 'I promise.'

The Crone gazed back out at the ocean. 'He broke his own mind.'

'Why would he do that?'

'To forget the truth.'

I grabbed one of her wrinkly wrists, turning her to face me.

'And *what* is the truth?' I snarled.

The Crone studied me a long time, then ran a finger through my hair.

'The war was too much for him. Too much suffering, too much death. Somehow, the Enemy was able to trick him, and he lost control of his powers.'

A frown formed on her brow. 'He caused the Drowning.'

26

The Drowning

Ellie slammed the book shut.

Her heartbeat crashed against her eardrums. She put a hand to her chest and took three deep breaths.

It was Seth.

Ellie rose unsteadily from her bed. A shred of moonlight dappled Seth's face, his breathing a gentle rise and fall, in time with the wash of the waves on the shoreline. The walls of the tiny room pressed in on Ellie, and she felt an overwhelming desire to be outside. She pulled on her coat and shoes, grabbed her cane, and hobbled down the stairs and out of the Vile Oak.

The sky was a blanket of infinite stars, casting silver light across the island and the sea beyond. Ellie wove through the Shambles, past sleeping cats and chickens, until her thoughts became too big and heavy and she slumped down on a drystone wall.

Seth had caused the Drowning.

He had made the seas rise, and destroyed the world as it was.

Seth. Her friend.

Ellie leaned forward, clutching her legs. She half expected the bleeding child to appear to mock her. But all she heard was the sound of the sea, and the pounding in her chest.

'No,' she whispered. 'The Crone said he was tricked.'

It was the Enemy's fault; it was *always* the Enemy's fault.

She turned to look back at the Vile Oak, its gnarled limbs curling out of the Ark's shadow. The little window of their bedroom was still dark. She had never felt so distant from Seth.

She sat, listening to the sea, trying to grapple with the huge, ugly thought in her head. Was he the person she thought he was? She glanced at the clock that hung from one of the branches. It was quarter to three already, almost time to meet Kate. She was nervous about waking Seth, but took a deep breath and began climbing the Shambles.

Seth was awake already, though, standing outside the inn, wearing a green cardigan.

'Oh, you're up!' said Ellie, forcing cheerfulness. She patted her coat pockets. 'Shall we get going? I think I've got everything I need.'

Seth looked uncomfortably at his feet. 'Ellie, I've been thinking. I don't think we should go tonight.'

'What?'

'I think we should leave. Leave this island forever.'

Ellie took a step back. 'We can't just leave. What about the friends you've made here? What about Viola?'

Seth shoved his hands deep in his pockets. 'I told you, Viola despises me.'

'She doesn't *despise* you.'

Seth turned his back on her, his shoulders shaking. 'Things will only get worse if we stay. We have to go.'

'And leave Kate to deal with this all by herself? We can help. We can reverse the famine. Once we prove that Loren poisoned the fields, I can use my machines to fix everything.'

Seth's lip trembled. He didn't seem able to meet Ellie's eye. 'I don't know why you care about her so much.'

'What's that got to do with anything? We're trying to help people.'

Seth turned sharply. 'No, you're trying to help *her*,' he said through gritted teeth. 'I don't trust her, Ellie. If she had to pick between you and being Queen, she wouldn't even hesitate.'

Ellie balled her hands into fists. Of course Seth wanted to leave. He lived in his own head, with his dreams and his visions. He didn't care about what Ellie wanted any more. She remembered the feeling that had overcome her before, looking up at the dark window, being so distant from him.

He was a *stranger* to her. Her whole body shook furiously. It was an effort to speak through her rage.

'You're. Just. Jealous,' she whispered. 'That I have a friend who's not you.'

Ellie turned and marched away.

'Ellie?'

'I *don't* want to talk to you, Seth.'

She stormed down through the Shambles, picking up her pace as she realized she was running late. She met Kate on the southern side of the island, by the entrance to the Kellerman Mines. Kate was kneeling on the paving stones in her blue cloak, straining to study the map in the starlight. She hopped up eagerly when she saw Ellie, then frowned.

'Where's Seth?'

'Not coming.'

'That's not like him. Is he still unwell?'

'No,' said Ellie, wiping a tear from her face. 'Come on, let's go.'

Kate watched her worriedly, then nodded and ushered Ellie into the tunnel. Ellie retrieved a lighter from her coat, filled with the last of the whale oil she'd brought from the City. She clicked it, and a flame burst out, bathing the craggy walls of the mine in flickering yellow light.

'Oh, I almost forgot,' said Kate, pulling one of the golden bracelets from her pocket and slipping it on to Ellie's wrist. 'I thought we both should wear them, so we can find each other again if we get separated. Are you ever going to explain to me how they work?'

'Oh, it's through a complicated machine,' Ellie said. 'That can, um . . . tell when one of the bracelets is nearby.'

'That's amazing!' said Kate. 'Can I see it?'

'Sure, it's, um . . .' She reached into her pocket. 'Here it is.'

'Ellie, that's a pencil sharpener.'

'Is it? I mean, yes, it is.'

'Ellie, are you sure you're okay?'

Ellie suppressed the urge to sob and threaded her arm through Kate's, holding it tightly. Kate shot her a concerned look, but took Ellie's hand and squeezed it, and suddenly Ellie didn't feel so alone any more.

'Come on,' said Kate. 'We don't need Seth grumping up the place, anyway.'

They wound through twisting tunnels, Ellie nervously eyeing the stalactites above and feeling her broken arm twitch.

'Um, do you know where we're going?' she asked.

'Of course!' said Kate, pulling out the map. Ellie held up the lighter, illuminating the routes that Seth had drawn. Kate pointed out the curving paths Loren's people had been taking. 'I compared your map to a map of the mines, and looked for places they overlap. That should show us where to get into Loren's tunnels.'

Ellie nodded thoughtfully. 'That's clever.'

Kate fiddled with a strand of hair. 'Well, we don't know if it worked yet.' She traced a finger along the map. 'This way.'

They travelled deeper into the mine, along rickety wooden platforms, picking their way between scattered tools and carts of rock.

'If I'm right,' said Kate, 'there should be a tunnel right round this corner that *isn't* on the mine map.'

Kate laughed in delight as a narrow passage appeared before them.

'Come on. I thought first we'd find out what secret Loren's been keeping hidden *here*.' She pointed at the X on the map.

The passage was rough and so tight that Ellie was surprised anyone larger than her had been able to fit through it. It veered left and right, and Ellie prayed she had enough whale oil in the lighter. Soon, the rock changed to cold brickwork.

'These tunnels are incredible,' Kate said, her breath flickering the scant flame of the lighter. 'How long has Loren been building them? How long have his *ancestors* been building them? Ah, I think we take a right here.'

Down the tunnel they found a staircase, which led them up to a rusty metal door. Kate opened it, and ushered Ellie inside.

The air was stale, with a reek like sweat and curdled milk. Ellie raised the lighter higher. In the corner of the room was an alcove with tall iron bars, spaced closely together. Something shifted in the shadows behind them.

Ellie yelped. Without thinking, she clicked off the lighter, plunging them into darkness.

'What are you doing?' said Kate. 'Put the light back on.'

Ellie stood frozen. 'I . . . I . . .'

Kate found Ellie's hand and took the lighter.

'There's nothing to be afraid of. Whoever they are, they're behind bars.'

There was a click, and Kate's face was revealed, bright yellow against the darkness. Ellie's heartbeat echoed inside her head as she stared at the man in the prison cell.

It was Hargrath.

The Volcano Court

Ellie clamped her hand to her mouth, her cane clattering to the ground. The light spilled up her legs and she was afraid it would reach her face too. She staggered back into the shadows, wincing as she slammed against the wall.

Hargrath's massive frame was crushed inside the cell. His black Inquisitor's coat was torn, his trousers dusty, his shirt flecked with dark splotches. His eyelids were crusted, struggling to reopen each time he blinked, and he hugged the shoulder where his missing arm would have been. He was as large as Ellie remembered, but without substance, like a tree that had toppled and rotted from the inside.

Kate stepped towards the cell.

'Who are you?' Her voice was deep and vibrated in the stone: the voice she used when she was being Queen.

Hargrath eased himself up on to his knees, resting his head on two bars. His skin was so clammy and fishlike, Ellie half feared he'd pour between the bars like water. A low gurgle rumbled deep inside him, then rolled from his lips like thunder.

'Inquisitor. Killian. Hargrath,' he said, pronouncing the words with great care, like they were all he had left.

'An . . . Inquisitor?' Kate said, shoulders tensing. 'So, you're from the Enemy's City?'

'It is NOT the Enemy's City!' Hargrath roared, and Ellie worried he would reach out through the bars and wring Kate's neck. 'We do not *serve* the Enemy. We *hunt* the Enemy!'

Kate didn't move an inch. 'Why has Loren imprisoned you?'

'He's a monster. He's insane. This whole *island* is insane. You should have just left me to do my work. Now she's out there, and soon *it* will return and destroy the lot of you, all you halfwits and barbarians.'

Kate lowered herself to Hargrath's eye level. 'You mean the Enemy?'

Hargrath's lip curled. 'You don't believe me. Loren didn't believe me, either, that such a frail little girl could be the Enemy's Vessel. None of them believed me! I told them – Lancaster's still alive. She escaped. The rope was cut.' A fly crawled across Hargrath's face, but he didn't seem to notice. 'Why would the Enemy drown itself? Why did we not find her body?'

Kate turned her head slightly, towards Ellie, and Ellie swallowed, her teeth chattering. She prayed Hargrath wouldn't follow the movement and spot her through the darkness.

'They didn't *want* to believe me!' Hargrath screeched. 'Even when that underwater boat of hers was seen heading south. But I'm going to find her. I'm going to break out of this place, and destroy her, and that preening idiot too!'

'The girl,' said Kate, her voice emotionless. 'Lancaster. Describe her to me.'

Hargrath bared his teeth. 'Short. Pale. Blonde hair, green eyes. A nose that goes to one side. Last time I saw her she walked with a cane.'

Ellie whimpered, and clamped her hand hard to her mouth, feeling tears on her fingers. Kate's face was a mask in the flickering light.

'You told Loren this?'

Hargrath lifted his chin, showing Kate the bruises and cuts on his neck. 'Yes.'

Kate turned, studying Ellie carefully. Ellie shrank backwards under her stare. She opened her mouth, her whole body compelled to deny the truth. They watched each other for a long moment.

Kate turned back to Hargrath. 'I'm sorry you've been so mistreated,' she said, her voice firm but kind. 'You were only trying to rid the world of evil. But your job is done. The Lancaster girl is dead.'

Ellie let out a small, sharp breath. Hargrath's eyes bulged. 'She is? How?'

'Loren killed her,' Kate said. 'I saw it myself. She's no longer your concern. Your hunt is over.'

Hargrath closed his eyes, and tears ran down his face.

'She's dead.' He slumped against the bars. 'Peace,' he whispered gratefully.

Kate rose. 'No,' she said. 'There will be no peace until Loren is dealt with.'

Hargrath nodded vigorously. 'Let me out, and I'll make him regret what he's done to me.'

'I will let you out,' said Kate, 'but not yet.'

'What? NO!' Hargrath thrust his hand between the bars, but Kate was too nimble, hopping out of reach.

'See? I can't trust you. I will send others for you when the time is right. In the meantime, you must not let Loren know anyone was here. Can you do that for me, Killian?'

Kate looked him deep in the eye, and he stared back at her, tears glistening on his cheeks.

'Remember my face,' she said. 'The next time you see it, I will give you the vengeance you desire.'

Hargrath frowned uncertainly, as if he couldn't figure out whether he was looking at a caterpillar or a butterfly. 'Who . . . who are you?'

'I am the Queen,' Kate said, and with a *click* she extinguished the lighter, plunging them into darkness.

'No, no, don't go!' cried Hargrath. 'YOU CAN'T LEAVE ME HERE!'

Cold fingers curled round Ellie's and pulled her away down tightening tunnels. Hargrath's raving grew distant.

'Kate?' Ellie said, her voice barely more than a whisper.

Kate clicked on the lighter, her golden eyes fixed on Ellie.

'Why didn't you tell me you're from the Enemy's City?'

Ellie hesitated, confused that *this* was her first question. 'I . . . I know how much everyone here hates it.'

'I see,' Kate said. 'I don't like being lied to, especially by you.' She smiled uncertainly. 'But I understand.'

'Wait, you're not worried about what he said, about me being the Enemy's Vessel?'

Kate's smile broadened. 'Oh yes, because you're so obviously a creature of pure evil. That poor man is clearly insane.'

Ellie let out a sigh, and almost broke into tears.

'Ellie? Whatever's the matter?'

'I just . . . I thought, after hearing what he said, that you'd never want to even look at me again.'

Kate took Ellie's hand. 'That is very silly. Now come on, the volcano's this way. We have to find evidence of Loren's secret council.'

She raised the lighter as they squeezed along a narrow corridor, which soon branched off in all directions.

'Wait.' Kate paused. 'What's that?'

Ellie listened, and after a moment she could hear it too: faint music echoing in the darkness ahead. They let the music guide their path, and the brickwork soon became coarse, jagged rock. The corridor vanished around them, widening abruptly into a damp-smelling chamber. Kate rushed onwards, looking up in surprise.

'Watch *out*,' said Ellie, pulling her back. Kate dropped the lighter and it fell down, down, into a vast dark pit.

'Th-thank you,' said Kate, swallowing as she stepped back from the brink. She edged towards a steep staircase that reared overhead towards the centre of the chamber, towards the music.

Ellie looked up. High above, a circle was cut from the darkness, and through that circle was a dark blue sky pierced with bright stars.

'We're inside the volcano,' Ellie whispered.

As they climbed, Ellie noticed many other staircases, all of them leading from different tunnels, rising to the same wide platform, where Loren sat on a low stool.

He was dressed in a silver gown and playing a silver harp, as if both he and the instrument were crafted from pure starlight. Hooded figures sat on a long stone bench wrapping round the edge of the platform, listening to Loren play.

Kate and Ellie ducked down, lying flat against the stairs so they could just see Loren's head.

'Is this a concert, Loren?' a deep voice rang out. 'Are we expected to sit silently while you play for us?'

'Wait, I know that voice,' Kate whispered. 'That's Emile Cassor. He's a member of my Royal Court. The wretched traitor!'

Loren continued to play, his eyes closed, head nodding in time to the music.

'Why *is* he playing for them?' Ellie whispered.

Kate narrowed her eyes. 'To show them he can make them wait as long as he likes.'

Finally, Loren let out a long sigh, and his hands came to rest against the harp. 'My friends,' he said. 'My dear friends. Please believe me – I am so sorry for what I have had you do. I have asked much of you – to steal, to lie, to riot and destroy. We have made our home a poorer place. But it is only temporary. For now, even those most fanatically loyal to Her Beloved Majesty are wondering whether She has the strength to lead our island. Now, they look for real leadership.'

Kate shivered. 'They're all *traitors*.'

'Let's call the Seven Sentinels,' said Ellie. 'Let's get as many people as we can and have them see this for themselves.'

She touched Kate's hand, but Kate continued to glare hatefully at Loren. 'Soon, our island will be governed well, and with strength,' he said. 'A Vessel our Queen may be, but a leader? It is time, my friends, for a new age.'

'NO!'

Kate's shout echoed up through the volcano, and Loren turned, his eyes widening slightly. He smiled. 'Well, well. Speak of the Vessel and She shall appear.'

'Kate!' Ellie cried, hobbling up the steps as Kate tore across the platform towards Loren.

'You *poisoned* the fields and the grain,' Kate spat. 'You started the riots. You robbed my people's homes!' She snarled at the hooded figures. 'You will all *pay* for this.'

The men shifted awkwardly, and some even stood to leave, pulling their hoods down further. Loren waved a hand.

'Friends, please. Sit, sit; talk among yourselves. Come, Divine One, speak with me.'

He sat down on the stool and took up the harp again. Kate clenched her fists and walked over, Ellie hurrying after.

'*What?*' Kate spat.

Loren dropped his voice beneath the chords of his harp. 'My Queen, I am sorry to tell you this, but you've made a grievous mistake in coming here.'

'Do these people know about your little book of *secrets*?'

Loren raised an eyebrow. 'Ah, that explains the break-in the other night. Some do. Most do not. I don't think I'd live long if I told everyone that I knew their darkest secrets.'

'How about *I* tell them, then?'

'You would embarrass me in front of my friends?' Loren shook his head sadly. 'And after I've done so much to help you.'

'You've done *nothing* to help me.'

Loren closed his eyes again as he played. 'My Queen, it is clear to me that the burden of leadership is breaking you.

It is etched in your face. Why not be free of it? Give me control.'

Kate laughed, low and humourless. 'I would have to die to do that.'

Loren waved a hand. 'Not at all. Name me your Royal Successor. Mark me as the next Vessel. Then, we can send you to a faraway island with your little friend here. I'll tell the people that you died peacefully, tragically young. I will use Ellie's machines to restore Shipwreck Island to its former glory. And you need never worry about anything, ever again.'

Kate bristled. With a sweep of her hand, she sent the harp flying to the ground. Loren blinked down at it, fingers frozen in mid-air.

'Not a fan of the harp, my Queen?'

'I am going to tell everyone on this island what you've been doing.'

Loren shrugged. 'They won't believe you – they love me too much. You need a good story, my Queen, and the truth does not make for a good story. Not always, anyway.'

He gestured towards Ellie. 'For example, I think they *would* believe me if I told them that the Queen's closest advisor is, in fact, from the Enemy's City.'

A slow smile spread across his face as he watched Kate stiffen. 'You didn't know, did you?'

'So what?' said Kate. 'It's not like she *is* the Enemy.'

'Of course not,' said Loren, looking Ellie up and down. 'Why would the Enemy choose such a feeble, broken creature for its Vessel? Still, what will the people say when they learn that a spy from the Enemy's City has been whispering in the Queen's ear? Why . . . they'll probably demand her head.'

Kate swallowed so hard that Ellie could see the ripple in her throat.

Loren righted his harp, running a finger over a chip in the wood. 'At the Festival of Life, in four days, before all the most powerful people on Shipwreck Island, you are going to name me as the next Vessel, and give me absolute power.'

'I will *never* do that.'

Loren rose. He pressed his hands together beneath his chin, considering Kate.

'You know, I've been wondering about something. It's a wild theory, but please indulge me. Why *is* it, exactly, that the harvests have been getting worse every year since your mother died, and you have done nothing to stop it? Could it be that you do not use your powers because you cannot? Could it be that you're *not* actually a Vessel?'

He looked Kate in the eye, smiling broadly. Kate glared back at him, her breathing unsteady. Her hands began to tremble.

Loren closed his eyes, nodding as if the music still played. 'Thank you, Kate. It was just a theory, as I said. Now it is . . . much more than that. Ellie's secret seems quite small compared to yours now, doesn't it?' He put a hand on Kate's cheek.

'Don't *touch* me,' Kate spat. She lashed out at Loren's face, but he grabbed her wrist, wrapping his other hand in her hair and lifting her from the ground. Kate screamed.

'No!' Ellie cried, rushing at Loren and swinging her cane at him. Loren tore it from her grasp, twirling it in the air then jabbing her hard in the stomach. Ellie keeled over, gasping for a breath that wouldn't come.

'LEAVE HER ALONE!' Kate roared, her face red as she clawed against Loren's grip. 'I will *rip* you apart. I will *burn* your name to the ground.' Loren's knuckles whitened as he pulled her hair tighter, and Kate screamed. 'I will destroy . . . *everything* that matters to you,' she hissed.

'That's not very queenly,' said Loren. 'Now, you will do as I ask. And you know what, since I'm so generous, I'll even have some actors pretend to be healed by you at the Festival of Life, to keep your horrid secret hidden. So play along, or I will tell everyone the truth − that you are powerless and your friend is a traitor.'

He put Kate down, and she fell to her knees, clutching her head.

'*Kate!*' said Ellie, crawling over to her. 'Are you okay?'

Kate nodded, unable to speak. She took Ellie's hand and squeezed it.

'MY FRIENDS!' Loren raised his hands in the air. 'Matters have progressed even faster than I'd hoped. We have an accord – in Her divine wisdom, our Queen has decreed that I shall be named Royal Successor. I will be the next Vessel to the God of Life.'

Kate sprang to her feet and ran at him, howling in anguish and trying to force him towards the edge of the platform. Loren laughed, then shoved Kate away. 'You don't understand, do you? I know the truth about you. *I* have all the power.'

He stepped over to Ellie, pulling a knife from his pockets and yanking Ellie up by her broken arm.

'NO!' Kate cried, a shout that chilled Ellie's blood. 'I'll do it! Please don't hurt her!'

Loren considered her a moment, then put Ellie down.

'Run along now, *Great Inventor*,' he said.

'I'm not leaving her,' said Ellie, standing over Kate.

Loren smiled. 'She'll be going *with* you. She has an important ceremony to organize. May I recommend that tunnel? It will take you to the shore. You can find your way home from there.'

Ellie and Kate put an arm round each other, then hobbled down the staircase towards the tunnel, Kate's ragged breathing loud in Ellie's ears. They were halfway down when Loren spoke gently.

'Kate, smile for me, would you?'

Kate gritted her teeth, then breathed deeply, letting her face go blank. She turned round.

Loren studied her carefully. Kate's lip twitched, and a tiny frown formed on her brow. She stepped forward, cleared her throat, and spat at him.

Loren shook his head. 'My friends, the Queen must be taught a lesson in power. Do not harm Her, under any circumstances. Kill Ellie Stonewall.'

'Ellie, RUN!' Kate roared, pulling Ellie down the steps. Hooded figures sprang after them.

'Give me a smoke bomb,' said Kate, as they hurtled towards the tunnel. Ellie rummaged in her pockets and shoved a small, marble-sized device into Kate's hand.

'Ellie, this is a marble!' Kate cried, but threw it anyway. It sailed beneath the hood of the person nearest, impacting like a hammer on stone, the man clutching his face as the others slammed into him.

'You go ahead,' said Kate. 'I'll hold them up. Get back to the palace as quickly as you can.'

'I'm not –'

'You heard Loren – they're not allowed to hurt me.'

'But –'

'Ellie, *go*!'

Kate shoved her hard, and Ellie raced along the tunnel, the pain in her leg searing with every step. Kate roared in fury behind her. Ahead, Ellie smelled salt and seaweed, and saw a pale light glimmering at the end of the tunnel. She burst out into fresh air and found a rocky shore around her; a black, lifeless sea stretched out ahead, lined by a faint pink light. She picked her way down the rocky side of the volcano towards the beach. She could hear the thud of boots behind.

'There's no way you can survive *this*,' said the bandaged child, sitting back on a mossy rock, waggling its toes. The soles of its feet were wet with blood.

Ellie hopped down from one rock to the next, searching for the easiest path. The child picked at a loose thread on its arm. 'Ask me, go on. I'll get rid of them for you. I can take care of Loren too, while we're at it.'

Ellie leapt from a high boulder down to the beach, crying out as her leg buckled underneath her.

'Come on, Ellie,' said the child. 'You've been ignoring me for too long.'

Shouts echoed from the tunnel. Ellie limped on along the beach, searching around for something, anything to help her. But she saw only rocks, and sand, and the bandaged child standing in the shallows.

'Go on,' it said, grinning its pointed grin and reaching out a pale, bandaged hand. 'Let's be friends again.'

A desperate impulse seized her, and she threw herself to her knees, dunking her head into the sea. The water rushed up her nose and down the collar of her shirt as she screamed Seth's name as loud as she could, bubbles spilling from her mouth.

Ellie pulled her head out, gasping for breath.

The child laughed. 'What was the point of *that*? You really think he's going to hear?'

Two hooded figures slid over the wet rocks towards her. Ellie limped into a run, pulling a smoke bomb from her pocket and slamming it hard against her chest. The smoke trailed behind her, and she glanced over her shoulder to see a young man with wild grey eyes, hood fallen back, coughing as smoke got in his lungs.

'This isn't funny any more, Ellie!' the child cried, stamping its foot. 'These people are going to kill you!'

Ellie turned a sharp bend, and saw on her left a low, grassy cliff face, painted pink by the sunrise. She looked for a way up to the street above, but her boot hit a rock and she tumbled across the sand, jagged rock ripping her clothes and skin.

More hooded figures raced towards her, knives drawn, whooping and laughing. The child knelt at Ellie's side.

'Save yourself,' its wet voice gurgled in her ear. 'Ask me.'

Ellie looked at the blades glinting in the sunlight. Her lips quivered, about to form the words.

'No,' she said instead. 'If I die, at least the world is rid of you . . . for a little while.'

She lay back in the sand, blinking at the rising sun. She thought of Finn, the two of them in their little rowing boat, eagerly scanning the water for fish.

And his smile.

She held that smile in her mind, as the footsteps drew near.

Leila's Diary

4,821 days aboard the *Revival*

Varu has good days and bad days. Today was a bad day so I dropped a bag of fruit and vegetables in front of him.

'Come on,' I said. 'We're going to give these out.'

'To who?'

'Dunno. Whoever needs them.'

We wandered the deep, gloomy corridors of the Ark that creaked like the bones of a weary old giant. We passed the cabin-houses of the fishing clans and the farming clans, but we found the most desperate and hunger-filled eyes down in the bottom decks, where the smell is worst and the people huddle like woodlice in the dark. The bag we brought was only so big and there were still too many hopeful faces watching us by the time it was empty.

'They're so hungry. It's not fair,' said Varu.

'The Ark-Captain and his men eat too much. Don't leave enough for everyone else. Come on.'

We wandered back up to the Sky Deck. Varu can walk and walk and not get tired, just like me. The wind ruffled his black hair as he looked at the sea.

'The Crone says you have the power to part the waves,' I said. 'To make land for the first time since the Drowning, for her to grow plants on. Do you think you can do it?'

Varu stared at the sea like it was a foul-smelling stew. 'I'd have to put my mind down inside it. Where all the dead voices are.'

'Well, I can sit with you when you do it, if that would help?'

Varu straightened, his eyes filling with amazement. 'Actually, I don't think I need to part the sea.'

'What?'

He pointed to the horizon. 'Out there. I can feel something. The sea wraps round it, like it wants to drown it. Only it can't.'

'What do you mean?'

Varu smiled. 'I mean ... there's land out there *already.*'

28

God of the Sea

The footsteps stopped.

Ellie sat up to find the hooded figures standing beside her. They weren't looking at her, but at the sea.

'What's wrong with it?' one said.

It was bubbling, like someone had lit a stove underneath the waves, gouts of water spurting high in the air. A mound of seawater began to grow, swelling upward like a hill, and the hooded figures jumped back.

'What's happening?' one shrieked.

Ellie glanced up, and her heart leapt.

Seth was standing atop the cliff, his hands held out at his sides. The blue mists swirled angrily across his skin, and there were dark pits where his eyes should have been.

'You were going to kill her,' Seth said. When he spoke, another voice spoke too, issuing from the sea itself: a low, ancient growl, so deep it made Ellie's bones tremble. The bulge in the sea was still growing: a mountain of froth and dark water, casting a long shadow across the beach.

'No!' said one man, pulling his hood back. She recognized him from his sword fight with Viola – he was only a few years older than Ellie. 'We were just going to rough her up a bit!'

He wasn't talking to Seth, but to the growing mountain of water. None of them had noticed Seth at all. His skin was already as pale as marble, except for the blue swirls, and Ellie feared what would happen if it got any paler. She rushed towards the cliff.

'LIAR!' Seth roared, and the waters did too. Ellie thought she glimpsed something beneath the surface of the growing mountain: a towering, spectral creature made of darkness, as tall as ten men.

One by one, Loren's followers fell to their knees, flinging back their hoods to reveal the frightened men and women underneath.

'Loren made us do it!' one shrieked. 'He said he'd make us rich!'

'Seth!' Ellie called, wedging her good arm into a crack in the cliff to heave herself upward. 'You've made your point, stop!'

The blue swirls on his skin now looked like swollen black blood vessels, coiling round his arms and neck as if to choke him. The creature in the sea lunged forward, and the men and women screamed. Behind it, the wall of water was growing higher, as wide as the island itself.

Seth fell to his knees. 'Stop . . . hurting . . . each other,' he said, his voice a pained whisper that was magnified a thousandfold in the echo of the sea.

'Seth!' Ellie cried. 'It's over – I'm okay!' She looked down at the people on the beach. 'Don't just stand there, run!'

At last, Loren's followers came to their senses, fleeing in both directions along the beach. With a gasp, Ellie heaved herself over the lip of the cliff and tumbled towards Seth. She cried out as she touched his hand, finding it cold as ice water. She stared into his eyes, but couldn't find anything of her friend.

'SETH!' she roared.

'They're . . . hurting,' he said, his face twisting with horror at whatever it was he could see. 'I have to stop it.'

The wall of water was rising higher, blotting out the light of the sunrise. The dark shape took another step towards the beach, still shrouded in the raging, twisting waters. It reached out a black claw towards Seth.

'NO!' Ellie screamed, holding Seth close. 'Get away! He's not yours to take.'

Again the ancient voice spilled from Seth's lips and the sea at once. 'He *is* me.'

Ellie grabbed Seth's face. The blue-black veins had covered him entirely; she didn't think his body would last much longer. She thought of what the Crone had said in Leila's diary. She battled against the urge to tell him – it was the worst thing she could think of to do to him, but the only way to save his life.

'Seth, listen to me. The Crone said that your mind is broken, and that to truly control your powers you must remember the truth of what you did.' She took a breath. 'There was a war, and the people you loved were in pain. I don't think you meant to, but . . . I'm so sorry, Seth. You caused the Drowning.'

The wall of seawater recoiled, roaring as if struck. Seth wriggled in Ellie's grip, muttering fretfully. The black veins released him, vanishing to nothing, and his eyes were his own again, wide and afraid. He gasped, like someone rescued from drowning, a sound that was at once heartbreaking and utterly human.

'No,' he whispered. '*No.*'

Behind them, the wall of seawater was swallowed back into the ocean. Of the dark creature, nothing could be seen.

'I did this?' Seth said, his voice childlike and terrified. He stared at Ellie, his lips trembling.

'Yes,' said Ellie. 'I'm so sorry.'

Seth stared at his hands, his mouth opening and closing. 'No.' He balled his hands into fists. 'I WOULDN'T!' he yelled, and the sea rumbled too. 'Ellie,' he whimpered. 'Ellie, how could I?'

'It was the Enemy,' said Ellie. 'I don't know how, but it tricked you. I *know* you, Seth. You would never have done it on purpose.'

Seth let out a cry that echoed across the empty beach, then keeled over, sobbing into Ellie's shoulder. She held him close.

'It wasn't your fault,' she whispered, over and over again. 'It wasn't your fault.'

29

Divine Act

How long they sat there, Ellie wasn't sure. The birds began to sing, and the skies grew light.

'Shall we go home?' she asked finally.

Seth sniffed and sat up. He gave a tiny nod.

'Are you okay?'

'Not really.'

Ellie squeezed his shoulder. 'Come on, maybe some orange-peel pie would help?'

Seth looked at her sharply through red-ringed eyes. 'I don't understand. Why aren't you afraid of me?'

Ellie shrugged. 'I told you – the Seth I know would never want to hurt anyone.'

'But I *did*. Just now. There was something inside me that wanted to kill those people.'

'And there's something inside me that wants to kill *everything*. But it's not me.'

Seth slumped forward, hugging himself. Ellie rubbed his arm; his skin was cold as winter frost.

'Come on, let's get you a blanket and some tea.' She looked along the beach. 'Though I need to find Kate. Loren told his followers not to hurt her, but I don't trust him . . . Wait, she was wearing one of the bracelets!'

She looked at Seth hopefully, and he looked back with sad, weary eyes.

'Sorry,' said Ellie. 'You probably don't want to be using your powers right now.'

Seth closed his eyes, and took a deep breath. 'There's someone in the street above. Darting in zigzags.'

Ellie helped Seth to his feet and they clambered up the rocky path towards the town. They found Kate in Arturo Street, darting in zigzags just as Seth had said, checking round corners and through windows. She turned, saw Ellie, and fell to her knees. 'Oh, thank goodness you're okay. I thought . . . I was *sure* . . .'

Ellie hurried over and hugged her. 'Are *you* okay?' she said. Kate was trembling like a frightened mouse.

Kate forced a smile, then shook her head. 'No. Loren's going to tell everyone I'm not the Vessel if I don't give him what he wants.'

'But he's got no proof! We're going to stop him,' Ellie said, squeezing Kate's arm. 'We'll tell everyone about that Inquisitor and –'

'If we do that, he'll reveal you're from the Enemy's City, and the people will demand your head. And he'll . . . he'll tell everyone the truth about me. It's over, Ellie. Like he said. His story is better than ours.'

Ellie gripped Kate's hand, but it was lifeless and stiff, and did not squeeze hers back.

'I . . . I need to get to the palace,' said Kate.

'Oh, oh right.' Ellie took Seth's arm, and he drifted along beside her. 'We'll come with you.'

Around them, the island was waking up: shouts and cries and the occasional bang of something heavy being dropped. Kate kept marching, eyes fixed ahead.

'Look,' said Ellie, 'I'm sorry I didn't tell you, but you understand, right? I mean, you kept secrets from me too!'

There was a smash of breaking glass. Kate frowned.

'Kate, we can still stop him. We *have* to. All that stuff about sending you to another island – he's lying. As soon as he gets what he wants, he's going to *kill* you.'

But Kate said nothing. She had stopped at the corner of the street, clasping her hands to her mouth.

Before them was a torn-up market street: ransacked shops and toppled stalls, people picking over them like ants over fruit. A sea of tumbling, tussling figures, faces sweat-smeared and wide-eyed and panic-stricken.

A man hefted a statue of the Queen and launched it through a shop window. He jumped inside, and moments later dragged out a bag of oats. The tiny shopkeeper chased after him, still in his dressing gown.

'No, stop – this is my livelihood!'

The thief pushed him, and he tripped and fell back through the window. Two women leapt upon the fallen bag of oats, scooping the contents up in their hands and filling their coat pockets.

A newspaper fluttered against Ellie's shoes.

THE INVENTOR HAS FAILED. LOREN SAYS: 'THE ISLAND IS DYING!'

Further up the street, a stallholder fought back against two men who were trying to get at the moneybox under his stall. They pinned him to the ground, then flung the box open, wrestling over the coins inside. One kicked over a basket of onions that rolled into the dirt. Three small children scurried about, gathering them up.

Kate rushed up the street. 'Stop!' she cried. 'Stop this!'

She ran at the two men still fighting over the moneybox, pulling at one's arm. The man growled and shoved Kate with his shoulder, and she rolled across the sandstone and into a patch of soil. Ellie left Seth on a bench and hurried to help Kate up. The knees of her trousers were torn and Ellie could see blood and grit in the skin underneath.

'I'm fine,' Kate said, turning back to the fight. 'Stop it!' she cried. 'As your Queen, I command that you end this madness!'

'Kate,' said Ellie softly. 'That's not going to help.'

'No, I *must* do something,' said Kate. 'My subjects, listen to me!' she roared, in the deep, commanding voice of the Queen. But when heads turned to see who was speaking, they saw only a girl caked in mud, her hair matted and her trousers ripped. 'I am your Queen,' she whispered.

'FRIENDS, STOP!'

The rioters froze. Ellie felt her stomach twist at the sight of Loren, spotless in his silver robe, touching the hands that reached out to him as he passed.

'You are afraid,' he said gently. 'I understand. I admit, even I was frightened by the sight of those barren fields, and the countless tales of theft and violence across the island. But know this, friends – help is on the way! I have just reached an agreement with Our Revered Queen; soon I shall take command of the farms, restoring them to their former glory with ingenious machines of my own invention!'

There were laughs of relief. The two men that had been wrestling now clapped each other on the back.

'But brace yourselves, my friends, for I have some even better news – and you lucky few are the first to hear it. At the Festival of Life in four days, the Queen shall mark *me* –' he took a long pause – 'Royal Successor!'

There was silence, and a few blinks, as if the crowd wasn't sure what this meant. Then an explosion of applause burst from those nearest to Loren and spread up the street, raging in Ellie's ears like a thunderstorm. Loren raised his hands for silence.

'This means that, should tragedy strike and Our Divine Queen pass on, I shall become the next Vessel to the great God of Life!' Loren beamed round at everyone, his cheeks flushed pink. 'In the meantime, with the powers granted to me as an official member of the Royal Family, I will put right the damage done to our beloved island. But look!' Loren's eyes had fallen on Kate, widening in delight. 'How fortunate we are!'

He walked down the street, placing a hand on Kate's shoulder. Kate stiffened, breathing in sharply as every eye turned to look at her.

'Don't *touch* her,' Ellie spat, and Loren held a finger to his lips.

'Friends.' He searched the crowd. 'You may find what I'm about to say shocking, but know that I would never lie to you. I am sure you have found yourselves wondering, in your darker moments: why does the Queen stay up in the palace? Why does She not come down to help us? Well, friends, it turns out She has been with you all along. The Queen of Shipwreck Island – Vessel to the Most Bountiful

God of Life – stands before your very eyes.' He patted Kate's shoulder. 'And this is Her.'

There was silence, broken only by the cries of seagulls. Kate stood deathly still. A mutter of uncertainty rippled through the street.

'I'm not lying to you, friends. This is the twenty-first ruler of Shipwreck Island. This is our Queen.'

A woman gasped and fell to her knees, clasping her hands together. 'Praise Her!' she cried. Others stared, confused, as if they thought this was a joke.

'Everyone, on your knees!' shouted the same man who'd barged Kate to the floor minutes earlier. He glared at those around him and they all dropped to their knees.

'Praise Her,' some murmured.

Loren bent towards Ellie, smiling broadly. 'On your knees, loyal subject,' he said softly.

Ellie stayed standing, glaring at Loren hatefully.

'Get down, child,' said an old woman behind her. 'Show your Queen some gratitude.'

Ellie dipped to one knee, as the man next to her began to weep. 'Praise Her!' he sobbed into his torn sleeve. 'Bless Her!'

Kate looked around at the crowd, tugging at her fingers one after the other.

'What are you doing?' she whispered to Loren, but Loren just winked.

'Show us your power!' cried a woman in the crowd.

Kate's eyes went wide. Ellie swallowed, and they stared at one another in horror. The crowd muttered and bit their fists in excitement.

'Yeah!' cried a boy. 'Make some plants grow!'

'Save us!'

'Stop this,' Kate hissed to Loren, trying to force a smile. 'Please, I will give you what you want. Just make them stop.'

Loren smirked. 'What a glorious idea, my friends.' He pointed to a patch of dried earth beside the street. 'Here, now, She will make the dead earth bloom with life. Praise Her!'

The crowd rose to their feet in excitement, bouncing up and down and clapping their hands. One man punched his fist into the air.

'Praise Her!'

'PRAISE HER!'

'Praise Her!' Loren echoed. 'Our great God-Queen will bring forth plants and flowers that have never before been seen!'

He clapped, and clapped, and the crowd clapped with him. Kate was flushed and trembling as if from a fever. Ellie wanted to reach out to take her hand.

'I think our Queen just needs more encouragement!' Loren announced. 'Did you know, She likes to be known as Kate to Her closest friends?'

Kate took a step back as the clapping grew louder and more insistent.

'Kate!'

'Kate!'

'KATE!'

Every face was smiling, Loren directing their cheers like the conductor of an orchestra: three hundred delighted people who had so recently been trying to rob one another.

'KATE!'

'KATE! KATE! KATE!'

Kate turned to the patch of soil. The people watched in hushed expectation.

Kate fixed her eyes on the dead earth. A tear rolled down her cheek.

Loren grinned. 'Ah well, I guess even Queens have bad days.'

The crowd laughed, and Kate stifled a sob, turned and staggered up the street towards the palace. One man shoved her back down towards the patch of dirt.

'Try again!' he cried. 'We're hungry!'

Kate stumbled, and Ellie leapt forward to catch her before she fell. Kate stared hopelessly at the ground.

'Now, friends!' said Loren. 'The Queen is clearly tired. Let her go, so she can rest. I'm sure she has plenty to think about.'

The crowd grumbled in disappointment and Kate rushed off up the street, not meeting anyone's eye.

'Kate!' Ellie yelled, hobbling to catch up with her. 'Kate, wait!'

But Kate was running now.

'Kate!' Ellie cried.

'Go away, Ellie!'

'But I want to help,' Ellie mumbled. 'You . . . you can trust me.'

Kate stopped running, and turned to look back at Ellie. She screwed her eyes shut, squeezing new tears down her cheeks.

'No, Ellie. I can't trust you. I can't trust anyone.'

Leila's Diary

4,822 days aboard the *Revival*

It took all night for Varu to decide exactly where the land was, but by the morning he was sure that the Ark was *not* heading towards it.

'Then we need to get the Ark-Captain to change course!' I cried.

'Be *careful*,' the Crone called after us, as we raced from the garden. We hurried up to the captain's quarters, crashing through the doors. For some reason, the First Mate was sitting in the Ark-Captain's throne.

'Where is he?' I asked.

'Who?'

'The Ark-Captain.'

'I'm the Ark-Captain.'

'No you're not.'

The First Mate smiled nastily. 'The old man was weak and foolish. He didn't believe me when I told him that the Enemy is onboard. Now he's at the bottom of the ocean.'

I swallowed, but tried not to look frightened. 'Well, whatever – you need to steer the Ark east. There's land out there.'

'What? Nonsense. No land left. Not taking orders from a child.'

'You've got to. Once we reach land, the Crone can –'

'Don't trust that Crone. How's she growing all those vegetables down in the dark, anyway? Sounds like the Enemy's work to me. You!' He pointed at three of his men. 'Bring me the Crone. Kill her if she struggles.'

I grabbed Varu's hand and we raced out of the Ark-Captain's quarters, his men clomping after us.

'We have to help her!'

'She's a Vessel – she'll be okay,' said Varu. 'We need to make sure the Ark is pointing in the right direction first.'

'But the wheel's in the Ark-Captain's quarters! We can't go back in there!'

'I don't need the wheel.'

I chased him up the stairs towards the Sky Deck, children shrieking as I barged through their game. Varu hurtled towards the prow. He flung out his hands, then his face twisted like he'd been stabbed in the heart. The sea rushed up the Ark's sides, roaring

322

and spitting. The Ark lurched, its hundred masts groaning in protest.

And then it started turning.

I wanted to clap and laugh and cheer. But Varu fell to the deck, his skin completely blue. He was icy cold, muttering in a horrible deep voice that didn't sound like him at all.

But the Ark was on a new course, cutting through the waves as fast as a swordfish. And there, in the distance, I saw it.

A dark peak that burst from the horizon.

An island.

30

A Better World

It began with the giggling servants in the steam-filled kitchens of the palace, then made its way by courier to the grand houses of the bankers and lawyers. It was draped out of windows with the morning's wet clothes, rising in the markets with the smell of sizzling fat, whispered politely in the libraries of the Academy. It echoed through the mines and cascaded down the steeply stacked streets of the Shambles to be hurled from the docks out to sea, yelled from one ship to the next:

Loren was to become Royal Successor.

The palace became a hive of constant business as servants prepared for the Festival of Life. It was to start with a massive feast, at which Kate would mark Loren as the next Vessel in the Ritual of Succession. Servants scrubbed every inch of the palace, from the bannisters to the bird cages.

Sculptors chiselled new statues of Loren to decorate the Divine Hall, while seamstresses sewed banners in the gold of his family crest.

The only person in the palace who had not been given anything to do, it seemed, was Ellie. This suited her fine, and the workshop buzzed and clanked as she tinkered away at her latest invention, while Seth sat silently in one corner, staring into space.

'Why don't you go and see Viola?' Ellie said, rubbing sweat from her forehead. 'It might be good to get some fresh air.'

Seth said nothing.

'You could go fishing with her? You'd love that.'

But Seth just hugged himself tighter, staring forlornly at the ground. Ellie picked an apple from the fruit bowl, leaving it at his side in the hope he might eat something.

The door creaked, and Ellie turned to find Kate hovering by the door. 'Hello,' she said bashfully.

'Um, hi.' Ellie's stomach squirmed. She'd not seen Kate since her humiliation in the Felicia Markets. 'I . . . I didn't think you'd . . . I mean, I'm glad –' She swallowed. 'It's nice to see you.'

Kate smiled weakly. 'You wanted to talk to me? Oh, hello, Seth. Is something the matter?'

Seth's mouth twitched.

'He's just, um, been a little under the weather,' Ellie explained.

Kate nodded and looked around the workshop. Ellie watched her, hot nerves rattling in her chest. 'Oh look – it's your old coat,' said Kate, clutching a flap of Ellie's grey coat.

'I was mending it,' Ellie said hurriedly. 'Not that I don't love the coat you made me. It's just so I have something warm for the winter.'

Kate frowned. 'It never gets cold here. Not like where you come from,' she added, and Ellie felt a stab of guilt.

'Kate, I'm . . . I'm so sorry. About the other day.'

'It's not your fault. What are these?' Kate asked, pointing to the odd flaps of silk that had been attached to the coat, and two long cords trailing from the arms.

'Oh, I, uh, I thought it needed relining,' Ellie said. This wasn't true, but the real reason was too embarrassing. 'Here, I have something to show you.'

She stepped over to a cart-sized bundle in the centre of the workshop, draped with an oil-stained sheet. She pulled the sheet aside with a flourish, revealing an immense, turtle-shaped contraption with leather flippers.

Kate's nose twitched. 'What is it?'

'A boat that can swim underwater!' Ellie announced. 'That way we can leave Shipwreck Island without anyone noticing us. I even know an island we can escape to – Seth and I slept there one night on our way here. It has fewer wolves than some of the others.'

Kate barely spared the boat a glance, instead inspecting the cages of mice and the vials of ground-up exotic plants.

'Kate?' Ellie said.

'I hope you've stopped eating this stuff,' Kate said stiffly, examining the brightly coloured vials.

'Mostly,' said Ellie, rubbing the back of her head.

'*Mostly?*'

'I've only been taking a *little* bit,' Ellie admitted, fidgeting awkwardly with her sling. 'To help my arm heal. Not enough that it turns my eyes red like before. Well, not *bright* red, anyway. But about the boat –'

'It was this one, wasn't it?' Kate said, picking up a vial of blood-red powder. 'I'm confiscating it for your own good. You don't know what long-term effects it might have.'

Ellie frowned but didn't argue. 'Now listen, I thought we could go tonight. Viola and her dad will help –'

'I'm not leaving, Ellie,' said Kate, pocketing the vial.

Ellie blinked. 'But you have to. If you make Loren your successor tomorrow, he'll have no more use for you. He'll kill you, Kate. You know he will. You can't go through with this.'

'If I don't, he'll tell everyone that I'm a lie.'

'You'd rather *die* than have people know you're not really a Vessel?'

Kate balled her hands into fists. 'I am not leaving this island, Ellie. I'll never abandon my people. Never.'

Ellie's eyes prickled. 'But –'

'Please, I don't want to talk about this. Why don't we build something together? Like we used to.'

'Oh,' said Ellie, feeling a tiny flutter of warmth in her chest. 'Well, you could help me put the finishing touches on the boat. Even if you don't . . . want to use it.'

'Actually, I was hoping to make something simpler. I've always wanted to learn to cook, you see. I thought we could make some sort of oven, one that you can turn on with a flick of a switch. For cooking things.'

Ellie's shoulders sagged. 'All right,' she said. 'Well, my mum had plans for a stove that was powered by burning gas. I think I can remember –'

'If possible,' Kate grinned, 'I'd prefer it doesn't explode spectacularly.'

Ellie smiled too, unable to stop herself. They set to work, cutting up squares of metal and fixing bolts into place. Seth sat in total silence, and occasionally Kate would glance worriedly at him then give Ellie a searching look. Ellie would just shrug. By five o'clock, they'd built a gas stove that reliably failed to explode, though it did make an odd smell, like burning dust.

Kate used it to cook pancakes for dinner, tossing them into the air, and they both laughed hysterically when she launched one with such force that it stuck to the ceiling. They sat together on the floor, eating the not-so-well-done pancakes with their fingers and a jar of fig jam. Kate declared the stove a complete success, then laid the last three pancakes by Seth's side.

'I hope you feel better soon,' she said, and Seth gave a small, grateful nod. After checking that the stove had cooled, Kate carried it in both arms to the door.

'Wait,' Ellie said hurriedly. 'Do you want to stay a bit longer? We could, um, we could play that game where we throw things at each other?'

Kate smiled sadly. 'That's not really a game for a Queen, Ellie,' she said, and turned to the door. 'I must go. Tomorrow, during the banquet, you will stay in here, under guard. I won't let Loren hurt you again.'

'*Wait*,' Ellie said, following her to the door. 'Please – leave with me, Kate. It's not worth staying. It's too dangerous!'

Kate stared at Ellie for a long moment. 'My people need me, Ellie.'

She left, and Ellie slumped down next to Seth. Her heart was like an anchor in her chest.

'I'm sorry,' Seth whispered.

They sat side by side in silence, Ellie listening to the ticking of the clock, counting down to the Festival of Life. Occasionally she glanced at Seth. Though he was still, Ellie felt she could almost hear his thoughts, tumbling and crashing like waves. She rested her hand on his.

'Seth, I know what it's like to blame yourself for something. But the shame will eat you up, if you let it.'

Seth pulled his hand away. 'This is different,' he said. 'Your brother's death wasn't your fault. I caused the Drowning.'

'We don't know for sure what happened. There's a lot in this world we don't understand. Even if it was your powers that caused it, that doesn't mean you wanted it to happen.'

'You saw what I did on the beach. I'm . . . I'm no better than the Enemy.'

Ellie felt a jolt of anger. She rose to her knees and stared into Seth's sullen eyes. 'Listen to me, you are *nothing* like the Enemy.'

Seth blinked, and sudden tears tumbled down his cheeks. 'I don't want this power, Ellie. I . . . I don't want to be a god.'

'I know,' said Ellie, sitting back down. 'And I don't want to be a Vessel. But we don't get to decide that.'

She let out another long sigh, staring up at the ceiling. This time, Seth put his hand on hers. He squeezed it, then winced and grabbed at his head. He took a shuddering breath.

'Seth? What is it?'

'It's Varu and Leila. They're in trouble. They're in . . .' He winced again. 'Pain.'

'That happened a long time ago,' Ellie said softly.

Seth gritted his teeth. 'No, it's happening *now*,' he said. 'I can . . . I can feel them in the sea. The memories. There are people hurting . . . always. Then, now, over and over and over again. It won't *end*.' He looked at Ellie, his face wet. 'And I'm part of it.'

Ellie pulled Seth into a tight hug. His breathing came in ragged bursts.

'Seth,' said Ellie, resting her head on his shoulder, 'please don't give up. We *have* to hope that we can create a better world than the one we have.'

'But you tried to make this island better, and they wouldn't let you.'

'So we'll keep trying,' said Ellie, pulling back and pressing her forehead to his. 'I nearly gave up once before, but you and Anna showed me that hope is always there, if you look for it. There *will* be a better world.'

'What better world? Where?'

'The one we'll make. It's there, Seth, I know it.'

Seth shook his head. 'I can't see it.'

'Well I *can*,' Ellie said defiantly.

He nodded, though didn't seem sure. He took a deep breath, some of the tension easing out of him. For a long time they sat there, and Ellie listened to the steady rise and fall of Seth's breathing.

'Your turn,' said Ellie, with a furtive smile.

Seth looked at her, then understanding dawned in his eyes. He stared at a flickering candle for a moment, thinking.

'I . . . I hope that . . . we'll find a new little island to live on. Where we can build you a workshop. Where I can have a boat to go out fishing in, and make us dinner. Where Anna and the orphans can come live with us.

Where nobody will chase us, and where the sea will be calm.' Seth closed his eyes. 'So calm we can hear the whales sing at night.'

Ellie closed her eyes too, and pictured it all, until she could almost feel the gentle breeze on her face and the sand beneath her feet. She reached into her pocket, pulled out her penknife, and carved an S into the side of a workbench, scoring a single line beneath it.

'You win.'

Seth smiled.

They sat together as the clock ticked into night. Eventually, Seth got to his feet. 'I think I'll go for a walk,' he said, putting on his shoes. 'Get some fresh air.'

'Do you want me to come with you?'

'No. You've helped enough. See you back at the Oak.'

He left the workshop, and Ellie felt immediately smaller without him. She stared at the new underwater boat, and her hand strayed to a hammer, consumed by a desire to smash it to tiny pieces. She'd been so sure Kate would come with them, but now that hope seemed so foolish, so childish, so embarrassing. She groaned, and felt more alone than ever.

She heard footsteps, and Seth put his head back round the door. He'd pulled on his green cardigan, and looked vaguely troubled.

'Ellie, I had an idea.' He stifled a cough, and Ellie worried he'd caught a chill from lying on the workshop floor.

'Maybe you should tell Kate about me. About what I can do. Maybe then she won't feel so powerless?'

Ellie thought about this, then shook her head. 'No. No we shouldn't — it's not safe for anyone else to know. Even Kate. They might not understand. They might think you're the Enemy again.'

Seth nodded. 'Okay.' He coughed. 'Are you sure?'

'I'm sure,' she said, and Seth shrugged and left the room. Ellie paced the workshop, trying to clear some of the clutter from the floor, her mind churning. She heard a persistent dripping, and worried that one of her chemical bottles had fallen over.

'A better world,' hissed a voice.

The bandaged child was sitting on a workbench, scratching at a leaky patch on its arm, dripping blood on to the floor. Its head was bent at an odd angle. Ellie turned away, deliberately ignoring it as she picked up a wrench and a jar of nails from the ground.

'You don't really believe that, do you?' The child grinned, blood pooling between its teeth. 'You thought *this* island would be a better world, and now look at it. Look at Kate. She's nothing more than Loren's puppet. Nothing but an empty —' the child licked its lips — '*vessel* for Loren's power. And soon, he'll have no need for her at all.'

The words were like the vicious stabs of a knife into Ellie's stomach. The child put both hands to its head, cracking it back into position. When it spoke again, its voice was stronger.

'He *will* kill her.'

'I . . .' Ellie stammered. 'I can stop – I can –'

'No,' said the child, sliding off the workbench and stepping towards her. 'You can't. You've failed. And if you don't ask for my help soon, you will lose her forever.'

Ellie closed her eyes, and pictured her brother. 'Finn,' she said.

The Enemy cried out, lurching backwards in a swirl of bandages, and vanished.

The warmth inside her cooled too soon, as the thoughts of her brother faded. She screamed in frustration, launching the jar across the workshop, where it exploded in a shower of glass, nails raining down on the floorboards. She curled her hands into fists, hating the Enemy for its very existence. Hating that it had made her its Vessel, and hurt her, and her friends, and so many people before them.

Hating that she had no choice but to ask for its help.

The Festival of Life

The Festival of Life was to start with a sumptuous feast in the Divine Hall of the palace. There would be five lavish courses, including a special cake, the eating of which would mark Loren as the Royal Successor. After that, Kate was to tour the island, pretending to cure diseases, with actors that Loren had no doubt blackmailed into secrecy.

The clock struck seven, and Ellie tied her hair back and changed into a white shirt and black skirt. She stuffed a pillow inside the lilac coat Kate had given her, laying it across the workshop floor, sticking yellow straw above the collar. Then, she threw a flash-bang at the wall.

It exploded with a *CRACK*, and the workshop door flew open. A Warden clattered inside, falling to his knees beside Ellie's coat.

'Oh no! Ms Stonewall, what happened to you?'

Ellie leapt from behind a cupboard and pelted through the door, locking it from the outside with the new bolt she'd attached the night before. She heard the Warden hammering his fists on the door as she raced along the corridor and up into the palace.

The Divine Hall was a sweltering mass of puffy sleeves and floppy hats, as nobles milled around, shaking hands and searching for their allotted seats. Four long mahogany tables were strewn with flowers of pure white and blood red, little golden basins for the washing of hands, and tall silver candlesticks already nesting in mounds of wax. The fifth table at the far end was perpendicular to the others, with two empty wooden thrones in the middle.

Ellie kept her back as straight as possible and tried to hide her limp as she joined a line of servants delivering jugs of water. She ducked from the line and between two nobles, who were taking in the Divine Hall's grandeur with theatrical gasps.

'Look at those silk tablecloths! Loren's outdone himself — you know I heard he provided all the flowers.'

'And the food too! He's really brought us back from the brink of disaster.'

It wasn't just the nobility who were present. There'd been a special lottery, and people from all over the island had been invited to share in the occasion – farmers and tailors and musicians and innkeepers.

'This is actually my third time in the palace,' Molworth was proudly telling the noblewoman to his right, who seemed disgusted to be seated next to someone who wasn't a noble, or even an adult. 'I'm extremely important.'

'*Molworth*,' Ellie hissed, ducking down at his side.

'Ellie? Why are you dressed like the servants?'

'*Shh!*' said Ellie. 'Act like I'm not here.'

Soon, every seat in the chamber was filled, save for the two thrones. A band played in the gallery above, a jaunty melody of cellos and violins. Guests muttered excitedly as the first dish was set before them: a single octopus tentacle, soaked black in squid ink and curled in a question mark upon a bed of pickled red cabbage.

'Young lady, what are you doing down there?' said an old nobleman to Molworth's left.

'Oh, just mopping up,' said Ellie, taking Molworth's napkin and dabbing the floor. 'This boy is *very* messy.'

Up and down the table, people slurped at tentacles, spraying squid ink on their napkins and faces. Ellie looked around, wondering why the Enemy hadn't appeared yet.

The Seven Sentinels stood before the great double doors. They stamped their feet once, and servants heaved the doors open.

And there were Kate and Loren.

Loren was dressed in a purple robe, his golden hair plaited into the shape of a crown. Perched in his hair was a violet glass bird. He reached for one of Kate's hands, but she clasped both firmly behind her back.

Kate's hair curled out in two great black tendrils behind her head, like horns. A circlet of silver was balanced on her forehead, her face decorated with swirls of white and purple make-up. Ellie marvelled that even on this day she somehow stood tall.

She wished she could reach out to her.

The guests stood, drowning out the music with their hearty applause. Kate drifted like a phantom between the tables, not meeting anyone's eye.

'It's Her,' Molworth whispered, watching Kate with wide, tear-filled eyes. 'It's *Her*,' he said, and clapped both hands to his mouth. Ellie did not think she'd ever seen someone so truly happy.

'Gosh, She looks awful,' whispered the old man next to Ellie. 'Like Her mother before She died. It's a good thing She's naming Her successor now, before She gets any worse.'

Loren stood in front of his throne, beaming and holding his hands out to the crowd, his cheeks rosy pink.

'My friends, welcome to my feast!' he cried. 'Well, well. Here we are, here we are!' He rubbed his hands together. 'Thank you for celebrating it with us – really, I couldn't be happier to have you here to witness my ascension to –' he paused for effect, biting his lip – 'Royal Successor!'

The explosion of applause was deafening. Noblemen punched their fists in the air – some even climbed on to their seats, shoving fingers in their mouths to whistle.

Loren waved them all down. 'There will be time for more speeches later, but first there's the matter of a feast, and, dare I say it –' he tilted his head forward and touched the tip of his nose – 'a special cake.'

There were more titters of laughter. A flicker of disgust crossed Kate's face.

'Why does he need a cake to become Royal Successor?' said Ellie.

Molworth tutted. '*Outer islanders*. Can't have a Succession Ritual without eating cake. It's tradition.'

'Laughter aside,' Loren was saying, 'I would like you all to know, here and now, that I could not be more delighted to be selected by Our Great Divinity as Her Successor. So that, should anything unexpected befall Our Beloved Queen, I will be here to take up the mantle of King. And now.' Loren squeezed Kate's arm, making her flinch. 'I believe Kate . . . haha.' He grimaced. 'I'm sorry, the *Queen* has a few words to say about me.'

Ellie tried to catch her eye, to mouth to her that she was going to fix things. But Kate was looking at her knees, her hands fidgeting under the table. She stood up, pulling one trembling hand inside the sleeve of her robe.

'Hello,' she said, in a distant voice. 'It is . . . so nice to see you all.' She cleared her throat. 'I couldn't be happier on this holy day.'

She forced a smile, and the crowd clapped and stamped their feet once more. Kate sat down, and her smile fell to nothing.

A second course was brought out: green soup with chicken heads floating in it. Molworth stared in disgust. 'I don't like rich-people food. Where are the oranges?'

'It's a real delicacy,' said the old man next to him, swallowing a chicken head whole.

Molworth rubbed his chin thoughtfully. 'It feels strange to be eating like this, when the rest of the island's going hungry.'

A third course arrived, and a fourth. Ellie watched Kate staring blankly ahead and occasionally muttering to herself. Loren and the nobles chatted as if she wasn't there, except when Loren pointed to her, like some expensive painting he'd won at auction.

Ellie rubbed her chest, her throat dry. She couldn't bear to do nothing as her friend was humiliated.

'Then it's time,' hissed a voice.

Ellie looked up. The bleeding child was sitting among the band above, legs dangling off the gallery. 'It's time to save her,' it said. 'I will take Loren away – I don't even have to kill him, if you don't want me to. Then you and Kate can get back to saving the island, and all can be peaceful again. For a time.'

Ellie swallowed. The violins struck up a rousing, upbeat tune. Every eye turned to the door.

'Oh, the cake!' said the old nobleman, bouncing in his chair.

A large platter was carried in by two servants. On it were six fat tiers of fruit cake, nestled in a bed of flowers, its surface covered with slices of strawberry and pineapple and nectarine. The servants set it down in front of Loren. He grinned brightly, picking up a knife. 'Time for the cake, and a song, I think!'

'And then our new successor!' yelled a noble from the back.

'Well, precisely,' said Loren. 'Speaking of which, would you do the honours, my Queen?'

He passed Kate the knife. She held it, poised over the cake, then sank the point in deep, cutting a narrow slice from one side.

'When Loren takes the first bite,' the old man whispered excitedly, 'he officially becomes Her successor! Of course, I *do* love the Queen, but I think Loren will be even better, don't you?'

Molworth snorted. 'No one could be better than the Queen.'

Kate lifted the slice on to a gold-rimmed plate. Ellie's fingers were sweaty, her heart quivering like a skittish bird. She glanced up to the gallery, and found the bleeding child watching her expectantly.

Kate presented the plate to Loren. A droplet rolled down her cheek, of sweat or tears, Ellie wasn't sure.

Ellie drew a tremulous breath and opened her mouth, to whisper her request to the Enemy.

Kate looked into Loren's eyes. A tiny smile crossed her lips.

The doors of the dining hall crashed open and a Warden stumbled in, a wild look in his eye.

'What is the meaning of this?' one nobleman yelled in outrage.

'Blasphemy! How dare you interrupt this great occasion!'

'Your Divinity!' the Warden cried. 'Forgive me, but I have urgent news.'

Loren rose from his throne. 'My friend, you are interfering with a holy ritual. Whatever this matter is, it can be resolved later.'

'My Queen,' said the Warden. 'We have apprehended a man. He . . . he . . .'

'What is it?' said Kate softly. 'Speak, my subject.'

The Warden took a deep breath. 'He says he's from the *Enemy's City.*'

Screams tore the air as men and women scraped backwards in their chairs. Ellie felt acid rise into her throat.

'Throw him in the dungeons!' roared one noble.

'Kill him!' cried another.

'My friends,' said Loren, 'be seated. We shall deal with this matter. No agent of the Enemy should be allowed anywhere near Our Beloved Queen. I suggest –'

'Bring him in,' said Kate, her voice filling the room. Ellie stared at her in surprise. She was so relaxed, like she'd expected the interruption.

'My Queen, I don't think this is wise –' Loren spluttered.

'My friends,' said Kate, rising from her throne, wearing a gentle smile. 'What a golden opportunity for Loren to prove he has what it takes to be our Royal Successor.' Her smile broadened. 'Do you think he can protect us from this evil man?'

'YES!' the old noble cried at the top of his lungs. 'Loren! Loren!'

Others around the hall took up the chant, and soon the walls reverberated with the cry.

'Now, friends,' said Loren. 'I am grateful for your support, but –'

He winced as his voice was drowned beneath the clamour. He turned to Kate, hissing something in her ear. Kate's smile did not waver.

Two more Wardens stepped inside, carrying a man between them. Ellie stood, trying to see through the crowd of guests clambering over their chairs to get a better look. She clutched her chest.

Hargrath looked even worse than he'd done when they'd found him in Loren's prison. The skin of his face was like paper, so tightly stretched Ellie could make out the shadow of his skull. He staggered beneath the weight of his coat, staring at the wall of faces surrounding him. They booed and hissed like he was the villain in a play.

The Wardens thrust Hargrath before Loren and Kate, the Seven Sentinels forming a line between him and the Queen. The hall fell silent.

'Very well,' said Loren, straightening up and glaring down at Hargrath. 'As an agent of the Enemy, I declare that you shall be executed immediately. *Sentinels*, take him away.'

But the Seven did nothing. Kate narrowed her eyes at the massive, broken figure before her.

'Why did you come here, stranger?' she said. 'Why did the Enemy send you to our island?'

Hargrath made a strange noise, halfway between a snarl and a whimper. 'I do *not* take orders from the Enemy. I am a member of the Most Holy Order of Inquisitors. I *hunt* the Enemy's Vessel.'

There were murmurs and whispers around the hall.

'We've heard enough,' said Loren, his cheeks now bright red. 'Take him away! He's clearly deranged.'

A noblewoman stood up, her face pale with fright. 'If he's hunting the Enemy's Vessel, then why did he come here?'

'My friends, really.' Loren held up his hands. 'We cannot trust a man from the Enemy's City to tell the truth. Everyone knows the Enemy is a master of deception and lies.'

Kate leaned forward, looking at Hargrath with a kind smile. 'Answer the question,' she said softly. 'Why did you come here?'

Hargrath's mouth twisted with hate. 'I followed the Enemy's Vessel.'

There was a moment's silence, then a hundred shrieks pierced Ellie's eardrums. She sank lower behind Molworth's chair, her skin flooding with ice. Was Hargrath about to reveal her true identity to everyone? Would Kate let him?

'If you followed the Enemy's Vessel,' Kate said, 'why haven't you caught them yet?'

Hargrath shivered, his face contorting with shame. 'Because I was prevented from performing my holy duty!' he spat. 'I was . . . captured.'

A horrible silence sucked at the chamber. All eyes were fixed on Hargrath.

'Now, friends, enough of this,' said Loren. 'You are letting yourselves get caught up in a fantasy.'

There were sharp *shush*es from around the hall, and Loren staggered back, as if no one had ever told him to be quiet before.

'Who captured you?' cried a woman.

Hargrath's head tilted upward. His red-ringed eyes narrowed. He lifted his arm, and pointed at Loren.

Everyone began talking at once.

Loren raised his hands. 'Friends, friends!'

'Is this true, Loren?' snorted a nobleman, standing up so quickly his wig fell off.

'Of course not, my friends,' said Loren. 'I would never have dealings with an agent of the Enemy's City – I would have turned him over for Royal Judgement! This man is clearly deranged, or perhaps an actor paid to defame me. I am not without jealous rivals, my friends.'

There was more murmuring and snorts of disapproval. Kate held up one finger, and the room fell silent.

'Why would Loren imprison you?' she said. 'What did he want?'

Hargrath shook, looking at Loren in fury. 'He wanted to know the identity of the Enemy's Vessel.'

A high-pitched ringing whined in Ellie's ears. Her vision went cloudy. She stared at Hargrath, her lips trembling. At any moment he would say her name.

'Why?' Kate asked.

'So he could kill her,' Hargrath said. He took a step towards Kate. 'She's dead.'

'*Dead!*' said Loren. 'She's not dead, she –'

Loren's eyes bulged, and Ellie realized he'd trapped himself – he couldn't admit knowing who the Vessel was without revealing he'd known about Hargrath this whole time.

'All right, fine!' he announced. 'You've found me out. I used this man to learn the identity of the Enemy's Vessel, so I could kill her. I didn't wish to court the glory – I am a humble man, after all. But I single-handedly fought and vanquished the Enemy, and now our island is safe.'

Kate turned to Loren, her expression cool. 'You cannot kill the Enemy, just its Vessel,' she said. 'There is only one person in the world with the power to destroy the Enemy, and that is me.' She faced the hall. 'My friends, you know the nature of the Great Enemy. As with all gods, when its Vessel is destroyed, its spirit searches for a new one. Loren has killed the Enemy's Vessel, so now its spirit is free, on *our* island. Soon, it will find another Vessel with which to wreak destruction upon us. Far from saving us, Loren has *endangered* us with his stupidity.'

There were moans of agreement. One man stood up and booed.

'Now, please, friends,' Loren stammered, licking his lips. His voice was hoarse. 'Please –'

Ellie glanced at Kate, who was shaking her head in theatrical disappointment. As the hall jeered at Loren, Ellie saw Kate's right hand leave the sleeves of her robe, ever so briefly, to hover over Loren's goblet of water.

'The Enemy, on our island!' cried a man, digging his hands into his hair.

'Friends,' Kate announced, raising her arms. 'I know how frightened you must be. Loren was foolish, yes. But know this: we will root out the Enemy's new Vessel, wherever he may lurk. I am your Queen. I will protect you.'

Panic turned to hesitant smiles, as the whole hall gazed at Kate. A man stood up in his chair.

'Praise Her!' he cried.

'Praise Her!' said another.

'PRAISE HER!' Molworth roared at the top of his lungs.

Ellie's heart thudded in her jaw. She tried to catch Kate's eye, to tell her to stop. Kate didn't understand what she was unleashing: she couldn't let fear of the Enemy reign across her island, like it did in the City.

'Thank you, friends,' said Kate. 'And do not judge Loren *too* harshly – he acted only out of a desire to protect the island.' Kate placed a hand on Loren's shoulder. 'However, I think we shall postpone naming him Royal Successor for a time. Under my tutelage, he will learn to do better, won't you, Loren?'

Loren swallowed. 'I, um, I . . .'

'Now, there is much work to be done,' Kate said briskly. 'Let's finish the Festival so we can begin the hunt for the Enemy's Vessel.' She pointed to Hargrath. 'This man has done us a great service, though he may be from the Enemy's City. Take him to the kitchens and see that he is properly fed. A solemn toast!' Kate declared, picking up her goblet in one hand, reaching under the table with the other. 'My friends – to the Enemy's end!'

There was a loud cheer and more chants of 'Praise Her!' Loren nodded uncomfortably, his golden hair in disarray.

'Yes, to the Enemy's end,' he croaked. He lifted his goblet and drained it in one, then slumped back in his throne.

Kate smiled, and for a moment her queenly mask fell and she was a girl again, cheeks flushed with excitement. Ellie noticed an odd smell, like burning dust.

'Now let us put this behind us and be merry!' Kate cried, clapping her hands together over the great cake.

There was a tiny *pop*, and berries and flecks of nut sprayed from the top, leaving a hole.

A brown head poked out, blinking its beady eyes. The dinner guests gazed in shock.

'Is that . . . a rat?' Molworth said.

Pop.

A second rat burrowed from the cake. Then a third, and a fourth. Then ten, all at once, the top of the cake splitting open in an eruption of strawberries and oranges and tiny pink noses and tails. The rats tumbled down the side, skittering across the tabletop. One man fell backwards off his seat.

And as the rats feasted on icing sugar, the candlelight bounced off a glistening, wriggling mass spewing from the hole they had left. A hundred fat, purple earthworms.

Kate staggered back, watching in terror as the worms spilled out over the top of the cake, as if they were fleeing from something beneath them.

Something hot.

'What's happening?' Loren shrieked, trying to scrabble up on his throne.

'Stop it!' said Kate, looking at Loren. 'How are you doing this?'

Loren gaped at her. 'I'm not doing anything!'

Kate put a hand to her mouth. 'Oh . . . oh no,' she gasped. 'No, it can't be.'

She raised a hand, pointing a trembling finger at Loren. 'That's why you did it. That's why you killed the Enemy's Vessel. So you could become its *new* Vessel.'

Fresh wails pierced the air, and guests fled their seats, gathering up their skirts and gowns and rushing to the other side of the room. Loren frowned at them, confused. But they could see what he could not.

Loren's skin had turned pale as snow. His eyes as red as blood.

His mouth opened and closed frantically. 'H-how, how *dare* you accuse me, you foolish *child*. These are lies, and I won't stand for them! My friends, let me tell you the truth about our Queen –'

Molworth leapt up on to his chair. 'The Enemy!' he shrieked. 'The Enemy has come!'

'He's the Enemy!' cried a nobleman. 'The Enemy's Vessel!'

'THE ABOMINATION IS HERE!'

'Protect the Queen!'

There was a thunder of clattering metal as a Sentinel vaulted over the table, grabbing Loren by the throat and raising him high in the air. Loren choked and batted uselessly at the armoured warrior, as nobles grabbed his arms and legs, rolling their sleeves over their hands to avoid touching his skin.

'I've got him! I've got him!'

'Don't worry, my Queen!'

In seconds, Loren was pinned to the floor by a hissing mass of frills and feathers, gagged with a large orange Molworth had produced from his pocket.

Kate climbed on to the table, glaring down at him. Ellie shivered, a squirming feeling in her stomach. She couldn't say what it was exactly, until Kate spoke, and Ellie realized that, for the first time, she was afraid of her.

'Take the Enemy's Vessel to the dungeons,' Kate said. 'At sunrise, he shall be executed before the eyes of the entire island. Then, I shall use my divine power to annihilate the Enemy that festers inside him, so that our island will be safe forever.'

The crowd cheered and Kate put a hand to her chest. 'Though know that I do this with a heavy heart, my subjects,' she said. 'For if I destroy the Enemy, I will have no power left to perform the Festival of Life. I ask you to decide – would you rather have the Festival of Life, or would you prefer I destroy the foul god that has tormented humanity for millennia?'

'THE ENEMY! DESTROY THE ENEMY!'

Loren and his jailers surged from the hall, pursued by the remainder of the guests. The doors swung closed with a crash, leaving Ellie and Kate alone. Rats picked at the cake crumbs. Worms wriggled off the tablecloth. Kate reached under the table, and Ellie heard the tiny click of the gas stove being turned off.

Kate sat down on her throne. She let out a long, satisfied sigh, stretching out her legs. Ellie watched her in astonishment.

'There,' Kate said. 'That was a better story than his, don't you think?'

Leila's Diary

4,822 days aboard the *Revival*

Huge waves rose around us and touched the sky, as the Ark cleaved through the sea.

'Varu, you need to slow us down!' I cried. If he didn't, I worried we would smash straight into the island.

But Varu was somewhere else. His eyes were blue all over and sounds were drifting out of his mouth, like the muffled screams of other people. I remembered what the Crone had said, how Varu could die if his mind got trapped inside the sea. I shook him but it did nothing.

The people on the deck stared at Varu in horror.

'It's the Enemy!'

'No!' I cried. 'Don't you see? Look – he's taking us to that island! We'll be saved!'

The island grew taller on the horizon every second, like a widening rip in the sky. The crowd gasped, and some began to cheer. Then the new Ark-Captain burst through them, swinging a big butcher's cleaver, his face veiny with fury.

'The Enemy must die!' he howled.

I jumped between him and Varu, but he bashed me aside. I fell across the deck and white blotches danced across my eyes. I looked up, and saw the cleaver fall.

A tiny bundle of rags flew from the crowd and grabbed the Ark-Captain's arm, and suddenly it wouldn't move. He growled, baring what teeth he had left, then swung a punch with his free fist. The Crone grabbed this arm too. I didn't know how she could be so strong. Varu moaned in pain. I tried to get to my feet to help him but the whole Ark shook and everyone fell to the deck.

The Ark-Captain reached Varu first, lifting him up by his neck, carrying him to the rail. I screamed and ran at them, but there was a huge *CRACK*, like the world ending, and I fell over again. There were shards of wood everywhere and people were crying out for each other.

The Ark-Captain still had Varu in his grip, ready to toss him overboard. There was a thick, wet thud, and the Ark-Captain dropped Varu, a confused look in his eyes. He tried to turn his head over his shoulder, like a dog searching for its own tail. The handle of the butcher's cleaver was sticking out of his back.

Then I saw the Crone, the countless lines on her face stretched in hatred. She leapt at him, snarling and wrestling him to the ground. He cried shrilly and pushed back at her and they both tumbled once, twice, and rolled over the side of the Ark.

The New Enemy

'You had this all planned,' said Ellie, her tiny voice echoing through the hall. 'Why didn't you tell me?'

Kate dabbed a finger in the cake crumbs on the table, unfazed by the worms wriggling by her plate. 'Oh, Ellie,' she said, 'I needed to focus on making sure it worked.'

'But I could have helped.'

'Ellie, it's *fine*. Loren is beaten, that's all that matters.' Kate grinned. 'Now we can get back to fixing the farms, and making my island whole again.'

Ellie stepped warily towards Kate, feeling strangely like she wasn't *allowed* to be near her any longer. 'You're not really going to have Loren executed, are you?'

Kate swung her legs over the arm of her throne, leaning back and closing her eyes. 'We'll see.'

'Please don't kill anyone.'

Kate opened one eye. 'Fine. If you insist. It was wonderful what I did, though, wasn't it? With the Inquisitor, and Loren's eyes, and the cake? I even sawed a square out of the table, so the stove would fit.'

'I don't know if *wonderful* is the word I'd use. It was certainly clever. I was so worried, though. I wish you'd told me what you were up to.'

'Just like you told me how you came from the Enemy's City?'

Ellie swallowed. 'We've both kept secrets from each other.'

'Yes, Ellie,' said Kate, sitting up in her throne. 'I kept secrets from you. Because I'm the Queen, and I will do whatever I must to keep my people safe.'

Ellie looked down at the floor. 'For a moment, I thought Hargrath was going to tell everyone that he was hunting *me*. I thought maybe that was part of your plan.'

Kate's face softened. 'I'd never do anything to hurt you.'

A rat sniffed Ellie's bare ankle, while two others chased each other under the table, splashing through puddles of red wine.

'Is that true?' said Ellie.

'Of course, Ellie,' said Kate. 'It's my duty to protect my subjects.'

A splinter of pain lodged in Ellie's heart. A subject. Not a friend.

'You know, we could still leave the island. Go somewhere else, and never come back.'

Kate's eyes widened. 'What? After all we've done? Ellie, why would you say that?'

'Because, I'm . . . I'm frightened,' Ellie whispered.

'I'll be fine, Ellie. No need to worry about me.' Kate folded her legs underneath her. 'Now come on, let's put all this behind us. I need you by my side.'

Ellie chewed her lip. 'Do you want me by your side?'

'Of *course* I do. Now stop being so gloomy. Everything's fine.'

Kate squeezed Ellie's hand and nuzzled her head into Ellie's shoulder. Her hair smelled of honey. Ellie could feel her smile against her neck.

But Ellie's heart was empty. She stared at the ruin of the beautiful cake in front of her, and its rotten, worm-filled insides.

~

That night, Ellie tossed and turned in bed, and was still awake when the sun rose. She should have been delighted – Loren had been defeated, and could never harm Kate again. But she couldn't stop thinking of what Kate had said.

I will do whatever I must to keep my people safe.

'It's fine,' Ellie told herself. 'She didn't mean it.'

'You okay?' Seth mumbled from his bed by the window.

'Oh, sorry – I woke you up,' said Ellie.

Seth turned over. 'I wasn't sleeping. What's wrong?'

'I'm worried about Kate. I feel . . . like everything's not really finished.'

High above them, a bell clanged, its deep peals shaking the branches of the Vile Oak.

'What's that?' said Seth.

Ellie pulled on her coat. The sound awoke horrible memories of being chased through the streets of the City by the Inquisition. She wedged her feet in her shoes and hurried for the door, grabbing her cane on the way.

'Hold on – I'll come with you,' said Seth. 'It might not be safe.'

'No . . . no, it's fine,' she said. 'Kate told me she was going to do this – she's breaking the news about Loren to the rest of the island. But I need to be with her. To make sure she doesn't *actually* have him executed.'

There was a clatter along the branch outside and Viola hurtled through the door, clutching a trembling Archibald.

'What's all that ringing about?' she said.

Seth hopped over, putting a shoe on. 'We're going to the palace to see.'

'No, *I'm* going,' Ellie told him.

'But –' Seth protested.

'She can look after herself, Seth,' said Viola, with a glare.

'Stay out of this,' Seth snapped.

'Don't tell me what to do,' Viola said. 'Though I guess that comes naturally to your lot, doesn't it?'

'My lot?'

'Yeah. Wanting to rule over people.'

'I don't want to rule over anyone! Why are you acting so weird?'

Viola spun to face him. 'Because you should have told me! How can I trust you when you kept this secret from me?'

Seth blinked. 'How I can trust *you*? You won't even look me in the eye!'

'Oh, STOP IT!'

Ellie's cry silenced them both and sent Archibald racing under Seth's bed. She was surprised to find hot tears on her face.

'This is stupid. The two of you were *best* friends – why are you acting like this? Viola, Seth's the same person as before; he's not pretending to be a boy, he *is* a boy. A wonderful, foolish boy who probably should have explained his powers to you before now.'

'Ellie, are you okay?' said Viola. They were both staring at her in shock.

Ellie wiped the tears from her face. 'Don't give up on a good friendship. Please don't.'

'We won't,' said Viola, gripping her hand. 'It's good to argue sometimes. Gets it all out.'

'Ellie, it's okay,' said Seth, his eyes wide. 'It was just a stupid argument.'

Ellie felt they were only placating her. She grabbed a chair and shoved Seth into it. 'You two are going to sit and talk this through. I want to hear you laughing and joking by the time I get back.'

She left the two of them, still staring at her, stunned, and closed the door. She waited a few moments, until she heard them cheerfully shouting at each other, then left the Vile Oak, her shoulders a little lighter than they'd been before.

The morning sun painted the Shambles a pale blue. A man lay sprawled across the paving stones, an empty wine bottle in one hand. 'Is that – are those the Festival bells?'

'The Festival's been cancelled, you drunken slob,' said a woman from her doorstep. 'Didn't you hear? Loren is the Enemy's Vessel.'

The man's eyes bulged. 'The Enemy? Here on our island? Oh, God protect us.'

'She did,' the woman said proudly. 'She's imprisoned him.'

The man sagged in relief. 'Well, either way – I'm going to need more wine.'

Ellie hurried up the winding streets towards the Ark. A young man burst into an alley full of anxious families in dressing gowns. 'News from the palace! He's escaped. Loren has escaped!'

Men and women gasped and screamed, clutching babies protectively to their chests. 'The Enemy is loose!'

Ellie's heart plummeted. Who knew what Loren might try now, what viciousness he might attempt in his

362

desperation? She hobbled along Revelation Boulevard towards the doors of the palace, grateful when the Wardens opened them for her without question.

'Kate?' Ellie called, her voice echoing through the Grand Atrium. 'Where is the Queen?' she asked the first Warden she passed.

Kate's head appeared over the bannister, bright-faced and smiling for some reason, still wearing her clothes from the banquet. She waved cheerily.

'Come on up!'

Ellie followed Kate into the huge chamber of stuffed animals, empty of people but for two Sentinels guarding the door.

'Why are you so calm?' Ellie asked, gasping for breath. 'Loren's escaped!'

Kate's smile widened. 'No he hasn't. He's still in the dungeons.'

'Then why does everyone think he's escaped?'

Kate bit her lip, like a child caught in an act of mischief. 'Because I've started a rumour that he has.'

She walked over to a tall machine next to the snow leopard, which Ellie recognized as a printing press. Kate picked up a piece of paper, displaying it proudly.

THE ENEMY, LOREN, IS LOOSE. THE QUEEN SAYS: 'HIDE INDOORS WITH YOUR LOVED ONES.'

Ellie sat down in a chair beneath the flying squirrel, her leg aching from the climb. Kate watched her with an expectant, excitable look.

'I . . . don't understand,' said Ellie. 'Why would you do this?'

'Just *imagine*. If the people think the Enemy lurks among them, they'll want someone to protect them. And who better than a God-Queen?'

A sudden cold was born in the deepest part of Ellie's chest. She rose from her chair.

'No.'

Kate frowned. 'No?'

'You can't do that,' said Ellie. 'You don't understand what fear of the Enemy can do – it's almost as bad as the Enemy itself! It turns people against each other. It breeds suspicion and violence and hatred.'

Kate stroked her chin. 'Oh,' she said disappointedly. 'But don't you see? If the people don't need my protection, I'll seem weak, and men like Loren will keep trying to steal my power from me.'

'You can't use fear to control people.'

Kate scoffed. 'It's not like I'm *really* putting the Enemy among them.'

'That's not the point! If you do this, people will suffer.'

'People *have* suffered, Ellie. And if Loren had got his way, even more people would have suffered.'

Ellie took Kate's hand. 'Please, I'm begging you – don't do this. We'll find a better way. You and me.'

'Ellie, you know the truth.' Kate's eyes flicked around the room. 'I'm not really a Vessel,' she whispered. 'I don't have any real power. This is all I can do. You're making a fuss over nothing.'

'No, I'm not,' Ellie said, her hands clenching to fists. 'Don't you see you're being STUPID!'

Kate straightened up. 'Ellie, please. I know it's a lie, but it's the only way to keep things peaceful and settled.'

Ellie closed her eyes. Her mind raced for ideas: anything to convince Kate that she was wrong. Instead, she remembered Seth's offer from two nights before, as he'd stood in the workshop doorway in his green cardigan.

Maybe you should tell Kate about me . . . maybe then she won't feel so powerless?

'You do have power,' she said.

'No, Ellie, I don't.'

Ellie took a step towards her. 'If you want it, you do. You have Seth.'

Kate narrowed her eyes. 'What are you talking about?'

'He's a god.'

Kate opened her mouth to speak, then closed it again.

'Not a Vessel,' Ellie continued. 'He's a true god in physical form. The same god from Leila's diary. Varu. With him by your side, you *can* perform divine acts, and no one will ever doubt that you're a god. You don't need to spread rumours about the Enemy for people to trust you.'

Ellie's nails dug into her palms. She imagined a future in which Seth and Kate were friends, bonded by their powers, whether real or not. She imagined the three of them sitting at a table together in the palace gardens, a gentle breeze rustling the bushes and flowers around them. Viola and Molworth were there, and Anna too, and they ate pancakes Kate had made and Ellie drank in their laughter and it curled up warm and snug by her heart.

But the real Kate was silent, staring up at the ceiling. Beyond the flying squirrel was a purple bird made of amethyst, a miniature of the God-Bird in her bedchamber. She frowned at it.

'So all those tales about the sea behaving strangely lately were true? And that's why those whales rescued us from Loren's men. Seth . . . is Varu?'

Kate clenched her teeth, and Ellie realized she wasn't picturing the same happy scene as Ellie had been. She was not picturing anything like it at all.

'Well, we don't know for sure,' Ellie said, her stomach twisting. 'He's not, I mean, he's . . .'

'I . . . I think I would like you to bring him here,' said Kate, and the hairs on Ellie's neck stood up; Kate hadn't used her normal voice, but her deep, queenly one. 'Would you please do that for me, Ellie?'

Ellie stepped back towards the door. 'Actually, I don't think it's a good idea for him to get involved in all this. Forget I said anything. He's happy just fishing, really.'

'Bring him. We will . . .' Kate gave her a tight smile. 'We will discuss how I can use his power. For the good of the island.'

Ellie and Kate stared at each other for some time. 'Please?' Kate said, using her soft, real voice this time. 'He'll be safe.'

'Okay,' Ellie managed at last, and forced a cheerful expression on to her face. 'Yes, I will bring him here. I'll go and get him now. I'll be back as soon as I can.'

Kate smiled again, and Ellie stepped carefully from the room. She turned and offered a friendly wave. And as the door closed behind her, she tore down the staircase as fast as her leg would allow.

Seth

For a third time, Ellie checked over her shoulder to see if one of the Sentinels was following her. She snuck through the servants' quarters, hurried along cramped passageways, and stopped by her workshop door. She lingered there a moment, wondering if she had enough time, then rushed inside, pulling off her lilac coat. It was light as a shadow.

She threw it aside and picked up her mother's old coat from the workbench, running a finger along the new stitches in the lining. She pulled it on, its weight comforting upon her shoulders. She stuffed the pockets with smoke bombs and flash-bangs, then released Molworth's mice, noticing with a stab of pain the smear of spilled jam on the floor, from when she and Kate had eaten pancakes. She ran from the workshop and up the servants' staircase, out of the palace and into daylight.

'Ellie!'

She heard a stifled cough and saw Seth waiting at the corner of an alleyway, wearing his green cardigan and a look of caring concern.

'Seth!' she cried, feeling a wave of relief followed swiftly by panic. She glanced nervously back at the palace. 'We need to leave – we need to get away from the island, right now.' A sob rose in her throat and she gritted her teeth, pushing it back down. 'Come on!'

They bolted through empty streets. The colourful window shutters had all been fastened shut, and several washing lines had come untied, laundry fluttering forgotten against the brickwork. The Azalea Markets had been abandoned in a hurry – a seagull pecked at a pearl necklace, while a cat licked a puddle of melting cheese. The only sounds were dogs barking in the distance, and the palace bell, which would not stop ringing.

'It's the City,' Seth said. 'It's just like the City now.'

Ellie grimaced, taking a pained breath. The sea appeared beneath them in the gaps between rooftops, green-blue and inviting.

'Oh, Seth,' said Ellie. 'I've been so stupid. I know you had good intentions, but I should've known better – I should have guessed how she'd react.'

'What do you mean . . . good intentions?'

'When you suggested I tell Kate you're a god. Now she's desperate for your power. I'm worried she'll hurt you –

369

maybe even kill you – if she thinks your spirit might pass to her. If she thinks she can become a *real* Vessel.'

Seth slowed a little. 'Oh,' he said.

'It's all right,' Ellie added, putting a hand on his arm. 'We're going to get as far away from here as possible. You should go to the docks and explain things to Janssen and Viola, tell them we have to leave.'

'But what about you?'

'I just need to pick up some things from the Vile Oak,' said Ellie, thinking of Finn's drawing that she kept on the mantlepiece. Seth stifled a cough. 'But you're much faster than me – you should run ahead.'

'Ellie, you don't need anything from the Vile Oak,' said Seth.

'I do!' she said. 'Finn's drawing is there, of him and me and Anna. I *can't* leave it behind.'

Seth coughed again, a sore, ragged sound.

'Are you all right?' said Ellie, frowning.

Seth massaged his throat. 'Fine,' he croaked. 'Really. But if Kate knows about me, we need to leave right now.'

'The Oak's on the way to the docks, it's barely a detour,' she said, feeling a rising unease. 'Seth, you know how important that picture is to me – it's a piece of my brother.'

Seth let out a loud, hacking cough that shook his whole body and almost forced him to one knee. He rubbed at his mouth, and when he pulled his hand away, Ellie gasped.

Part of his cheek had peeled off, dangling in an odd, paper-like curl.

'S-Seth?' said Ellie. She took a step closer, inspecting the curl of skin. There was no blood underneath, only what appeared to be . . . fabric.

She stiffened. '*No.*'

Seth slapped the flap of skin back into place, grinning at her uncomfortably. 'Don't worry about that,' he said. 'Come on, let's get going!'

Ellie gripped her cane, feeling like she was about to fall through the paving stones beneath her.

'It was *you,*' she said. 'It was you who came back into the workshop the other night, after Seth had gone. Who told me to tell Kate about his powers. It was *you.*'

'Ellie, I . . . what are you talking about?'

'No. No!' Ellie smacked her head in anger. 'How could I have been so stupid? Wait . . .' The street spun round her as memories flashed past, her mind racing to fit the pieces together. 'That day I set off the bomb in the mine – the day I got taken to the palace – I saw Seth with a group of boys and girls, having fun without me. That's the whole reason I ran away, the whole reason I was anywhere *near* that mine in the first place! But Seth wasn't sitting with them, really, was he? Nobody was sitting with them. It was just you.'

'Of course it was me!' he said. 'Me – *Seth.* You're talking madness, Ellie!'

'And it was you who almost got us caught that night in Loren's mansion! And then, when Seth refused to come with me to the volcano, and we had that argument – I was just arguing with you!'

Ellie found she couldn't breathe. 'It was all you. Making me feel like Seth didn't care about me. Pushing me more and more towards Kate. It was even *your* bloody footprints that led me to her, the day we first met. You *wanted* me to be her friend.'

'Oh, Ellie,' Seth said, 'I really think you're letting your imagination get the better of you.'

A surge of anger throbbed through Ellie's veins. He looked at her with big doe eyes, still holding the loose piece of skin against his cheek.

'*Finn*,' Ellie whispered.

More skin peeled away, falling like ribbons to the paving stones. Frayed bandages spilled out from underneath, dripping with thick blood. Seth frantically grabbed at the coils of skin, trying to claw them back again. Ellie took a step towards him.

'FINN!' Ellie roared, letting her brother's memory fill her mind.

The Enemy hissed and the last of its skin fell away, revealing the bandaged child beneath. It writhed in a hideous dance before twisting in on itself, folding and collapsing until there was nothing left but the sound of Ellie's heavy breathing.

She felt sick. All this time, she'd thought the Enemy was too weak to hurt her, but it had found a way. And she'd been stupid enough to *let it*. Ellie rubbed tears from her cheeks, but more kept coming. A terrible realization was rising inside her. She glanced up at the tumbledown rows of the Shambles and spotted the Vile Oak.

'Seth!' she cried, breaking into a run. 'Please be okay, please be okay, Seth.'

Her foot caught on a broken paving stone, and she tripped on her bad leg and fell to her knees with a cry of pain.

'Ellie!'

Her heart leapt as she saw Viola and Molworth racing down the street towards her. Viola helped Ellie to her feet, picking up her cane.

'Where's Seth?' Ellie cried. 'Are you okay?' she added, noticing a nasty bruise on Viola's cheek, and Archibald trembling on her shoulder.

Viola's lips paled. 'The Seven came to the Vile Oak.'

'What?'

'No!' Molworth cried. He was clutching a little medallion of the Queen that hung from a chain round his neck, shivering.

'It *was* them, Molworth. You saw them.'

Molworth shook his head vehemently. 'It wasn't the Seven, it can't have been! They must have been imposters. The Queen would never do anything bad.'

'Don't be stupid,' said Viola. 'The Queen's not who you think she is.'

'She wouldn't,' said Molworth, stroking the medallion. 'She wouldn't.'

Ellie held a hand to her face, her lungs heaving too quickly for her to catch her breath. 'She's got Seth. What have I *done*?'

'Ellie, why does she want him?' said Viola.

Ellie felt hot tears dribble between her fingers. 'She knows he's Varu,' she whispered. 'She might hurt him. Maybe even kill him.'

'She WOULDN'T!' said Molworth. 'She's the Queen. She's a god. She's *good*.'

'She's just that girl Kate,' Viola told him. 'And she's taken Seth prisoner.'

'No, that's not the Queen,' Molworth said, closing his eyes. 'She's not the Queen,' he whispered. 'Not my Queen.'

'She *is*, Molworth,' said Viola, but he just turned away, eyes closed, whispering to the medallion in his hand.

'She's not. She's not. My Queen is good.'

Viola looked up at the Ark. 'Let's get the fishing clans – they won't have set sail yet. My dad can rally the sailors. We can rescue Seth.'

'No – people will get hurt.'

'*Seth* will get hurt, Ellie, if we don't do anything. Let's go to the docks.'

Ellie shook her head and touched her leg. 'I'll slow you down. I'm going to go to the palace. I have to try and . . . help Kate see sense.'

'All right. I'll bring as many sailors as I can.'

'Don't try to fight the Wardens or the Seven Sentinels. There's a secret entrance to the Ark in the abandoned butcher's shop on Leona Street. Take Molworth – he knows the inside of the palace by heart. He's obsessed with the place.'

Viola looked over her shoulder, to where Molworth sat on a wall, wiping his eyes.

'I'll talk to him,' she said, then gave Ellie a tight hug. 'Be careful, Ellie.'

'You too.'

Ellie limped up the street, glancing back to see Viola pressing Archibald into Molworth's hands, then sitting down next to him and hugging him close. Molworth stroked the kitten's ear, and gave a tiny smile.

~

Ellie's journey back to the palace took a lifetime. The streets were empty but for her, some cats and the occasional furtive, nervous face in a window. A newspaper fluttered across the paving stones.

THE ENEMY, LOREN, IS LOOSE. THE QUEEN SAYS: 'HIDE INDOORS WITH YOUR LOVED ONES.'

A cold shadow engulfed her, and Ellie looked up at the looming Ark. She crossed an empty street, passing the shop where she and Kate had once eaten their weight in honeyed nuts, then, heads full of sugar, attempted to skip-rope – in Ellie's case, unsuccessfully.

Ellie swallowed, forcing the memory down, down, down, carrying on towards the palace gates. The Wardens admitted her with a nod. Inside, the Great Atrium was illuminated by the new morning light, sunbeams stabbing through the many hundred windows. All that moved were glowing dust motes; there wasn't a person in sight. Not a sound but the hammering of Ellie's heart.

She climbed the stairs, and with every painful stab in her leg, a fresh, happy memory of Kate tormented her. At last, the double doors to Kate's chamber loomed before her. She took a long breath and held out her free arm, trying very hard to imagine another hand reaching to take hold of hers. And when she looked right she could almost see him: sandy blonde hair, green eyes, and a loving smile.

She nodded to her brother in gratitude, and wiped the tears from her cheeks.

She reached for the golden door handle.

Leila's Diary

0 days on the new island

The Ark ended up almost vertical when we crashed into the island. I clung to the torn stump of one of the masts, afraid that if I didn't I would fall to my death. People were lying all over the deck, clinging to wreckage or each other and moaning from cuts or bruises or worse. I wanted to weep for the Crone but knew I had to find Varu first.

I grabbed a length of rope and tied it round the mast stump, lowering myself down the Sky Deck, calling out Varu's name. My own voice sounded scared to me and got worse every time I cried out. I had a big cut on my leg but there was no time to care.

I found him draped round another mast, limp as seaweed. His eyes were closed but his skin wasn't blue any more.

'Varu!' I cried, lifting him off the mast and holding him in my arms. He wasn't bleeding and all his limbs were in good shape. 'Varu? Varu, wake up! You did it!

You sailed us to a new land! You've saved everyone – we'll be able to grow proper crops, and there'll be more space for us to live and everyone will be happy again. And you and me can train those killer whales and we can all go out hunting together! It's all better. You did it, Varu. You did it . . .'

I don't know why I kept talking and talking, because I think a part of me knew already that he was dead. Eventually I was still talking but there were tears all over my cheeks, and then I was trying to talk but just sobbing and sobbing instead with my head on his chest, because he had died to save us all and it wasn't fair.

I heard a cry. It wasn't a person – I knew right away it was larger and greater and much more powerful. I caught a flash of purple up in the masts, and thought I saw feathers too. Then the cry came again, and the most beautiful thing I've ever seen flew from one end of the Ark to the other, wings spread wide. As it passed, everyone turned to look, and the people who'd been moaning in pain weren't moaning any more. Flowers of every colour bloomed from the allotment patches dotting the deck. The cut on my leg was gone.

I looked down at Varu hopefully, expectantly, because surely if the bird could heal then it could . . .

'Varu? Varu!' I shook him. 'Come on, please, come on.'

The colossal bird landed in the rigging above, folding its wings and looking down at me with impossible eyes, dark as whirlpools. 'Bring him back,' I told it. 'BRING HIM BACK!'

A voice spoke. I thought it was right by my ear, then realized it was in my head.

I cannot bring him back.

'Why not?' I shrieked at the bird. 'You've got to!'

The sea overcame him. His soul is still not mended, and he was not ready to control his powers. But do not weep, child. He will return, in time.

'But he was *hurting*,' I sobbed. 'It's not fair – he died saving everyone. We have to help him!'

That is beyond both of us now, child. But I feel . . . one day, there will be someone who can heal him. One who can give him hope. Do not fear for his fate, brave Leila. Now, we must look to ourselves. A new day dawns, and we shall meet it together.

'What do you mean . . . together?'

The bird's eyes filled my mind.

I mean, I am in need of a new Vessel.

34

The Great Inventor

Kate stood tall between the golden spiral staircases, beneath the glittering God-Bird. She wore her black dress, her purple make-up reapplied, her hair still curled in two horns. She was as unmoving as the armoured Sentinels standing round the chamber, her large golden eyes watching Ellie impassively.

Seth was on his knees at her feet, hands bound, breathing heavily. He had a cut on his brow, an angry red bruise across one cheek. Kate had her sword drawn, and was holding it to Seth's neck.

'Ellie,' said Seth, his voice hoarse. 'Ellie, *run.*'

Ellie took a step forward, but a cold metal hand gripped her shoulder. She glanced back to find one of the Seven standing right behind her.

'Why are you doing this?' she said.

Sadness flickered in Kate's eyes. 'I'm sorry, Ellie, but this is the only way. Seth won't use his power willingly. So I need to force him somehow.'

Ellie frowned in confusion, then the armoured hand gripped her shoulder so tightly that she screamed, falling to her knees.

'NO!' Seth cried. 'DON'T HURT HER!'

'If you don't want me to hurt her,' Kate told him, her voice breaking slightly, 'then you must do as I ask.'

The hand released Ellie, and she sobbed, rubbing her shoulder.

'Please, Kate,' she said, trying to locate the sadness she'd seen a moment before. 'You don't have to do this.'

Kate straightened, her expression hard and mask-like. 'You don't know what I have to do.' For a long moment, she stared at the God-Bird above her, then back at Ellie. 'Seth is going to part the seas. From here to the Enemy's City.'

Seth's eyes filled with wild horror.

'What?' Ellie cried. 'Why?'

Kate took a deep breath. 'The underwater place where my mother was stripped of her powers lies somewhere between here and there. I'm going to find it, and restore the divinity that is rightfully mine.'

Ellie felt a spark of hope. 'But if *that's* what you need *I* can get you down there! We can use my underwater boat!'

'No, I need Seth.' Kate licked her lips hesitantly. 'Going north will mean getting very near to the Enemy's City.

But if there's no sea, I'm safe from their fleet. And the City will be unable to defend itself.'

Ellie's stomach lurched. 'Wait . . . what do you mean, defend itself?'

Kate's knuckles blanched round the hilt of her sword. 'Imagine, Ellie, how strong I'll seem when I conquer the Enemy's City.'

'No,' Ellie whispered. She thought of Anna, saw blood pooling between the cobblestones of Orphanage Street. 'No!' she cried. She inched closer to Kate, but was wrenched back by the Sentinel. 'You can't. You don't *need* to prove anything any more. They love you here! Everyone loves you!'

Kate stared forlornly at the ground. Her sword dropped from Seth's neck. She looked up into Ellie's eyes, and Ellie tried to pour their whole friendship into her gaze.

Kate turned her head aside. She nodded.

The Sentinel took Ellie's bound arm in its armoured fist, then gripped so tightly Ellie felt her bones crunching. Her vision went white and she screamed and screamed, knowing only pain until a voice called out from a far distance.

'Stop! Stop hurting her!'

'Then *do* it,' said Kate. 'It's your fault she's hurting.'

'STOP!' Seth roared.

The pressure released and Ellie sobbed in gratitude, the sudden ache in her arm almost pleasant.

'I'll do it,' Seth whispered, looking at Ellie with tear-filled eyes.

'Seth, don't.'

Seth stared at Ellie for a long moment, then closed his eyes.

There was a hollow, unendurable silence. Kate stared fixedly at the window, tapping her sword point against the floor. Seth's brow twitched, and Ellie winced as guilt coiled in her gut. She had done this.

Kate gestured for one of the Sentinels to hold Seth, then stepped over to the balcony. 'Why is nothing happening?'

'Please,' Ellie gasped. 'Please don't – something this big, it could kill him.'

Seth's eyelids scrunched tighter, his lips pressed into a thin line. Tiny swirls of blue swam across his hands and his neck.

Kate's eyes widened as she stared out the window. 'The sea is frothing,' she said eagerly. 'Does that mean it's working?'

Ellie watched Seth in fear. New swirls burst upon his skin like silent fireworks.

'It's getting lower,' said Kate.

Ellie strained to see, but was pinned in place. Kate blinked in astonishment, bouncing on the balls of her feet. 'The water is *parting*. It's working!'

Then she slowed, clutching the balcony rail.

'What's going on?' she said. 'It's getting *higher*.'

The windows rattled, the statues of Kate's ancestors shivering. Then, an impossibly deep, ancient sound issued from Seth's throat. His eyes opened wide, but Seth was not looking out of them. They were entirely dark blue.

The light in the chamber dimmed, and faint screams echoed from the island below. The grip on Ellie's arm loosened, and she rose to her knees to see better.

'What . . .' Kate whispered.

The sea was a shimmering wall of dark water that touched the sky, towering above the Ark. The Sentinel clutching Seth brought a sword to his neck, looking to Kate for instruction.

'Don't!' Ellie cried. 'If you kill him, the sea will crash down on us. He's losing control of his powers. You have to let me talk to him.'

Kate stared at Seth, her eyes flicking between him and the window. At last, she nodded, and the grip on Ellie's shoulder released. She stumbled across the chamber and fell beside Seth's limp body, as another bone-trembling rumble issued from his throat. She hoisted him on to her lap, placing a hand on his cheek. His blue skin was icy cold against her fingers.

'Seth, Seth, it's me,' she said, turning his face up towards her. Her teeth chattered as she tried to speak through her terror. 'It's Ellie. I'm here.'

Seth's eyes stared uncomprehendingly. Raspy mutterings spilled from his lips, as if a chorus was crying out from deep inside him.

'Please, Seth – I'm here, I'm here.' She took his hand in hers, rubbing the back of his icy hand with her thumb. 'Stay here, stay here, stay here.'

The chamber grew darker, darker, darker.

'Stay here, stay here, Seth. Stay here with me.'

The world rumbled and roared all around. Seth went limp, nearly sliding from Ellie's grasp. She gripped him tighter. '*Please*, Seth,' she said. 'Please don't go. Please don't leave me.'

Her tears dripped on to his face. She heard a slight intake of breath. Seth spoke in the merest whisper.

'I feel it, Ellie. I feel all their pain.'

'I know,' said Ellie. 'I know. But please, there's more in this world than suffering. There is, I know it.'

Seth's face scrunched up and he let out a pained gasp, like someone's last breath escaping. 'I . . . I can't see it . . .'

'I know, but stay with me, and we'll find it together. I promise.' She put a hand to his cheek. 'Please, Seth.'

The swirling, depthless blue storm in Seth's eyes cleared ever so slightly. He gazed at her for many long seconds. Then, a tiny smile formed on his lips.

'Yes,' he whispered. 'Now I see it.'

The corners of Ellie's mouth twitched, and she almost smiled, despite herself. The roaring outside calmed. Ellie was aware of daylight all around, but kept her eyes on Seth the whole time, as the roiling patterns on his face slowed, grew small, then vanished entirely. His eyelids closed, and his head lolled back. Ellie felt for his wrist, sighing as she found his pulse.

She looked up to see Kate standing above her, watching with a strange, faraway look. There was a clatter of heavy footsteps, and the doors swung open, admitting the sound of distant shouts and clashing metal. A silver-armoured Warden stood breathless and sweating in the doorway.

'The sea!' she cried. 'The sea!'

'We know,' said Kate. 'What's all that noise?'

'We're being attacked,' she said. 'There are hundreds of people downstairs, sailors, I think – we don't know how they got inside. But, Your Divinity – the sea!'

Kate snarled, then looked round at the Seven.

'Get down there. Deal with the attackers! You, keep her here.' She pointed to the Sentinel holding Ellie, as Ellie batted uselessly against their metal shoulder. 'I will speak to these people.'

Six of the Seven rushed from the chamber, while the remaining Sentinel wrenched Ellie away from Seth's prone form. A furious shout echoed up from downstairs.

'THE REVOLUTION HAS COME!'

Kate paused by the door, looking at Ellie for a fleeting moment. She opened her mouth to speak, but as she did, Seth's eyes flashed wide, and he flung one hand out towards the Cabinet of Tears.

There was an angry tinkling of glass and the cabinet doors flew open. A hundred vials of false tears tumbled from the shelves in a glittering cascade. Ellie thought they would smash to the floor, but instead they curved upward like a wave, spinning across the chamber. Kate yelped as one struck her in the head.

The rest flew at the Sentinel like a flock of birds. Ellie dropped to the ground, covering her head as tiny shards showered all around her. The Sentinel released Ellie, arms raised in defence.

'Ellie, RUN!' Seth roared.

Ellie grabbed for her cane and staggered to her feet, racing up one of the spiral staircases towards the window above. She risked a glance down. The water soaking the Sentinel was coalescing, reshaping into a shimmering ball that rushed up the gap beneath their helmet. They fell on all fours, pawing at their throat. There was a muffled sound of choking.

Ellie and Seth's eyes met briefly, before he fell on his back, eyes closed.

'Seth!'

Ellie hesitated, desperate to rescue him. But Kate was heading towards the staircase, sword in hand. Ellie moaned, flinging open the window and climbing out over the balcony railing.

She landed among the field of squat, featureless statues that dotted the sloping surface of the Ark's hull. Ellie gritted her teeth, gingerly navigating her way down between them until she could see over the edge towards the ocean. She gasped.

The sea had parted.

Two immense walls of blue-black water faced one another, their insides seething with raging, flickering currents like bolts of lightning. Between them was the sea floor – a craggy red-brown expanse of earth, glistening wet and striped green with moss and seaweed, clouded here and there by patches of swirling mist. The chasm was wider than the island itself, and got wider as it stretched north to the horizon.

Hinges squeaked and Ellie looked up to see Kate stepping out on to the balcony. She stopped abruptly, eyes wide in wonder. She grinned at Ellie.

'It worked,' she said. 'He actually *did* it.'

For the merest second, Ellie forgot what had transpired in those last few hours, and it was like the two of them were friends again. Then, a vice closed round her heart, as if her own ribcage was crushing it. She steadied herself with her cane, feeling dizzy. What was it, she wondered? Then she looked at Kate, and realized.

Kate was lost to her forever.

'WHY HAVE YOU DONE THIS?' Ellie hurled the words at Kate, the anger tearing through her body, setting her bones alight. 'We could have made this island such a wonderful place. You've destroyed *everything*!'

Kate looked at Ellie in surprise, then waved her away. 'Ellie, you're being dramatic. Now come back inside before you get hurt.' She glanced down at the flaky statues and masonry. 'You know this surface isn't stable.'

Ellie took a step further away. 'You hurt Seth. You could have killed him!'

Kate let out a small laugh, and Ellie's heart burned with fresh rage.

'Is *that* what you're angry about?' Kate said. 'He seems fine! Anyway, it doesn't matter now. He's done it. There's no reason to hurt him again. And I need him alive to keep the sea like this.'

'He's not a *tool* for you to use.'

Kate rolled her eyes and climbed over the balcony, landing delicately among the statues. Ellie took another step backwards.

'That's all I was to you,' Ellie said. 'A tool to help you keep your power.'

'Ellie, now *stop* being ridiculous,' Kate said sternly, moving between the statues towards her. 'You know how dear you are to me.'

'Then why did you hurt Seth?'

Kate blinked rapidly, her lips tightening. 'Ellie, stop being a brat and come back in!'

'You've still got your sword out,' Ellie said, nodding at the shining blade.

'That's because I'm worried you might do something foolish!'

Ellie hobbled away, the ground curving steeply beneath her feet as she put more statues between them. 'You know,' she said, tasting tears on her lips, 'I thought . . .' She opened her mouth, but the words clogged inside her throat. She breathed, and tried again. 'You were the most important thing to me.'

Kate's eyes widened for a moment, then flickered shut.

'I wish they'd never done this to you!' Ellie yelled. 'I wish you'd never become a Queen!'

'Ellie,' Kate sighed. 'If I wasn't a Queen, I would be nothing at all.'

'That's not true,' Ellie sobbed. 'You'd be my friend.'

'Ellie, you're being –'

As Kate took another step forward, there was a sharp crack of splitting stone, as a statue loosened by her foot. Kate slipped and fell hard on her side.

'Oh,' she said, in mild surprise.

'Kate!' Ellie leapt forward, but Kate slammed into another statue, which snapped under her weight. She rolled faster down the side of the Ark, tearing at crumbling statues as she fell, spraying up lumps of clay then vanishing over the edge. Ellie heard a scream that turned her heart to ice.

'*No!*' Ellie cried, falling to her knees. She took three terrified breaths, clenching her hands to fists. She closed her eyes. 'SAVE HER!'

The screaming stopped.

Ellie took another breath.

She dared to open her eyes.

Kate was lying in front of her, right where she'd first fallen. She looked about in a daze.

'How . . . how did I . . . ?'

Ellie swayed. Her body felt empty, her head heavy.

'I was . . . falling,' Kate said. 'I was falling, and then I wasn't.'

Sweat trickled down Ellie's brow. She shivered.

'That's . . . impossible,' Kate said. She stood slowly, then her gaze flickered to Ellie. Her eyes widened. 'It was you.' She stared at Ellie with catlike focus. 'You saved me.'

'I . . . I . . .'

'The Inquisitor was right about you,' Kate whispered. 'That's why you're so clever, isn't it? How you made all your devious inventions.'

Ellie flinched. Her mouth felt full of salt.

'You're the Enemy's Vessel. Aren't you, Ellie?'

Ellie shook her head feebly. She tried to say *no*, but a sob constricted her throat.

Kate glanced around, her gaze landing on her sword. She bent to pick it up.

'Please,' Ellie managed, head swimming. 'I'm . . . I'm not dangerous. I'd never do anything to hurt you.'

Kate held up the sword between them, pointing the tip at Ellie's heart. Her hand trembled only slightly. 'I know that, Ellie,' she said. 'But imagine what I could do with the Enemy's power?'

Ellie froze, as she realized what Kate intended.

'Kate, please. You don't want this. If you kill me . . . Believe me — being the Enemy's Vessel is the most terrible thing you can imagine. It would destroy you.'

Kate's face was blank, her voice hollow. 'It hasn't destroyed *you*. I think I'll manage.'

'No, no, it will tear you apart.' Ellie's eyes stung with tears. 'It will take all your shame and your doubt and your regret and it will *break* you!'

'Oh, shut *UP*, Ellie,' Kate said, and swung her sword.

It missed Ellie by an arm's length, and they both stood there, unable to move, watching the sword between them and struggling to believe what had just happened.

Ellie took a deep breath. 'Did you . . .' She swallowed. 'Did you ever love me?'

Tears shone on Kate's eyelashes. 'I . . . I don't know, Ellie. I'm not sure how that's supposed to feel. I'm so sorry.'

She lowered her sword, and her shoulders sagged. Ellie took a slow, careful step towards her.

Kate's eyes snapped up to hers, ringed red. 'But I *need* that power.'

She lashed out with her sword and Ellie threw up her cane in defence. Kate's sword bit again and again, and Ellie yelped as her cane split in half. She staggered to the side, and Kate mirrored her movements, tripping against a statue. As she recovered, Ellie put five steps between them, and hurled a smoke bomb right at Kate's face.

Kate caught it, and it did not explode. 'Ellie – you've nowhere to run, and you can't fight me; I'm hardly even trying. Please, just make this easier for us.'

Ellie slid her feet into two loops at the bottom of her coat. 'I can . . . I can run.'

'What are you talking about?' Kate said, watching her with a bemused expression. 'You have a limp and a broken arm.'

Ellie undid the knot at her neck that held her sling in place. It fluttered away in the breeze, and she stretched out her left arm, feeling the fresh air wrap round it, wriggling her fingers.

Kate's eyes widened. 'That powder of yours worked?'

Ellie nodded, holding back fresh tears. 'I wish you had trusted me,' she choked. 'We could have done so much good together.'

With that, Ellie turned, took a few fast, reckless steps –

And jumped from the Ark.

The screaming wind tore at her face, whipping her hair against her neck like cords of rope. The rooftops of the Shambles rushed up to meet her. Ellie stretched out her arms and legs, and pulled at the cords in the sleeves of her coat.

The heavy outer layers ripped away, spraying smoke bombs and flash-bangs that detonated in bursts of cloud and light in the streets below. Between her arms and legs were two long pieces of silk that tautened as they captured the rising air – not like wings but something else, something she might never have dreamed of had she not seen them once on a squirrel.

The world below was still rising, rising, yet somehow, it had stopped rising so quickly. Shipwreck Island slipped beneath her, and she flew over the muddy-red valley Seth had created, the flanking walls of water roaring in her ears.

There was a crackling rip, and Ellie gasped as the silk on her right side gave way. Her bad leg seared in agony as the force of the wind wrenched it at an angle, sending her tumbling towards the valley below.

She wrestled with another cord at her waist as the wind tried to snatch it from her grasp. She tugged it sharply and a parachute exploded above her, swallowing up the air and yanking her suddenly skyward. Legs dangling, Ellie drifted, sinking steadily to the muddy ground, landing in the shadow of a tall craggy rock encrusted with seaweed and pale pink coral.

Ellie's world spun as she crashed into the mud, her good leg racing to keep up with the ground as it sped beneath her, her bad leg falling behind. She tripped and plunged through the gloopy slurry, rising out of it with a wet *pop*, disentangling herself from the strings of the parachute. She pulled off the tattered remnants of her coat, throwing them to the ground with a strangled shout.

She staggered forward, trying to push down the pain in her heart. A half-sob broke from her lips, and she took a deep breath and counted to ten.

A shadow crossed her vision. She held her hand up against the sun, and saw a silhouette standing atop the tall rock. Tiny frayed bandages fluttered at its edges.

'Go away!' Ellie snarled.

'Oh, Ellie. I'm so proud of you. You did it. You did it.'

'Leave me alone!'

'You *saved* her, even though she was going to kill you. And now . . . you've made me *so* strong.'

A cloud passed before the sun and Ellie saw the bleeding child smiling down at her. Only it wasn't bleeding any more. Its bandages were clean. There was colour in its lips, and its hair was no longer matted but neatly tied up in a ribbon of bandage. It stood tall.

'*FINN!*' Ellie roared, taking two steps towards it.

The child flinched, as if struck by a sharp gust of wind. It looked about itself. 'Well, isn't that interesting?'

'FINN!' Ellie roared again, trying to summon every happy thought of her brother that she could. 'FINN! FINN! *FINN!*'

But the only thing she could picture was Kate.

The child laughed in delight. It was a new sound – not the hacking laugh of the bleeding child, or the musical laugh it had used when it had been Finn. All the same, it sounded oddly familiar to Ellie.

'Now listen,' it said, 'I have something to show you.'

'Why isn't it working?' Ellie cried hoarsely, her throat raw and sore.

'You thought you could defeat suffering. You thought you could save this island, save *her*. But now . . . this island is as bad as the City. And all because of you, dear Ellie. You. You. You.'

The child raised a hand to its face, and tugged at a frayed twist of fabric by its ear. The material began to unravel.

With the first inch, a sliver of pale, freckled cheek was exposed. Then the bandages round its body unravelled too, revealing thin freckled arms and curly, dirty blonde hair that fell past its shoulders. One green eye, then another. Small lips and a dimple on one cheek. A nose that curved slightly to one side.

The Enemy looked down at Ellie, smiling a kind smile. It hugged its shoulders, cradling itself adoringly.

'*You*,' it said, in Ellie's voice.

Ellie took a step back, her breath coming quickly. She put a hand to her tangled, muddy hair. The Enemy stroked its own gleaming curls. Ellie touched a finger to her nose, and the Enemy did likewise.

It hopped backwards off the rock, and when Ellie blinked it was standing right next to her. It put a hand to her cheek. Somehow, the hand was warm.

'You keep trying to fight me,' it said. 'Maybe it's time you remembered – all the bad things that happen to you are your own fault.'

'*Your* fault,' Ellie spat.

'Our fault,' said the Enemy, blinking at Ellie with her own green eyes.

Ellie tried to picture Finn again – his sandy hair, his warm smile, the two of them fishing in their little rowing boat. But Kate pursued her everywhere she turned. She thought of when they'd played together in the workshop, flinging nuts and bolts across the room. She thought of Kate crying as Ellie hugged her. She thought of Kate chasing her across the surface of the Ark, and of Kate with her sword at Seth's throat.

And of Seth, as Ellie held his limp body in her arms.

And of Seth, and the tiny smile he had given her as his eyes gazed into hers.

Yes, he had said. *Now I see it.*

Ellie looked at the Enemy, and it looked back curiously, a happier, healthier replica. An Ellie who had never known suffering.

'No,' she told it.

The Enemy smirked. 'Ellie, you've lost everything.'

'No, I *haven't*. The seas are still parted, and that means Seth is still alive. And someone needs to warn the City that Kate is coming.'

'I won't let you do that. Don't forget, I have a wish to make now.'

'You'll never get the chance.'

'Ellie, I don't think you understand –'

Ellie seized the Enemy by its throat. It tried to resist, pawing at her grip, and Ellie saw the exact same pattern of freckles reflected on the backs of their hands, the same wiry fingers. But the fear in the Enemy's eyes was its own.

'I *do* understand,' she told it. 'Kate's mother was a Vessel. But then she was taken to a place beneath the sea, and

398

suddenly she wasn't a Vessel any more. The god was gone. Do you know what that means?'

The Enemy laughed, even with her hands round its throat.

'Oh, Ellie, what a strange fantasy.'

'It's not a fantasy. Look around. With the sea gone, I should be able to reach it on foot.'

'You'll never find anything,' it hissed.

Ellie shoved the Enemy away, bending to untangle her frayed, muddy coat from the parachute strings.

'Altimus Ashenholme found something out there,' she said, gazing at the horizon. 'Somewhere even gods can die. That's where I have to go.'

Ellie pulled on the rags of her coat and took her first steps north, through the shimmering shadows cast by the walls of roaring sea.

'Maybe I can't destroy suffering,' she said, as the Enemy followed after her. 'But I can destroy you.'

SHIPWRECK ISLAND

YOUR QUESTIONS ANSWERED

Read on to discover the inspiration
behind *Shipwreck Island* and more
about author Struan Murray.

1.

HOW DID YOU FIND WRITING SHIPWRECK ISLAND COMPARED TO ORPHANS OF THE TIDE?

They were such completely different experiences. *Orphans of the Tide* was written over five years, with lots of time to step away from it and think about what was working and what wasn't. But it was also scary at times because literally *anything* was possible. With *Shipwreck Island* I already had the main characters, and a lot of the plot was already seeded in the first book, so there wasn't so much possibility of the unknown. However, I had only a year to write it, so it was something of a rollercoaster to get it all done in time!

2.

WHAT WAS YOUR INSPIRATION FOR SHIPWRECK ISLAND?

After writing the City, I was really keen to explore a place where the people *worshipped* the god living amongst them, rather than fearing it. I imagined it as cheerful and colourful, and full of life and music, in complete contrast to the City. Mediterranean islands were a big inspiration, especially places like Malta, which inspired the feel and the visuals of the streets. For the Queen and her noble court I read a lot about King Louis XIV, also known as 'The Sun King', and the complicated etiquette at his court in Versailles. I had also discovered that the mining of bird-droppings has been a major industry throughout human history, with the existence of 'Guano Lords' at one point, so obviously that had to go in as well . . .

3.

FANS LOVE THE CHARACTER
OF ELLIE – WAS SHE INSPIRED
BY A REAL PERSON?

She began life as an attempt to write a
story about a young Leonardo da Vinci,
but swiftly became her own person! I
loved the idea of an 'eccentric genius' child
character with a head full of ideas but who is
struggling with a dark secret that weighs on
her every moment. Some of her habits are
inspired by me . . . she's very messy, and cares
little about her appearance, and she's always
eager to prove to people that she's clever,
even if it gets her into trouble.

4.

WHERE DO YOU DO YOUR WRITING?

I really like writing in cafes and libraries, as I find it comforting to have lots of people and noise around me when I write. However, much of *Shipwreck Island* was written during the 2020 lockdown, so I had to improvise. In the summer I actually took to writing in a sunny park beneath a tree, which is a lot less comfortable than it sounds. The insects didn't seem to care that I needed my own space.

5.

IF YOU WERE STUCK ON SHIPWRECK ISLAND, WHAT THREE THINGS WOULD YOU WANT TO HAVE WITH YOU?

Sunscreen, definitely, because I have red hair and freckles and so get sunburned even on a cloudy November day. Also a notepad, so I can carry on doodling and writing to keep my brain active. And some smoke bombs, in case I need to run away from the Inquisition.

6.

WHALES FEATURE A LOT IN
BOTH ORPHANS OF THE TIDE
AND SHIPWRECK ISLAND.
HAVE YOU EVER SEEN ONE IN REAL LIFE?

Never! It has always been my biggest dream
to finally see one, and I think it might be too
much for me to handle when it finally happens.
The closest I've come is seeing a forty-foot long
whale shark at an aquarium in Japan. I stood
there for three hours (I'm not exaggerating), just
gaping at it, until my friend got angry with me
and demanded we leave.

7.

WHEN DID YOU FIRST REALIZE YOU WANTED TO BE A WRITER?

I was always drawing and writing silly stories when I was at school, including a comic book about a group of talking animals that I sold for 20p, to help pay for a serious Pokémon trading card obsession. A couple of years later, I wrote a series of detective stories for my uncle Hank, and he seemed to get such a kick out of how unnecessarily violent they were. It was a great feeling to have someone really enjoy something I'd written, and I knew I had to keep doing it.

8.

WHO IS YOUR FAVOURITE NEW CHARACTER IN SHIPWRECK ISLAND*?*

Molworth was a big surprise, and ended up my firm favourite. Like Anna in the previous book, he just sort of sprung to life on the page. He was originally going to be a grumpy, cynical but good-natured old man, until I realized it would be much funnier if he was a grumpy, cynical but good-natured twelve-year-old, who for some reason owned his own pub.

9.

WHAT WAS THE MOST CHALLENGING SCENE TO WRITE IN SHIPWRECK ISLAND?

Kate was a complex character to write, and her two sides – the frightened, lonely girl and the frightening, otherworldly queen – were hard to balance. The scene where she turns on Ellie was particularly challenging, because it had to be entirely believable that she would throw away the only friendship she'd ever had, so she might finally have the powers of a god.

10.

Ellie's mission now is to find the mysterious place
where Kate's father, Altimus Ashenholme, was
able to destroy the god that lived in Kate's mother.
Ellie believes that if she can find this place she will
be able to destroy the Enemy once and for all.
However, Kate is now hellbent on leading an army
to the City, to conquer it and prove she is a true
queen. And, of course, the Enemy has plans of its
own, and will be doing everything it can to stop
Ellie in her mission. Fortunately, Ellie will have the
help of her friends from both Shipwreck Island and
the City, including one particular red-headed girl
with a fondness for violence . . .